weeds

weeds

by

EDITH SUMMERS KELLEY

Afterword by Charlotte Margolis Goodman

THE FEMINIST PRESS

AT THE CITY UNIVERSITY OF

NEW YORK

Published by The Feminist Press at The City University of New York
311 East 94th Street, New York, New York 10128-5684

First Feminist Press edition, 1982

03 02 01 00 99 98 97 96 5 4 3 2

LC number: 81-22061
ISBN 1-55861-154-1

The Feminist Press would like to thank
Helene D. Goldfarb, Joanne Markell,
and Genevieve Vaughan for their generosity.

Frontmatter text designed by Nicola Ferguson

Printed in the United States of America
on acid-free paper by McNaughton & Gunn, Inc.

CONTENTS

WEEDS

CHAPTER I

BILL PIPPINGER was counted to be as good a neighbor, as bountiful a provider and as kind a husband and father as was to be found in the whole of Scott County, Kentucky, according to local standards of goodness, kindness and bountifulness. He had never been known to refuse a neighbor the loan of anything that he owned, from his pocket knife to his team of mules. He was prompt with neighborly assistance whenever there was any big job to be done, such as a smokehouse to move or a hog to butcher. If he saw his neighbor's ox or his ass fallen down by the way, he heeded the Bible injunction, of which he had never heard, not to hide himself from them, but surely to help his brother to lift them up again. And if he saw his brother's ox or his sheep go astray, he brought them again unto his brother; for he was one of the few strictly honest farmers in Scott County. Unlike most of his neighbors, too, he was a man of peace. He never sought a quarrel and always avoided one if possible. He had never in his life pulled a gun on a man, an unusual record for a native of rural Kentucky, brought up from boyhood in the time-honored tradition that the pulling of guns is a manly sport.

His wife had little cause for complaint against him, for he hardly ever got drunk oftener than once a month at the Georgetown Court Day. He saw to it that there was always, or at least nearly always, at least one fat hog in the pen waiting to be butchered at Thanksgiving or Christmas. He aimed every spring to raise enough corn so that there would be plenty to feed the hens, to fatten his hog or hogs and to furnish material for the daily cornmeal cakes until next season's crop came on. If Bill did not always succeed in this laudable endeavor, the blame was not laid at his door by his neighbors and certainly not by himself. If there came a dry spell that withered up the corn just as it was filling out in the ear, it wasn't Bill's fault. And if a rainy season set in and kept the ground so wet that he couldn't get into the patch with a cultivator, it was none of his doing if the weeds grew so fast that they soon overtopped the corn. Bill was not the inventor of weeds nor of their nefarious habit of growing faster than corn. Under such circumstances reflections like this gave him much peace of mind and spiritual comfort. There was considerable satisfaction in being able to shift the blame onto the Almighty; and there was still further repose of spirit in the thought that no effort of his own weak, human frame could undo the damage done by the will of that all-powerful being. If the corn crop was light, it was light, and that was all there was to it; and there would be that much less corn to shuck out and that much less fodder to haul in.

There were of course other matters pertaining to the farm over which Bill could exercise more control than he did over the rain supply. On these latter his mind could not repose with the same peaceful abandon; hence he did not concentrate upon them. The fences that needed mending, the manure that ought to be hauled out, the brush that should be cut out of his pasture to give the grass a chance to grow: these things preyed more or less upon Bill's mind, but he did not allow them to annoy him too constantly. After all, he told himself, there was just so much that one man could do on a place. A man couldn't be hauling out manure and cutting brush and mending fence all at the same time; and there was no use in worrying because everything was not kept up to the top notch. Besides, a fellow had to have a little rest now and then and a chance to visit with his neighbors, or what use to be alive at all?

Bill dearly loved to rest and visit. They were his favorite

pastimes and indeed about the only ones that the circumstances of his life offered to him. To sit on a rail fence or a hitching post with a chew of tobacco in his cheek, a bit of wood in his left hand and a jack-knife in his right, and pass the time of day with all and sundry who happened by, was as much as Bill asked of life. Whether the place was his own barnyard or Jim Townsend's blacksmith shop or Peter Akers' general merchandise store in Clayton made no particular difference to Bill so long as he could sit and chew and whittle and talk. He was built long and rickety, nondescript of feature, but with a bright twinkle of humor and kindliness in his gray eyes; and his tall, narrow-chested figure was a frequent sight about the lounging places of Clayton.

The main trouble with Bill was that along with nine-tenths of the rest of humanity, he had missed his calling. He was by nature a villager, not a farmer, and the great regret of his life was that he had not been a blacksmith. He had mastered the trade through sheer love of it and had become the best of non-professional blacksmiths. He shod his own horses and the horses of all his neighbors, asking them nothing in return but the pleasure of their company while he worked. To have a little shop of his own in the village whither the farmers would come from six or seven miles around, bringing their horses and all the news and gossip of the neighborhood, that had always been Bill's unrealized dream. Chance, however, that wayward arbiter of the fates of all of us, by making Bill the son of a farmer and the husband of a woman who had inherited a farm, had spoiled a good blacksmith to make a poor farmer. It did not occur to him to repine or cry out against his lot or consider himself in any way a blighted being on this account. He merely cast a momentarily envious eye upon Jim Townsend, the blacksmith, whenever he happened to see him, and went on farming—after a fashion. He was a gentle, kindly and sociable soul, and the good will of his neighbors meant more to him than anything else on earth except his family.

His family consisted of his wife and five children. Aunt

Annie Pippinger, a small, inconsequential woman in the early forties, was all one color, like an old faded daguerreotype. She may have had some claims to prettiness in the days when Bill courted her; but they had long since gone, leaving her a bit of drab insignificance. Crawford, the eldest boy, was surprisingly handsome and quite as surprisingly indolent of mind and body. The twins, Luella and Lizzie May, were thin, sickly-looking little girls. Lizzie May was pretty in a pale, blond, small-featured way. Luella had a long, pale face, drab hair and dull gray eyes; and her mouth hung open as though she had adenoids. Judith was the third girl, born two years after the twins. After her there was an interval of four years marked for Aunt Annie Pippinger by two miscarriages and a stillborn infant. At the end of this interval a child was born who grew into a chubby, round-eyed, stupid-looking little boy named Elmer.

These children played and quarreled and made discordant, schoolyard noises in the dooryard of a little, three-room shanty standing upon forty-seven acres of heavy clay land which Aunt Annie Pippinger had inherited from her father. The front yard had been plowed up at some time or other but never planted to anything; and the result was a plentiful crop of ragweed, yarrow and pink-blooming soapwort. Two or three rose bushes clung to the broken picket fence and made it gay in June; and by the front door there was a large bush that bore beautiful creamy roses, tinged in the bud ever so slightly with delicate pink. By the back porch a lilac bush as tall as a small tree made April fragrant for the Pippingers.

The back dooryard was beaten bare and hard by the playing feet of children and the dumping of endless tubs of soapsuds and pans of dishwater. A discarded cookstove lying on its side against the back wall of the kitchen, formed the nucleus for a pile of rust-eaten pots and pans. Beyond the bare spot, a fringe of mustard, ragweed, and burdock reached to the picket fence. Along this fence a dozen or so stalks of holly-hock bloomed in summer gorgeously pink and scarlet against a blue sky. The smoke house and the back house occupied opposite corners of this yard, a well worn path through the weeds leading the way to each.

A stone's throw beyond the picket fence stood the barn, a structure that had been in need of repairs these many years, and part of the roof and sides of an old wagon shed. Here, too, was the horsepond, overhung by a big weeping willow, and a small corral that Bill had built for the milking of the cows. Beyond rose a grassy slope dotted with locust trees. A few straggly apple and peach trees, mostly sprung from seed, grew here and there in odd corners.

The Pippinger farm, like all the rest of the land immediately about it, consisted of hills sloping more or less gently into each other, so that there was no level ground to be found anywhere. This was characteristic of the whole of Scott County. Everywhere there were hills: steep hills and gentle hills, high hills and low hills, plowed hills, and grassy hills and weed-covered hills, but always hills. These hills sometimes ran in long ridges across the land with hollows on each side and other hills sloping up from the hollows. The only level land was the narrow strips at the bottoms of these hollows made by the washing down of soil from the hills.

A great deal of otherwise good land was spoiled in this way. If the hills were kept in bluegrass or sweet clover, they "stayed put." But when they were plowed for corn or tobacco and afterward left to grow up in weeds, the heavy rains cut deep gullies in their sides and washed the good soil to the bottom. This was the case with most of the Pippinger acres. There was only a small amount of land left that was smooth enough to be plowed for corn. Ever since the family had moved onto the place, which was when Crawford was a baby, Bill had talked about how he was going to "stop up them gullies an' put in sweet clover." But each year the gullies wore deeper and each year Bill talked less about reclaiming them. There was still enough pasture, however, for two cows, Roanie and Reddie and a team of gray mules that answered, though sometimes reluctantly, to the names of Tom and Bob. Scratching and cackling hens made the barnyard lively; there were geese on the horsepond; and a few turkeys ranged in the surrounding fields and grew fat on the corn and alfalfa for miles around.

This was the center of the universe for the Pippinger children. Here they played the games that they had learned in the schoolyard: "Blind Man's Buff," "Tag," "Tom, Tom, pull away," and "Little Sally Waters." They made playhouses in fence corners where they treasured up bits of colored glass and stones glittering with mica. They hunted for the eggs of hens that had stolen their nests. They stalked the turkeys to find out where they were laying the precious turkey eggs. They stood around their mother as she churned and with greedy little fingers scraped off the spattered blobs of butter as they appeared on the dasher stick and the churn top. When house-cleaning time was come and their mother had the front room carpet out on the line, they crept in between its dusty folds and crawled gleefully up and down making the mild April evening vibrant with their shouts and laughter. They gathered wild raspberries and blackberries in summer and in autumn hickory nuts and black walnuts. They brought up the cows for the milking and exemplified the phrase, "Straight from producer to consumer," by milking into their own mouths. They made dandelion chains in spring and burr baskets in autumn and scattered the silky fluff of ripe milkweed pods into the sunny autumn air. They held buttercups under each other's chins to see if they liked butter. They quarreled over the possession of playthings and other subjects of childish dispute. Sometimes they fought savagely and kicked each other's shins and made vigorous attempts to scratch and bite, then ran crying and complaining to their mother.

A radius of some eight or ten miles about the farm formed their entire world. Within this circle was Clayton, the source of groceries, candy and Christmas toys, as were also the homes of the various grandparents, aunts, uncles, and cousins with whom they visited. Almost every Sunday, and sometimes on a week day, Bill would hitch up Tom and Bob to the spring wagon as soon as the morning chores were done, and the whole family, dressed in clean denim and starched calico, would jog away over the winding dirt road to the home of one or other of their kin for an all-day visit. The parent Pippingers sat on the seat in front, which was padded with a couple of old patchwork quilts; and the children made themselves comfortable seats in the thick straw of the wagon body.

So they would drive out into the sunshine, up hill and down hill, across rickety wooden bridges, around gentle bends and sharp turns, past corn patches and tobacco fields and long stretches of land grown up in weeds and brush; through little groves of second growth maple and hickory, past old log houses and weathered frame shanties and big tobacco barns and occasional large, more or less pretentious dwellings surrounded by lawns, till they came to grandad's or Aunt Abigail's or Cousin Rubena's, and there halted for the day.

It was not considered necessary to warn relatives that on such and such a day they were to receive seven all-day visitors. Such an idea had never occurred to Bill or his wife or any of their connections. The Pippingers themselves received many such guests, and were quite as glad to be visited as to visit. There was no sin greater than the sin of being stingy with your time, your food, or your work. To intimate by word, deed, or look that visitors were not welcome was unthinkable in the social circle in which Bill's family and their kin moved.

When the visiting Pippingers reached their destination, whether it was grandad's or Aunt Abigail's or Cousin Rubena's, the procedure was always the same. Everybody, men, women, and children, came out to the wagon to welcome the visitors. There would follow a few moments of general kissing, handshaking, comments on the weather, and mutual inquiries concerning health. Then the men unhitched, put up the mules, and retired to the barnyard to chew, whittle, and exchange silence-punctuated views on the three main topics of common interest, the weather, the crops, and the neighbors. The children straggled after them or ran to the wagon shed to see the new litter of puppies or started a game of "Hide and Seek" in the dooryard. Aunt Annie Pippinger went with the womenfolk back into the house, where, having laid aside her sunbonnet and jacket, she immediately started to scrape potatoes, cut string beans, peel apples, or otherwise help with the preparations for dinner.

The whole day was spent in this way. The men loafed in the barnyard; the children played or hung in semi-boredom about their elders; the women cooked and washed dishes in the house. And when these tasks were done and the kitchen floor swept, they sat down stiffly on straight-backed chairs, smoothed their aprons and talked about the price of calico, the raising of chickens, the recent sudden death of Uncle James Cruikshanks, the stroke that Aunt Jenny Boone had had last week, and other such topics.

The only break in what would seem to an outsider an interminable stretch of tedium was the dinner. This usually consisted of salt hog meat, fried or boiled, potatoes and some other vegetable, followed by a heavy-crusted apple pie or a soggy boiled pudding. If it were summer or autumn there would likely be a big platter of "roastin' ears," sliced ripe tomatoes, or sliced cucumbers and onions in vinegar. Everybody ate plentifully and silently, and as soon as the meal was over the men slouched back to the barnyard.

When the sun began to slant low in the western sky, Bill would at last bring the wagon around. Aunt Annie Pippinger would put on her sunbonnet and jacket, and the children, seeing the mules hitched up, would straggle up one by one from their play. There would be a long family gathering about the wagon before the visitors drove off; for nothing having to do with social intercourse is ever done in a hurry in rural Kentucky. They had had all day to talk to each other, and they had repeated the same things many, many times over. It was getting late, too, and there was a long drive ahead of them and all the chores were waiting to be done. But still there could be no hurried leave-taking; there was no precedent for such a thing. So they all stood about the wagon and exchanged some more prophecies about the weather and some more comments on Aunt Jenny Boone's stroke and Uncle James Cruikshank's sudden death. And then there would be a long silence. And at last, in the midst of the silence, Bill would gather up the lines. Then, having allowed a decent interval to elapse, he would give the lines a gentle shake and clear his throat.

"Waal, I guess we'd better be a-hittin' the high places. It'll be dark agin we git home an' the chores'll be to do by lantern light. Is all them young uns in there back, or are we a-leavin' some of 'em behind? Waal, anyway a couple or three more ner less don't make no p'tic'ler odds. Come over all."

"You come agin," the visitees would chant in chorus; and followed by this never failing invitation to return the Pippinger coach and pair would trundle out of the barnyard.

The remaining important factor in the life of the Pippinger children was school. Bill himself like many of his neighbors could neither read nor write, and hence was very firmly convinced of the benefits to be derived from an education and determined that his children should have the best that was to be had. Nothing, therefore, except bad weather, was allowed to interfere with their regular attendance at school. The school was two miles from the Pippinger farm. It was a small, whitewashed, oblong box standing close to the road in the midst of a circle of bare, beaten ground. A grove of stately maples and beeches, fringing the bare spot, made a fine place for "Hide and Seek."

Inside a small pine kitchen table formed the teacher's desk, which stood on a slightly raised platform. There were the usual jackknife-carved double wooden benches and the inevitable lithographs of Washington and Lincoln. Some admirer had contributed a large, impressive print of Roosevelt, which had been given the place of honor immediately over the teacher's desk. A large map of the United States, printed many years previously and much yellowed by age, hung between the windows on one side. These, with the blackboard, were the only mural decorations.

Here Lena Moss, an anemic little girl of eighteen, still a child herself in mind and body, who had been educated for a year and a half at the Georgetown High School, did what she could to drill the three R's into the somewhat blockish heads of about twenty children ranging in years from five to the still tender age of the teacher herself.

Fortunately Lena did not have much trouble with discipline. Her pupils were not, like little city hoodlums, vulgar and boisterous with the life of the streets. Nor were they like the children in smaller towns, who are quite as vulgar and boisterous and are held less in control because their school "system" is perforce less ironly rigid than that in the big cities. Lena's pupils were mostly inbred and undernourished children, brought up from infancy on skim milk, sowbelly, and cornmeal cakes, and living on lonely farms where they had no chance to develop infantile mob spirit. They were pallid, long-faced, adenoidal little creatures, who were too tired after the long walk to school to give the teacher much trouble. The slang, rag, and jazz, which standardize vulgarity in the towns and cities, penetrated to this out-of-the-way corner only as faint, scarcely-heard echoes. The phonograph and the colored "funny sheet" were unknown. Hence, Lena, though she did not know it, had much to be thankful for. The loud munching of apples, the shuffling of feet, the occasional throwing of spit-balls, or exchanging of scribbled notes were the main breaches of a discipline which was never at any time at all rigid. There was one pupil, however, who often gave the teacher a good deal of trouble; and that, strange to say, was a girl. She was Bill Pippinger's youngest daughter, Judith.

Judith was a lithe, active, slim little creature, monkey-like in the agility with which she could climb trees and shin up poles and vault over fences. Her bare, brown toes took hold like fingers. There was something wild and evasive about her swift, sinuous little body, alive with quick, unexpected movements, like those of a young animal. She was like a naughty little goblin that springs up mockingly in your path and before you can reach for it has run up a tree or vanished into the thicket. These characteristics of her body were somewhat contradicted by her face, vivid and bold in color and outline and habitually serious. Her eyebrows were black and straight and rather too heavy; and beneath them her gray eyes were dark, clear, and steady. She had a way of seeming to look through and through you when she fixed you with even a passing glance. These qualities of elusiveness and boldness seemed bafflingly interwoven in her character and made her a hard pupil to deal with. Lena never knew what to expect from her.

Without doubt the troublesomeness of Judith was partly due to the fact that she was better fed than most of the other children. Bill was one who never stinted his children in their food if he could possibly help it. When there was a shortage he let it affect his own plate. The Pippingers were not so saving as most of their neighbors; they did not take every ounce of butter to the village store to sell at fifteen cents a pound. Eggs, too, were not entire strangers to their table. The fact of comparatively good nourishment did not, however, explain away all of Judith's bad conduct; for the other Pippinger children, fed on the same fare, were model pupils in the school. There was something then in the girl's own inherited nature that made her different from her brothers and sisters and from the docile, mouse-like little girls and boys who sat beside her on the school benches.

In backwoods corners of America, where the people have been poor and benighted for several generations and where for as many generations no new blood has entered, where everybody is cousin, first, second, or third, to everybody else for miles around, the children are mostly dull of mind and scrawny of body. Not infrequently, however, there will be born a child of clear features and strong, straight body, as a reminder of earlier pioneer days when clear features and strong, straight bodies were the rule rather than the exception. Bill Pippinger had two such children, Crawford and Judith. Crawford was, like many of the good-looking children of the neighborhood, merely an empty shell. He had inherited the appearance of some pioneer ancestor without any of the qualities of initiative and energy that had made him a pioneer. Judith, however, was quite different. Sometimes when she was bringing up Roanie and Reddie from the pasture at a fast trot or driving the mules out of the cornfield with much whooping, arm-waving, and bad language, Bill, watching her dynamic, long-legged little figure, would say with a sort of restrained admiration: "Land, that little gal's got life enough for a dozen sech—too much life, too much life for a gal!"

CHAPTER II

FROM early babyhood Judith had shown signs of an energy that craved constant outlet. From the time that she began to creep about on an old quilt spread on the kitchen floor, she was never still except when asleep. She soon passed the boundaries of the quilt, then of the kitchen, and began bruising her temples by pitching head first from the rather high doorstep. After two or three accidents of this sort, she mastered the art of crawling down the steps backward, and could soon do it with surprising agility. She did not creep on her knees, but went on all fours like a little bear, her small haunches high in the air. Soon, with this method of locomotion, she was going all over the yard and even following her father out into the cow lot, sticking close to his heels like a small dog. After she learned to walk the farm could no longer contain her, and she was many times brought back home by neighbors who happened upon her as she strayed away along the roadside.

As she grew older, she showed a strong interest in all living things about the farm. She followed after her mother when she went to feed the chickens, slop the pigs, and milk the cows. She watched her father hook up the mules; and when he plowed trotted along behind him in the furrow for hours together. She was great friends with Minnie, the big Maltese cat, and gave an excited welcome to each of her frequent litters of kittens. Perhaps more than any other animal on the farm she loved old Bounce, the dog, a good-natured and intelligent mongrel, mostly shepherd, brindle of color and growing with age increasingly lazy of habit. She was jubilant when a hen that had stolen her nest would come proudly out from under the barn or behind the pigpen clucking to a dozen or so fluffy little yellow-legged chickens, all spotless and dainty. Once she came upon a turkey's nest in a weed-shaded corner of the rail fence and, stooping with breathless excitement, saw

15

that the little turkeys had just that day come out of the shell.
They peeped at her from under the old turkey hen, not with
the bright, saucy looks of little chickens, but with shy, wild,
frightened eyes, like timid little birds. Even better than the
turkeys and chickens, Judith liked the little geese. They were
so big and fluffy when they came out of the shell, and such a
beautiful, soft green; and they waddled and bobbed their heads
so quaintly, as they moved in a little, compact band over the
bluegrass that they loved to eat. They were prettier still when
they sailed, like a fleet of little boats at anchor, in some quiet
corner of the creek, the sun flecking their green bodies with
pale gold as it blinked at them through the boughs of the overhanging willow tree.

She was absorbed in all the small life that fluttered and
darted and hopped and crawled about the farm. The robins
and finches that sang and built their nests in the big hickory
tree by the gate; the butterflies, white, yellow, and parti-
colored, that fluttered among the weeds and grasses; the big
dragonflies with gauzy wings iridescently green and purple in
the sunlight, that darted back and forth over the brook: these
little creatures, with their sweet voices, their gay colors and shy,
elusive ways, entered into Judith's life and became a part of
it. The grass and the bare ground, too, were alive for Judith,
alive with the life of beetles, crickets, ants, and innumerable
other worms and insects. The toads that hopped about in the
evening were her friends; and when she happened upon a
snake she did not scream and run as Lizzie May would have
done, but stood leaning forward on tiptoe admiring its colors,
the wonder and beauty of its pattern and the sinuous grace of
its movement until it wiggled out of sight in the grass.

She loved fish, too: the long, slinky pickerel that live where
the pond is full of reeds and water lilies, the whiskered catfish
and the beautiful perch, banded with light and dark green, as
though they had taken their colors from the sun-flecked banks
along which they lived. Better than these big pond fish, because they were smaller and nearer and so more intimately
hers, she liked the little "minnies" that lived in her own creek.

From time to time she had been lucky enough to secure a minnow, which she would bring home triumphantly in a salmon can. She would set the can down on the doorstep, fill it up with fresh water from the cistern and sprinkle the water lavishly with bread crumbs for the minnow's refreshment. Then she would sit with the can in her lap and lovingly watch the little dark, sinuous body slipping about beneath the bread crumbs.

The next morning she would find the little fish that only yesterday had been so dark and graceful and lively, lying inert and white-bellied among the sodden bread crumbs at the top of the water.

Then the pitiless grip of self-accusing horror and remorse would tighten on Judith. It made her leaden-hearted to think that she had been the cause of the death of this happy little creature that had seemed to love its life so well. Anguished in spirit, she would make frantic efforts to revive the minnow by supplying him with fresh water and bread crumbs and restoring him to his living position in the water, valiantly opposing her eager endeavors and warm pity against the iron inexorableness of death. But all in vain! The fresh water and bread crumbs always failed to interest him; and as soon as the anxious fingers that held him back upward were removed, he would turn up his little white, pink-veined belly to the fresh morning sunshine that would never gladden him again. Sadly Judith would own her defeat at last and, sick at heart with a sorrow too deep and real for childish tears, she would bury her hapless victim in a tiny, flower-lined grave, resolved that she would never again be so cruel as to catch a minnow. But in a few days, with the easy forgetfulness of childhood, she would slip away to the creek, salmon can in hand; and the old rapture and the old agony would sway her too eager soul all over again.

It seemed to Judith at such times, as she would sit on the doorstep staring dismally into vacancy, that not only in relation to minnows, but to everything else in life, she was foredoomed to failure—failure disastrous not only to herself but still more so to the objects that she tried to befriend and benefit. Mud turtles brought from the swampy land near the creek and kept in a soap box in the yard always died. Butterflies imprisoned in an old, rusty bird cage, though watched and tended ever so carefully, always died. Grasshoppers that she tried to domesticate by keeping them in a pasteboard box with holes punched in it, even though tempted with raisins filched from her mother's pantry and called by the most endearing of pet names, always died. Beautiful, fuzzy, amber-colored caterpillars, treated in like manner, always died. The little girl, sitting meditatively chin on hand, wondered vaguely why all her efforts should be followed by such a curse of blight and disaster. One day she heard, coming nearer and nearer, the sound of sharp, shrill voices and harsh, staccato laughs which she recognized at once as those of boys. Peering through the tall weeds, she saw coming along the road the two Blackford boys, Jerry and Andy, who lived about half a mile farther along. They had with them a small, forlorn, white kitten, which, after the manner of boys, they were amusing themselves by torturing. Just as Judith looked, Andy gave its tail a sharp tweak; and the miserable little thing whined piteously and looked about in a feeble, watery-eyed fashion, for a way of escape. Then Jerry caught up the little creature by its limp tail and whirled it around and around in the air, shouting inarticulately, like the young savage that he was.

When Judith saw the hapless plight of the kitten, a spirit of uncontrollable horror and rage born of horror entered into her. The mother feeling, an instinct which rarely showed itself in her, would not let her see this little animal tortured. Her face blazed scarlet, her eyes flashed with a wild glitter, her long arms and legs grew strong and tense. She dropped her basket, leapt the picket fence and rushed upon the boys like an avenging Fury, her knife in her hand.

"You let that cat alone! Give it up to me! How dare you hurt a poor little helpless cat? By gollies I'll cut you! I'll kill you! Oh! Oh! Oh! Oh!"

The "Oh's" that Lady Macbeth uttered as she walked in

her sleep were not more full of tragic horror than were Judith's as she brandished her knife to right and left in a frenzy of tumultuous emotions. Her long black pigtails, tied at the ends with bits of red grocer's twine, bobbed wildly in the air. Barefooted and bareheaded and wearing a faded and torn blue calico dress, she was yet in spirit a very queen of tragedy as she lunged with her kitchen knife and called down imprecations upon the heads of Jerry and Andy.

Her fury daunted the boys. They had had differences of opinion with Judith before and they knew how she-devilish she could be when angry. They had had experience of her biting, scratching, kicking, and hair-pulling as well as of the hard blows of her strong little clenched fists. While dodging one of the lunges of the knife, Jerry let go of the cat; and Judith instantly snatched it up and stood at bay, the knife poised in one hand, the cat in the other.

"Naow then, one of you jes dass come near here an' I'll run this knife right in yer guts! See if I don't!"

Jerry and Andy showed some sense of the value of discretion. They made no step forward, but stood where they were and bandied compliments.

"You wait till we git ye comin' home from school, ye little slut!" threatened Andy.

"Guess I'll wait a spell, too," retorted Judith, sticking out a viperish red tongue. "I'm not a-skairt of you ner ten more like ye. I can lick any kid in yer family; an' my father can lick yer father, too."

"Oh, can he so?" mocked Jerry. "Mebbe he'd better come over an' try!"

"He don't need to. He wouldn't dirt his hands to touch yer greasy ole dad. But he could if he had a mind to."

"I know sumpin 'bout you! Ah ha, I know sumpin 'bout you!" caroled Jerry derisively.

Judith had begun to lose interest in the verbal encounter.

"Aw shet up yer dirty mouth!" she snapped disgustedly, as she crawled back into her own yard through a hole in the picket fence.

The boys went on down the road walking backward, their fingers to their noses, calling after her in diminishing chorus.

"Cowardly kids! Cowardly kids! Cowardly kids!" returned Judith scornfully, until the enemy voices could no longer be heard.

When she got back to the house she set down her basket by the kitchen door, carried the kitten into the kitchen and got it a saucer of milk. Its eyes were bleared and abject in expression, its sharp little bones almost stuck through its dingy white fur; and its discouraged little tail, tangled with burrs, drooped pitifully.

Judith examined the frail joints of its legs and was immensely relieved to find that none of them were broken. Their intactness seemed to her a miracle; for they were so thin and small and delicate that it seemed as though the slightest blow or pressure would crush them. She shuddered as she felt these fragile joints; and through her whole body there surged a great ocean of tenderness and pity for this defenseless little creature. She experienced a vague, but overwhelming sensation of its pitiful helplessness against all the great, cruel powers of nature, which seemed to be conspiring against it. A clumsy foot, a slamming door, the fall of a flatiron from her mother's ironing board: these and a thousand such could cruelly mangle its frail body and even crush out its tiny spark of life. With a blank, painful, discouraged ache in her heart, Judith wondered vaguely why the whole world should be so rough and cruel and hazardous a place for kittens and minnows and all small, unbefriended things. She did not know that she was precociously experiencing the feeling of many a young mother who, with the birth of her helpless firstborn, feels in one overwhelming rush all the tragedy of weakness in a world where the weak must acquire strength or perish.

The very ugliness of the little thing endeared it to her; for it was a pitiable ugliness, an ugliness born of hunger and ill-treatment. Tenderly she stroked its mangy little head and vowed that she would take care of it and stand between it and the cruel world all the days of its life.

In the morning as soon as she awoke her thoughts flew to
the kitten. She scrambled into her clothes and ran out into
the yard, glancing about the empty kitchen as she passed
through. For a long time she searched in vain and was beginning to think that the kitten had wandered away when of
a sudden down at the foot of the hill she stopped in amazement and horror. Here in the heavy clay land beside the
creek was a little pool that she had hollowed out the day
before and into which she had put four live minnows. The
flowers that she had planted around it had all wilted and fallen
over. Some were lying flat on the muddy ground, some trail-
ing lifeless in the water. Their bright yellows and purples
and pinks had all faded into a common drab. On the edge
of the water sat the white kitten. And even as she gazed with
horror-dilated eyes it fished up a live minnow with its paw and
crunched it mercilessly between its small, strong jaws. In a
dazed, half-hearted way Judith looked down into the water
of the pond and saw that there was now nothing there—
nothing alive—only the pebbles and mosses and half dead
water plants.

Silently she turned and ran away, far, far away from the
unspeakable kitten and the dead flowers and the empty pool
and all the hideous horror of it.

From that day she never again felt the same poignancy of
distress at the sight of suffering and death among animals.
As she grew more intimately into the life of the woods and
the fields and the barnyard she learned to take for granted
certain laws of nature which at first had seemed distressingly
harsh and cruel. She became resigned to the knowledge that
the big fishes eat the little ones, that the chickens devour the
grasshoppers, that Bounce, the gentle and affectionate, would
kill rabbits and groundhogs whenever he could get hold of
them: that in all the bird and animal and insect world the
strong prey continually upon the weak. It was hard at first
to see Minnie's whole litter of kittens but one dropped into a
bucket of water and drowned and to watch her father lead off
to the butcher the calf that for two months she had been feed-

ing and petting. But these things happened so often, and the law of the survival of the fittest was so firmly established a part of the life of the farm that she soon learned to accept it with equanimity. She might have been slower in learning this lesson if she had been given to self-deception. But she could never lull her sensibilities with this so commonly used opiate. She insisted upon standing over the bucket in which the kittens were drowned and upon knowing exactly what was going to happen to the calf. Soon she discovered that however many little fishes were eaten there were always plenty more; that an endless number of birds and butterflies and grasshoppers sang and fluttered and jumped through the summer days regardless of the depredations of their enemies; that there were always more kittens and calves being born. Without putting the thought into words or even thinking it, but merely sensing it physically, she knew that in the life of nature death and suffering are merely incidentals; that the message that nature gives to her children is "Live, grow, be happy, and obey my promptings." The birds and chickens and grasshoppers all heard it and Judith knew they heard it. Judith heard it too. As she trotted to school in the clear, sun-vibrant air of the early morning, or brought up the cows through the sweet-smelling twilight, or picked blackberries on the edge of the sunny pasture, nature kept whispering these words in her ear. It is given to few civilized human beings to ever hear this message. Perhaps in that generation Bill Pippinger's girl was the only human being in the whole of Scott County who heard and heeded these words: "Live, grow, be happy, and obey my promptings."

For a number of reasons religion never became a part of Judith's life. The Pippingers were not a church-going family nor were many of their neighbors. The consolations of religion were sought more by the village people who had no morning and evening chores to do and were handy to the churches. A deep-seated, if rather vague respect remained, however, in the mental make-up of these country folk for the religion of their fathers. An ill-defined fear, a dim hope, and a few inhibitions remained of the once more vigorous religious life. Judith sensed these things as she grew into girlhood; but they could find no foothold in the healthy vigor of her spirit.

Once when she was ten years old, she went with the rest of the family to a camp revival meeting where the preaching evangelist described with lurid language and fear-compelling inflections the last judgment day and the tortures of an eternal damnation in a hell burning forever with fire and brimstone. The task of browbeating an ignorant audience was apparently one that the preacher enjoyed mightily; for he went at it with tremendous vigor and zest. At times his voice sank to an awe-inspiring whisper, then rose to a demoniac shriek as he sought to bully and terrify his hearers into a state of nerve collapse. Judith listened with eyes that showed more and more of the whites. The lurid pictures were printed instantly on the sensitive plate of her keen imagination. She took the preacher seriously, literally, which fortunately few in the audience appeared to do. She looked around at their stolid, peaceful faces and felt somewhat reassured. Perhaps it wasn't true after all.

On the way home she asked her father if what the preacher had said was true.

"Waal, I reckon it is an' it ain't," answered Bill, spitting over the side of the wagon. "Mebbe Uncle Ezra Pettit is a-goin' to the hot place. An' I kinder hope he is—not wishin' 'im no bad luck. An' Sam Whitmarsh'll like enough pull up there too. Lord knows he's done enough dirty tricks to deserve to fry good, an' on both sides. An' Uncle Ezry'll be mad whichever place he goes, 'cause he'll have to leave his money an' his land behind. But anyhow me ner mine hain't a-goin' to no hot place, ner nobody else that tends their own business. Git up, Bob! Lord love them mules, they're a-comin' to be slower'n the seven year itch."

Her father's unconcern greatly allayed Judith's apprehensions; but the picture drawn by the evangelist was too fresh and vivid to be forgotten at once. That night Judith dreamed that the end of the world had come. Portentous curtains of black, like a hundred thunder storms in one, hung from the sky. Stabbing the blackness came one sharp arrow of crimson light, glowing, intense, and awe-inspiring. Slowly and dreadfully the arrow lengthened, widened, gathered blinding light and burning heat. The judge of the world was coming in his majesty to sit upon the judgment seat. People rushed from their houses and tried to hide in haystacks, under piles of old lumber or in the rooted-out holes beneath hogpens. Judith herself, with a despairing realization that the worst had really happened and that the world would never again be peaceful and sunshiny, ran out into the dooryard. At that moment the air was split by a terrible blast from Gabriel's trumpet. The blast woke Judith and turned out to be only her father passing the window and blowing his nose onto the ground between his thumb and forefinger.

It was an immense relief to Judith to find that it was only a dream, that the sun still shone and the birds sang and her mother was frying corncakes for breakfast and Craw was chasing the big black hog out of the yard and everything was going to be the way it was before.

CHAPTER III

BUT with the growth of this harmony with natural things,
Judith developed a constantly growing tendency to clash with
the life of the school and the home kitchen and the kitchens
of the various relatives with whom the Pippingers visited. She
was considered by her aunts and other female relatives "a
wild, bad little limb," and her contempt for the decent and
domestic scandalized them more and more as she grew older.
Lena Moss could not for her life understand how it was that
Judith had learned to read and write and figure better than
almost any other child in the school; for she was anything but
studious. In fact she never seemed to pay the slightest attention to her studies. She flatly refused even to try to learn
Lena's long and carefully prepared list of all the counties and
county towns in Kentucky; and the battles of the Revolu-
tionary and Civil wars, with their accompanying dates, found
no lodgment in her mind. Instead of applying herself to these,
she munched apples, chewed slippery elm and sassafras, stared
idly out of the window, bedeviled the child who sat in front of
her, cut folded bits of paper into intricate designs or drew pictures on her slate, the desk, the seat, the floor, the back of
the pinafore of the girl in front, any available space within
her reach.

These pictures were the curse of Lena's existence. They
were to be found everywhere: on the desks, the walls, the floor,
the blackboard, the window casings. Outside they decorated
the whitewashed wall of the school building, the tops of big
flat stones, the fences, the trunks of trees where the bark had
been stripped away, every place where a piece of chalk or a
bit of black crayon could function.

The pictures, invariably of human beings or animals, were
usually comic, satirical or derisive. That they showed great
vigor and clarity of vision would have meant nothing to Lena

even if she had known it. They were, in her phraseology, "not nice!" They were frequently disrespectful. The morning after the visit of the county superintendent, a large picture in white chalk was found on the blackboard wickedly caricaturing the features of that august personage. The picture was done in profile and exaggerated irreverently the large, bulbous nose, the receding forehead, and the many chins reaching around to a fleshy, pendulous ear. Poor Lena was hard put to it to find a way to control this unruly member of her school. Having much less force of character than her pupil, the advantage of years and vested authority availed her little.

When asked why she had done thus and so, Judith's almost invariable reply was: "Cuz I had to."

"Judy, why hain't you a better gal at school?" Bill asked one morning, trying to look sternly at his favorite daughter across the mush and milk. "Lizzie May says the teacher has a heap o' grief with you. Why don't you mind the teacher, Judy?"

"I do mind her, dad—all I can," Judith returned without looking up. She had the syrup pitcher in her hand and was absorbed in pouring sorghum onto her plate in a very thin stream. Presently she set the pitcher down and handed the plate across the table to her father.

"There, dad, ain't that a good mule? I drawed 'im with the blackstrap. Lizzie May couldn't draw a mule like that."

"Ner I don't want to neither," put in Lizzie May disdainfully. "You otta see, dad, sech pitchers as she draws all raound the school, an' makes fun of everybody: the teacher an' the sup'rintendent an' her own relations an' all. She'd otta think shame to herse'f!"

Bill was proud of his girl's ability to draw, but felt it his duty to discourage her choice of subjects, seeing that the same seemed to be so universally condemned.

"What makes you draw them kind o' pitchers, Judy?" he asked.

"Cuz I want to," replied Judith a little sullenly. "I see things; an' when I see 'em I want to draw 'em."

"O law, she don't see no sech things, dad! Haow kin she? Nobody else sees 'em!" exclaimed Lizzie May, outraged. "Why, the idea of her sayin' she sees sech things!"

"Aw, shet up, Liz, an' tend yer own business!" snapped Judith, flushing red with sudden anger. "Jest cuz you don't see nuthin don't mean nobody else does."

She pushed her chair back from the table and began to gather together her school books, slamming them on top of each other with angry energy. Bill said no more; he was not a disciplinarian.

"It's your turn to wash the dishes, Judy," reminded Luella, who was busy helping her mother put up the midday lunch. "Lizzie May washed 'em yestiddy an' I did 'en day before."

"Why don't Craw have to take his turn washin' dishes?" inquired Judith, who was still nettled from the recent argument.

"Craw's a boy. Boys don't wash dishes," adjudged Luella in a tone of dead finality.

"I don't see why he hadn't otta," continued Judith, as she slapped the plates together. "Far's I c'n see he ain't no good fer nuthin else."

The subject of this conversation, engaged in his favorite occupation of doing nothing in a rocking chair by the stove, looked at his sisters with a mild, impartial eye and said nothing. He was safe and aloof in his masculinity.

"Land, hain't that a nice pattern this platter is burned into, Elly!" exclaimed Judith, examining a small platter which she had just picked up from the table. "Look here at all the nice squares an' di'monds—an' all jes as even!"

"I don't see nothing nice about it," said Luella with a half glance at the platter. "It's burned so's it won't never come white agin. It was you done that, Judy, puttin' it in the oven with them slices o' hog meat on it an' fergittin it till the grease was all burnt into smoke. An' sech a stink as it made when mammy opened the oven door! A person could hardly git their breath."

"Well, I like it anyway," said Judith cheerfully. "It's a good thing somebody likes these old, cracked-over plates, cuz most all of 'em is cracked over. I have lots o' fun lookin' at 'em an' seein' all the diff'rent patterns they git burnt into."

"Yes, an' that's why it takes you so long to wash up the dishes. If you don't hurry you're a-goin' to be tardy for school. The rest of us is a-fixin' to start naow, an' you'll have to run to ketch up."

"I ain't a-goin' to ketch up if I don't want to," returned Judith. "An' if I'm tardy, you hain't got no call to be a-frettin' yo'se'f."

This sort of bickering between Judith and her sisters went on daily in the Pippinger home and increased as the children grew older. Luella and Lizzie May, good, right-minded, docile little girls, looked down upon Judith from the height of two whole years of seniority and felt it their duty to try to make her as good, right-minded and docile as themselves.

There was a half-story attic above the three ground rooms occupied by the Pippingers, and this attic was the girls' bedroom. Here the three slept together in a big wooden bed made all of twisted spirals. The bed had a straw tick and in winter many thicknesses of patchwork quilts. In summer one quilt was enough and often too much; for the windows were small and the roof low; and on hot, breathless nights no air seemed to enter. In summer the bedbugs came out of the walls and Aunt Annie Pippinger saturated the bed once a month or so with kerosene and corrosive sublimate, the odor of which lingered for many days after the application. Between the windows stood an old cherry chest of drawers which had once been a handsome piece of furniture, but was now much scratched and scarred by hard usage. Each girl had one of the three drawers, and here they kept their clothes and treasures.

Luella and Lizzie May had each a pincushion of silk patchwork in the then popular "crazy" style, and fatly stuffed with bran. Luella had a box the lid of which was encrusted with small shells surrounding a red velvet pincushion shaped like a heart. In this box she kept carefully folded bits of silk, velvet and lace; locks of hair cut from the heads of all her relatives, wrapped in tissue paper and labeled with the name of the grower, glass beads, fancy buttons, Christmas cards, pressed flowers, small empty scent bottles and the like. Lizzie May had a similar accumulation but hers was housed in a box with a colored picture on the lid. This picture showed a young lady dressed in a very low-necked pink satin evening gown and a white fur muff and scarf, adjusting a pair of skates on pink satin slippers in the midst of a snowy winter landscape powdered with frosting to make it more realistic. Lizzie May liked this picture very much. She often took out the box just to gaze at the lovely pink satin evening gown, the delicate hands and the pink satin slippers.

Poor Judy had no such treasure box. She often looked at her sisters' collections with envious eyes and wished for as much as two minutes together that she too had some nice things. Somehow she had never been able to collect things. Her drawer contained nothing but her little old frocks and underwear and holey stockings thrown together in a tousled heap, and perhaps a few pine cones and clam shells and odd pebbles that she had picked up from time to time.

There were several colored pictures on the walls, mostly calendars of previous years, much fly-specked and yellowed on the edges. One of these, an advertisement for some kind of corset, represented the upper two thirds of a young woman with bright pink cheeks and golden hair, attired in a chemise and a straight-front corset and holding an Easter lily in her hand. On one side of the chest of drawers was an old, much faded chromo showing a child with a tremendously large head, dressed in skin-tight red satin breeches and pale blue coat with lace ruffles in front looking at a kitten which was playing with a pink ball on the floor. This picture was enclosed in a frame the ends of which stuck out beyond the picture, forming little crosspieces at each corner. On the floor were several pieces of frayed rag carpet and before the bed an oval braided rag mat.

Luella and Lizzie May spent a good deal of their time in this sanctum, "redding up," looking over their treasures, exchanging confidences and sewing patch-work blocks. But Judith

hardly ever went into the room except to go to bed. She liked
her father's company and her father's occupations better than
those of her sisters. She stood at his side and watched him as
he nailed the bright new shoes with the bright new horseshoe
nails onto the hoofs of Tom and Bob. When he said, "Whoa!"
she said "Whoa!" with a faithful echo of his tone and inflec-
tion. She loved to hear the cheerful strokes of the hammer
and watch the sparks fly from the piece of old railroad iron
which Bill used as an anvil. When he stretched a piece of
wire fence she was there to hand him the wire stretchers, the
pliers, the hammer, the staples. And whenever he mended
spots in the old rail fence she caused Bill much inconvenience
by insisting on lifting one end of each rail. She liked to watch
and help him when he had a job of carpentry to do, a bench
to make, or a shelf or some new chicken coops for the spring
broods. She ran and fetched the hammer, the nails, the brace,
and bit. She held the ends of boards while he nailed them,
dragged up more boards; and all the time she watched eagerly.
As he worked Bill chewed tobacco and whistled and now and
then broke out into a rather tuneless attempt at a song:

> Grasshopper settin' on the sweet petater vine;
> Turkey gobbler come up from behin'
> An' peck him off'n the sweet petater vine
> In the mo'nin', in the mo'nin'.

Judith pirouetting about, would sing the song after him, but
with the correct time and tune.

"Seems like you c'n beat yer dad at singin', Judy," Bill
would say proudly. "I never was one that could hang onto a
tune. After a bit, somehaow, it'd allus git away from me.
Hand me them there pinchers—the little uns with the shiny
ends onto 'em."

Judith liked to work around the mules and was soon en-
trusted with the task of leading them to water and pitching hay
into their manger. In the stable she would get down the curry
brush and comb from the beam where Bill kept them and curry

them down with many shouts of "Whoa, ye bugger!" and "Git araound there naow!" When there was an errand to do at the neighbor's, she would ride Tom or Bob barebacked, guiding the old mule proudly with tightly held bridle reins. She liked to go with her father in the spring wagon when he went to Clayton or Sadieville or took corn to the mill to be ground. The clear morning sunshine, the sweet air, the life of the woods and fields all about them mingled exultantly with the rattle of the wagon as it jolted over the ruts in the dirt road, the strong, horsey smell of the mules and the grinding creak of the brake as Tom and Bob held back on the steep hillsides. Perched beside her father on the seat, she insisted on driving and was indignant when Bill would take the lines from her hands at the top of a steep hill or on the approach of another team.

Whenever they met a neighbor or relative—and almost everybody they met was a neighbor or relative—Bill would rein up the mules, the other team would pull up alongside, and there would be a long spell of roadside visiting. There would not be much said, but it would take a long time to say it; and Judith would sometimes grow impatient.

"Dad, why do you stop so long an' talk to folks on the road?" she would ask.

"Why-ee, I dunno. I allus done so ever sence I was a boy, an' my dad allus done so afore me. I like to know haow folks is a-comin' on. You wouldn't have me drive right on with nuthin but a 'Howdy' would you? 'Twouldn't be neighborly."

The mill was a mile or so beyond the village on the bank of a pleasant little stream which furnished it with water power. It was built of logs mortared with mud, and grass grew in the chinks. It was a very small mill the single business of which was to grind corn into meal for the corn cakes of the neighborhood. When Judith and her father would drive up, everything would be silent; not a sign of life but the turning wheel and perhaps a chicken pecking along the path or a pigeon cooing from the roof.

"Hey, Dave! Hey, Dave!" Bill would call, as he tied the mules to the hitching post. Presently Dave Fields, the miller, would come hobbling down the path from his house which stood a few rods away hidden among locust trees. He was a shriveled little old man with one leg shorter than the other from rheumatism and a pair of merry blue eyes twinkling from under bushy white eyebrows.

"Waal, howdy, Bill. Purty weather we're a-havin' naow. Yer folks all smart?"

"Yaas, we keep middlin' smart. How's yo'se'f an' the woman, Dave?"

"Oh, we git about; we git about. But we hain't what we onct was, Bill. The woman had one o' them asthmy spells last week; an' my rheumatics keeps me purty stiff. But of course we're a-gittin' old. We can't complain. Haow much corn you got?"

"Oh, mebbe a couple o' bushel," Bill would answer, lifting the sack out of the wagon.

"Waal, Judy, an' hoaw're you a-feelin' to-day? You're a-growin' to be a great big gal. You'd best stop here with me an' mammy. We hain't got no little uns no more."

And the old miller would chuck the little girl under the chin good-naturedly, as she looked at him with wide, questioning eyes.

Then the mill would be put in operation and Judith would be fascinated by the sight of the golden meal pouring into the hopper.

When the corn was ground, the old man took a tenth for his share and put the rest back into Bill's sack. Then, but with no unseemly haste, the meal was lifted into the wagon and the mules untied and turned in the direction of home.

"Waal, Dave, you an' yer woman come over."

"Yaas, we'll be along by there some day. You come some Sunday an' stop all day with us."

And at last they would go rattling away up the hill toward Clayton.

Then to Peter Akers' general merchandise store to buy flour

and sugar and coffee and a ten cent sack of candy for the children. There were always a few loungers here and even in midsummer they stood from force of habit about the tall, rusty, pot-bellied stove, spitting tobacco juice into the little sawdust yard which surrounded it. While her father made his purchases and passed the time of day with the loungers about the stove, Judith would walk about looking at the bright-patterned calicoes and chintzes ranged on the shelves, the shiny dippers and saucepans, the straw hats and piles of blue denim overalls, the brooms standing upside down in a round rack, the gleaming hoes and rakes and shovels with bright-painted handles. Around the walls just below the ceiling ran a frieze of galvanized washtubs and tin plated boilers. The showcase stood on the counter near the door, and Judith, having passed all the other things in review, would flatten the end of her small nose against the glass looking at pink and yellow cakes of scented soap, barber's pole sticks of candy, bottles of ink, silk ribbons, tooth brushes, pads of letter paper, alarm clocks, pocket combs, and sheets of tanglefoot fly paper, arranged much as they have been here enumerated. She never tired of doing this. To her the store was a vast emporium capable of satisfying every human need or whim. She rarely teased Bill to buy her a ribbon or a toy, partly because she knew that he needed the money for horseshoe nails and flour; and partly because there was nothing here that she really wanted very much for herself. She felt no acute need in her own life for any of the contents of the showcase; but she regarded them none the less with deep respect and admiration.

Often Peter Akers, a baldish, pot-bellied man with a flabby face and old-fashioned sideboards, would lean across the counter with professional affability and chuck the little girl under the chin.

"Waal, Judy, you like to come in taown with yer dad? You'd best stay here an' keep store with me. Wouldn't you like to help keep store?"

Judith, looking straight at him with level, grave eyes, would answer never a word.

Then over to Jim Townsend, the blacksmith, to get some plate shoes in case a neighbor should come with a job of horseshoeing to do. Once Jim looked admiringly at Judith, whom he was really seeing for the first time, although she had been there dozens of times before.

"You got a handsome gal there, Bill," he said.

"All my gals is handsome," answered Bill complacently. "But this one here is more a boy'n a gal. She's her dad's hired hand, she is. She helps me shoe the mules, she does."

"Waal, waal, so she's a blacksmith's helper! I'm needin' a hand. Wouldn't ye like to stay here an' help me shoe hosses, eh, little gal?"

Judith looked him through and through and made no reply.

"Dad, do folks really want other folks' chillun to come an' live with 'em?" she asked her father, when they were back in the wagon.

"No, Judy, I can't say they do," Bill answered. "Other folks' young uns is gener'ly wanted 'bout as much as other folks' ailments."

"Then why do they keep a-askin' me to come an' live with 'em?"

"Oh, I dunno. It's jes a way they have. They done like that when I was a lad too."

"I wish they wouldn't," said Judith.

Then, as they drove back home through the sleepy heat of the noonday, Judith would grow hungrier and hungrier and her one thought would be of dinner. She could smell it as soon as they pulled up in the barnyard: boiled hog meat and mustard greens and young beets and potatoes. How good it tasted when at last she had a heaping plateful in front of her with a generous tin mug of cool skim milk to wash it down!

Judith liked best of all the autumn season, when the sky was a hazy, tender blue and the mellow sunshine lay like a film of golden tissue over all the earth. Then there were plenty of apples to munch; and she could go out into the garden and pick the big, red, juicy tomatoes and eat them alive, as it were, before they had been slaughtered by her mother's paring knife. Then the corn stood in the shocks and the big, yellow pumpkins lay scattered among the stubble, suggestive of plenty. The hickory nuts and black walnuts began to drop from the early frosts, the trees turned bronze and russet and scarlet and the warm air was full of bees and butterflies and other humming, buzzing, fluttering things. The tobacco fields lay brown and bare and deserted; but from the big tobacco barns there welled forth a fragrance that was for these Kentuckians, the soul of autumn. Oozing out into the golden sunshine from every crack in the great structures, it exhilarated like an elixir, like a long draught of some rich, spicy wine. The big doors, left open to allow a free current of air, showed the long, yellowish-brown bunches hanging thick-serried in the fragrant gloom.

It was an intoxication to her at this time to be alive, to gather and eat the good things that the earth so generously provided, to see the autumn glory of the woods and roadsides, to feel the glow of the sun, the warmth of the earth under her bare feet, and to sniff in the spicy exhalations of the great barns.

On these autumn days the sun sank early; and this was the time that the Pippinger children most enjoyed their play. There was something about the chilly drawing-in of these October twilights that made them want to leap and run and throw their arms about and utter wild, animal-like noises into the gathering night. Judith was always the leader in these games, and her wild abandon easily infected the others. Round and round the clothesline prop they would fly in the game of "Go in and out the Windows," and "The Farmer in the Dell," the long braids bobbing, the boys' shirttails, escaped from their overalls, flapping in the wind with the girls' petticoats. Then, tiring of this, there would be "Hide and Seek," "Tom, Tom, pull away," and the inexhaustible "Tag."

Minnie, the cat, liked these evenings too, and so did her kitten and the white cat that Judith had rescued from the Blackford boys. The cats, like the children, were filled with a spirit of kobold friskiness, as though their evening bowl of skim milk had gone to their heads. In daytime they did nothing but stretch, sleep, yawn, and wash their faces in the sun; but the chill of the autumn evening brought to them also the spirit of adventure. In their strong, slinky litheness, they jumped and darted and climbed; and the children watching them envied them their perfect unison of body and spirit. Minnie, in spite of all her years and the many times that she had been a mother, was a kitten again. Nothing would do her but she must run clear to the top of the clothesline prop, scratch mightily with her front claws as though sharpening them, then make a sudden leap to the grass and circle about like a mad thing. Her kitten darted up into the lilac bush and peered down at the children with glowing topaz eyes, then whisked away to circle after its mother. The white cat, frisking in and out among the shadows, made the children think of ghosts.

Often a wind would spring up out of the west as the twilight thickened, and the young Pippingers would run in the face of it, their hair blown back, their arms waving wildly, their voices ringing shrilly into the autumn night: little Valkyries of the hills.

Once, as they were playing a ring game by the barn, a big red moon rose over the brow of the hill and showed their dancing figures silhouetted sharply in black on the barn wall. The weird little shadow figures seemed like a troop of goblin companions that had come to join their play. The more wildly they pranced and threw their arms about, the more reckless and drunken grew the little shadow creatures on the wall, stimulating them in turn to a still greater frenzy of abandon. The wind blew in their faces and brought subtle whiffs of fragrance from the big tobacco barn down the ridge. The other children soon forgot this evening; but to Judith it remained always as one of the exalted moments of her life.

When the children were called in to supper after these autumn orgies, they would come with ruddy cheeks and blazing eyes. Bill, looking about the table, would say with satisfaction: "Them young uns ain't a-lookin' poorly. Guess we won't need to call in the doctor for 'em yet a spell."

The little glass lamp would be lighted in the middle of the oilcloth-covered table; and there would be fried potatoes and a big red platter of sliced tomatoes and roastin' ears steaming hot—a delicious meal!

The winter season was not such a happy one for the Pippinger children. Usually the weather would be warm and pleasant and the roads dry up to Thanksgiving or even later. But then would come the inevitable heavy frosts, followed by thaws and the cold, dismal rains that lasted sometimes for days together. Then the young Pippingers had to stay home from school and time hung very heavy on their hands. They bickered and quarreled and yawned and stared idly out of the window at the drearily falling rain and the dismal expanse of mud that would be there till the April sun dried it up.

Sometimes when the house grew too unbearably dull and small, they threw their coats over their heads and plodded through the heavy mud to the barn to play in the corn fodder and consort with the mules and chickens. It was a great relief to their mother to get them out of the house. Around the barn, the sodden stable dung made a lake of stinking filth and the children had to step very carefully from stone to stone to avoid sinking into it. Inside it was fun for a while to jump about in the clean fodder, to curry the mules and climb on their backs, and to hunt for eggs in the loft and on the top of the beams. But they soon tired of this and trooped back to the house, bringing with them their boredom and a quantity of sticky mud which refused to wipe off on the dirty bit of folded rag carpet before the door.

When the rainy spell was over Mrs. Pippinger heaved a sigh of relief and started them off to school again. Dressed in faded caps and little made-over, outgrown coats, too short in the sleeves and too tight across the chest, they trudged through the mud, glad to be away from the dreary house. When they got to school they were tired to the point of exhaustion; and the mud, which had splashed over their shoe tops, was drying in grayish flakes on their stockings. A tremendous wood fire, built by some of the older boys, blazed in the big box stove and made the room so hot that the children, tired from their long walk and entering that close, heated atmosphere from the chilly freshness of the outdoors, almost fell asleep over their copybooks.

It was worse still as the winter advanced and snow began to fall. The melted snow mixed with the mud and made a thin, oozy, penetrating slush, which usually meant wet feet for the Pippingers. It was not always possible for Bill to provide five new pairs of shoes and five new pairs of rubbers or overshoes with the oncoming of the bad season. And so the shoes were often broken and the rubbers worn into holes in the heels, which gave an easy entrance to the cold winter slush. For this reason and because the air of the schoolhouse was kept so close and overheated, coughs and colds were of very frequent occurrence. The winter, in fact, was one long stretch of barking, sniveling, wheezing, and nose-blowing, with sometimes a more severe attack which kept one or other of the children from school. Mrs. Pippinger always kept on hand in a stone jar a homemade cough syrup consisting of butter, sugar, and vinegar. It did not seem to have any very great curative effect on the coughs and colds; but the children were always glad to take it because it tasted so good.

Then too, as the winter advanced, the pantry and smokehouse grew more and more empty. "Roasin' ears," tomatoes, cucumbers and such garden delicacies were gone with the early frosts. Sweet potatoes, dried out on a shelf behind the kitchen stove, lasted a while longer, but were soon eaten up. White potatoes, cabbage, and pumpkins lasted till about Christmas. After that the frost always got what was left of them, as the Pippingers had no cellar. Christmas, too, saw the last of the apples; for Kentucky is too far south to grow good winter apples. The cured and smoked hog meat hanging in the smokehouse sometimes lasted till spring; but more often it was gone by February. The few jars of jam and cans of peaches and blackberries that Mrs. Pippinger managed to put up through the summer were turned into empty bottles almost before the frost came. Then began a long, lean season of mush and milk for breakfast, corn cakes and drippings for dinner, and corn cakes and sorghum for supper. If Bill could get a job stripping tobacco or shucking corn, there would be some canned goods and a side of bacon from Peter Akers' store. But usually the tobacco was all stripped and the corn all shucked before the lean season came on. Sometimes there was a job of hauling to be had. But the hauling jobs were so few and scattered that they did little more than provide the Pippingers with the occasional sack of flour to make the Sunday and holiday treat of hot biscuit. Bill made special efforts to keep flour in the house, for he did dearly love a light hot biscuit.

CHAPTER IV

THE winter that Judith was twelve years old was an unusually bad one. For days the heavy rains fell drearily over the sodden earth. The all-pervading mud went everywhere in the house, in spite of Mrs. Pippinger's housewifely efforts to keep it out. It dried in light gray flakes on the floor, the rungs of chairs, the lower parts of walls and doors and furniture, wherever careless passing feet smeared it off. When Mrs. Pippinger swept it rose in a fine, dry, choking dust that filled the air and then settled thickly on every object in the room. Luella and Lizzie May were kept busy dusting and shaking the dust-filled rags out at the door. The air of the kitchen was damp with steam from wet coats and overalls hung to dry behind the stove. The woodbox was full of sodden, half-rotten fence rails or newly cut green wood, both of which required the greatest coaxing to induce them to burn. Usually the fence rails had to be dried in the oven. They shed rotted scraps over the oven and the floor and the steam of their drying rose up and joined the other exhalations.

When the rain stopped it always turned cold and a piercing, bitter wind came out of the north. For two or three days it stayed cold, then grew mild and cloudy; the wind changed into the south-east and the fine, penetrating rain began all over again.

One bleak, windy day in February the children came home from school to find their mother with a very bad cold. She had done a big washing the day before, had gone out warm from working in the hot suds and got chilled hanging out the clothes in the bitter wind. She was hot and feverish from the cold, her head ached and her chest was tight. Before going to bed Bill made her rub her chest well with skunk grease and take a tablespoonful of castor oil and a good dose of the sugar and vinegar cough mixture.

40

In the morning she was still poorly and the twins, now grown into a sense of responsibility, insisted on her remaining in bed. They sent Judith and the boys off to school and stayed at home to take care of their mother and do the work. By evening she was much better; and the next day she got up and went about her work as usual.

But two days later, when the children came home from school, she was worse again. She had a high fever, could eat nothing, and failed to make her usual resistance when Bill and the twins insisted on her going straight to bed.

The next day she was no better. The twins stayed home again and Bill drove over and fetched her half sister Abigail.

Aunt Abigail's children were grown and so she could be spared to help in time of sickness. It was for this reason and this only that Bill went for Abigail instead of for Cousin Rubena or Aunt Libby Crupper.

"I might a knowd," she snapped, as she climbed into the wagon, "that Annie'd be daown sick. She don't never take no care of herse'f; an' them folks that don't take care of theirselves makes a heap o' trouble for others. An' I declare with all them near growed-up young uns she works jes as hard as if they was still babies. You an' her has allus babied yer chillun, Bill. They ain't never been made to learn to work the way they'd otta."

Bill made no reply. He always avoided argument with Aunt Abigail. She was the sort of person, not infrequently found in out-of-the-way places, who combines great narrowness with great strength of mind. To a lover of domestic peace and harmony she was not comfortable to live with.

She was considerably older than her sister, a thin, painfully tidy little person with bright, hard, shallow black eyes, a close-shut, thin-lipped mouth and shiny black hair drawn tightly back into a knot that looked as hard as granite. When she took off her jacket and sunbonnet and the many folds of scarf wound round and round her head and neck, she disclosed a spotless checked dress and a white apron with small black polka dots, faultlessly starched and ironed. The apron was frilled and rounded at the corners. The strings, tied in a careful bow in the back, were ample and rustling with starch. Aunt Abigail was very particular about her aprons.

She bustled into the room where her half sister lay in bed restless and feverish.

"Waal Annie, you sholy are a-lookin' bad; an' all, as I ses to Bill, jes 'cause you don't take no care of yo'se'f. The idee of a-goin' aout drippin' with sweat from the washtubs an' hangin' out clothes in this weather when you don't have to! What's all them gals here fer, anyway? Can't they hang aout their mammy's washin' when they git home from school? Law, when I was their age I was a-doin' the washin' an' a-hangin' it aout an' a-cookin' an' a-scrubbin' an' a-milkin' four caows fer dad an' the boys after mammy was took away. Wait till them young uns finds aout what it's like to be without a mammy, an' they'll soon feel the diff'rence."

Aunt Abigail's manner of saying this last almost suggested that she hoped that such time would soon arrive.

The worst thing about Aunt Abigail was her voice. It was even more nasal than that of most Kentuckians; and her a's were harder and flatter. It was hard, shallow, and piercing, like her eyes, and absolutely without depth or resonance. It was as soulless as the hammering of a poker on a tin stewpan. It rang and vibrated through the three rooms of the little log house like a call to arms. The Pippingers all shrank from it but took it for granted because she was their aunt.

"I'd best go on to Clayton, naow I'm hitched, an' fetch Doc MacTaggert," said Bill, looking tentatively at his wife.

"Nothin' o' the kind, Bill! I don't need no doctor. I ain't got but a bad cold, an' I'll be all right in a day or two. You ain't a-goin' to fetch no docter." Mrs. Pippinger's voice had a ring of genuine alarm.

"Waal, I dunno," hesitated Bill, appealing with his eyes to Aunt Abigail, who was bustling about the room setting things to rights.

"If ye'd ast me, I'd say Annie'd otta have a doctor," said Abigail. "But of course folks allus knows their own business

best. I don't never advise people, so's they won't have a chanct
to turn back on me an' say, 'I told ye so!' "

Still Bill hesitated, looking from one woman to the other.

"No, Abigail, I really ain't so bad as that," placated her
sister. " 'Tain't nothin' but a hard cold. An' I think mebbe
if Bill would chop the head off that rooster—the little un that
don't seem to be good fer nothin'—I could take a little chicken
broth."

So Bill went to slaughter the inadequate white rooster and
Aunt Abigail hastened to see to it that there was hot water
to scald him.

But when the chicken broth was made Mrs. Pippinger could
eat none of it. The next day she was no better; but still she
made alarmed resistance whenever Bill suggested going for a
doctor. Aunt Abigail sent home for some more dresses and
aprons and prepared to make a stay of it.

Two days later she was so much worse that Bill did not stop
to argue with her but hitched up and drove to Clayton for Dr.
MacTaggert. Aunt Abigail busied herself mightily putting a
clean gown on Mrs. Pippinger, clean sheets and pillow slips on
the bed, clean towels on the washstand, in preparation for the
august visit.

The doctor came, a bald, dust-colored little man with spec-
tacles and an air of patient resignation to his lot. He took her
pulse and temperature, asked about her bowels, listened at
her chest, and said that she had congestion of the lungs. From
a black leather satchel he took out two bottles of medicine,
some pills in a little brown box, and some pills in a small envelope. On the labels of these·he wrote directions for giving
them and left them with Aunt Abigail, saying that he would
call again day after to-morrow. When he was gone they all
experienced a sense of great relief, as though the necessary
thing had now been done and the sick woman would at once
begin to get well.

But Mrs. Pippinger did not get well; and when Dr. MacTaggert paid his second visit she was half delirious. He looked
serious and concerned and left several more medicines with

more complicated directions for administering them. Aunt Abigail, who always prided herself on her devotion to duty, carried out his instructions with scrupulous exactness. She was also very particular about excluding draughts and in fact all outside air. With great care she pasted up the cracks about the two small windows.

There followed a long period when Mrs. Pippinger alternated between being very sick and not quite so sick. The house was kept unnaturally tidy. The children moved about on tiptoe and spoke in whispers. Judith and the boys stayed outside or in the barn as much as they could. The rooms were full of the smell of strong medicines and ointments. Neighbors and relatives came bringing presents of soups and jellies and pickles and such bedside delicacies, which the children ate with subdued relish after their mother had refused them. The air was full of anxiety, of restlessness, of a sense of waiting, as though the regular flow of life hung for a time suspended and everybody was waiting with half-taken breath for the signal to breathe and live again.

When Bill came in from the barn after the evening chores were done, he pulled off his shoes very quietly and went about in sock feet. Sometimes he went to his wife's bedside and sat silently watching her flushed, restless tossing, or talked with her for a while in low tones if the fever was gone and she was lying pale and quiet. Then he would go back into the kitchen and sit by the stove with his quid of tobacco in his cheek, now and then lifting the lid nearest him to spit into the wood fire. He was a man of clean habits and hardly ever spat in the woodbox. Often he would sit like this till long after his usual bedtime, to be roused at last by Aunt Abigail's strident tones.

"Well, land sakes, Bill Pippinger, if you hain't a-settin' there yet! You'd otta be in bed this hour an' a half. If you're fixin' to be over bright an' early to help Andy Blackford butcher hawgs to-morrow mornin' you'd best be a-gittin' some sleep else ther'l be no rousin' you in the mornin'."

Thus exhorted, Bill would grunt sleepily, slouch to his feet, stretch, yawn, wind the clock, whittle a few kindlings for the morning and retire into the little back room where the air was already heavy and stale from the breathing of Craw and Elmer.

In spite of the occasional days when she felt better and talked about getting up, Mrs. Pippinger grew steadily worse. There were whole days now when she lay in a semi-stupor only rousing a little to smile feebly if Bill or one of the children came to her bedside. She had grown very thin, and her hands that lay on the quilt were white and transparent.

One day on leaving the doctor took Aunt Abigail aside and said in a low tone: "I'm afraid there's not much hope that she'll live through it. If she's in pain and her breath comes hard, give her one of these."

And he handed Aunt Abigail a little envelope containing small, white pills.

Her stupor increased very noticeably after this and she was hardly ever conscious. The neighbors came in and took turns sitting up with her to relieve Bill and Abigail. They moved her bed into the kitchen for greater warmth and convenience of waiting on her; and there she lay day after day more like a dead woman than a living one.

One very cold day her breathing was loud and sonorous like snoring. It echoed all through the stagnant air of the little house. When the doctor came that afternoon he took Bill and Aunt Abigail aside on the way out.

"It isn't likely she'll live till morning," he said.

Bill did not answer; he went to the barn to do his chores. Aunt Abigail hurried back into the house with the air of one who has work to do.

Aunt Sally Whitmarsh came that night to sit up. She was an elderly woman with crafty eyes and rather handsome regular features that were always set and composed, as though she were sitting in church listening to a sermon. She was not so thin as most of her neighbors and her skin was white and fine and almost free from wrinkles.

Then when the supper table was cleared, the dishes washed and the children in bed, and the watchers were settling down for the night, the doorknob turned and old Aunt Selina Cobb stood in the doorway.

She came in with teeth chattering, the remains of an old Paisley shawl drawn tightly about her head and shoulders. A blast of icy air swept in after her.

"Land, but it's a-goin' to be a cold night!" she quavered, as she drew off two pairs of ragged mittens and warmed her withered, claw-like hands over the stove. "It'll like be zero afore mornin'."

She was a tiny, dried-up creature, not more than four and a half feet high and so thin that there seemed to be nothing at all between the yellow, wrinkled skin and the bones beneath. The eyes, as in many old people, showed the only remains of youth and life. They were bright and brown and looked about the room with birdlike alertness. Her movements were sudden, quick and nervous, like those of a person living always at high tension. Her calico dress, when she took off her jacket, was seen to be patched in so many places and with so many different kinds of goods that it was idle to speculate as to its original color and pattern. Her apron was even more patched than the dress. The patchwork garments were clean, stiff with starch and smoothly ironed.

"She's bad off to-night, ain't she, poor thing?" said Aunt Selina, stepping from the fire to the bedside of the sick woman.

Aunt Sally Whitmarsh moved to the bedside and stood beside her. "Yes," she said in a low voice, "she's bad off. The doctor don't think she'll last through the night."

"Eh, dear! Well, well, poor Annie! It seems like yestiddy she was a little gal a-runnin' araound bareleggèd."

"Yes, an' we two stood together at her weddin' here in this very house. You mind that day, Aunt Selina? It don't seem no time sence."

They could see their breath in the cold air about the bed. Their teeth began to chatter and they went back to rub their hands together over the stove, then settled down in kitchen chairs close to the warmth.

"You'd best be a-gittin' to bed, Bill," advised Aunt Abigail.

"You can't do nothin' fer her, an' the rest of us'll set up."

Bill was sitting beside the woodbox, between the stove and the wall, apart from the three women. When Abigail spoke he cleared his throat, recrossed his legs, and said: "No, I guess I'll set."

They settled down to wait. Outside it was growing steadily colder. An icy wind was sweeping down from the north, whistling about the decayed old house, rattling window sashes and worming its way through every chink and crevice. It whispered eerily behind the ugly old wall paper and fluttered little loose fragments like struggling wings. Long dust webs clinging to the ceiling above the stove swung to and fro in the draught like clotheslines on a windy day. The loud, sonorous snoring sound filled the room and dominated the hushed voices of the woman about the stove. The little glass lamp threw its dim yellow light over the oilcloth-covered table, threw its dim reflection to the low ceiling and left the rest of the room in deep shadow. They sat waiting.

As the night wore on, the breathing of the dying woman grew gradually less noisy. The creeping cold crowded the three women more closely about the stove and the lid was often lifted to put in more wood.

Gradually the breathing grew fainter, so that it ceased to dominate the room and became scarcely audible even when listened for. The clock struck three slow strokes. Still the women huddled about the stove and Bill sat silently beside the woodbox and the scarcely heard breath fluttered on the lips of the dying woman.

Suddenly she gave a short, quick gasp. Aunt Abigail got up quickly and stood for a moment by the bedside, long enough to make sure that she was still breathing.

"If she lives past four," she said, turning away with a slight shade of disappointment, "she'll likely last another day. This is the time they most gener'ly go."

A movement passed almost imperceptibly through the group about the stove; but no one spoke.

"Waal, I'm ready to be took when my time comes," went on Aunt Abigail, coming back to her seat by the stove. "And when I'm gone it hain't a-goin' to be said of me that I didn't do my duty in times o' sickness an' death. I bin real bad lately with them liver spells I git, an' I was in the very midst o' puttin' up new paper on the front bedroom—it's a awful nice paper an' one that won't show dirt, a chocolate ground with kinder red flowers on it. But when Bill come a-drivin' over with word that Annie was down sick, I put my things right on an' come back with 'im. An' I hain't bin home sence."

Still they sat about the stove and dozed and talked and waited. It seemed as if the faint breathing, the ticking of the clock, the crackling of the fire, and the low intermittent drone of the women's voices would go on forever.

"If the signs tells true, there'll be other deaths among the hills this winter," went on Aunt Abigail, looking from one to the other of the little group. "The dawgs has been a-howlin' awful this winter. Well, the Lord gives an' the Lord takes away; an' none of us knows when our time is a-comin'. When you settle on a spot fer Annie's grave, Bill, you'll want to see that there's a piece left alongside fer yerse'f to lay beside her."

Bill shifted his legs and grunted. The grunt might have meant anything.

There was a low moan. This time they all looked toward the bed for a moment, then sank back into the old positions. Again a faint, rattling gasp. Aunt Abigail got up from her chair with ill-concealed alacrity. Aunt Sally and Aunt Selina looked at each other, then toward the bed, and rose and followed her lead. Once more a faint, guttural gasp came from the dying woman's white lips. Aunt Abigail bent over her, her hand on her pulse, and listened. Then she turned back the covers and placed her hand upon her sister's heart. There were a few moments of heavy silence broken at last by the voice of Aunt Abigail, who spoke with a certain subdued sharpness and authoritativeness. "It's time to stop the clock. Annie's gone!"

Preparations for the funeral began at once. The children, confused and bewildered, were dazed more than grieved by their mother's death, the full gravity of which they could not realize in the midst of Aunt Abigail's hectic hurry and scurry. There was much to be done. The girls' Sunday dresses of red cotton crêpe must be dyed black, their hair ribbons likewise. Aunt Abigail stood over the boiling dye in the wash boiler and stirred and lifted the goods with two long smooth pieces of broom handle till they were funereal enough to satisfy her. Then she soused and rinsed them through many waters and hung them dripping on the line, three sad little black garments, weeping as it were for their own dismal transformation. Lizzie May went out and looked at them and burst suddenly into loud weeping at the sight of what had so lately been the three pretty little red dresses that their mother had made for them. She could not have told whether it was for the dresses or her mother that she was crying. Then the dresses had to be pressed by Aunt Abigail's swift, capable hands. And the boys' Sunday clothes and Bill's Sunday suit— the one he was married in—had to be aired and pressed also.

"Air you sure yer dad's got a fine white shirt?" asked Aunt Abigail, looking up at Luella from the suit she was pressing.

Luella was washing dishes. She let her hands rest idle in the dishwater for a moment.

"Dad's got a fine shirt," she answered promptly, "but it's stripèd."

"Is the stripes black?"

"I couldn't say fer sure if the stripes is black or navy blue."

"Well, you'd best fetch it here an' let me look at it, Elly, 'cause if the stripes hain't black it won't do fer 'im to wear at his own wife's funeral," opined Aunt Abigail.

Luella wiped off her hands and brought the shirt, which Aunt Abigail, after careful inspection at the window, pronounced to be satisfactory.

"The stripes is black all right. It'll do," she approved, handing it back to Luella, who folded it away again in the drawer.

Bill went about in a dazed way, hardly conscious of the life about him. He did the chores about the barn and chopped the wood mechanically from force of habit. When he was spoken to he did not hear. He looked haggard and grief-stricken.

"He feels bad, don't he, poor man," said Aunt Mary Blackford, looking out of the kitchen window at his stooping figure straggling aimlessly toward the barn.

"Yaas, he grieves some," admitted Aunt Abigail. "But he'll be a-lookin' araound fer another afore the year's out. That's haow men is."

The neighborhood for miles around came to the funeral. The hitched buggies filled the barnyard and were strung out for some distance along the side of the road. The women wore their black mourning clothes, with little white aprons tied about their waists. Some of the men had on their wedding suits. Some wore ill-fitting readymades bought from the mail order house after a good crop year. Others came in clean overalls and corduroy jackets lined with sheepskin. All were shaved, sleek-haired and serious-looking. When they had tied their horses, they gathered together in little knots in the barnyard talking in low tones, not about the dead, but about the price of hogs on the hoof, the long, hard winter that it had been this year, and the best way of preparing a tobacco bed. At a sign from the undertaker, they filed respectfully, with bared heads, into the little front room whither their womenfolk had preceded them.

The long coffin stood on a trestle in the middle of the room. It seemed tremendously large and imposing. The mouse-like little woman was claiming more attention now than she had ever done in all the forty-odd years of her drab existence. Bill sat at the head, staring straight before him. The children, with red eyes and dazed, frightened faces, sat along one side. Aunt Abigail and several other near relatives, with solemn faces and handkerchiefs in their hands, completed the circle about the bier. The other mourners stood or sat against the walls. Several of the women were crying. The three women who had laid out Aunt Annie and had not shed a tear at her death, were all weeping copiously now.

The preacher was young, insignificant, and ineffectual, a poor wisp of humanity, who had probably drifted into preaching because it was the only thing that he could do, and had been elbowed into this remote corner by the law of the survival of the fittest. In the flat, empty voice of one who has sounded no depths of life, he spoke feebly of the virtues of the "dear departed sister," offered a sort of canned consolation to the "bereaved husband and children," and mumbled a few concluding words about the "hope of a glorious resurrection."

Then Jabez Moorhouse rose to the six feet three inches of his height.

"Friends an' neighbors," he said, standing simply with his hands in his pockets and speaking in the tone of one talking across the kitchen stove, "the Reverend Mister Spragg has spoke the blessin' of the church over Aunt Annie Pippinger that lies here in the coffin. But not many of us is church goers an' the Reverend Mister Spragg is not much acquainted among us. The Bible says, 'Out of the abundance of the heart the mouth speaketh.' So I can't let this moment go by without risin' to my feet to offer our respects as friends an' neighbors to the memory of one o' the kindest, best-hearted and hardest-workin' wimmin in the whole of Scott County. Solomon, the wise man, says, 'The heart knoweth its own bitterness.' An' we all know that talk don't do much to help them that suffers. But I feel I speak for all of us here when I say how sad we feel for Bill Pippinger an' for these motherless little uns an' how we're all a-standin' here ready to do what we kin to make this loss easier for him to bear. Amen. Let us all sing, 'Nearer, my God, to Thee.'"

Most of the women were crying now and the men clearing their throats and furtively wiping their eyes with the backs of their hands. But they all joined bravely if haltingly in the old funeral hymn, as Jabez' deep, sonorous voice leading them filled the little room.

Nearer, my God, to Thee,
Nearer to Thee,
E'en though it be a cross
That raises me;
Still all my song shall be
Nearer, my God, to Thee,
Nearer, my God, to Thee,
Nearer to Thee.

With the end of the hymn the mourners passed about the coffin to take their last look at the dead, then went out respectfully and left the family alone.

On the way out to form the funeral procession, the Reverend Spragg touched Jabez Moorhouse on the elbow.

"I—I wonder if you would mind reading the service at the grave? You could do it as well as I can. You know I preach in three churches and they're a long way apart and it keeps me busy going between them, especially with the roads so bad. It's a long way to the graveyard and I have to preach at seven to-night in Mayville Junction."

The little preacher was embarrassed, apologetic, but anxious to be released. He pressed a leaflet containing the service into Jabez' hand.

"All right," said Jabez, not without a trace of condescension, "I'll do it. But you don't need to give me no book." He handed back the leaflet.

The long, cold drive seemed as though it would never end; but at last they got to the little graveyard, a few white and gray stones and painted wooden slabs crowning a hill. Here they climbed out of the buggies and stamped up and down a bit to limber up their numb feet and stiff legs.

Then they gathered about the open grave, Bill and his children nearest, the others clustered about them in a silent group, the men holding their hats awkwardly in their hands, and Jabez Moorhouse spoke over the dead what he remembered of the graveside service.

"Man that is born of woman hath but a short time to live

and is full of misery. He cometh up and is cut down. He fleeth as it were a shadow.

"Forasmuch as it hath pleased Almighty God of his great mercy to take unto himself the soul of our dear sister here departed, we therefore commit her body to the ground."

He said it tenderly, as one who has come to realize that to be committed to the ground may be sweet, soothing, and desirable.

"Dust to dust, ashes to ashes, earth to earth."

It was over and they turned away.

But there was one to whom the thought of the lonely grave was anguish. It was when they were getting into the wagon for the long drive home, and the other mourners were letting their thoughts dwell with pleasant expectancy on fried side of hog and corn cakes, that Bill spoke for the first time since they left the house.

"Well, young uns, you hain't got no mammy now." His voice broke and he dropped his face in his hands and shook with sobs. The children gathered about him, wailing dismally. It was a long time before he could control himself enough to gather up the lines and say: "Git up there," to Tom and Bob.

CHAPTER V

FOR a while it was very dismal and lonely in the Pippinger household. Bill continued to send the children to school and made shift to do the housework as best he could in his slovenly male fashion. When the little Pippingers got home from school in the gathering dusk of the gray winter afternoon, there was no mother briskly baking fragrant cookies or frying corn cakes and sizzling strips of sowbelly. The untidy kitchen, already in twilight, was usually empty, with Bill choring about the barn or away doing a day's work somewhere in the neighborhood. If he happened to be in the kitchen, he sat hunched over the stove in a half stupor, his quid of tobacco in his cheek, his eyes fascinated by the gleams of fire that could be seen through the open sliding draught in front. The twins, now become the housekeepers of the family, would bustle about, polish the lamp chimney and light the lamp, brush the ashes from the stove and the hearth with the turkey feather duster, sweep up the floor and get together the evening meal. Judith helped, but only under direction. She had to be told to run and fetch the side of bacon, to get out the mixing bowl and big spoon for the corn cake batter, and to wash the milk strainer, which Bill had not washed clean in the morning. Elmer and Craw generally went with their father to help milk and do up the barn chores; and Judith went too whenever she could slip away from the twins.

On Saturdays the twins, with Judith's somewhat reluctant help, cleaned house thoroughly, repairing with feminine housewifely zeal the ravages of a week of slipshodness. They polished the stove, scrubbed the table and the floor, dusted the shelves, swept the bedrooms, beat the dust out of the rag mats, and hung out the bedding to air. Sometimes when they were busily at work, Bill would come into the kitchen, glance about and ask, "Where's your—?" then leave the question

54

unfinished, suddenly remembering that she was not there and never would be there again. He had always been in the habit of asking for her this way whenever he came in and did not see her at once.

As time went on and the March sunshine warmed the earth into life, Bill became more cheerful. Everything takes heart in the spring; and Bill too felt the warmth of the sunshine in his bones. Like his children, like Tom and Bob and the cows and the geese and the chickens and the grass under his feet, he lifted up his face to the light and breathed deep of the warm, sweet air. He stretched, yawned, shook from him the heaviness and lethargy of winter, and felt once more that it was good to be alive. On those rare, delicate days in March when the earth is full of a promise of spring, a promise more intoxicating than any fulfilment, he whistled and sang again as he trudged round and round the field in the long furrow getting the ground ready for the new corn crop. So the shadow of death passed from the Pippinger family.

All his thoughts now were of his children, all his planning was for them. They were in school, all five of them; but Craw and the twins would graduate this year. After that everything would be easier. Craw would be at home to help him on the farm and the twins would keep house. Then with Craw's help he would get the farm back into good shape again. The land was good; and if he could once get the washes filled up so that it could be plowed, he and Craw would raise as good a crop of tobacco on it as Uncle Ezra Pettit or old Hiram Stone or any of that lot that felt themselves so much better than other folks because they had the time and the money to keep their ground in shape to raise good tobacco. Yes, Bill would show them all right. In the cool, invigorating March air and heartening sunshine he felt himself filled with a boundless zest for work and achievement.

Things went better with the Pippinger family after the twins were through school. Little women already, with a natural zest for housekeeping, they polished the milk pans, cleaned the cupboards, churned the butter and washed and

rinsed and blued the clothes, all the time clacking cheerfully
about their work and about the new dresses they were making
and the coats they were planning to have before winter came
on and the new shoes they would get when dad got paid for
his last job of hauling and the Fair at Cynthiana, to which
they were all going, dad having promised each of them a quarter to spend. Already, too, they had a nose for gossip and
loved to talk about the neighbors and their doings. Again
and again they told each other how stingy Uncle Ezra Pettit
was and how meanly the Pettits lived in spite of their big
house and all their land and money.

Judith was such poor help about the house that the twins
soon stopped bothering with her and did the work themselves,
only insisting that she look after her own clothes and take her
turn at washing the dishes, a job that none of them enjoyed.
These tasks done, she was left free to follow her father about
the barnyard or run the woods and fields. Soon, however,
because she was not lazy and took a deep interest in the farm
animals, she made herself useful by taking over most of the
out-of-door chores. She brought up the cows and milked
them, fed the pigs, took care of the little chicks and saw that
all the broods were cooped for the night. She hoed in the
garden and kept the rows of beans and turnips thrifty and
free from weeds. Like a lynx following its prey, she stalked
the turkey hens and found their nests; and she would go out
in any kind of storm to save the tender little turkeys from
the wetting that would be their death.

Living so intimately in the life of the barnyard, the mysteries of sex were not mysteries at all to her, but matters of routine to be dealt with in the same matter-of-fact fashion in
which you slopped the pigs or tied the mules to the hitching
post. She knew all about the ways of roosters with hens.
She saw calves born and testicles cut from squealing pigs,
from young bulls to change them into fat steers and from
young stallions to make them tractable in harness. These
things interested her, but not more so than other barnyard
activities. She was strangely free from precocious interest in

sex matters. At school she ignored the small dirtiness that lurks wherever many children are gathered together.

From her own and the neighbors' barnyards Judith had picked up all the profanity and obscenity that is a part of the life of such places, and she used it freely, joyously and unashamedly. Bill's mild remonstrances, "What kind o' talk is that for a little gal?" and the horror of the twins had no effect upon her.

"I should suttenly think shame to myse'f, Judy, if I was you," Lizzie May would say, "to talk that air way. What makes you go fer to do it?"

"Well, Craw talks that way, an' the Blackford boys does, an' dad does too when he's with other men. I ain't no diff'rent from them."

"In course you're diff'rent; you're a gal."

"Well, anyway, I don't feel like one," Judy would answer unrepentantly.

If she could have put into words what she vaguely felt, she would have said that the language of the barnyard was an expression of something that was real, vital and fluid, that it was of natural and spontaneous growth, that it turned with its surroundings, that it was a part of the life that offered itself to her. The prim niceness of the twins, suitable enough to them in the world that they were making for themselves, was for her a deadening negation of life. To have to be correct and decent in her speech was the same as being forced to sit motionless on a straight-backed chair in the front room when she was consumed with a longing to run and jump and whoop and chase the dog and play at "Hide and Seek" around the barn.

Craw was at home now and able to help his father. But the plans that Bill had made in the invigorating coolness of early spring did not bear much fruit. It was one thing to plan work and quite another thing to do it when the dog days came and the sun baked the hillsides. Then as he hoed out weeds or followed the cultivator in the the heat of the day, and the sweat rolled down his body in scalding streams, he felt less enthusiastic about raising a big tobacco crop. Indeed, the task of reclaiming the farm was so big and formidable that it would have discouraged a much more energetic man than Bill. It was easier to do jobs of hauling and the like, and so make enough money to pay the store bill. Bill had always been partial to jobs of hauling. This also suited Craw, whose mind was of the routine sort, incapable of planning or grasping any enterprise however small. Craw was sixteen when he left school, a big, good-looking, good-natured, well developed fellow, but slow as a tortoise. He could follow the plow or drive a team or do any simple task assigned to him, but of initiative he had none. With Craw's help Bill increased his acreage of corn considerably and hauled out his long accumulated barnyard manure onto the corn field, thus getting a much better yield. But neither of them broached the subject of raising tobacco. Craw, growing rapidly stronger and bigger, soon began to "work out," and earned his seventy-five cents a day from Uncle Ezra Pettit or old Hiram Stone or any of the neighboring tobacco planters who wanted a hand. He was a good, steady, plodding worker, and the neighbors who employed help soon learned to call upon him. Proud in the possession of money, he liked to patronize his sisters, and brought them home occasional presents of scented soap, white muslin shirtwaists and imitation jewelry for the pleasure of listening to their excited squeals of delight and feeling male and superior. Pretty soon he got to going with a girl; and after that he never brought his sisters anything.

It was a matter of great wonder and amazement to Bill how quickly the children grew up. Up to Annie's death he had regarded them as mere babies. After that they seemed to become young men and women all of a sudden. Two years after their graduation from school the twins were wearing long dresses and putting up their hair; and Lizzie May had a "feller" coming to see her every Sunday. She had known him all her life, but had become friendly with him at a party the winter before. His name was Dan Pooler and his folks lived over near Dry Ridge. He came in a red-wheeled buggy which he had carefully washed down and polished the day before;

and he and Lizzie May would drive forth grandly. Lizzie May was very proud of her swain's good looks and store clothes and of the shiny, red-wheeled buggy. When Craw guffawed and spoke of him as "Dam Fooler," and when Judith teased her wickedly about him, she became very indignant and haughty.

Judith, too, was rapidly growing up. She had become such a tall, straight, handsome girl, with such strong, free gestures and such a ringing, careless laugh, that Bill's heart swelled with pride when he saw people turn to look after her on the streets in Clayton. She was learning, too, to smile at the young men, and practising whenever occasion offered the arts of banter and coquetry.

She began to develop an interest in clothes, and brought to the neat, but uninspired dressmaking of the twins a sense of form, color, and picturesqueness.

"You know, Lizzie May, you ought to wear soft, sleazy things an' have 'em nice an' full. Get a blue voile—not a real light blue, but 'that there new Alice blue. You'll have to send off for it to get the right color. An' make it with the waist crossing in front an' a real full skirt an' a sash tied in a big bow at the back. Then you'd look so nice that Dan Pooler'd jes have to ast you whether he wanted you or not."

"You shet up an' tend yer own business, Judy," Lizzie May answered. Her uncertain relations with Dan were making her somewhat irritable. But she heeded the suggestions about the dress and followed them out as best she could.

"An' I'm a-goin' to have me a new petticoat that won't be like nobody else's petticoat," Judy went on. "I thought it out las' night afore I went to sleep. I'm a-goin' to get some red turkey cotton, real bright, an' have it in points all araound the bottom an' make three black French dots in each point. I bet when you two see it you'll both want one like it."

"You'd better be thinkin' of havin' yo'se'f a warm jacket agin the time winter comes on," said Luella half reprovingly yet betraying more than a gleam of interest in the prospective petticoat.

"I'm a-goin' to have braown ve'vet collar an' cuffs on my new jacket," put in Lizzie May.

So they would sit together stitching and planning and chattering happily over their few yards of cheap cotton goods. The mail order catalogues had of late years come to take a large place in the lives of the Pippingers and their neighbors, much to the disgust of Peter Akers, whose store was shrinking instead of growing. They were a source of endless interest to the girls, especially the twins. In the winter evenings when the lamp was lighted they would bring these enormous books to the table and turn the endless pages, never tiring of the pictures of slim, simpering, abundant-haired young women arrayed in coats, suits, sweaters, dresses, aprons, nightgowns, corsets, chemises, union suits: every kind of garment that goes upon the female figure. The gorgeous colored pages held them longest and often caused Lizzie May to gasp with admiration and envy.

"My, I wish I was as pretty as that and had that blue silk dress!" she sighed, pointing out the object of her envy to Luella.

"Oh, land, you're much better lookin' than that gal, Liz!" Judy exclaimed, looking over her shoulder. "She's got an awful smirk!"

Lizzie May, though not entirely convinced, patted her blond hair with a gratified expression.

Bill and the boys looked at the pictures of men in overalls and work shirts, tools, wagons, buggies, harness, and farm machinery. Sometimes Craw would hesitate over the pages of ladies in underwear, then blush furiously and turn quickly to the mowing machines if he thought that any one was noticing him.

The books served many purposes, all and more than does the daily newspaper in homes where the newspaper enters. The old ones were used to light fires, to wrap up winter pears, to paste over broken window panes or cracks in the wall. In the backhouse they did duty as toilet paper. And Craw, beginning to smoke cigarettes, wrapped the crumbled native leaf in a bit of the margin and puffed away with the air of one conscious that he has attained man's estate.

It was about this time that Judith and the twins took to using tooth brushes. But the boys, exhorted to do likewise, poohooed such vanities.

"Mebbe you gals needs to hoe out your teeth," Craw would say condescendingly, "but my mouth's clean, same's the rest o' my insides."

The summer that Judith was sixteen she came home from Sadieville one afternoon in a state of excitement.

"What d'ye think I'm a-fixin' to do, dad? I'm a-goin' over to Aunt Eppie Pettit's to work out. Aunt Eppie come out to the road as I was a-drivin' past an' she ses would I like to come over to her place to work. She's got hired hands a-eatin' there, and four cows to milk, an' she ses there's too much work for Cissy an' would I come for a spell. She snapped her false teeth at me a time or two, but I didn't mind. I 'member haow when I was little I used to think she was a-goin' to bite me; but now I ain't a-skairt of her. So I told her, yes, I'd come; an' I'm a-goin' to git a dollar a week. Elmer's plenty big enough to do my chores, so I kin be spared easy enough."

She said all this almost in one breath. Bill, who had been chopping stove wood, stood with one foot on the chopping block and looked at her with a mixture of surprise and disapproval.

"Pshaw, Judy," he exclaimed, spitting disparagingly into the chips. "What do you want to be a-goin' there fer? I wouldn't if I was you. My gal don't need to go a-emptyin' nobody's slops, let alone old Ezra Pettit's. I wouldn't do no sech thing."

"Oh, but I'm a-goin', dad. I told her I'd come. Craw works out an' earns money, an' I want to earn some money too. If I stay there ten weeks I'll have ten dollars, an' that'll buy me my clothes an' shoes fer the winter."

Bill saw that she was quite determined, so he made no further opposition. A couple of days later he drove her and her satchel of clothes over to Aunt Eppie's place, which was about a mile and a half away on the road toward Sadieville. The road they traveled was known as the Dixie Pike. It was the main highroad between Cincinnati and Lexington. Before the Civil War it had been the coach road between these two cities; and the very old folk still told tales of prancing three-team coaches and gay horseback parties galloping by. Now one met mostly the wagons and buggies of tenant farmers, with an occasional automobile or a covered wagon occupied by gipsy folk or horse traders.

The house of the Pettits was a long, white, rambling, leisurely looking place with green shutters and a wide porch supported by square white pillars. It had been built in ante bellum days for people of a leisurely habit of life. It stood some distance back from the road, and between the road and the house stretched a neat bluegrass lawn dotted with flower beds and shade trees. A low stone wall separated the lawn from the roadside. From the rear came the cackle of hens, the cooing of doves and the scream of a peacock. Basking in the morning sunshine the place looked gracious and peaceful.

Bill reluctantly deposited his daughter and her satchel at Aunt Eppie's gate.

"Don't take no lip from nobody, Judy. You've allus got a home to come back to," he advised, as he turned the mules' heads toward home.

Judith swung briskly up the flat stone walk, through the chinks of which grass was growing, then around by the little side path to the kitchen door. Here she found Cissy rolling pie crust on a floury baking board. She and Cissy were old acquaintances. Judith sat down by the table and they chatted together till Aunt Eppie came in.

Cissy was a middle-aged woman of spare figure, dull eyes, neatly combed hair and blurred, nondescript features. There was nothing about her to notice or remember. Some explanation for this lack of personality might be found in the fact that she had been working for the Pettits since she was nineteen years old. During that time she had never had as much as a mild flirtation with any man, nor had she ever been further from the Pettits' kitchen than Sadieville. For over twenty years the life of Aunt Eppie's household had been her life. She had gone there a timid young orphan girl; and in the unbroken routine of these twenty years had become a dull middle aged drudge. Each week she had received her dollar, and she was reported to have money "loaned out." Judith looked at her and thought of this report and envied Cissy. Her young mind perceived nothing of tragedy in Cissy's long years of celibacy spent in the routine of a stranger's kitchen. The only thought that passed through her head as she sat there in her radiant youth was: "My, if I only had all that money she's saved, wouldn't I have me nice clothes!"

Aunt Eppie bustled into the kitchen and was pleased to find Judith.

She was a tall, large-featured bony woman and had a protruding chin and a wrinkled, thin-lipped mouth that shut together with the strong, swift motion of a snapping turtle. The click of her false teeth lent realism to this motion and caused her to strike terror into the hearts of small children toward whom she tried to be affable.

"Well, naow, that's a good gal to come like you said you would," she condescended. "So often these hired hands promises to come an' that's the last you see of 'em. Cissy, you take her up to your room an' show her where to put her things. She might as well sleep with you an' save dirtyin' up two pairs o' sheets, let alone the wear an' tear on 'em. An' after that she can he'p you git the apples ready fer the pies an' shell the peas and scrape the taters fer dinner. An' mind you, scrape an' not peel 'em, Judy, 'cause they're jes new out o' the ground. It's a sin to waste the best o' sech taters by peelin' 'em."

With the adaptability of youth Judith drifted easily enough into the life of the Pettit family. She left most of the indoor work to the patient Cissy and busied herself with the cows, the chickens, the turkeys and the garden, as she had done at home. She and Cissy did most of the work. Aunt Eppie believed herself to be still a hard worker, but in reality she spent most of her time bustling from one place to another bossing the girls, Uncle Ezra, and the farm hands. She was always nosing out all sorts of small, neglected matters and calling them to the attention of the neglecter.

"Ezry, don't you fergit to fix that garden fence this mornin'," she would shout into Uncle Ezra's ear at breakfast. "The hens is a-gittin' in an' a-eatin' into the hearts of all my beets."

"An' Judy, don't fail to coop up all the settin' hens when you gather up the eggs. I don't want to raise no more chicks this year. What with the price of eggs so low it don't hardly pay to feed hens." She sighed heavily. Any mention of money loss, real or fancied, always brought this sigh to her lips.

When she was not busy directing the other members of the household, she read the "Country Gentleman," whose rosy tales of phenomenal success on the farm excited her interest and envy, made log cabin blocks for bedquilts or cut and sewed carpet rags. She already had carpets enough to keep the whole house thoroughly padded for at least a quarter century, but she could not bear to see the rags go to waste.

She was one of the few remaining members of the old "first families" of Kentucky. Her haughty aquiline nose, broad brow and penetrating eyes showed that she had intellect and breeding. In the old days, several decades before the Civil War, her father had purchased hundreds of acres in Scott County for twenty-five cents an acre. He cleared the land, realized about a hundred dollars an acre out of the timber and still possessed his hundreds of acres of fine clay loam, virgin soil, only needing the seed to produce enormous crops of almost anything. So he became rich and built this leisurely white mansion. The war brought disaster and poverty. Aunt Eppie's father was one of the few landed proprietors who did not move away but remained to begin life over again as a poor farmer. In the school of penury, Aunt Eppie, applying her superior intellect and energy, proved to be all too apt a scholar. She learned not only to be saving but to be niggardly and penurious.

Uncle Ezra had been one of Aunt Eppie's father's hired

hands. He was of much commoner clay than his wife and with age had become a mere clod. Almost as deaf as one of his own well planted fence posts, he heard nothing nor cared to hear. He spoke rarely and in half articulate grunts. His one thought in life had always been how to get the most out of his land, which was not his, but Aunt Eppie's, as she was not slow to remind him when the occasion arose. Now that he was too old to work hard he spent his days puttering about the fields and the barnyard watching, always watching. He had the reputation of being the hardest man to work for in the whole of Scott County and he paid the lowest wages.

Once in a while Aunt Eppie's brother, Hiram Stone, ate a meal in the house. He was a spare, silent man. Since his wife's death many years before he had lived attended by one old servant, in the big, rambling house on his estate. Nobody quite knew how he passed his days. He had been seen to read, to cultivate a little patch of vegetables and flowers, and to smoke meditatively on the back porch. In his youth he had been sent away to college. He always employed an overseer and had very little to do with his tenants. Nobody ever called him "Uncle Hiram." This was because he lived his life to himself and his life was not their life. He was not niggardly and interfering like Uncle Ezra and many of the other landlords. He allowed his tenants to keep a cow and pasture it on his land. He put no limit to the number of their chickens and turkeys. Yet the tenants distrusted and avoided him. They would rather work under Uncle Ezra, because he was one of themselves and they understood him.

It caused Aunt Eppie endless worry and chagrin to see the way her brother mismanaged his land. The overseer was letting it all, she said, and the tenants did as they liked and stole from him before his very face. It was a shame and a disgrace.

She said as much to him time and again. But he went his own way. He treated her always with politeness and deference and only smiled gently and enigmatically when she nagged him. The smile drove her to distraction.

Though the Pettits owned over a thousand acres of good

land and lived in a house of seventeen rooms and were said to have money in all the banks in Scott County, their way of life was not different in any essential from that of their tenants. It was even more stark and barren and sordid than most, for in the humbler homes there was sometimes love and fun, and here there was neither. The meals were eaten in dull silence except when Aunt Eppie remembered something that somebody hadn't done or when the hired girls and farm hands, who ate from the same oilcloth as their employers, got to sparring with each other.

Two hired hands ate at the dinner table, but got their breakfasts and supper at home. These were Jabez Moorhouse and Jerry Blackford, second son of Andrew Blackford, who owned a small farm next to the Pippingers. Jabez, who, when not drunk, usually held his peace, rarely spoke at the table except to ask for another portion of string beans or to have the sorghum pitcher passed to him. When he raised his head from his plate his rather vague blue eyes seemed to be either turned inward or looking at something a long distance away. Jerry, who had come successfully through his cat-torturing period, had grow into a quiet, decent, clean appearing young fellow, blond and ruddy like David of old and good to look upon in his strong young manhood. He was not more given to conversation than Jabez.

Fortunately for Judith the blight of bareness and dullness that lay over Aunt Eppie's household did not extend to the barnyard. There the morning sunlight fell as goldenly as in princes' courtyards. The geese were as dignified, the turkeys as proud, and the hens as busy as any others of their kind, and Judith enjoyed ministering to their needs and watching their ways.

The turkeys, fifty odd of them, had been little fellows when Judith came, with flat tortoise bodies and long necks, and Aunt Eppie let them wander at will among the beets and cabbages. Whenever they saw a bug or a fly they darted forth these long necks with a quick, snakelike movement and rarely failed to catch their prey. Soon they grew too big to be allowed in the garden and roamed the alfalfa and corn fields for their food. As they grew toward maturity sex divided them into two groups. The female turkeys kept together in a small, silent band and devoted themselves mainly to the business of eating, while their brothers preferred to loaf in the barnyard. A spot speckled with light and shade under a row of locust trees was their favorite promenade. With their tails spread fan-shape, their wing feathers scraping the ground, their heads and necks brilliantly blue and red and the little wormlike appendage above their beaks inflated and pendulous they would pace grandly up and down with a slow, dignified movement. The sun, striking along their satiny backs, made their feathers gleam with changing tints of rose, gold, green, and copper.

When they grew tired of the parade they loved to slip away and steal food that they knew was not intended for them. Aunt Eppie's grapes and peaches were their favorite tidbits. While feeding on these delicate morsels they talked to each other with little congratulatory gulps of delight like water gurgling out of the neck of a bottle. Then Judith would run and chase them out of the orchard, and they would all stretch out their necks at her and gobble together in indignant chorus.

It seemed a pity that so much beauty, pride, and joy in life should go to tempt the cloyed palate of some smug bishop or broker who had, compared with the soul that had lately animated the bit of white meat on his plate, but a poor notion of what it was to love, to play, and to enjoy the sun and the fruits of the earth.

"It's a shame fer folks to eat sech critters," Judith thought one blue September morning, as she watched the turkeys parade under the locust trees.

She had been slopping the pigs and was leaning on the railing of the hogpen looking at the turkeys beyond. A female turkey that had strayed from her sisters was among them and trying to make her escape. Each time that she made a move to go away, the young Toms for pure devilishness would intercept her by stepping in front of her, like a pack of village boys teasing a little girl. When she at last made her escape and flew back to her sisters, they all reached out their necks and gobbled after her derisively. Jerry and Jabez, starting out to the field where they were cutting tobacco, came and leaned for a few moments on the railing beside Judith.

"Do you know what them young Toms reminds me of?" said Judith, looking at Jerry with an eye not entirely free from the self-consciousness of sex. "They make me think of a pack o' fellers a-standin' raound the street corner in Clayton or Sadieville of a Sunday afternoon dressed in their good clothes, a-swellin' up their chests an' a-cranin' their necks after every gal that goes by, an' then a-blabbin' together about her after she's gone a-past. They'd otta think shame to theirselves for bein' so vain an' idle. There's the turkey hens all out in the field a-eatin' corn so they kin grow up quick an' lay eggs an' make more little turkeys, so Aunt Eppie an' Uncle Ezra kin have more money to put in the bank. That's haow a turkey'd otta act, 'stead of enjoyin' his own vain life."

She laughed and looked quizzically at Jerry.

Jerry had no rejoinder to make. He was not quick at repartee. But he was young, healthy, and handsome; and as he looked from the turkeys back to Judith, the smile on his lips and the answering look in his eyes made words an impertinence. Jabez looked at the turkeys and at the boy and girl and laughed an amused, indulgent laugh. He was fifty-five and had long known the way of a turkey in the sun and the way of a man with a maid.

"The young Toms'll be cut off in the pride o' life," he said in his rich, sonorous voice, "an' jes as well for them that they air. An' the turkey hens'll live to raise up families. An' the families they raise'll repeat the same thing all over agin, an' so on world without end. Amen. Solomon was right when he said there's no new thing under the sun, an' that which has been is that which is a-goin' to be. An' yet each new batch takes as much interest in livin' as if they was the only ones that had ever lived an' was a-goin' to keep on livin' forever. It's the same with folks. Hain't that so, Jerry?"

Jerry had not heard a word of what Jabez had said and

Jabez knew he hadn't. He had slyly filched two hairpins out of Judith's hair, had stuck them behind his ears and was pretending to march away with them.

"You gimme back them hairpins, Jerry Blackford. I've got on'y five an' my hair won't stay up with three. You'd best hand 'em over, 'cause I kin give you a black eye quick as look at you."

She tried to get hold of Jerry's wrists. Jerry got hers instead and they struggled together laughing. After a while he let go of her wrists and allowed her to capture the pins.

"You'd best git along to work," she cried, flushed and sparkling. "Uncle Ezry'll be out here in a jiffy an'll want to know why you ain't to field."

"Yaas, the old groundhog'll be diggin' out afore long," grumbled Jabez. "Come on, Jerry, folks has gotta have their terbaccer. Judy, you go in an' tell Cissy to cook us a dern good dinner."

As Judith turned away from the hogpen, bucket in hand, she almost ran into a lean, spry old man, who had come up silently behind her, his steps making no noise on the scattered straw and chaff of the barnyard.

"Howdy, Uncle Sam. Haow's Aunt Sally?"

His face darkened slightly. "Oh, she keeps smart. Is Uncle Ezry anywheres hereabouts?"

"He's mos' likely in the kitchen warmin' his feet," said Judith. "Every mornin' he has to warm his feet the longest time afore he'll step outdoors. He sets there with his sock feet on the oven shelf, an' sets an' sets. An' Cissy has to go raound him every time she wants to git to the cupboard. She says sometimes she thinks he's *never* a-goin' to git up an' go aout where he belongs. I'm glad my feet ain't allus a-cold."

"That's haow you young uns allus is," answered Uncle Sam. "No feelin's for the sufferin's of the old." It was plain from Uncle Sam's way of speaking that he did not class himself among the aged.

"Andy Blackford was a-tellin' me that Uncle Ezry had some alfalfy hay he wanted to git shet of 'count of needin' the barn room. I'm a bit short o' hay this year an' I thought I'd come daown an' see if I couldn't make some sort of a deal with him." By this time they had reached the kitchen door. Uncle Sam stepped inside and found Ezra, as Judith had predicted, sitting with his feet on the oven fender, his suspenders down, his long. gray face set and motionless. He turned his head as Uncle Sam darkened the sunny doorway.

"Waal, Sam."

"Waal, Ezry. Purty weather we're a-havin'. I hain't seed a purtier September since '83, the fall afore the coldest winter we ever had to my knowin'. An' this summer's crops is the best there's been this nine year. Corn's made an' terbaccer's made; but we'll be needin' a good rain soon to freshen up the pastures."

Uncle Ezra did not hear a word of any of this, so he grunted for answer in a non-committal manner. His feet being now roasted to a turn, he fished out his congress shoes from under the stove and drew them on slowly and methodically. Then he got up, hitched his suspenders over his stooping shoulders, took down his hat from its peg by the side of the door, and stepped out into the sunshine followed by his visitor.

The two old men passed out of the garden gate and walked across the barnyard side by side.

"I hearn you had a part spiled stack of alfalfy hay you was a-wishin' to git shet of, Ezry."

Uncle Sam said this not in his former conversational tone, but in a loud shout close to Ezra's ear; for it was intended to be heard.

"Part spiled nuthin! There hain't a leaf of it spiled. It's all good, clean alfalfy. On'y reason I want to sell it, I got plenty hay this year, an' I'm a-goin' to be needin' the room in the terbaccer barn."

"I hearn it was part spiled," shouted back Uncle Sam with brazen conviction. "Anyway, let's have a look at it, Ezry."

The two men, the one with bent back and plodding legs, the other almost as straight and spry as a youth, walked side by side down the ridge path to Uncle Ezra's biggest tobacco barn.

To the right of them lay Ezra's gently rolling blue-grass pasture dotted with cattle and sheep. To the left stretched his dark green alfalfa fields, his corn, ripe and ready to be cut, and his field of ripe tobacco, the broad, tropical looking leaves now turned to a rich golden color. Part of the field was already bare; and in the distance Jerry and Jabez could be seen going down the rows with their sharp tobacco knives. With one stroke they split the stalk of each plant, with the other they severed it from the root. The cut plants drying on the tobacco sticks set at intervals along the rows, trailed limply, waiting to be hauled in.

Arrived at the tobacco barn, they found the alfalfa stacked in a close-packed pile in one corner.

"Why, there hain't much hay here!" shouted Uncle Sam, kicking disdainfully into the pile. "It's loose as kin be. There hain't no weight there. It wasn't tromped when it was put in. I bet I cud haul the whole thing away in two loads."

"Two loads!" snorted Uncle Ezra. "Why, Sam Whitmarsh, there's a good seven ton o' hay there if there's a paound. It's packed close as it kin be packed."

Uncle Sam kicked into the hay and succeeded in finding near a crack in the wall a small mildewed spot.

"It's spiled, Ezry, same's I said it was," he shouted triumphantly. "Look ye here! All along these cracks the rain's beat in an' spiled it. An' there's no tellin' haow far that there mildew goes. Spiled alfalfy hain't no good fer nuthin'."

"Now, Sam, there ain't no use in your a-talkin' on like that," said Uncle Ezra in the tone of one who deals with facts. "You know well nuf there hain't but a handful of it in that corner that's been teched by rain."

"An' see here," went on Sam, "this hay must o' laid two or three days afore you raked it. Why, half the leaves is off. An' I bet it had a rain onto it, too, while it laid on the graound. Look what a dark color it is. Good alfalfy hain't that color."

"It didn't lay ner it didn't see no rain," exclaimed Uncle Ezra, his voice harsh with indignation. "You know yerse'f, Sam, I cut an' hauled that hay latter part of las' July; an' there didn't a drop o' rain fall after the ninth. The alfalfy's a good color if ye see it in the light."

"Looks to me like it's a bit woody," mused Uncle Sam, rubbing a scrap between his thumb and forefinger. "An' here's seed on some of it. You was a bit late a-cuttin' this hay, Ezry."

"Naow, Sam Whitmarsh, you know well's I do, I cut this here hay in the bloom." Uncle Ezra's hands were beginning to tremble with exasperation. "Why, I 'member you come by one Friday when we was a-cuttin' an' you said what fine alfalfy that was."

"Haow do I know this is the same alfalfy, Ezry?" queried Uncle Sam, darting a swift look from his keen blue eyes. "Don't look to me like it is. An' I see jes lots o' weeds through it, too. Part of it hain't good fer nuthin but beddin'. Well, Ezry," with the tone of one coming at last to the crucial point, "what're you a-askin' for it?"

There was a long, ruminating pause. The subject of price could not be approached without deliberation befitting its importance.

"Waal," hesitated Uncle Ezra at last, "you've said every dirty thing you kin think of to say about the hay. But the hay's good hay jes the same; an' you know it well's I do. An' if I had a place to put it I wouldn't sell you nary pound of it fer no money. But bein' as haow I gotta have the room in the barn, I'll take forty-five dollars, an' you do the haulin'. An' that's dern cheap hay I'm a-offerin' you."

"Cheap, Ezry! Before you'll git anybody to give you forty-five dollars fer that there little mangerful o' spiled hay, your new barn'll fall to pieces from old age. An' I guess neither you ner me'll be here to see that happen, Ezry. Be reasonable now, Ezry. You know there hain't but a ton an' a half there. I'll give you twenty dollars fer this here little handful o' hay a-laying before us. An' that's a-payin' you twict over."

"Twenty dollars!" shrieked Uncle Ezra. "Why, there's seven good ton o' hay there. An' hay's worth sixteen dollars a ton at the cheapest. I ain't wishin' to give the hay away. If every leaf of it was spiled it'd be worth more'n that to me to put under my grapes an' peach trees."

"All right, Ezry. Like enough you'd best use it fer that. 'Tain't no good fer nuthin but manure an' beddin' anyway. I don't know as I'd want to bother hookin' up to haul it away."

Uncle Sam made as though to leave the barn. Ezra weakened. He was very anxious to get rid of the hay; he needed the barn at once for his tobacco. And buyers for hay, he knew too well, were not to be readily found at this time of year. Also he knew from sad experience the effect of alfalfa upon tobacco when the two were left in the same barn together. He had been prepared to make some sacrifice; but he shrank from making the sacrifice that Sam demanded of him. Because, what would Aunt Eppie say?

He turned away shaking his head with a final movement, as though negotiations were ended. But Uncle Sam, casting at him a searching, sidewise glance, saw the look of irresolution pass across his face.

"You won't take twenty, eh, Ezry? Then what will you take?"

There was a long pause.

"Waal, I'll take thirty."

The four words dragged themselves with the greatest reluctance from Uncle Ezra's lips.

There was another long pause. Uncle Sam spat deliberately, took a fresh chew of tobacco, and looked out across the landscape meditatively through the big barn doors.

"I tell ye, Ezry," he said at last with great deliberation. "Nobody hain't a-buyin' hay this time o' year. An' if you leave the hay here an' put yer terbaccer in, the terbaccer'll like enough heat an' spile. An' even if it don't heat an' spile, it'll turn dark, sure's yer shirt's on yer back. An' you know what price dark terbaccer fetches. Naow, Ezry, seein' we've allus been good neighbors together, I'm willin' to split the diff'-rence with ye. Twenty-seven fifty I'll pay ye right here in cold cash. Will ye take it?"

Uncle Ezra looked beaten and utterly miserable. "Oh, I s'pose so," he grunted at last.

Uncle Sam had come prepared to clinch matters. He pulled out from his hip pocket a roll of bills, selected two tens, a five, and a two; then fished around among his loose change till he found a fifty-cent piece, and laid the whole in Uncle Ezra's reluctant, yet eager, hand.

Aunt Eppie was waiting anxiously for the result. She had watched the men set out together.

"Did he buy it, Ezry?" she queried excitedly, as soon as her husband appeared in the dooryard.

"Yump."

"Haow much did he give fer it?"

"Twenty-seven fifty."

"Twenty-seven fifty! Do you mean to tell me, Ezry Pettit, you sold that five ton o' good hay fer twenty-seven dollars an' fifty cents, an' hay worth sixteen dollars a ton if it's worth a dollar! The poorhouse is where we'll all end up if that's the way you're a-goin' to go on!"

"Waal, I had to git shet of it; an' nobody's a-buyin' hay naow."

Uncle Ezra was too sick at heart to enter into a quarrel. He walked away as the easiest way of ending the argument, disgusted at the unreasonableness of womankind.

Uncle Sam, the veteran bargain driver, was as gratified as a boy who has just traded a watch that won't go for a shotgun that will. It was a feather in his cap to get the better of old Ezra Pettit. He bragged about it far and near and received congratulations from all the neighbors. There was nobody for ten miles around who did not enjoy a joke at the expense of Uncle Ezra. Being a wag, Uncle Sam could not resist the temptation to get some fun out of his deal. So he hauled the hay away in many lightly-piled loads, craftily built to look much larger than they really were. These loads got on Aunt Eppie's nerves. When the eleventh load trundled by the kitchen window, she shrieked hysterically: "Well, Ezra, ye might as well lock the doors an' pull daown the blinds! The poorhouse is the place fer us!   There goes Sam Whitmarsh with another load o' hay!"

Judith tittered immoderately behind the pantry door.   But Cissy, being a serious and right-minded servant and a stranger to a sense of humor, felt deeply concerned at the loss of her master and mistress, considering it in some degree her own.

CHAPTER VI

THEY had a long, beautiful fall that year. The warm, still sunny days followed each other week after week without a break, until it seemed as if there could never be wind again nor rain nor snow. In the mornings when Judith stepped out into the yard the grass was covered with flimsy gossamer webs encrusted with dewdrops, each one a rainbow in the sun. The beds of geraniums and the bank of scarlet sage along the stone wall seemed to grow each day a richer red. The morning glory vines over the back porch were full each morning with fresh bloom. In colors from faint blue to deep purple, from pale pink to rich rose, delicately veined and gleaming faërily with dew, they lifted up their frail cups to the sun that in a few hours would bring them death. Judith loved to look at the morning glories; yet they gave her a feeling of sadness. They were very silent, these mornings. No birds spilled music into the sunshine. Only a few crows cawed over distant fields. It had been a bountiful year and maturity and plenty were on every hand. The geese, the turkeys, and the chickens were full grown and the proud young males were fat and ready for the market. The hogs in the pen were getting all they could eat. Often they were too lazy to stand up to eat and munched their corn lolling luxuriously on their haunches. Much of their time they spent in sleeping. When they awoke they stretched, snorted, and rolled blissfully in the mud and straw, feeling the warmth of the sun on their bodies and the satisfying comfort of a full belly. By Thanksgiving they would be ready for the butcher's knife. There was a great abundance of tomatoes, cabbages, pumpkins, cornfield beans, everything that flourishes in the good clay soil of Scott County. Corn had been good and the cribs were full. Tobacco had been
76

extra good and Uncle Ezra's great barns were packed to the doors and filled the air about them with exotic fragrance.

There was much pickling, preserving, and canning done in Aunt Eppie's kitchen, for she hated to see anything go to waste. The savory smell of catsup and chili sauce in the making and of vinegar cooking with spices to pickle the pears and peaches streamed out of the door and whetted the appetite of passers-by. It was impossible for Aunt Eppie's family to consume all these bottled delicacies during the winter. Hence her cellar was crowded with the accumulation of many years. Still she insisted on making more each year. When the plenitude of peaches or grapes or cucumbers was so great that it was a human impossibility to can them all, she gave of her surplus to the tenants, grudgingly, yet with a certain Lady Bountiful pleasure in bestowing favors, and always with many admonitions as to the sin of improvidence.

"It's a sin for sech things to go to waste," she would say. "I'm sure I've give away twenty bushel this year if I've give one. An' all the tenants could have 'em jes as plentiful as us if they'd only plant 'em an' tend 'em. I do think it's a shame for folks to live like hawgs from hand to mouth an' never plant a tree ner a bush ner hardly a tater to put in their mouths. Jes look at all these tenant houses! Not a fruit tree ner a berry bush ner hardly as much as a row o' beets an' cabbages! The shiftlessness of some folks is sech that it's a wonder the Lord A'mighty don't send a plague on 'em."

As the weeks went by Jerry began to follow Judith with his eyes and to think about her when she was not in sight. She seemed to have become all at once a much more interesting person than the little black-haired tomboy that he had played and quarreled with ever since he could remember. One October evening when he came up from work and Judith was in the barnyard milking, he lingered about after putting up the horses, pretending to tinker with the harness. It was past the time to go home and he was hungry as a bear; but something held him. Judith got up from the red and white cow and went to the Jersey, the milking stool in one hand, the bucket in the other. Jerry followed her with his eyes. She had on an old blue cotton dress with a long tear in one sleeve and her arms and neck were bare. Her arms and neck looked very beautiful to Jerry.

When she had finished milking the Jersey she got up, kicked the milking stool over toward the fence where the cows would not step on it, and turning to go to the house saw Jerry still pretending to work with the harness.

"Well, Jerry Blackford, hain't you got started fer home yet! Haow long d'ye think yer mammy'll keep yer supper hot fer ye?"

"Till I git there," answered Jerry, coming up beside her.

The horses, as soon as the harness fell from them, had gone at once to the horsepond and taken a long, satisfying drink, then trotted back to the barn to munch the good alfalfa hay that Jerry had pitched down for them. It had been a warm, lazy day. The sun had just set and the evening was still, blue and luminous. Three two-year-old colts that had been brought up for the night, feeling the stimulation of the cool air, began to frolic about the barnyard. They began by rolling in the loose straw and chaff, turning over and over on their backs and waving their hoofs foolishly in the air. Then one colt scrambled to his feet and raced to the gate, the others after him. Back they came from the road gate to the other gate leading into the field, then round and round the barnyard snorting and neighing, their heads and tails high, their manes flowing, their hoofs pounding rhythmically, their beautiful, strong, sleek bodies taut with the joy of the gallop. The work team, having eaten a good supper, trotted out from the barn and joined in the fun with as much zest as the colts.

In the middle of the barnyard stood Charlie, Uncle Ezra's old white mule. He was too old to do much work and was usually left out at pasture. To-night Uncle Ezra had brought him up because he was going to use him in the morning to help haul in corn fodder. Being old and white, he always looked rough and dirty; and he had an ugly bare spot on one shoulder where the harness had rubbed off the hair. His under lip had grown loose and flabby and sagged down, giving his face a sullen look. Isolated by his age and his kind, he stood perfectly motionless, his knees bent like those of an old man, his head low, his haunches slack, his whole body sagging, and took not the least notice of the horses galloping about him. In joyous madcap career they raced in front of him, behind him, all around him; but he neither stirred nor raised his head.

"That's haow folks is when they git old," said Jerry, looking meditatively at the ancient beast.

"Yaas, an' ain't he for all the world like Uncle Ezry? Seems to me them two has growed to look alike, they bin so long together."

"The colts hates him 'cause he's old and 'cause he's a mule," mused Jerry, "an' he hates the colts 'cause they won't leave him have no peace."

Judith had taken from the pocket of her dress a stub of green crayon and begun to draw on the whitewashed fence post. Jerry watched her and saw the profile of Uncle Ezra appear in green on the white post, then beside it the profile of Charlie the mule. She had skilfully modified the features just enough to best bring out the points of resemblance.

"See, hain't they like as twins? They're both the same dirty gray color, both got the same hangin' under lip an' hook nose an' the same big ears."

"An' both is deaf as posts," laughed Jerry.

Judith had her back to him admiring her handiwork. He wanted to lean forward and kiss the white nape of her neck. Instead, he turned about and started off for home.

.   .   .   .

A little before Thanksgiving there came a cold, heavy rain, then a blighting frost that killed the morning glories and the geraniums and blackened everything in the garden except the beets and cabbages. A strong, cold wind blew the trees bare in a single night, and the whole aspect of the world was changed. Two days ago it had been summer. Now it was winter.

It was not so pleasant for Judith at Aunt Eppie's after the

cold weather came. Driven in for warmth from the deserted and windswept barnyard, she found little to interest her in the stuffy, overheated kitchen or the bare, cold bedroom that she shared with Cissy. As the days grew colder, the sitting room took the place of the porch. Here a hideous product of modernity known as a "base burner" was pressed into service. It stood on a square of ornamental zinc placed over the rag carpet and kept clean and shiny by Cissy's floor rag. It was covered with knobs and scrolls and glorious with polished nickel. All around its fat belly it had several rows of little mica windows. When a fire was lighted in this gorgeous crematory and fed with a bucket of cannel coal, mined in the neighboring state of West Virginia, it made the room so hot that Judith had to gasp for breath.

As the days grew colder, Uncle Ezra spent more and more of his time sitting silently with his feet on the fender of the majestic base burner.

The afternoons were short now, and it was night long before the chores were done. The last thing at night Judith had to milk the cows, feed the pigs and calves and shut up the chickens. When at last she came in shivering out of the dark and cold, there was no steaming hot coffee waiting to hearten her, no bacon sizzling in the pan, no biscuits fluffy and fragrant from the oven. The deserted kitchen was bleak in its chilly neatness and a leftover meal was coldly set forth on the table in the sitting room: cold vegetables and bacon left from dinner, cold biscuits and corn cakes, cold water and cold skim milk to drink, a cheerless and uninviting spread. This had been Aunt Eppie's custom from the beginning of time, and there was never any breach in its observance. As soon as the great base burner of the sitting room was put into operation, the kitchen fire was allowed to go out immediately after dinner, and it was not lighted again until next morning. Aunt Eppie, in explaining this custom, always made a great deal of the fact that it saved work for Cissy. What of course it did save was fuel. A tiny lamp set in the middle of this chill-inspiring table irritated the eyes with its feeble glare and served only to make darkness visible. Aunt Eppie possessed a large, round-burner lamp with a polished nickel bowl and a "hand painted" china shade. This lamp was a present from one of her married children. She prized it greatly but never lighted its oil-consuming wick except when she had visitors of importance.

When the silent and cheerless supper was over and the dishes gathered up and washed, everybody went immediately to bed.

"Never be out o' bed at eight ner in at five," was Aunt Eppie's oft repeated motto; and winter and summer this rule was rigidly observed. In the bitter winter mornings as well as in the radiant dawns of summer, the whole family turned out at a quarter to five. They ate breakfast by lamplight. Then while Cissy and Judith washed the dishes, Aunt Eppie and Uncle Ezra sat over the base burner waiting for daylight. With no light in the room but the glow from the mica windows of the stove, the two old people sat in unbroken silence, slaves to their lifelong habit of thrift.

The dreary monotony of this manner of life soon palled upon Judith and she decided to leave Aunt Eppie's service.

"I'm a-goin' back home nex' Satiddy, Aunt Eppie," announced Judith, when one Saturday evening she received her dollar as usual.

"What, a-goin' home, Judy! There hain't nuthin fer you to do at home, an' you won't be earnin' a cent of money. What's the idee of a-goin' back home?"

Judith looked straight at Aunt Eppie with her dark, level eyes.

"I'm a-goin' home 'cause I want to," she said with unashamed simplicity.

"You'd best stay right where you are," advised Aunt Eppie. "Look at Cissy that's been a-workin' for me so long, haow well fixed she is. She's got money loaned out an' a-bringin' her in five per cent interest. You could do jes as well as her if you'd be willin' to stay here an' tend your work, 'stead o' goin' off an' a-loafin' round yer dad's place an' finally a-marryin' some good-fer-nuthin tenant farmer. You'd best stay here, Judy, an' learn to be a good thrifty housekeeper like Cissy."

Aunt Eppie said this last with a certain clinching finality, as though it had been quite decided that Judith was to stay. A more timid and impressionable girl might have been influenced. But Judith, heeding only her own inner promptings, could be neither tempted nor bullied by Aunt Eppie. When the following Saturday arrived she collected her dollar, packed her satchel, climbed onto a wagon that was passing on the way back from Sadieville and was jolted toward home.

Aunt Eppie looked after her with an aggrieved expression.

"That's jes haow it allus is," she remarked to the faithful Cissy, as they turned back together into the kitchen. "They hain't got no notion what's good for 'em. You no sooner get 'em trained into your ways than they're up an' gone. Thankless an' shiftless—all of 'em."

She went back to her sewing in disgust, meditating bitterly that they would now have to pay a male hired man four times what they had been paying to Judith.

Judith was glad to get back to the humbler but warmer atmosphere at home, and the folks were glad to have her back. She made Bill and the boys roar again and slap their sides with delight when she imitated Aunt Eppie's shriek of terror at the fear of the poorhouse. She spread out on the table her accumulated wealth amounting to sixteen dollars; and delighted the twins with a present of three dollars each to buy them stuff for a new dress. To Elmer she gave a dollar to buy him a popgun and reserved the rest of the money to spend riotously on clothes for herself.

"An' we'll all have new dresses for the party," exulted Lizzie May. "Poolers is a-going to have a party Christmas Eve an' we're all bid to go. But we'll have to hurry to git the dresses done."

Unable to wait a minute longer, the girls drove to Clayton first thing next morning and selected the material for their dresses. They chose cotton voile as being the prettiest, most party-like material to be had for the sum that they were able to spend. Lizzie May selected a delicate pink. Luella's choice was a medium blue with darker blue shadow bars running through it. Judith's was a red and white check. They were delighted and voluble over their purchases. They felt gay and festive and full of holiday spirit, like boarding school girls on a visit home. On the way home they all tried to talk at once and laughed so much that Tom and Bob, disturbed by the unusual hilarity behind them, kept looking around inquiringly trying to see what was going on. As they jolted at a fast trot past the Pettit place, Aunt Eppie peered out of the kitchen window.

"There goes them Pippinger girls, an' I'll bet they've spent most every cent Judy's earned while she's been here," she said to Cissy, turning away from the window with her heavy money sigh. "It beats me haow extravagant an' shiftless folks kin be. They don't seem to ever have a thought that there's another day a-comin'."

That very afternoon the girls started to make their dresses. They could hardly wait to eat and wash the dishes.

On Christmas Eve, when they were dressed ready for the party, they felt somehow like different beings, as though they were not workaday people at all but ladies who had always worn new, fluffy dresses, white stockings, and shiny shoes.

It was a drive of three miles to the scene of the party. Then the mules had to be hitched to a fence post at the top of the ridge and the remaining quarter of a mile made on foot. The descent into the hollow where the Pooler house stood was too steep and narrow to attempt with a wagon at night. Tom Pooler, the father of Lizzie May's sweetheart, was a tenant of old Hiram Stone and lived in one of Hiram Stone's tenant houses. Like most of the other tenant houses in Scott County, it was built close to the acres of tobacco land with which it belonged. Proximity to the main road was a matter not taken into account.

By the light of two lanterns the Pippingers proceeded on foot down the steep, scarcely marked wagon track that led to the house, the girls carefully holding up their skirts and stepping daintily so as to avoid the mud. The night was mild and bright with stars. As they walked a light wind blew in their faces and the dead leaves rustled under their feet. As they approached the house, they saw light shining not only from the windows but from many little square chinks in the walls. The reason for these little golden squares of light dated back to the building of the house several years before. Tom Pooler had made an arrangement with Old Man Stone's overseer to build the house if Stone would supply the lumber. The overseer supplied green lumber. Tom set to work briskly to build the house and soon completed the twelve by fourteen packing case which in that locality is called a house. All went well until the green boards began to shrink. Then Tom approached his landlord's manager in this wise:

"Whatcha gimme green lumber to build that 'ere house fer? The boards is shrunk naow so's a man might jes as well be a-livin' in a corn crib. You could throw a dawg through any o' them there cracks atween them shrunk boards. You'll have to gimme some more lumber to fix it, else I hain't a-goin' to stay on there nary week."

The overseer grudgingly supplied another load of lumber, with which Tom set to work to make the house tight and shipshape. This time he nailed the boards crosswise. They turned out to be as green as the first lot; and in a few months they had shrunk away from each other, leaving the house dotted with little square holes. "I'll fix that," said Tom to himself one Sunday morning, and started toward the corn crib. He soon came back with a wheelbarrow load of corn cobs and started to drive them into the holes and break off the ends. For an hour or so he worked busily driving in cobs and breaking off the ends. When he was called to dinner he surveyed the results of his work and saw that he had mended only a small patch of the great chequered expanse still gaping with holes. In the afternoon he began again, but with diminished energy. Along toward four o'clock the weariness of well doing suddenly came upon him. There were too many holes.

"Aw, hell, let 'er go the way she is," he muttered disgustedly, and felt in his pocket for another chew of tobacco.

It was to this house of many little golden windows that the Pippingers were now coming in the darkness. Arrived at the door, they turned their lanterns low and set them beside several other low-burning lanterns that stood in a little cluster against the house wall. Pushing open the door and entering without knock or ceremony, they found themselves in a stifling hot room crowded with people. The dim glare of two small kerosene lamps seemed a brilliant illumination after the darkness of outside; and for a moment they were dazzled.

Addie Pooler, the eldest girl, came forward and escorted Judith and the twins to a shedlike leanto back of the house where the Pooler boys slept and which was now doing duty as a dressing room. Here the four youngest Pooler children were already asleep all in one bed, two at each end, under a quilt roughly constructed of various sized pieces of dark colored goods cut from the less worn portions of men's old coats and trousers. Several sleeping babies were disposed here and there about the room on improvised beds made of overcoats or laprobes. The girls put their coats and scarves on another large bed already piled with outdoor clothing, patted their hair a little in front of the small, face-distorting mirror over the chest of drawers, and followed Addie back into the kitchen.

Here the party was not yet under way. The women and girls and small children of both sexes were sitting or standing self-consciously about the walls. For the most part they sat bolt upright and stared straight ahead of them. Now and then they eyed each other covertly. Sometimes a woman would speak to her neighbor in a hushed voice and thus start up a small whispered conversation; but of general talk there was none. Almost all of them, daughters and mothers alike, were painfully thin, with pinched, angular features and peculiarly dead expressionless eyes. The faces of the girls wore already an old, patient, settled look, as though a black dress and a few gray hairs would make them sisters instead of daughters of the older women.

Tom Pooler, the host, a little man, red-faced and choleric like a bantam fighting cock, the possessor of a tremendous ego, sat in a round-backed armchair by the stove and spat tobacco juice into the wood box. His feet in heavy gray cotton socks were comfortably extended upon the fender. He was the center of a group of older men who stood and sat about the stove spitting tobacco juice and discussing the same things that they always did. The young men were nowhere to be seen. They were all standing outside with the lanterns.

All at once the door flew open and Jabez Moorhouse came in with his fiddle.

Jabez was in the best of spirits. He had taken a drop before he started, had had several pulls from the bottle on the way over to keep out the cold, and was feeling in holiday spirit. He was much in demand at gatherings like these on account of his ability to play the fiddle and call off the dances; and his response was usually a ready one. But he never went without a flask of good corn whiskey in his pocket to blur his eyes and his mind and nimble his fingers and his feelings.

"Waal, naow, gals, whatcha doin' here anyway? Settin' all raound solemn, like you was to a buryin'?"

He opened the door and held it open while he called out into the darkness:

"Hi there, you backward young fellers! Air you a-goin' to set aout on the doorstep with the dawgs all night? Come along in here an' pick yer gals fer the fu'st dance."

They came pouring in, elbowing and shoving each other and uttering loud guffaws to cover their embarrassment. They were healthier and less angular than the girls and the look of premature age had not been stamped upon their features.

"Naow then, you good lookin' gals, git up onto the floor; an' if a partner don't pick you, you pick a partner. This here is leap year anyway. Besides it's allus the wimmin that picks the men, though they try to make out it hain't. I say every gal that wants to git a good man step out onto the floor. An' every gal that wants to stay a old maid keep a-settin' by her mammy."

Nobody was offended by the crassness of Jabez' exhortation. It was what they had all been waiting for. This crude joviality and the smell of corn whiskey that was beginning to pervade the atmosphere soon cured the young fellows of their bashfulness, and there was much pulling and pushing of the girls from their seats, which they pretended to wish to retain.

Jabez had stationed himself in a corner and was tuning his fiddle.

"Naow then, all aboard! Form a line daown the middle; a lady an' a gent, a lady an' a gent. Gents to the right, ladies to the lef'. Swing yer partners."

He broke into the tune of one of the square dances familiar in that neighborhood, and the feet of the young men and girls followed him. Awkwardly and haltingly enough they stepped the first figure. The girls, with their angularities sticking out of their skimpy, ill-fitting dresses, moved at first as though from the pulling of wires. The young men slumped and floundered, lost their partners and got tangled up in the chain of dancers and had to be untangled again. As they warmed to the music, however, the feet lightened, the arms limbered, and self-consciousness was forgotten.

The men about the stove kept the fire well stoked and the room grew hotter and hotter, especially to the dancers. Dance followed upon dance. Tobacco smoke and the fumes of corn whiskey filled the stale air. The cheeks of every one were blazing from the heat and closeness. The children in the chairs were all asleep, leaning against their mothers. The older men in the corner by the stove watched the dancers and talked and spat tobacco juice into the wood box. They spat so much tobacco juice that the wood was covered with it. Fortunately it was the spitters who had the job of putting the wood into the stove, so it was their own affair. For the dancing girls in their slippers and light dresses, their feet and hearts beating time to the music, the spit encrusted wood box did not exist. With the beautiful ability of youth to ignore the ugly and sordid, however near at hand, they danced and laughed and coquetted with their partners, feeling in this their hour far removed above the humdrum of their lives.

The two prettiest girls in the room were Bill Pippinger's daughters, Lizzie May and Judith. Lizzie May, with her pale pink dress, cornsilk hair and small, dainty features, made one think of a wild rose. Dan Pooler could not take his eyes from her and insisted on being her partner in every dance, until toward the end of the evening the two disappeared entirely from the dancing floor. Judith in red and white shone in her dark loveliness like a poppy among weeds. Something more than her beauty set her apart from the others: an ease and naturalness of movement, a freedom from constraint, a completeness of abandon to the fun and merrymaking, to which these daughters of toil in their most hectic moments could never attain. Somehow, in spite of her ancestry, she had escaped the curse of the soil, else she could never have known how to be so free, so glad, so careless and joyous.

This difference from the other girls singled her out for comment more than once; and the comment was always adverse, less from maliciousness than from lack of comprehension; although envy, naturally enough, was not absent.

"My sakes, Judy Pippinger'd otta think shame to herse'f," whispered Jenny Whitmarsh to Esther Pooler, "the way she goes on with the fellers!"

"If Judy's poor mammy was alive, she wouldn't like to see her a-goin' on in that way," sighed Aunt Mary Blackford to Aunt Maggie Slatten. "That way o' carryin' on ain't a-goin' to bring her to no good."

The men about the stove had by this time passed the bottle several times and were filled with good feeling and reminiscences, as they watched the dancers passing in a far-off blur. The young men too had occasionally slipped aside to enjoy a swig with a companion, and were becoming bolder and more demonstrative in the dance. From time to time the talk of one of them slipped past the bounds of the decent and caused the cheeks of his partner to flush still redder.

As they danced the old game of "Skip to ma Loo," everybody sang noisily:

> Dad's ole hat an' mam's ole shoe,
> Dad's ole hat an' mam's ole shoe,
> Dad's ole hat an' mam's ole shoe,
> Skip to ma Loo, ma da'lin'.

In the pauses of the dance, the voices of the men about the stove could be heard growing louder and more vociferous, as the bottles became lighter.

> I'll git another one better'n you,
> I'll git another one better'n you,
> I'll git another one better'n you,
> Skip to ma Loo, ma da'lin'.

Aunt Nannie Pooler, a wizened, bent little woman, the mother of eleven, now began to spread out the refreshments on a table in a corner. Some of the older women got up and assisted her. The Poolers were noted for their improvidence and their lavishness in entertaining. Soon the table was spread with layer cakes, cookies, corn cakes and plates of cold fried chicken. The smell of bad coffee boiling on the stove had permeated the room for some time. It was now poured into cups, mugs, bowls, glasses, anything that would hold liquid, and the guests invited to step up and partake.

"Yaas, we eat at our haouse," Tom Pooler's voice could be heard saying loudly. "An' anybody comes in our doors, neighbor or stranger, goes away with his belly full."

"Whose hencoop d'ye reckon old man Pooler reached this fried chicken out'n?" asked Edd Whitmarsh of young Bob Crupper, when the two had retired to the back stoop to enjoy chicken washed down by a swig of whiskey.

"Whosever it was he had 'em fed fat," answered Bob, devouring a piece of the breast with great satisfaction. "I sholy

do love a fat chicken. I kinder hope the joke was on Uncle
Ezry."

With the leg of a chicken in one hand and a corn cake in
the other, Jabez, now blissfully intoxicated, stood beside the
table and rallied the girls as they came up. Most of them
were too excited to care for food and Jabez knew it.

"Waal naow, Judy, my gal, hain't you a-goin' to do nothin'
but nibble at a half of a wing, like you was a mouse on a pantry
shelf? I seen you a-dancin' that fast an' a-laughin' that hard,
a body'd think you'd be clean wore out an' a-needin' vittles.
If you'd worked that hard at the washtub, I'll bet you'd be
a-wantin' to eat a' right."

Judith's cheeks were scarlet and her dark eyes blazing.
She looked at him from under her straight black eyebrows
with the peculiar level gaze of hers. Even in the excitement
of the moment there was something calm and critical, almost
cold in that clear, unwavering look. She had always resented
the self-appointed privilege of the old to make sport of the
young.

"When you was seventeen did you eat hearty at parties,
Uncle Jabez?"

Jabez did not notice the question. "Land, Judy," he said
meditatively, "it makes a body feel old to see haow quick you
young uns grows up. It seems like only day afore yestiddy
you was a little brat a-crawlin' raound on the kitchen floor.
When I'd step into yer dad's to see about borryin' a tool or gittin' shoes put onto a hoss, I'd have to walk careful to keep
from settin' my foot daown on yuh. An' naow here ye be a
tall, growed young leddy; an' if there's a handsomer gal in
Scott County I'd like to have her showed to me."

Just then Jerry Blackford came up, grabbed Judith on both
sides of her red and white checked waist and whisked her
away to another corner of the room.

The music and dancing began again after Jabez had finished
his chicken leg and ended in a wild, helter-skelter scramble,
the young men chasing the girls around and around the room,
catching them and kissing them with loud, resounding smacks.

The girls exchanged slaps for kisses, and the sound of female fingers ringing on male cheeks peppered the air.

"Young folks to the wall; ole folks to the middle," called out the voice of Jabez. "This is dad's an' mammy's turn naow. Step out here you ole timers an' show the young uns haow we used to dance when we was lads an' gals."

Tom Pooler could be heard pulling his shoes out from under the stove.

"Yaas, by gollies, let's show 'em haow we done a barn dance. We hain't so stiff with rheumatics but what we kin step a figger yet, hey, Nannie?"

The other men about the stove shambled after Tom to the middle of the floor. The older women, exhorted by their daughters and husbands, were at last persuaded to forsake their chairs and join the circle.

Although nearly all of the "old folks" were under fifty and most of them in the thirties and forties, it was a scarecrow array of bent limbs, bowed shoulders, sunken chests, twisted contortions, and jagged angularities, that formed the circle for the old folks' dance. Grotesque in their deformities, these men and women, who should have been in the full flower of their lives, were already classed among the aged. And old they were in body and spirit. It was only on such rare occasions as this that the stimulation of social feeling and corn whiskey incited them to try to imitate with Punch and Judy antics the natural gaiety of youth.

"Yaas, we'll teach 'em haow to step a dance," cried Andy Blackford, the father of Jerry, floundering into the wrong place in the chain and grabbing the wrong partner with his great, seamy, wart-covered hands. "This is haow we done it in the old days, hain't it, Aunt Susie?"

The skinny, dried-up, little women in their black dresses and white aprons did not get much enjoyment out of the dance. There was neither lure nor mystery about the other sex for them any more; and they were disgusted and nauseated by the foul whiskey breath that spewed out upon them from their partners' mouths. The thought of the hard-earned money thrown away upon said whiskey did not tend to make them more cheerful. They went through the dance as they had gone through everything else since childhood, as a matter of course, because the circumstances of their lives demanded it of them.

Toward the close of the dance, Tom Pooler fell sprawling upon the floor. The drink had gone to his legs as well as to his head. He took the fall as an unwarranted insult to his dignity and scrambled to his feet flushed with whiskey, importance and indignation.

"I tell ye, I'm a baar in the woods, I am. Nobody don't dass say nuthin to Tom Pooler that he don't wanta hear— not Ezry Pettit ner Hiram Stone ner none of 'em. I don't take no sass from nobody no matter haow much land they got. I bet I cud lick any man in Scott County. I tell ye I'm a baar in the woods."

"You shet up yer mouth, ye dern ole fool an' don't git to quarrelin' in yer own house. Whatcha drink all that whiskey fer?" admonished Aunt Nannie in a loud whisper close to his ear. He glared at her with small, fiery, bloodshot eyes, like an angry old boar at bay. She met the glare firmly and calmly. Under her cold gaze that had restrained him so many times before he calmed down. But for a long time he kept muttering to himself: "I'm a baar in the woods, I am. Yaas, sir, I'm a baar in the woods."

The young people had paid no attention to the dancing of their elders. They had slipped away into corners and were absorbed in their own affairs.

The party was over with the old folks' dance. There was much sorting out of clothing, wrapping up of sleeping babies and shaking of older children to get them wide enough awake to walk to the wagons. No one told the host and hostess that they had enjoyed themselves; such things went without saying. When the Pippingers were all ready to start and had at last selected their own lanterns out of the bewildering cluster by the door, Lizzie May was not to be found anywhere. They waited and called. By and by she appeared around the corner of the house; she had been saying good-by to Dan. She seemed flustered and excited.

After they had reached the wagon and were driving along the ridge road, they heard Jabez, who was striding home across fields, singing ebulliently as he walked:

> Possum up the 'simmons tree,
> Raccoon on the graoun';
> Raccoon says, "You son of a bitch,
> Throw them 'simmons daown."

The night was still, mild and bright with stars. There was a clean smell of earth and dried leaves. The song came across the fields out of the darkness, rich, clear and mellow. A soft, cool wind blew in their heated faces; and the stars twinkled down through the tracery of bare treetops.

"Ain't Uncle Jabez awful!" sighed Luella, snuggling down into the straw. "He kin play the fiddle good; but land he does use sech langridge."

"Oh, don't think yerse'f so nice, Elly," snapped Judith, who had loved the sound of the singing. "His langridge hain't no worse'n other men folks'. On'y the song hain't true, 'cause a coon kin climb a tree jes as good as a possum any day."

CHAPTER VII

LIZZIE MAY could hardly wait till she was alone with her sis‑
ters in their attic bedroom to tell them that Dan Pooler had
asked her to marry him. They were going to try to go to
housekeeping in the spring.

The following Sunday afternoon when Dan and Lizzie May
were out driving, Jerry Blackford came over to the Pippinger
place. There was nothing unusual about this. Since they
were mere babies the Blackford boys, Andy and Jerry, had
been in the habit of coming over to play with the Pippingers.
This time, however, Jerry came alone. And instead of being
in overalls and torn shirt, he was wearing his new brown mail
order suit, a black derby hat, a "biled" shirt, and a resplendent
tie of red and green stripes. He walked up the wagon drive,
hesitated for the fraction of a second before the little picket
gate that led into the dooryard of the house, then walked on
into the barnyard. Here he found Bill, Uncle Sam Whitmarsh,
and Uncle Amos Crupper sitting on the chopping log chewing,
whittling, and spitting. It was late December, but the day
was mild and the sunshine pleasant to sit in. A Sabbath after‑
noon calm permeated the pale sunshine and the still, birdless
air. A few crows cawing reproachfully over the stubble of
the deserted cornfield, only intensified the silence. Between
the men and the barn, Craw and Elmer were playing a game
of catch with a homemade ball of twisted rubber and string.

"Where be ye a-goin' in yer Sunday clothes, Jerry?" in‑
quired old Amos Crupper, looking up from his whittling.

"No place."

"Aw, come on naow," rallied Uncle Sam Whitmarsh, with a
twinkle in his keen gray eyes. "A young feller don't stretch
on his Sunday best jes to tramp the roads. You're a-goin'
sparkin' some gal."

"I hain't neither. I'm a-goin to hev a game o' ketch with

94

Craw an' Elmer. Come on, Craw, pitch 'er to me, an' we'll make it a three-handed game."

By and by Judith came out to the well to get a bucket of water. Jerry glimpsed her out of the corner of his eye as she worked the pump handle up and down. But he was careful not to turn his head in her direction.

"Jerry Blackford's aout there in all his Sunday clothes a-playin' ketch with the boys," she announced to Luella, as she set the bucket down. "I wonder where he's been to."

Jerry played catch until it was chore time. Then he went home, passing the house with his head turned in the opposite direction. Judith and Luella, peering out of the kitchen window, saw him go.

For four successive Sundays Jerry repeated this performance. By the second Sunday the girls had formed a pretty shrewd notion of the reason for his peculiar behavior.

"I'm jes a-goin' to set still an' see haow long he keeps it up," said Judith wickedly, as she sat by the kitchen window trimming a hat with peacock feathers that had molted from the tail of Aunt Eppie's peacock. "I'm a-goin' to sew the feathers all raound an' raound the brim, Elly; an' then have some a-droppin' daown behind. Won't it make a nice hat?"

The longer Jerry continued to come on Sundays in his best clothes, the more amusement he provided for Judith. She felt gratified by his attentions; but she took no interest in him any more than in any of the other young fellows of the neighborhood, with all of whom she dearly loved to coquette. So she was not at all impatient at this slow courtship. She liked to go out and draw water or hang something on the line in order to see Jerry turn his head away from her. Often she found it necessary to go into the barnyard to feed the chickens or slop the hogs; and would stop and exchange a few casual words with him for the pleasure of watching his embarrassment and enjoying his discomfiture when she turned away.

On the fourth Sunday, as Jerry was hanging about the barnyard with the boys, he saw Dick Whitmarsh drive up to the Pippinger door in a newly-washed buggy. In a few moments he was galvanized to see Judith come out, radiant in her Sunday best, with the peacock hat glowing iridescently above her black hair. She and Dick got into the buggy and drove gaily away.

Jerry went home almost immediately, feeling like a small rooster that has been chased out of the cornfield by a larger one. He savagely pulled off his good clothes, put on his comfortable old overalls, went out to the barn and fell to cursing and currying the horses with all his might.

The next Sunday Jerry appeared in the Pippinger wagon drive very early in the afternoon. He was driving Jinny, the spirited four-year-old bay mare; and the Blackford family buggy was washed and polished to resplendence.

"Hey, Judy!" he shouted in loud, careless-like fashion from the buggy seat.

He had to shout three or four times before the door at last opened and Judith appeared on the threshold.

"Say, Judy, wanta come—ahem—fer a little drive?"

Jerry was so much embarrassed that he choked in the middle of the invitation and had to clear his throat.

"I'd like to go all right, Jerry; but I promised Dick Whitmarsh I'd go with him this afternoon."

"But—uh—I'm here first, hain't I?" countered Jerry, beginning to feel indignant.

"Waal, s'pose you air! No little bird told me you was a-fixin' to come. An' I promised Dick las' Sunday I'd go with him agin to-day."

"Waal, I'll be damned!"

Jerry muttered this to himself, staring straight before him with blank, unseeing, disappointed eyes.

By this time the whole Pippinger family had collected in the dooryard and were looking at Jerry, the glossy bay mare and the newly washed buggy with the intentness with which children regard a circus parade. He looked up from his blank stare at nothing and encountered their six pairs of eyes all fixed upon him with cool, dispassionate appraisal. Then he caught a glimmer of amusement in Bill's eye and Craw winked at him significantly. He felt like a grasshopper impaled on a darning needle with a circle of boys watching its efforts to escape.

The sound of buggy wheels rattling through the Pippinger gateway made him turn his head; and he saw Dick Whitmarsh driving in.

He passed with his head down and his eyes on the dashboard and made no response to Dick's cheery "Howdy, Jerry." When he was out on the road, he turned the mare's head in the opposite direction from home, whipped her up into a gallop and used freely in muttered imprecations all the bad language that he had ever heard.

About two miles away he saw ahead of him the great gaunt figure of Jabez Moorhouse stalking along the roadside. He had slowed up by this time and was feeling somewhat calmer.

"Git in an' ride, Uncle Jabez," he said, pulling up beside his former working companion.

Jabez clambered into the buggy and disposed his long legs as best he could. He was slightly under the influence of corn whiskey and the smell of it was upon his breath. He pulled out a bottle from his hip pocket.

"Have a drink, Jerry," he said, handing it to the younger man.

Jerry took a long pull at the bottle.

"Where be you a-goin' in yer good clothes, with yer buggy an' mare all slicked up so neat?"

"No place."

"Aw, don't go to tellin' me that. I been a young feller too in my day. What gal air you a-sparkin', Jerry?"

"No gal."

"Jerry, 'tain't no youst fer the young to try to hide things from the old. They been through it all. You might as well own up you're on the track o' some wench. What's her name?"

"Aw, shet up, Uncle Jabez. You know I hain't a-sparkin' no gal."

Jerry looked straight ahead of him at the moving haunches of the mare.

"Have another drink, Jerry."

Jerry took another long pull at the bottle, and felt much better. Jabez also helped himself before returning the bottle to his pocket.

"Jerry," went on Jabez, after a long silence. "The old likes to give advice to the young—not that they look to see 'em take it o' course. For, as the Bible says, they got ears but they hear not. Jes the same, even if I'm a-talkin' to deaf ears, I gotta have my say. Jerry, don't have nothin' to do with wimmin. I've had a right smart of experience with 'em, an' I kin tell yuh, an' it's the livin' truth, all wimmin is harlots."

Jerry stirred uneasily and seemed about to open his mouth.

"It's the livin' truth, Jerry, my boy." Jabez' vague blue eyes took on a prophetic look, as though he were a seer of old exhorting the heedless to look to their ways; and his deep voice fell into the rhythmic chant of the inspired man. "Don't go after none of 'em, I tell yuh. Wimmin'll deal treacherously with yuh, Jerry. Their lips drops honey an' their mouths is smoother'n oil; but in the end they're bitter as wormwood an' sharper'n a two-edged sword. The Bible says so, Jerry; but that hain't the way I found it out. Yaas, Jerry, they're all deceitful. They'll all eat an' wipe their mouths an' say they hain't done no sin. Keep yerse'f clean of 'em, my boy."

"All wimmin hain't harlots," answered Jerry slowly and with conviction.

There was something in what Jerry said and his way of saying it that brought Jabez back to the matter of fact.

"Aw, hell," he laughed, in the tone of one descended suddenly to earth, "what youst to tell a husky young buck like you not to go after the wimmin? Might as well speak to the grass an' tell it not to grow in May. Have another drink, Jerry."

They each took another long pull at the bottle and then drove for some time in silence.

"Is she dark or fair, Jerry?" asked Jabez out of the silence.

"She's dark," admitted Jerry, the mellowing influence of the whiskey beginning to overcome his boyish bashfulness and natural taciturnity. "But her skin hain't dark. On'y her eyes an' hair is dark. Her skin is all creamy colored an' her cheeks is pink like brier roses. No, not like brier roses—a pinker pink—more like peach blossoms."

"Huh," grunted Jabez thoughtfully. " 'Tain't Judy Pippinger, is it?"

"Yump." Then after a pause, "Would yuh say Judy Pippinger was a harlot?" Jerry looked belligerently at Jabez.

The older man was too surprised by the question even to notice the young fellow's attitude of challenge. He gave a start of shocked astonishment.

"A harlot! My gawd no, Jerry. Judy Pippinger hain't but a little gal! I allus liked that little gal. She seems more like a boy. It's on'y lately she's begun to know she's a gal an' not a boy. Too bad she hain't a boy."

He fell silent for a time, musing.

"Waal, haow's the courtin' a-comin' on?" he asked at last. "Is the day set yet?"

"No, it hain't."

Jerry's face assumed an expression of sullen disgruntlement. Jabez looked at him keenly out of the corner of his eye.

"Have another drink, Jerry."

Both men had another drink, and there fell another long period of silence.

"Where's the hitch, Jerry?" asked Jabez at last.

By this time the whiskey had thoroughly warmed Jerry through and through. The landscape was beginning to look blurred and far away; and he felt shut in with Jabez in a warm atmosphere of congeniality and comradeship. He began, haltingly at first, to tell his friend his troubles. Gradually his trickle of speech flowed more freely; then burst suddenly forth, like a stream that has broken a dam, and rushed in a torrent of picturesque curses on the head of Dick Whitmarsh.

Jabez laughed the loud, carefree laugh of inebriation.

"Why, Jerry, you bin a heap too backward," he cried, slapping his friend on the back till Jerry winced, "an' Dick Whitmarsh has sure got the start of you naow. The on'y thing fer you to do is to come up on him from another d'rection an' s'prise the enemy when he hain't a-lookin' fer yuh. Not all the courtin' is done in buggies, Jerry; though a feller born an' bred in Scott County might think so. It don't have to be done in buggies. An' Judy Pippinger 'specially hain't a gal to be courted in a buggy. You go to meetin' her accidentally when she's a-drivin' up the caows or a-stalkin' them turkeys over the hills an' hollers, an' I'll bet you'll ketch up with Dick in no time, even if he has got a head start. If yuh must go a-courtin', as I s'pose yuh must, yuh might as well go in fer to win. Good luck, Jerry!"

They had reached Jabez' house, a melancholy little weathered frame shanty shaded by two sorrowful hemlock trees that stood out blackly against the gray sky. Jabez leapt from the buggy.

Jerry turned the mare's head toward home. Knowing where she was going, she fell into a fast trot without any encouragement. The short winter day was already graying to a close and it was chore time. As he drove along over the half frozen ruts of the road, his imagination was aflame with the suggestions that Jabez had thrown out. The corn whiskey gave warmth and color to these imaginings.

The effect of the corn whiskey soon wore off, but not of Jabez' suggestions; and Jerry was now in no mood for delay. He had held off quite long enough, he told himself. The very next evening, as Judith was driving up Spot and Blackie, the successors of Roanie and Reddie, Jerry met her coming along the ridge path. She had on Craw's cloth cap, an old canvas coat of her father's and Craw's rubber boots. Shining out from this rough frame, her girlish charms looked all the more alluring to Jerry.

"Howdy, Jerry. Where you a-goin?"

"I'm a-lookin' fer our red an' white heifer. She's strayed away some place an' we hain't see hair ner hide of her since yestiddy mornin'."

"I didn't see no signs of a strange caow back yonder. But mebbe she's there. If she is she'll be in the holler by Uncle Jonah Cobb's place, 'cause you kin see all the rest from the ridge. Well, I gotta be a-gittin' on. Git along there, Blackie. It'll be dark afore I git milked. Good-by, Jerry."

"I don't reckon she's in the holler. Anyway it'd be too dark to see her agin I got there. I guess I'll go on back home."

He turned and walked by Judith's side.

They walked along the ridge path together behind the cows. Neither of them spoke a word. Before they reached the Pippinger barnyard, Jerry vaulted a rail fence and went off toward home across fields. Judith looking after him noticed with what agility he leapt the fence and how light and springy was his step as he strode away across the deserted corn fields. Yes, she admitted to herself, he was, as Lizzie May had said, much better looking than Dick Whitmarsh. On the whole she thought she liked him better than Dick.

The next evening he met her in the same place.

"Howdy, Jerry. You still a-searchin' for that red an' white heifer?"

She looked at him with laughing challenge in her dark eyes. Instantly he was put at ease by this frank admission of things as they really were. She had placed him where he wanted to be. He turned and walked beside her.

On the third evening he took her hand in his and they walked along together swinging the joined hands between them like two children. Her restless, work-hardened hand, neither small nor delicate, nestled comfortably in Jerry's large, warm palm. There was something comforting, something restful and satisfying about that firm, enfolding male pressure. Her hand, lying in his, felt relaxed and at peace, like a child rocked by its mother.

On the fourth evening it was raining in a fine, mild drizzle. The damp air made Judith's fresh pink cheeks fresher and pinker. Last year's dead leaves were soggy under their feet. In a little grove of second growth maples and beeches, Jerry released her hand and slipped his arm around her waist underneath the coarse old canvas coat. The exquisite curve of her body intoxicated him. A surge of desire swept over him and he took her in his arms and kissed her passionately on the lips.

She kissed him back with answering passion. For a long time they stood together in the soft drizzle, the shade of the beeches and maples deepening about them into twilight gloom.

It was all easy after that for Jerry. It was a speedy, simple, natural courting, like the coming together of two young wild things in the woods. Jerry, who was of a practical turn of mind, immediately began to plan for their future.

"I think I'll sign a contract with old Hiram Stone for next year, Judy," he said to her one spring evening, when they had met down by the brook in the hollow, a spot that they had chosen as a trysting place. "It's too late to get any land for this year. But next first of March we'll move into a little home of our own. Won't that be nice, Judy?"

"I dunno if it'll be nice or not," doubted Judy, looking straight at him. "I hain't never been very fond of keepin' house, Jerry."

She had a disconcerting way of stating a disagreeable fact quite baldly and then nailing it to his consciousness by looking him through and through with those clear, level, gray eyes of hers. He felt saddened and frustrated by her lack of enthusiasm for the little home on which he had pondered so fondly. Instinct told him what to do on such an occasion. He took her in his arms, kissed her, fondled her, made her love him. Then the feeling of unity came back and they were at peace again.

"You know," he went on, "old man Stone has got the best land anywheres around here. An' if I kin raise about five acres of tobacco on his ground, we'll be able to lay by a little money, Judy. An' after a few years we kin buy us a little place of our own. I don't want to be like all these poor devils that lives all their lives from hand to mouth a-workin' on somebody's else's ground an' never havin' a foot o' land that they kin call their own. It hain't no way to live, Judy. You an' I'll do better'n that. I want to own my own place; so if I don't like a feller's looks I kin tell him to git off of it."

Jerry took on a male and belligerent expression. Judith looked at him and laughed mockingly.

"You look jes like a Tom turkey with its head a-swellin' up with blood," she teased. "Why does a man allus like to feel hisself big an' important an' better'n every other man? You 'member Uncle Tom Pooler at the party. 'I'm a baar in the woods, I am. Yaas, sir, I'm a baar in the woods!' " She imitated his whiskey-fuddled mutterings. "An' you men hain't the on'y ones," she went on. "All male critters is the same. Look haow proud a Tom turkey struts, an' haow a big rooster cranes his neck an' crows an' chases the smaller roosters out o' the yard. An' look haow two big, bellerin' bulls'll fight jes fer the love o' fightin'. Wimmin hain't like that, allus makin' the most o' theirselves. They tend their own business and let other wimmin tend theirs."

"The hell they do so," countered Jerry. "Aunt Sally Whit-marsh was into our place las' night, an' I jes wish you cud a heard her. I was in the little room off the kitchen a-shavin' an' the door was open atween. An' if Aunt Sally wa'n't a-spit-tin' out pizen about the neighbors acrost the kitchen stove to mammy, then I don't know a dirty tongue when I hear it. The ugly thing about wimmin is they never say a thing right out an' have done with it, like a man does. They jes set with their hands in their laps an' say a little bit an' leave the rest to the other woman's dirty 'magination. An' my own mammy herse'f hain't much better'n the rest. I don't like wimmin, Judy. There's sumpin' small an' mean an' underhand an' foul about most all of 'em. Uncle Jabez was purty nigh right when he told me they was all harlots. You're the on'y woman I know that's got a man's ways, Judy. You hain't spiled."

The year passed quickly for them both in their delirium of early love. Accident was kind to them and did not thrust upon them with untimely speed the physical results of the sweet intimacy that they enjoyed. So they did not have to hasten their marriage, and the neighbors were deprived of a juicy bit of scandal. In February Jerry procured a license; and one day late in the month they drove over to Clayton and, through the medium of Obe Applestill, local Justice of the Peace, they secured the blessing of the law on their relations. After that Jerry did not rest easy until they were in a home of their own.

In early February Jerry signed a contract with old Hiram Stone.

The house that he was to have was a little two-room frame shanty in a deep hollow between two hills and about half a mile from the main road. The five acres of tobacco ground and the ten acres of corn land that were to be in Jerry's charge for the year, lay close at hand. The little cabin was more attractive than most of the tenant houses in Scott County, bare, boxlike sheds, most of them standing starkly on barren hillsides or marshy stretches, as though the hand of some careless giant had scattered them with no thought whatever of the use that they were to serve. Jerry had picked the house from three because he wanted to bring his bride to something that looked like a home. Two tall hickory trees rose high into the air and intertwined their branches above the little house. It nestled comfortably under the hill. The low roof projected over the eaves and gave it a snug, homelike look. Inside it had a fireplace, though a small and crude one. Some former tenant had planted a lilac bush by the door; and a grape vine clambered over a rude trellis at one end. A little brook trickled through the hollow a few rods away and made pleasant murmurings.

Jerry had "worked out" during most of the year and had assiduously saved money. Judith too had worked again at Aunt Eppie's for several months and with her savings had bought bedding, towels, a dress or two and a few pieces of coarse muslin underwear gaily strung with crass pink ribbons. Jerry's mother had contributed two new patchwork quilts. Luella had made her a nice warm comforter tied with red wool. And Aunt Abigail, much to Judith's surprise, had come forward with one of her best Log Cabin quilts.

"This here quilt," she said, unfolding it impressively, "was patched by me when I was a little gal on'y fourteen year old.

Gals don't patch quilts naow like they did when I was young. I've allus took good care of it, an' I want you to do the same, Judy. When you have a pack o' young uns of yer own, don't let 'em ramp an' tear all over it. Nothin' ruins a quilt quicker'n young uns a-pitchin' an' a-scramblin' a-top of it. If they've got to pitch an' scramble, let 'em do it on the grass or on the floor an' not a-top o' this here good quilt."

"Naow, Judy, we don't want to buy no new furniture," Jerry had said, when they were planning for their home. "New furniture costs too much. You can't git a new cook stove under about twenty-five dollars. An' at a sale you kin pick up one jes as good fer about eight or ten. Same with tables an' beds an' dressers. You kin git all sech plunder fer nex' to nothin' at sales. Fust sale there is anywhere within ten miles we'll go."

A short time after this a sale was advertised. Uncle Nat Carberry, who lived over near Dry Ridge, had died at the age of eighty-three, leaving his farm, stock, and personal possessions to be divided among his eight children. Everybody for miles around knew about the sale and nearly everybody was going whether they wanted to buy anything or not.

When Jerry and Judith got to the scene of the sale there were already many buggies and wagons hitched to the fence. One lonely automobile, a Ford, belonged to Pete Whitmarsh who was overseer for Hiram Stone. It was quite generally whispered of Pete that he managed to get away with a good deal more than his wages.

It was a mild, springlike day in late February, with the young grass already showing green in damp sheltered spots. The men were in the barnyard. The women and children were mostly clustered about the door, going in and out of the house, looking at the things set out for sale, peering into this and prodding at that with discreet curiosity. When they got tired of doing this, they sat down stiffly on the chairs that were for sale and stared straight ahead of them. They were dressed primly in their best clothes, with clean aprons and smoothly combed hair.

The house, a very old one, was much fallen into decay. Since his wife's death some twenty-odd years before, Uncle Nat Carberry had lived in it quite alone. The repairs that he had made during that time had been of a makeshift character.

"It'll last fer as long as I'm a-goin to need it," he had been in the habit of saying for the last twenty years, whenever he pasted paper over a broken window pane or stuffed rags into a chink in the wall where the mud had fallen away. Now at last he needed it no more.

The household goods had been moved out into the yard. The heirs, the old man's eight children, were keeping a watchful eye on them to see that nobody stole any of the smaller articles. A walnut dropleaf table covered with a square of hideous yellow oilcloth worn through at the corners, was spread with coarse white earthenware dishes, a few pieces of old blue willow ware, an eight-day clock, a handful of wooden-handled steel knives and forks, a few bits of cheap glassware, two small glass lamps and a pair of beautiful brass candlesticks. Near by stood an old horsehair-covered walnut couch with broken springs and stuffing sticking out through many holes in the horsehair; a mahogany chest of drawers, solid and massive, but much scarred and with most of the drawer knobs gone, a walnut bedstead and a few chairs.

On a battered kitchen table was massed a collection of smoked-up pots and pans, bowls, skillets, strainers, and the like. Underneath stood kegs, buckets, crocks of various sizes, stone jugs, and other cellar accumulations. Several dozen balls of carpet rags that had been sewn by Uncle Nat's wife before she died and had lain in the bottom of an old chest ever since, were piled in a clothes basket.

Jerry and Judith strolled about among the things looking them over. They came to an old rocking chair of hard maple. The back, high and comfortably curved, was of woven cane. The original cane seat had long since given out and been replaced by narrow strips of horsehide neatly interwoven in basket fashion. The curved arms were worn paintless and smooth and polished by the laying on of many shirt sleeves.

"That's a good lookin' chair," said Judith, regarding it. "An' I bet it sets comfortable."

"But don't let's buy it, Judy," whispered Jerry. "They say Uncle Nat died in it."

"Why, Jerry Blackford, don't be silly. What odds if he died in it or not?" she scoffed. "Hain't people allus a-dyin' in beds? An' folks keeps on a-sleepin' in 'em, don't they? It's a nice chair, an' I'm a-goin' to try to hev it."

All at once the auctioneer was heard calling: "Oh yes, oh yes, oh yes, all ye good people." Obe was proud of his legal language. He mounted upon a box beside the kitchen door. "Naow ladies an' genlums, the terms of this here sale is as follers: Everything under five dollars, cash. All over five dollars, note payable in six months at six per cent interest, said note to be endorsed by a responsible party ownin' property an' acceptable to the executors of Uncle Nat Carberry's will. Uncle Nat Carberry is gone to his long rest, an' we're here this afternoon fer to sell his goods. Naow what'll ye gimme fer this here skillet? It's a good, old fashioned steel skillet—no flimsy sheet iron stuff—an' it'll fry yer pancakes the way ye like 'em fried, nice an' braown on the outside an' done clear all the way through. What, nobody won't gimme a bid on this here skillet? All right, we hain't got no time to waste a-foolin' over this small stuff. It's gotta go quick. Hand me that there iron stew pan. Naow here's yer stew pan all ready to make the mush an' milk fer breakfast or bile the taters fer dinner. Who'll gimme a bid on the two of 'em?"

"Ten cents."

"All right, take 'em away. Ten cents; an' Jerry Blackford is the buyer. Goin' to housekeepin', Jerry?"

Jerry blushed furiously and set the skillet ana pot back in a corner beside the fence.

The auctioneer was Obe Applestill, local Justice of the Peace, who had lately performed the marriage ceremony for Jerry and Judith. Obe was a general utility character of a sort that is to be found in most rural communities, one of those legal hangers-on that one finds in very small towns. He functioned as Justice of the Peace, Notary Public, insurance agent, tax assessor, real estate broker, auctioneer, and in a number of other allied activities. He was a little man with a jolly round face, keen bright blue eyes and a mouth shrunken from missing teeth, which he was always wetting with his tongue. Every few minutes this small red tongue would dart forth adder-like, make a quick circle around his lips and then retreat again behind the snags and withered gums of his mouth. He wore a pepper and salt suit whose creases were of the body rather than of the pressing iron; and his hair, which had not been cut for some time, was beginning to follow the curve of his ears. He was something of a wag, was fond of a joke and a drop of whiskey, and knew everybody within ten miles of Clayton.

"Naow, gimme a bid on this here pair o' brass candlesticks like granmammy used to light the haouse with. Nobody don't hardly use a grease lamp like this no more; but they're mighty handy to pick up to go to bed with. You don't have to bother with no lamp chimney. Who'll gimme ten cents for 'em?"

He waited for a few seconds with the candlesticks in his hand.

"What, hain't this pair o' candlesticks wo'th ten cents to nobody. All right, hand me some o' them plates to go with 'em."

One of the eight children, a middle aged woman with pinched features, handed up a couple of coarse white plates.

"My, it looks like everything's a-goin' to go awful cheap!" she sighed dolorously.

Obe rattled on until he had sold all the household goods. They sold for almost nothing, as such things always did. The heirs looked on in dismay. Glad to be rid of this "wimmin's plunder," Obe led the way to the barn where the stock, tools and implements were waiting for him. Most of the women did not follow to the barn but remained sitting or standing stolidly about the house, waiting for their menfolks to come back.

The men who swarmed after Obe to the barn looked like a throng of animated scarecrows. Unlike the women, they had not dressed for the occasion; but had come in the clothes in which they had been following the plow or hauling out manure onto the tobacco ground. Their ancient garments, mostly bleached to a common drabness by exposure to rain and sun, were torn and patched in the most unexpected places. Long, straggly hair hung about the filthy necks and ears and over the frayed collars. There were gaunt, gawky bodies, small, shriveled, distorted bodies, bent shoulders, slouching legs, and shambling feet. The faces, most of them with weirdly assorted features, were skinny, pinched, and bleary-eyed. Only a few of the young men were straight and ruddy and shone out healthy and wholesome from their dingy clothes.

At the barn were several sets of harness in different stages of decay, hoes, rakes, pitchforks, tobacco knives, a few tools, and a great pile of scrap iron, which latter Obe bought himself because in addition to his other activities he handled junk. There was also an old buggy, a sled, two wagons, and a plow.

The men strolled about among these things looking them over critically, shaking wagon wheels to determine the play, examining the prongs of pitchforks, and straining bits of the harness to see how rotten the leather was.

Obe soon got rid of this accumulation and led the way around to the hogpen where there was a black sow ready to farrow and another black sow with eleven little pigs squealing about her. The men crowded about the hogpen. The livestock always excited their special interest and brought the liveliest bidding.

"Naow then, who'll gimme a bid on this here black sow ready to farrow? She's a-goin' to have pigs any day naow; an' every one o' them little pigs'll be ripe fer butcherin' agin nex' Thanksgivin' Day comes raound. They'll git along nice through the summer on scraps an' weeds an' dishwater; an' agin fall comes you'll have yer corn to fatten 'em. They won't cost ye much to keep. Gimme a bid."

"Five dollars."

"Five dollars! Why, any one of her shoats'll be wo'th five

dollars afore long. Somebody gimme a real bid on this here hawg."

At last the bidders reached nine dollars.

"Nine I'm bid. Naow gimme nine-fifty."

Uncle Sam Whitmarsh, who had been bidding on the hog against Tom Pooler, turned away and spat disgustedly into the straw.

"No, by Gawd, I don't pay no nine dollars fer no brood sow. I'm done."

Obe glimpsed him with his watchful little eyes and knew that the top figure had been reached.

"Nine-fifty, nine-fifty, nine-fifty. Hain't nobody willin' to bid nine-fifty on this fine brood sow all ready to farrow? Is she a-goin' to be give away at nine dollars? You all through? You all done? Watch aout! Daown she goes, an' sold at nine dollars to Tom Pooler. You've got a mighty good hawg there, Tom; an' you got 'er dirt cheap."

After the other sow had been sold the two cows were driven out of the barn and the men formed a circle around them. They came out sniffing the air and looking all around with startled eyes, frightened by the solid human fence that hemmed them in on all sides. One was a big, angular brindle cow with a great sagging udder showing signs of advanced age. Nobody wanted an old cow nor a thin cow; so she sold for only twenty-three dollars.

The other was a young Jersey heifer with her first calf at her heels, both of them slim, deer-like little creatures with large, liquid eyes. This cow was the subject of some lively bidding.

"What am I bid fer this here purty young heifer with her first calf by her side?" Obe started out.

The bidders ran the cow up to seventy-five dollars. Here the bidding lagged. Uncle Amos Hatfield, Sam Whitmarsh, and Ezra Pettit were bidding.

"Seventy-five," called out two of the bidders almost in one breath.

"Seventy-five. I'm bid seventy-five. She's a-goin', she's

a-goin', she's a-goin'. You all through? You all done? Sold to Amos Hatfield for seventy-five dollars."

"Hey," called out old man Pettit in an aggrieved tone. "I jes done gone bid seventy-five on that air caow. What's the reason Amos Hatfield gits 'er?"

"Sorry, Uncle Ezra; I didn't hear yer bid. Did anybody else hear Uncle Ezra bid seventy-five on the caow?"

There was no response.

"Ye'll have to learn to talk laouder, Ezra."

Obe smiled wickedly. The crowd snickered. Ezra turned away muttering disgustedly. Obe was occasionally suspected of playing favorites in this way and sometimes aroused considerable bad feeling. But when the joke was on Uncle Ezra everybody sided with the auctioneer and the other fellow.

The door into the horse stall was now thrown open and the horses came out. One of the old man's grandsons, a handsome, dark-eyed boy in a ragged red sweater, rode one and led the other. The men formed a wider circle to give the animals room to show themselves. There was no male inhabitant of Scott County who did not consider himself an expert judge of horses. Around the circle of onlookers went an increased buzz of talk, a craning of unshaven necks, a fastening of critical eyes on the horses and a great deal of emphatic spitting.

"Naow then," bellowed Obe, girding himself for the grand finale of the sale. "I'm a-goin' to sell ye the best team o' work hosses this side o' Cynthiana. They're five an' six year old, not a day more. Uncle Nat Carberry raised 'em hisse'f from foals an' he raised 'em careful. Nobody in Scott County knew better haow to raise an' break a colt than Uncle Nat. There hain't spot ner blemish on nary one of 'em. If anybody here'll point me spot or blemish on ary one o' them hosses, I'll hand him a ten dollar bill out o' my own pocket."

Obe reached down in his hip pocket, brought out a small roll of bills, flourished them for a moment or two and put them back. In the meantime the horses, ridden and led by the boy in the ragged red sweater, had been trotting around and around the enlarged ring. They were gray horses of the Percheron breed, strong, stockily-built animals with broad backs, heavy haunches, and gentle, if rather dull faces.

Obe's face glowed with genuine pride and enthusiasm as he waited for the bid.

"Hundred an' fifty."

He ran the horses up to two hundred and eleven dollars. There for some time they hung. Judith and Jerry, leaning over a bit of rail fence side by side, were flushed with excitement. Their healthy young faces shone out vividly by contrast with the faded scarecrows about them. Jerry was bidding on the horses.

"You'd best get 'em, Jerry, they're good uns," Judith whispered excitedly in his ear. "Don't let Edd Whitmarsh git away with 'em."

"Two hundred an' twelve. I'm bid two hundred an' twelve. Naow gimme thirteen, gimme thirteen, gimme thirteen. You don't wanta be unlucky? Waal gimme fourteen then, gimme fourteen, gimme fourteen, gimme fourteen."

His practised eye saw that the bidding was over.

"Air these fine hosses a-goin' to sell fer two hundred an' twelve dollars? Don't nobody want a extry good work team? Two hundred an' twelve I'm bid. Uncle Nat'd turn in his grave if he cud see me a-sellin' his good team fer two hundred an' twelve dollars. You all through? You all done. Watch out! Daown she goes an' sold to Jerry Blackford fer two hundred an' twelve dollars. Jerry, if you live to be a hundred you won't never own a better work team nor what you got right naow. Take good care of 'em, Jerry, an' they'll treat you good."

The sale was over. Obe, flushed with his exertions and the few drinks of whiskey that had been handed to him, took out his big red handkerchief and wiped his face. The crowd began to disperse.

When Jerry and Judith came to load their wagon they found that they had almost equipped themselves for housekeeping. They had bought the mahogany chest of drawers for a dollar and a half, and the walnut bedstead for a dollar, four rush-bottomed chairs for twenty cents each and the old cane-backed rocking chair for fifty cents. Judith had secured some of the blue dishes, not because she knew them to be of any value, but because they looked and felt nicer than the coarse white ware. In addition to these, they had an assortment of pots and pans, stone jars, kegs and the like.

Together they loaded their new possessions onto the wagon. Jerry tied his horses behind, and they rattled away toward home. The boy and girl were excited and jubilant over these treasures passed on to them from the ancient dead. All the way back they chattered together, planning for their new home. It was one of those mild clear February evenings that show already the lengthening of the days and give a subtle promise of spring. Bare trees and barns and little houses, standing out against the pure sky, made an ever-changing series of silhouette pictures for them as they drove along. Before they reached home the sun had set, and the evening star beside a slim new moon was silver in the deepening blue. Sheep bells tinkled across the darkening fields, the smoke of supper fires rose up into the still air; and out of the sky a great peace seemed to descend and brood over the earth and the affairs of men.

CHAPTER VIII

MOVING into the new home was an exciting adventure for Jerry and Judith. Neither of them was much past the playhouse age, and this first home settling was like the realization of their childhood longing to have a great big playhouse with things in it that really worked. Together they set up the newly-polished cookstove, which they had bought for eleven dollars at a later sale. Jerry put up shelves and drove in rows of nails, while Judith arranged the blue dishes and the shiny tin saucepans. Jerry, who was a good amateur carpenter, made a big bench for the washtubs and a baby bench to hold the wash basin and soap saucer. It was unusually warm for March, warm enough to have the door open. Judith polished the cobwebby little windows so that more sunlight could come in, and it fell in golden squares through the clean panes and in a slanting oblong through the open door. As Jerry worked on the benches just outside the door and Judith bustled about inside, they were continually thinking of important things to say to each other and rushing to the door to say them. The bright new shavings from Jerry's plane caught the sunlight and gave out a clean, fresh smell. Grass was springing up green through the dried growth of last year. Every few moments the trill of a meadow lark fell like a rain of bright bubbles through the sunny air. Robins were flitting about prospecting for a good place to build; and crows in the distance cawed their joy at the return of warmth and food.

The ancient chest of drawers was refurbished. Jerry had screwed empty spools into the places where the drawer knobs used to be and covered the whole with a coat of brown varnish paint that made it shine again. In the big drawers Judith folded away their clothes and spread one of the new red-bordered towels over the top. On the walnut dropleaf table she

114

laid a square of glossy new oilcloth. She made up the bed with the new sheets and the bright patchwork quilts. The old rocking chair in which Uncle Nat had died was gay with a bright chintz cushion. Thus the old man's possessions, already hoary with experience, took on a new outside gloss and began a new life, like an elderly widower who marries a young wife and for a little while shakes off the accumulations of the years and almost fancies himself young again. Drinking coffee from chipped and cracked blue cups a century old, Judith and Jerry laughed and chattered with no thought that those who had first drunk from these cups, perhaps as young and gay as themselves, were long since turned to dust in some neglected graveyard.

It was astonishing how much they could laugh. They laughed when the sizzling hog meat spat hot grease into their faces. They laughed when Jerry leaned too heavily on the table leaf and almost overturned it. They laughed when they saw flies buzzing in the sunny window pane, a sure sign of warm weather. They laughed when the new butcher knife fell on the floor and stuck daggerwise into the soft pine board. And when there was nothing whatever to laugh at, they laughed at nothing whatever, because laugh they must.

The first sleep in Uncle Nat Carberry's walnut bed was disturbed by no ghost dreams of the tragedies, comedies, and tragi-comedies that had been witnessed by that ancient piece of furniture. If old beds and chairs, like old houses, are haunted, it is to the lonely and the disillusioned that they reveal themselves. Before young lovers they stand abashed and hug their secrets to their bosoms. The old bed received them in its arms as though they were its first pair of lovers. And when at last they fell asleep under the gay patchwork quilts, they slept as soundly as two children until the early March dawn brought them their first waking together—supreme of moments!

But life could not be all play for Jerry and Judith, nor did they in the least expect it to be so. Work had never as yet showed its ugly side to them, hence they had no dread of it.

They were accustomed to work and expected to do so all their lives as a matter of course. How else could they use up all the abundant strength and energy that surged each day as from an inexhaustible wellspring into their young bodies? So on the third morning Jerry harnessed up his new team and went forth whistling to plow the land that was to be put into corn. Judith watched him disappear over the brow of the ridge, then went back into the house and washed up the dishes and set the rooms to rights. Having done this she went out again into the sunny dooryard.

She had always disliked the insides of houses. The gloom of little-windowed rooms, the dead chill or the heavy heat as the fire smouldered or blazed, the prim, set look of tables and cupboards that stood always in the same places engaged in the never ending occupation of collecting dust both above and beneath: these things stifled and depressed her. She was always glad to escape into the open where there was light, life, and motion and the sun and the wind kept things clean. So, having done up her morning chores, she went out into the yard and busied herself with building chicken coops out of packing boxes. She worked away happily, unmindful of the passing of time, until she was startled to hear the rattle of harness and Jerry's voice calling "Whoa," to the horses.

"My land, if I hain't clear fergot to put on a single bite o' dinner," she gasped, as she raced into the house and stuffed kindlings into the cold cookstove.

When Jerry came in after unharnessing and feeding the horses, she was frantically beating up cornmeal batter, and the sliced meat was sizzling in the frying pan.

"Didn't I tell you I was no good of a housekeeper," she laughed, as Jerry caught her in his arms and kissed her. "I was a-buildin' chicken coops, an' I done gone clean fergot all about dinner till I heard the harness a-rattlin'. An' I was a-goin' to make you a biled puddin' to-day an' cook some o' that cabbage Aunt Eppie give us. The Pettits has got so much cabbage left over this year they're a-feedin' it to the hawgs. Naow we can't have nothin' but hog meat an' cakes."

"Hog meat an' cakes is plenty good enough fer me," opined Jerry. "If you cook 'em they'll taste to me better'n biled puddin' and cabbage cooked by the Queen o' Sheba. Anyhow we'd otta be glad dad turned loose o' the hogbellies. Most folks eats corn-meal an' coffee three times a day this time o' year."

The strong salt pork and fried corn cakes, washed down by something that Peter Akers sold as coffee, a concoction at once rank and insipid, tasted delicious to their healthy young appetites. Laughs between the bites of corn cake, ecstatic giggles mingled with the salt pork and kisses that spilled the coffee from the cups, glorified their little meal into a feast royal. When it was over, Jerry went back to his plowing; and Judith, having washed up the dishes, put on her sunbonnet and jacket and walked over to see Lizzie May.

Lizzie May had been married to Dan Pooler for over a year. They lived about two miles away on the Dixie Pike in one of Uncle Ezra Pettit's tenant houses. It was a gaunt, two-story box standing bleakly on the top of a hill. Not a tree stood anywhere near and it looked as lonely as a water tank at a desert railway station. Its four weather-grayed sides were turned sullenly to the four winds.

Lizzie May was sitting by the stove sewing carpet rags. Her cotton dress was fastened at the throat with a little brooch of washed gold and imitation jewels, a present from Dan before their marriage; and she was wearing one of the fancy little frilled aprons that she loved to make. She was several months advanced in pregnancy and was not looking well. Her pale, small-featured face showed lines of endurance, and already a look of age was pinching the youthful curves.

"Why, Lizzie May, you don't look a bit pert. What's the matter?" inquired Judith, as she flung her hat and jacket into a chair and sat down opposite her sister. The younger girl's presence seemed to shed a warmth and radiance about the prim little room that enfolded and enhanced everything except her sister sitting coldly opposite her.

"Oh, I dunno. I s'pose it's my condition," answered Lizzie May languidly and a little importantly. "My stomach **don't** bother me no more; but my back feels weak most all the time and pains me a good deal some days." She launched into a detailed description of her symptoms which Judith, who had scarcely had a pain in her life, could not follow with much sympathy or understanding.

"You need to git out more, Lizzie May," she rallied, "and not hang in the house so much. I'd feel sick too if I stayed around this kitchen as much as you do. You don't hardly never go to dad's any more, an' I s'pose you won't come to see me naow I'm gone to housekeepin'. I'm sure I don't see what keeps you inside here all the time. You hain't got much to do. 'Tain't like as if you had milk to handle an' turkeys to chase."

"Mebbe you don't think I got much to do, but I do," answered Lizzie May, bridling. "You wait till you been a-keepin' haouse yo'se'f fer a spell. Agin I scrub this floor every second day an' polish the stove twict a week an' sweep an' dust an' wash an' iron an' bake bread an' cook the meals an' scour the black off the pans, I don't git much time to go a-gallivantin'."

"But you don't need to scrub the floor an' polish the stove so often. The way you keep 'em shined, anybody'd think you et off of 'em 'stead of off the table. You know what you make me think of, Lizzie May? You act jes like if a little tame rabbit would shet itself in its cage an' never came aout an' then spend all its time a-workin' hard to keep its cage clean."

Lizzie May pursed her prim little mouth with a superior air.

" 'Taint no use fer you an' me to argy over sech things, Judy," she said haughtily. "We got dif'rent notions about haow a house otta be kep'. Fer me, I like to see things nice an' I'm allus a-goin' to try to keep 'em nice. I like to do housework; an' even though I don't allus feel well, the work wouldn't bother me a bit, if I didn't have other troubles."

She sighed heavily.

"What other troubles have you got?" asked Judith incredulously.

"Oh, I have lots of other troubles. You'll have 'em too, naow your married. For one thing, Dan goes off fox huntin' nights an' nights an' leaves me here alone, an' I git that skairt. You wouldn't believe all the noises there is when anybody's alone at night. Night afore las' I was sure I heard somebody a-walkin' raound an' raound the house. I was in bed, an' I pulled the quilts up over my head an' tried to fergit it; but I kep' on a-hearin' it. At las' I couldn't stand it no longer, an' I got up an' looked out the winder; an' it was only Uncle Jonah Cobb's ole mare Betsy that had broke through the fence an' was a-wanderin' raound an' raound the house a-eatin' grass. But it give me a awful scare jes the same. Things like that makes a person nervous."

"Nonsense, Lizzie May! You born an' raised here to be askairt to stay alone in the house nights! Why, who's ever been bothered in their house that you ever heard on?"

Lizzie May had to admit that she had never heard of any of the neighbors being attacked at night in their homes; but nevertheless she was afraid.

"Them dawgs too," she went on. "He's baound to keep 'em all. You know how I've allus hated a haound. The meal they eat is enough to fatten a hawg. An' of course it's me that has to cook it fer 'em. An' another thing, when he goes fox huntin' I never know if he's a-goin' to come home drunk or sober. Whenever he gits with Edd Whitmarsh, the two of 'em jes drinks theirselves as full as ticks. An' we can't spare the money neither. If I spent the same money on clothes for myse'f or the baby that's comin' he'd be the first to say it was a awful extravagance. I wonder why men allus has to drink? Us wimmin git along without it. An' no matter if there hain't money in the house to buy a sack o' flour, they kin allus find some to spend on whiskey. One night las' week Dan come in so drunk he jes laid hisse'f daown on the mat beside the bed with all his clothes on an' declared up an' daown he was in bed. An' I had to take off his shoes an' his clothes an' pull an' 'yank an' pretty nigh kick him afore I could git him to crawl up into bed. I tell you I was that disgusted. If I'd a thought married life was a-goin' to be anything like this, I don't think I'd a been in such a hurry to git married. There's times when I wish I was back home with dad agin. It wa'n't like that in the books we used to read. You 'member them books?"

Lizzie May named several novels by such purveyors of roseate fiction as Bertha M. Clay, Mary Jane Holmes and Laura Jean Libbey, which in ragged paper covers had found their way into the Pippinger home.

"Yes, but in them books it allus ends when they git married," Judith reminded her. "They never tell what happens after. All they say is that they lived happy ever after."

"Yes, an' they're allus about rich people," chimed in Lizzie May. "I did used to love to read them books an' fancy I lived like that. I guess rich husbands is dif'rent. It must be awful nice to be rich."

She sighed and her blue eyes looked wistfully out of the window, where white clouds could be seen chased by the March wind across a bright blue sky.

The shriek of a whistle pierced the air, and a train half a mile away roared along the track on its way to Lexington. Through the little window the smoke from the engine could be seen in a white, moving column.

"Wouldn't it be nice if we was all rich an' ridin' away through the country on that big train!" she sighed. "When you're poor an' stuck allus in the same place, life gits to seem so dull."

In Lizzie May's imagination only the rich and happy rode on trains. She figured riding in a train as a sumptuous and palatial progress toward some idyllic pleasure goal. The reality of smoke, cinders, stale air, germ-infested plush, and filthy floor, tired women and dirty children, staid spinsters, and sleek commercial travelers with fat necks, dingy people hastening anxiously to deathbeds or drearily to new jobs: all this was happily unknown to her. Her eyes followed the white moving column of smoke hungrily, wistfully.

"Yes, it must be awful nice to be rich," she sighed again, as the column of smoke disappeared.

"Yes, I s'pose it *is* nice to be rich," rejoined Judith, with just a momentary far-away look in her eyes. "But somehow it don't bother me much that I hain't rich. I have lots o' fun a-doin' and a-makin' things. All this mornin' I built chicken coops. I got six dandies. No rat'll git my chicks this spring. An' I'm a-goin' to buy three settin's o' turkey eggs from Aunt Maggie Slatten an' set 'em under hens. If they're raised by a old hen they don't wander off so far when they're growed an' git ketched an' stole. An' nex' winter when I have to set in the house an' the evenin's is long, I'm a-goin' to sew me rags fer a carpet too. I've begun savin' 'em. Them's awful nice rags you got there. Haow did you manage to git 'em all sech nice colors?"

Lizzie May's face brightened and the wistful look disappeared.

"Yes, if I do say it, I got nice rags. I cut 'em jes as fine an' even as I can; an' then I tie 'em in bunches an' dye 'em the color I want. These yaller ones is dyed with cream o' tarter an' potash, like Aunt Abigail showed me haow to do. An' the blue ones I done with real strong blueing water. For the other colors I bought the dye. You kin dye a whole lot o' pink with one package o' red dye. I'm a-goin' to have Aunt Selina weave the carpet strip猫d: yaller, blue, pink, green, an' red; yaller, blue, pink, green, an' red. All along like that. It'll be nice an' bright an' cheerful. I want to try to have my front room real nice. Dan's Aunt Carrie give me a pair of lovely lace curtains fer the winder; an' I got three cushion covers patched. One of 'em is all silk, with flowers embroidered on nearly every piece. Lemme show it to you."

She ran into the other room, brought forth the "crazy" monstrosity and spread it with pride before Judith's admiring eyes. The joy of achievement, the rich glow of the creator gloating over his creation, filled her with warm radiance.

"My it *is* nice," exclaimed Judith, reverently feeling the smoothness of the silk and satin pieces with the tips of her fingers. "I'm a-goin' to make me one when I git enough silk pieces saved—if I ever do."

Encouraged by this admiration, Lizzie May brought out the

other pillow tops together with the coarse imitation lace curtains, and spread them gleefully before her sister. She was a child again in the delighted ownership of these "pretty things." Judith, too, was filled with childish envy and emulation. Together they exclaimed and rhapsodied over the colors, the embroidered flowers and the fine herringbone stitching done by Lizzie May's painstaking little hand.

"They're awful nice to have," said Judith, with an intake of the breath. "But somehow I've never had much patience to make sech things. I've allus liked better to draw pitchers of hosses an' dawgs an 'mules an' folks that looks like 'em. I do love to draw sech things yet. But of course they hain't pretty. Mebbe now I'm married I'll take more interest in sewin' an' makin' nice things for the house."

"Of course you will, Judy," encouraged Lizzie May, with more than a touch of patronage.

CHAPTER IX

CONTRARY to Lizzie May's predictions and somewhat to her disappointment, Judith failed to suffer from the marital troubles that increasingly vexed her own life. Jerry proved to be, at least according to Lizzie May's standards, a much better husband than Dan. He did not care for the sport of fox hunting, so there were no hounds to bay around the house at night and greedily lick of the corn meal that could ill be spared. He never went anywhere in the evenings, and he had not been drunk a dozen times in his life. Lizzie May had to admit to herself that Judy, the wild and harum-scarum, who was capable of almost any foolishness, had made a much more sensible choice than she. But of course it was nothing but luck, she told herself. She felt in a vague, half acknowledged way that she had a quite justifiable complaint to make against the powers that be because chance had favored the irresponsible instead of meting out just reward to the careful and prudent. This did not mean that she would have been willing to exchange Dan for Jerry. She would have scorned such an opportunity. Dan was Dan. He was the man who had courted her. He was hers. But she would have liked to borrow some of Jerry's qualities and insert them craftily into Dan's character, making him over into a husband more contributory to her comfort and convenience.

All that summer, in spite of the toil of the field, Judith was joyous and radiant. And she worked hard. She could not take the matter of earning a living as seriously as did Jerry; but she caught some of the infection of his ambition to raise big crops and lay by money for a home of their own. So she worked in the corn and tobacco as determinedly as he, stopping only to cook their simple meals and wash up the few dishes, with an occasional day off for washing clothes. Besides helping Jerry in the field, she looked after her chickens and turkeys and made a kitchen garden near the house in which she raised beets, cabbages, beans, tomatoes, and other vegetables to take away the curse of bareness from their table.

The first big job of the season came in May. This was the tobacco setting. Late in February Jerry had made the tobacco bed. It was nine feet by sixty feet and it lay in a sheltered hollow sloping gently to the south. To kill the weed seeds Jerry had burnt the bed by covering it with old fence rails and setting them on fire. Then he had raked the ashes into the ground and made the earth as fine and smooth as sand. Into this he had sowed the small, almost microscopic seed, had tramped it well into the ground and spread over the whole a tightly stretched covering of cheesecloth to protect the young plants from wind and frost. According to the custom of tenant farmers' wives in the tobacco country, Judith had planted on the edges seed of tomatoes, peppers, and cabbages to make plants for the home garden.

It was a dry spring that year, and Jerry had had to work hard to keep the plants alive. Again and again, after his day's work was done, he had trudged to and fro between the nearest spring and the tobacco bed carrying big buckets of water to the thirsty young plants. Jerry found to his dismay that it took a great many buckets of water to wet a nine by sixty bed. At last in late April there came several days of gently falling warm rain and the plants took on new life. By the middle of May they were lush and lusty and ready to be set when the right weather conditions arrived.

The big rain came the last week in May, bringing the much desired "season." Little showers had fallen from time to time, but they were not enough to wet the ground deeply. Jerry was beginning to grow uneasy and had been scanning the weather signs with an anxious eye for many days. On the evening of the twenty-fifth, as he drove his horses up from the field where he had been cultivating corn, the sun sank behind an opaque wall of sickly yellow cloud. Looking about Jerry saw the sky overcast in every direction with a uniform pale gray. Birds flew low under the heavy gray canopy. The whistle and rumble of a train several miles away sounded distinct through the still, brooding air; and as he walked along the top of the ridge behind the horses he heard twice the harsh cry of a woodpecker.

"We'll have a terbacker settin' rain afore mornin', Judy," he said, when she came out to help him put up the horses. "Everything says so."

Before they went to bed that night the rain began. Jerry went out and fixed the drain of the eaves trough so that the water would run into the cistern. The next morning it was still coming down in a warm, steady downpour. All day it fell in the same soft, gently-falling stream, like a blessing upon mankind, not from a self-centered Hebrew deity, but from some sweet natured and generous pagan god.

"Bejasus, this'll fetch things along, Judy," said Jerry, who was busily nailing soles on Judith's shoes beside the kitchen window. "Land, haow everything'll pick up after this rain! I sholy do love to see things grow in spring. An' about tomorrow afternoon we kin go to settin'."

The next morning dawned blue and warm, full of birdsong and the scent of wet growing things. The ground was dank with rain, but by afternoon Jerry thought it would be dry enough to begin setting. After breakfast he went to the tobacco bed to pull plants and Judith got on one of the horses and rode over to her father's to get Elmer to come and "drop." As the horse trotted along the top of the ridge and out onto the sodden "pike" full of puddles, she breathed deep of the fragrant air, felt the sun's warmth on her back and shoulders and almost fancied that she was a plant that had sucked in the life-giving rain and was preparing to raise its blossom to the sun.

She returned before long with Elmer, now grown into a loutish chunk of fourteen, all hands and feet and appetite. Elmer rode upon Pete, a young mule that Bill had bought to take the place of Bob, who had died the year before of old age. Pete was of a rich chestnut color, glossy, handsome, and liquid-eyed. He was also intelligent with the super-equine intelligence of a mule. He had a way of laying back his ears ever so slightly and looking at any one who approached him with a backward-sidewise glance of mingled playfulness and suspicion. It made Judith laugh to see him do this.

"Land, Elmer," she exclaimed, as they were putting up the horse and mule in the shed, "if that critter, Pete, hain't got the look of Uncle Sam Whitmarsh, I never seen two folks that looks alike. Uncle Sam has got jes that same way o' lookin' at you sharp an' sidewise an' yet smilin', as though he kinda suspicioned that you was a-tryin' to git the best of him, an' yet he wanted to be good friends an' have some fun with you too. An' if Uncle Sam could move his ears I'm sure he'd lay 'em back jes a little. They say animals can't smile. But if that mule hain't a-smilin' then what is he a-doin'?"

She patted his glossy neck admiringly. He flicked his ears and looked at her in his characteristic way, then poked his soft nose into her face.

"He's durn hard to ketch up in paster," grunted Elmer. "You come up alongside of him with the bridle, an' he gives you that 'ere look, an' fust thing you know he's a quarter of a mile off. My legs is run clean off since we got him."

After dinner the tobacco setting began. Elmer had the easy job. With a basket of plants on his arm he went along the rows that Jerry had laid off with the plow and dropped the plants at intervals of about eighteen inches, dropping two rows at a time. Jerry and Judith followed behind, each taking a row, and set the plants in the ground. They worked at first with their fingers, until the skin began to wear away. Then Jerry whittled two round, sharp-pointed sticks, and they used these instead of the fingers. With the sharp stick they made a hole in the wet earth, set the plant into it and pressed the earth down about the roots with their fingers.

At first they went along the rows gaily, rallying each other and trying to see which could work the fastest. Sometimes Jerry would get a little ahead and look back teasingly. Then Judith would make her fingers fly and outstrip him and laugh back at him from under her big blue sunbonnet. They soon stopped this, however, and fell into the regular, clockwork routine of those who go through the same set of motions many hundreds of times over, only now and then standing erect for a moment to straighten their cramped legs and ease their aching backs. Very soon they had no energy left to laugh or even talk and plodded along the rows doggedly, silently, seeing only the wet ground and the plants that were to be put into it. The muscles of their legs grew sore and strained from the unusual exercise of constantly kneeling and rising, kneeling and rising. The ache in their backs became sometimes unbearable; and the backs of their necks, held always at tension and beat upon by the hot sun, throbbed with a dull, continual pain. The moisture rising from the soaked ground made the heat heavy and enervating. Their hands cracked and stiffened. The wet clay stuck in layer after layer to their heavy work shoes until they found it hard to lift their feet, and had to stop often to scrape away the caked mud. Elmer, who was barefoot, got along much better. When the strain of constant bending became unendurable and they stood up for relief, the earth swam about them and for a moment everything turned black. They reeled, righted themselves, and went at it again.

They drank enormous quantities of water. Elmer, who was not kept so busy as the other two, had the job of bringing water from the spring in an earthenware molasses jug with a corn-cob stuck in the neck for a cork. The cool water tasted delicious.

They kept this up until after sunset, as long as they could see the ground and the plants, for no moment of the precious "season" must be wasted. When at last they stopped for want of light and dragged their mud-encrusted feet up the hill and along the ridge toward home, no one of the three spoke a word. Spattered with mud from head to foot, they walked with bent heads and sagging legs, like horses that have tugged all day at the plow through ground too hard for their strength.

"My land, I'm glad I don't have to set terbaccer every day," said Judith, as she fried the cakes. "I'm gonna make the coffee jes three times as strong to-night."

After they had eaten and drunk several cups of the rank decoction, they went immediately to bed. When they closed their eyes they could see nothing but tobacco plants standing up stiffly out of wet clay. They fell asleep with this picture painted on the insides of their eyelids.

Jerry had set the alarm clock for three. They seemed to have only just fallen asleep when its insistent ting-a-ling startled them awake. The early dawn was already melting the darkness of the room. Jerry jumped out of bed and in a few seconds had put on his shirt and overalls and was lighting the fire.

"Land alive, I wish I didn't have to get up," yawned Judith, stretching her slim young arms above her head. Reluctantly she put her feet out on the rag mat beside the bed, yawned, stretched, and began to put on her clothes. Elmer, who was still fast asleep in the other room, had to be shaken into consciousness twice before he crawled sleepily out and felt around on the floor for his overalls. They all washed on the bench outside the door, splashing the water about plenteously and rubbing vigorously with the towel to get the sleep out of their eyes. Soon Judith was frying the cakes, and the smell of boiling coffee filled the kitchen. They ate from the unwashed dishes of the night before. After the cakes and coffee they felt better and all three set out together for the tobacco field. This time they all went barefoot.

When they began to work, they found themselves so stiff in every bone and muscle that it seemed at first as if they could not possibly go on. After a while, however, they limbered up and managed to get through the morning. But the afternoon seemed as if it would stretch into eternity. The sun beat down fiercely. The mud caked thicker on their feet and the skin wore thinner on their aching fingers. Twice Judith collapsed and had to go and lie in the shade until her strength returned and the intolerable ache in her back and neck subsided a little. Jerry tried to persuade her to go back to the house and let him and Elmer go on with the setting; but she scorned his male assumption of superior strength and endurance. At last the sun sank and the cool evening air revived them a little. Gradually the sky paled, the light grew dimmer, and darkness closing in upon them made the green of the young plants intense and vivid. Still they worked on. At last they began to stumble over clods in the darkness and Elmer could no longer see to separate the plants from each other.

"Thank God we can't do no more to-night," said Jerry, in a tone of intense relief. He rose, straightened his strong young shoulders and surveyed the field.

"We got purty nigh an acre an' three quarters set," he announced. "An' the season's over. Agin to-morrow it'll be too dry."

"Gosh, I'm glad it will," said Judith, rubbing her bare feet on the grass to scrape away some of the caked mud.

Elmer went home that night the proud possessor of a dollar, and Jerry did not set the alarm clock. When they awoke next morning, the sun was high in the sky.

"Ain't you glad you don't have to set terbaccer to-day, Jerry?" said Judith, stretching luxuriously.

"You damn betcha I am," answered Jerry. "But there hain't no rest for the wicked. I gotta git into that corn right away if it's to be saved. The weeds'll grow like wildfire after this rain."

There came a second fairly good rain in early June, and they were able to set another acre of tobacco. A week or so later, it rained for a day and a night; and Jerry, going out next morning to see how deeply the rain had penetrated, was jubilant over his findings.

"She's soaked good, Judy," he called exultantly. "Even if the sun shines hot we'll be able to finish settin'. You git Elmer over this mornin' an' I'll pull plants."

He went off immediately after breakfast to pull plants; but in half an hour he was back, full of anger and disgust.

"You know what's happened, Judy? Somebody's stole near all our plants. There hain't plants left to set a half an acre, an' them's little bits o' runts no good fer nothin'. All them

nice big strong plants is took. An' I'm purty nigh sure I know
who took 'em, too; an' it's Luke Wolf. He was too damn lazy
to water his bed there when it was so dry in April, an' his
plants didn't do no good. He didn't have hardly nothing in
his bed. So after I found the plants was stole, I clim up on
the brow o' the ridge an' looked over; an' there sure enough
was him an' Hat a-settin' fer dear life. They had that half
witted brother o' Luke's a-droppin' fer 'em. I had a good
mind to go daown an' tell 'em to gimme back my plants. But
there 'tis. I can't prove he took 'em; but I know damn well
he did."

"Ain't that a mean shame!" exclaimed Judith. "An' after
all how hard you slaved to save them plants! An' we can't
git plants nowhere else, cause nobody hain't got plants this
year, count o' the dry spring. You had the finest bed anywheres araound."

"We'll have to put it in corn," said Jerry disgustedly. "An'
the corn'll be so late the frost'll take it. If I'd a knowed, I
might a saved myse'f the work o' plowin' an' harrowin' the
ground. But that's haow it goes. A man works hard to do
sumpin for hisself an' his fam'ly, an' then some lousy, thievin'
neighbor slinks in an' gits away with it. It sholy is discouragin'."

Judith tried to console Jerry and tried for his sake to appear
as indignant and disgusted as he over the loss. But it was
not in her nature to take material loss so seriously; and she
felt secretly relieved to think that she would not have to set
any more tobacco that year. She was ashamed of this feeling,
for it seemed like rank disloyalty to Jerry; but she could not
help entertaining it.

Luke and Hat Wolf lived in a little ramshackle frame shanty
in one of the neighboring hollows. They were a young couple
not many years older than Jerry and Judith; but they had
been married and had been raising tobacco on the shares for
three or four years. They had a well sustained reputation
for almost superhuman meanness and stinginess.

They were a pair of young giants. When they drove together in their buggy the springs sagged and passers-by felt sorry for the horse. Luke was a big, stupid looking lout, with small blue eyes and beefy jowls. He could neither read nor write; although Hat had been heard to say on different occasions that Luke could read "some kinds o' print." The kinds that he could read, however, did not include the kind universally employed.

Hat, a big, coarsely made, gipsy-like girl, was, to use her own phrase, a "great reader." She subscribed to a monthly magazine called "The Farm Wife's Friend," which cost her twenty-five cents a year. When she found the magazine in her mail box she took it home eagerly, full of delicious anticipations, and read it from the name in fancy print across the top of the first page to the last advertisement on the back sheet. It was printed in the vilest manner on the sleaziest of paper. Sometimes parts of it were so badly printed as to be illegible. It contained two or three sentimental love stories describing doings of people in high life. These stories abounded in beautiful heroines with delicate hands that had never approached a dish rag or a hoe handle, noble heroes and wicked, but fascinating villains. They opened to Hat a vista of unexplored possibilities and caused her to sigh over her own lack of opportunity.

Almost as engrossing as the stories, were little articles on how to get the best results with turnips, how to make the eyes sparkle, how to keep little chicks from getting head lice, how to remain always a mystery to your husband, how to keep sheets from fraying at the hems, how to make five hundred dollars out of a flock of fifty geese, how to tell fortunes with the tea cup, how to polish cut glass, how to keep the hands dainty and delicate, how to live so that the world is sweeter and sunnier for your presence, how to make orange marmalade out of carrots and how to treat a cow with a caked udder.

All of these "useful hints" Hat read with avidity, and many of them she tried to apply in her own household. She spent hours messing over a stew of mutton fat and cheap perfume in an attempt to make a homemade cold cream for beautifying the skin. After it had stood for a few days it turned rancid and she had to throw it out to the hogs. She became enthusiastic over the possibility of making a big income from geese, set a hundred eggs and hatched out seventy-five little geese, only to have the foxes feed fat on her flock. She mixed up the decoction to make the eyes sparkle; but it hurt her eyes and interfered with her sight. So she used it only once. She tried on Luke the receipt for remaining mysterious; but she was forced into the strong suspicion that he never even knew that anything unusual was affecting him in any way.

These failures did not, however, discourage her in the least. She read and experimented with the next month's collection with unabated enthusiasm. The magazine was her romance, her religion.

There were short poems in the paper, too. "Be a Beam of Sunshine," "Keep Smiling all the While," and "Never Let the Tear Drop Dim Your Eye," were characteristic titles. One poem, which made a deep impression on Hat, celebrated the joy of washing clothes. It described the deep satisfaction to be derived from rubbing, rinsing, bluing, and hanging out the family wash on the line. The constantly recurring refrain was, "And the Wind is Right to Dry." As Hat rubbed out her own faded cotton dresses and aprons and scrubbed manfully on the sweaty collars and wristbands of Luke's work shirts, even when she punished the washboard with his heavy denim overalls, stiffly encrusted with mud and axle grease and many other varieties of filth, and soused them up and down in the dirty, stinking, mouse-gray water, the words of this little poem lilted rhythmically through her mind, and she almost fooled herself into thinking that washing Luke's overalls was a delight. Who can say that the mail order sheet does not bring joy and comfort into the rural home? Nevertheless, Hat was glad when Luke came home one day with the information gleaned from Columbia Gibbs that overalls last twice as long if they are never allowed to see water.

The feature of the "Farm Wife's Friend" that caused her the most deep-seated excitement was the advertisements. The big black type exhorting the reader to "Send no Money," "Win Health and Happiness Without Cost," "Stop Suffering," "Send Two-cent Stamp and Know Your Future," "Make Big Money by Pleasant Work in Spare Time," these caused Hat to get down from the clock shelf the pen, the bottle of ink, and the letter paper and write to such of the advertisers as most appealed to her imagination.

It is true that the answers were usually disappointing. One brought a sample of kidney remedy, for which Hat, never having had any symptoms of kidney trouble, could find no present use. She laid it away carefully, half hoping that she or Luke might need it at some time in the future. The "Pleasant Occupation in Spare Time" people always required you to buy some complicated and expensive apparatus before you could begin to earn money with it. This was the last thing that Hat was prepared to do. She derived her greatest satisfaction from the firms that told your fortune for a dime or read your horoscope if you told them the date of your birth and the color of your eyes and hair; and from those that sent free samples of cosmetics, remedies for chicken diseases and gaudy calendars and bookmarks. There was no thrill in her life greater than that of finding a package in the mail box addressed to herself, of carrying it home in delightful suspense and at last opening the package in secret to see what it contained. The joy of getting something for nothing and of being in secret communication with unknown people appealed both to her cupidity and her thirst for adventure. Luke was not a partner in these pleasures; and as he could neither read nor write, she had no difficulty in keeping him in the dark regarding her correspondence.

Besides the "Farm Wife's Friend," and the carefully studied current almanac, Hat had other literature. She had a book called "Lena Rivers," in a tattered yellow paper cover, and another book entitled "No Wedding Bells For Her," in no cover at all. These two books she had read through at least a dozen times. She had a paper bound dream book which interpreted dreams, not as Professor Freud would do, but in a way much more satisfying to Hat. As she dreamed a good deal, she consulted this book frequently.

The remaining book, and the one that she valued most of all, was a small, much thumbed volume that had lost its cover and its first seven pages. This book was called "Old Secrets and New Discoveries." There was something about the magic word "secret" that made the book especially precious to Hat. Between its covers, or more accurately speaking, between its eighth and its last page, was contained knowledge universal.

On page eight there were given directions "How to Charm Those Whom You Meet and Love." This little article Hat knew by heart.

"When you desire to make any one 'Love' you with whom you meet, although not personally acquainted with him, you can very readily reach him and make his acquaintance if you observe the following directions: Suppose you see him coming toward you in an unoccupied mood, or he is recklessly or passively walking past you, all that remains for you to do at that moment is to concentrate your thought and send it into him, and, to your astonishment, if he was passive, he will look at you, and now is your time to send a thrill to his heart by looking him carelessly, though determinately, into his eyes, and praying with all your heart, mind, soul, and strength, that he may read your thought and receive your true Love, which God designs we should bear one another. This accomplished, and you need not and must not wait for a cold-hearted, fashionable and popular Christian introduction; neither should you hastily run into his arms, but continue operating in this psychological manner; not losing any convenient opportunity to meet him at an appropriate place, where an unembarrassed exchange of words will open the door to the one so magnetized. At this interview, unless prudence sanction it, do not shake hands, but let your manners and loving eyes speak with Christian charity and ease. Wherever or whenever you meet again, at the first opportunity grasp his hand in an earnest, sincere and affectionate manner, observing at the same time the following important directions, viz: As you take his bare hand in yours, press your thumb gently, though firmly, between the bones of the thumb and forefinger of his hand, and at the very instant when you press thus on the bloodvessels (which you can before ascertain to pulsate) look him earnestly and lovingly, though not pertly or fiercely, into his eyes, and send all your heart's, mind's and soul's strength into his organization, and he will be your friend, and if you find him not to be congenial you have him in your power, and by carefully guarding against evil influences, you can reform him to suit your own purified, Christian, and loving taste."

Hat loved to read the recipes for anchovy paste and artichokes served with hollandaise sauce, and eagerly devoured the directions for serving a formal dinner of eight courses to a party of twelve guests. Her inability to apply this information did not greatly trouble her. But when she read aloud to Luke the "Hunters' and Trappers' Secrets," she felt somewhat aggrieved because the knowledge thus obtained did not result in an immediate increase of rabbits and muskrats and an equally rapid decrease of the foxes that slaughtered her geese; and her opinion of Luke, always a low one, dropped a peg lower.

On one occasion, when he appeared to have gotten the worst of it in a horse trade, she upbraided him bitterly for not having applied the information contained in her book.

"Huh," retorted Luke, glaring at her across the supper table. "Anybody'd think to listen to you that that measly little half-page in that 'ere damn book o' yourn tells all there is to know about a hoss. Why, I know more about hosses, jes from handlin' 'em, than the print in all yer books together cud tell."

"Well, then, if ye know so much, why did you let 'em put over a lame hoss on ye?" she flashed angrily.

"Land alive, woman," Luke's tone was high pitched with exasperation, "do you s'pose Gad A'mighty c'n tell a lame hoss when he's shot full o' stuff to make him so's he hain't lame? Haow cud I know he was lame when he wa'n't lame when I traded fer 'im? Besides, naow, I've looked him over,

I know jes what's wrong with him. He hain't got but a little start of a ringbone; an' I kin burn that out an' have 'im cured in a month. Wimmin like you makes a man sick. You hain't got sense to pound sand with all yer books."

"Oh, hain't we though? Well, I hate to think o' the filthy, foul-livin' critters you men'd be if it wa'n't fer us wimmin. You'd go right back to be savages; an' you hain't fur off from it naow."

Hat also considered herself something of a musician, performing by ear on a fiddle handed down from her grandfather, who had been a fiddler and a caller off of dances.

When Jerry and Judith came to live in the neighborhood, Hat was the first to call upon the bride. Life was lonely back in the deep hollow where she and Luke lived, far from even the sound of a passing wagon; and the company of Luke had long since ceased to be stimulating. Last year, too, all the near neighbors had been old people. Hat was glad that somebody young and lively had come to take the place of the doddering old Patton couple who had lived there the year before.

Not many days after the new arrivals had moved in, Hat appeared one afternoon in the dooryard. She was dressed for visiting. She had on a clean pink and white checked frock and the inevitable little white apron. On her head was a starched pink sunbonnet. She was a tremendous creature, both tall and stout, and her skin was coarse. But she looked handsome in a dark, bold, gipsy-like way. Judith, who was neither small nor delicate, looked like a frail blossom beside her.

"Well, if it hain't Hat Wolf!" exclaimed Judith, who was bringing a bucket of water from the cistern. She set the bucket down and hastened to meet her visitor.

"My, but I'm glad you've come to live here, Judy," said Hat, with genuine enthusiasm. "Las' year I got so's I wouldn't come over here no matter haow lonesome I was, 'cause old Aunt Jinny Patton wouldn't do nothing but set an' sigh an' say she knew the Lord was a-goin' to take her soon. Old people is that tiresome. Naow you an' me, when we hain't got much to do, kin visit each other. An' I'll lend you my books an' you kin lend me yourn; an' we'll sew rags together an' have good times. You know it gits awful lonesome in these hollers, an' anybody needs neighbors. Tain't like livin' on the pike."

Judith proudly showed Hat her new chicken coops, the four dozen hens that her father had given her, the place that they had selected for a garden spot and the shepherd pup which a neighbor had given them, a fluffy ball of black and white silk, trimmed, as nature knows how to trim, with soft tan. Then she led her into the house and showed her, piece by piece, all her wedding finery, her new sheets and towels and her bright bedquilts. Hat examined all these things with deep interest and exclaimed over them with unfeigned admiration. In the intervals of looking at the things to which Judith called her attention, her bold black eyes travelled about the room and took in every detail of its floor, walls, and furnishings. Nothing escaped her. She was alive with that small curiosity so frequent in farmers' wives, which causes them to take note of the smallest minutiæ of their neighbors' interiors. When she went away she carried in her mind an exact photograph of Judith's two rooms and of her dooryard. She even knew that Judith's clothesline was a wire and not a rope one. Such capacity for detail does solitude engender in the female mind.

"Well," she said at last, when she was prepared to leave, "I'll have to be a-gittin' along back home. I got a right smart o' little chicks hatched out an' I want to raise every one of 'em an' make as much as I kin this summer. It gits dark early in our holler, an' the rats begin to run around most afore the sun's gone. So I'd best git back an' git the chicks cooped up. I can't trust nothin' to Luke. Come over, Judy."

"Yes, you come agin, Hat."

CHAPTER X

THE summer days came and went, bringing with them the usual routine that goes with the raising of tobacco in Scott County. After the plants had been set they wilted and looked as though they were dying. Many of them did actually die and had to be replaced by new plants. For about three weeks they scarcely seemed to grow at all. Indeed, they appeared to shrink, rather than grow; for the outer leaves died away leaving only the heart alive. All this time, however, the young plants were establishing themselves, accommodating their roots to the new soil and putting down deeper shoots into the ground. All at once, and with one accord, they began to grow with great rapidity. The small specks of green rose and spread, the leaves lengthened and broadened; and in a few weeks plant touched plant and shaded the ground.

When the plants were about three feet high, Jerry and Judith went through the rows "topping" them. With the thumb and forefinger they pinched off the central bud which, if allowed to grow, would shoot up and develop into flower and seed. This made the plants shorter, broader, and stockier and sent all the life into the great, succulent leaves. When Jerry and Judith worked at this task, their hands became covered with the thick, sticky, yellow juice of the plants. It took several changes of water to wash away this rank, poisonous sap; and the remaining stains were slow in wearing off.

The tobacco worms, too, were things that had to be contended with. All other plant pests leave tobacco alone, preferring more wholesome pasture. But there is one worm especially created to feast upon the tobacco plant. To this creature the deadly juice of the leaves means health and plenty. It resembles a tomato worm, but it is larger, longer, greener, and more many-legged. If it is allowed to live, its depredations are tremendous. Every week or so Jerry and Judith went through the tobacco plants with an old tin can in one hand and a stick in the other and knocked these offending vermin into the cans. When the rounds were completed they took the cans home and burned their contents in the cookstove.

It was not enough to cultivate the tobacco with the plow. It had to be hoed, too. To make its best growth each plant required individual attention. They chopped the ground about the plants with great hoes made especially for heavy work. The hard clay, baked flinty by the hot sunshine, resisted the hoes with all its might. It always seemed to Judith that her row would never come to an end. And when, after slow and toilsome progress, she at last reached the end, there were innumerable more rows waiting to be done. She was forced to admit that Jerry was her superior in the tobacco field. He could hoe three rows while she was doing one; and at evening, though tired, he was by no means at the end of his strength. It was very hot in the southward sloping field. The sun beat down mercilessly and the plants exhaled a heavy, sickening odor. She could feel the sweat standing out on her face, and rolling down her legs. It tickled and irritated her skin, and now and then she stopped to scratch viciously. Sometimes the acrid streams poured into her eyes and for the moment blinded her. When a breeze sprang up and swept across the tobacco field, its touch on her wet body made her feel almost cold. After it had died away the heavy quiet fell like a great, stifling blanket over the earth and it seemed twice as hot as before. Still she and Jerry plodded on with the patient persistence of those born and reared to a life of toil.

Not much visiting went on between Hat and Judith that summer; for the tobacco field claimed them both.

But Judith was young and buoyant. Tobacco did not have to be hoed every day; and these seasons of hard and continuous toil gave to the less strenuous days something of the feeling of holidays. In spite of the tobacco crop, life remained full of pleasures for Judith. She liked to work in her garden and see the beans and peas and cabbages making sturdy growth under her care. She liked to feed her chickens and turkeys morning and evening and note how fast the little chicks and young turkeys were growing and how strong and firm were their bodies. She liked to set hens and care for the little chicks after they came out of the shell. She planted morning glories and nasturtiums about the house and trained them up on rude trellises made of tobacco sticks. The summer was full of radiant mornings a-quiver with sunshine with sweet smells and the carolling of birds, and cool, quiet evenings when she and Jerry sat together on the doorstep through the slow-falling midsummer twilight until the familiar outline of hills and trees melted into a blur of darkness and the last sleepy twitter of little birds drowsed into silence. To Judith, as to the growing plants and the wild things of the fields and woods, the sun still meant joyous life and growth, its absence, peace and sleep. She was not much more given to thinking than was the mocking bird in the hickory tree over the house; and she enjoyed her life even as he.

In September the tobacco ripened. The leaves turned from green to a rich gold and the crop was ready to harvest. Jerry refused to let Judith help with this strenuous task and hired his brother Andy instead. When the two men came in from the field after "cuttin'" their hands, faces and clothes were smeared thickly with the sticky tobacco sap and its rank odor filled the kitchen.

After the tobacco had been allowed to wilt in the field, they hauled it to Hiram Stone's nearest tobacco barn, a big structure built on the top of the ridge about half a mile from Jerry's field.

It was a great relief to Jerry when the last load was hauled in and hung up. So many things can happen to spoil a tobacco crop that he had lived in constant anxiety ever since the plants had been set in the ground. The weather had favored Scott County that year, and the tobacco was heavy and of fine quality.

"Naow, by gollies, if she don't up an' heat in the barn the crop's made," he said to himself.

The outdoor work with the crop was over and the rest was on the knees of the gods. Jerry now had his corn to work with. As he cut the corn and stacked it in shocks, and as he and Judith together shucked out the ears, Jerry watched the weather with an anxious eye. If there came a warm, damp day, he grew uneasy; and a succession of warm, damp days sent him to the tobacco barn to examine anxiously the yellowish-brown bunches and open the doors wider so that the air could circulate more freely.

"If she heats an' spiles now after all our work, won't it be a dirty shame?" he said to Judith one day, when she had accompanied him on one of these visits.

"I wonder if there's anything the matter with the terbaccer, Jerry? It don't somehow seem to smell right to me," said Judith, sniffing the air critically. "I allus did love the smell of terbaccer a-dryin' in the barn. But this kinda makes me feel sick to my stummick."

"Smells all right to me," opined Jerry. "Smells durn good." He sniffed again.

"Must be sumpin wrong with your smeller, Judy."

"I dunno what's wrong," doubted Judith, "but it sholy hain't got a good smell to me."

As the days passed, Judith began to notice that other things besides the tobacco had a queer, unnatural, slightly nauseating smell. She supposed at first that she had eaten something that had disagreed with her and that the effect would pass off in a day or so. The trouble, however, grew worse instead of better. It came on so slowly, so subtly and insidiously, that she was in its grip before she fully realized that there had been a change. She thought that the first time that she had noticed anything unusual in her feelings was the day at the tobacco barn. But she could not be sure. As she looked back she imagined that she had felt other queer sensations even before that. The beginnings of the strange disease were shrouded in mystery.

Some canned salmon that they had for dinner a few days after the visit to the tobacco barn did not taste good at all.

Judith could not understand why. She had always loved canned salmon. It was a store delicacy rarely indulged in and hence much relished by the rural population of Scott County.

"What's wrong with this here salmon, Jerry?" she asked, turning it over listlessly with her fork. "It hain't spiled, an' yet it don't taste good, nohaow."

"Tastes good to me," said Jerry. "I cud eat a barrel of it. Gimme yours if you hain't a-goin' to eat it."

She gave him what was left on her plate and he ate it greedily and finished the can.

"I'm afraid you've worked too hard in the field this summer, Judy," he said anxiously. "I hadn't otta let you."

"I don't hardly think it's that," she answered languidly. There was no trace left of her usual animation. She seemed a different person.

As day after day passed and she got no better, she began to realize that a great change had taken place in herself and in the world about her. Nothing seemed at all the same. The fields and lanes, the dooryard, and particularly the house, were full of lurking, insidious stenches that attacked her on every hand and turned her stomach. Everything that she looked at seemed to have something ugly and repulsive about it. The very morning glories and nasturtiums were gaudy and tiresome and the smell of the nasturtiums sickened her. She particularly loathed the sights and smells of the kitchen and fled from them as often as she could. The odor of frying fat, of burning wood, or of beans boiling on the stove sent her reeling to the outside. There she gulped great draughts of the pure air, and as she grew calmer, breathed long and deep until her nausea had subsided. She found that she suffered much less when out of doors and would have stayed there all the time if she had not had to cook for Jerry. She did it as long as she could hold out. But sometimes it was too much for her, and she had to lie down in the bedroom and let Jerry find himself something to eat as best he could.

She detested the kitchen. The oilcloth-covered table, the blue dishes formerly so much prized, the coffee pot, and the big white water pitcher were objects of loathing to her. She hated the sight of the calendars and little pictures that she had tacked on the walls. There was one picture that particularly irritated her, though she could not have told why. It was a still life representing dead grouse and partridges lying on a table. One day she took the picture down from the wall and stuffed it into the stove, getting at least a momentary feeling of satisfaction from hearing it crackle up the stovepipe.

There was one dish that seemed to her especially odious, a berry bowl that Lizzie May had given her as a wedding present. It was made of imitation Tiffany glass, and she had thought it lovely until this strange malady had seized upon her. Now she could not bear to look at the crude bronze and green and purple lights that it cast at her. It seemed an evil and poisonous thing. She poked it into the bottom of one of the bureau drawers and covered it up with sheets and pillow slips.

Jerry, too, came in for his share of the general odium. She developed a great dislike for certain little inoffensive habits that he had, such as rubbing his hands together over the fire, whistling loudly as he went about his chores and teasing the pup for the fun of hearing him growl and snap. When he kissed her, which she now rarely allowed him to do, she was conscious with a shiver of repugnance that he needed a shave and that he had been chewing tobacco.

One afternoon, when existence about the house seemed intolerable, she put on her sunbonnet and started out on the cowpath that led along the top of the ridge and down into the hollow where Hat and Luke lived.

Hat was plucking geese in the back dooryard. This side of the house was littered with an accumulation of broken boards, rusty pieces of scrap iron, old rags, papers, empty bottles, discarded cooking utensils and rusted-out tin cans. Hat was not the pink-and-white vision that she had been on the day when she had first visited Judith. She wore a ragged calico wrapper, faded by much sun and many washings, into a dismal drab. About her waist was pinned a greasy gunny sack to serve as an apron. The short ends of her coarse black hair hung in uncombed rattails about her face; and her great feet, planked firmly on the ground with the toes turned in, were bare and very dirty. Her clothes, her hair, and her perspiring face were powdered thickly with the down from the feathers which fell like snow about her and frosted the ground for yards around. Between her knees she gripped the goose's head and with her big, coarse hands plucked away great handfuls of the soft, white, fluffy down from the breast and under the wings and stuffed them into a stiff paper flour sack that stood open at her side. The goose struggled and squawked mightily. Hat only gripped the prisoner more firmly between her great knees and went about her task more vigorously.

As Judith came up she was greeted by a strong smell of pigsty. Luke had had a good corn crop and was fattening several hogs that fall. Three or four lean hounds that were slinking about the dooryard barked in a perfunctory, spasmodic way, then relapsed into silence. Hat stopped for a moment to try to brush away with her down-covered hand some of the fluff that clung irritatingly about her eyes.

"Land alive, Judy, I sholy do hate to pick geese," she gasped. "I git all het up, an' then the durn stuff sticks in the sweat, an' you wouldn't believe haow it itches me. But it's gotta be done, an' there hain't nobody else that'll do it. Feathers is a good price this year. An' when *these* feathers is turned into money, it's *me* that's a-goin' to handle it. Las' time we sold feathers, Luke he got holt o' the money an' that's the last I ever seen of it. An' it was me that raised 'em an' fed 'em an' picked 'em an' done every durn thing."

Hat's voice trembled with anger and self-pity. Judith opened her mouth to start to say something; but Hat did not wait to hear what it might be. She was seething with a sense of wrong and glad to have somebody in whom to confide.

"The men sholy do have it easy compared with us wimmin, Judy," she continued. "Here all this summer I worked like a dawg in the terbaccer a-settin' an' a-toppin' an' a-hoein' an' a-wormin' an' a-cuttin'; an' all the fore part o' the winter I'll spend a-strippin'. An' then along about Christmas Luke'll haul the terbaccer off to Lexington an' sell it an' put the money in his pocket an' I won't never see a dollar of it. An' if I even want a few cents to buy me calico for a sun-bonnet, I gotta most go daown on my knees an' beg for it. I work jes as hard in the crop as he does. An' then what does he do while I cook an' wash dishes an' clean the house an' do the washin' an' tend the chickens an' turkeys? He feeds an' tends the hosses. That's what he's got to do outside of his crop. He hain't never picked a goose in his life; an' he wouldn't pick one if they died for lack o' pickin'. He says pickin' geese is wimmin's work. I tell you what I'm a-goin' to do. Nex' summer I ain't a-goin' to touch hand to his corn ner his durn terbaccer crop. If pickin' geese is wimmin's work, settin' an' hoein' terbaccer is man's work, an' he kin do it hisse'f 'ithout any he'p from me. I'm jes sick an' tired of slavin' like a mule an' gittin' nothin' fer it."

She paused on the brink of tears. A large tortoise shell cat arched her back and rubbed herself against the legs of her mistress, then reached up her head and sniffed delicately at the goose.

"An' then," she went on in the next breath, "with all his huntin' foxes most every night an' keepin' all them lazy haounds a-slinkin' raound the place an' a-eatin' up the feed the chickens otta have, he can't keep the foxes from gittin' my geese. Las' night when I went to ketch 'em up to coop 'em I found my biggest goose was missin'. An' this mornin' when I was a-lookin' up my turkeys, sure nuf I come on the feathers jes over that little hill yonder. I was that vexed an' disgusted. Think of it! Him an' all his durn haounds to-gether ain't as smart as one fox! An' what's he a-doin' naow, while I'm a-slavin' an' a-sweatin' over these geese? He's a-standin' yonder by the shed a-chawin' terbaccer an' a-gassin' with young Bob Crupper. He's been there in that one spot this good two hours, an' he'll be there like enough till chore time to-night. Men makes me sick; always a-sunnin' their-selves around the barnyard like flies on a dunghill."

She stopped, exhausted by her passionate jeremiad, and relaxed her hold upon the goose, which she had finished plucking. It ran off squawking indignantly. She made a vain attempt to scatter the down from about her nostrils by blowing upward, then brushed her nose frantically with her furry hand. "Ouf," she puffed, irritated beyond endurance by the clinging stuff.

Judith looked in the direction of the wagon shed and saw Luke and Bob Crupper leaning in easy attitudes against an old spring wagon that was drawn up outside the shed. From time to time they changed the weight of their bodies from one leg to the other or spat idly into the scattered straw. As she was looking, she saw Bob Crupper turn his head in her direction for a moment and then say something to Luke. Luke made some reply, and she could see the two men laughing together. Hat, too, had noticed the little pantomime.

"I wonder what them two was a-sayin'?" said Judith, casting another look in the direction of the two men.

"Sumpin nasty, I'll betcha," snapped Hat in a tone of disgust. "When men gits to laffin' together you kin be sure one or 'nother of 'em has come out with some dirty talk."

Judith knew that there was much truth in Hat's accusation; and she had a momentary feeling of curiosity as to what had been said, for she felt sure that it had been about herself.

Hat went to the coop to get another goose and came back carrying the big white bird with its head under her arm. The intelligent creature seized a moment when Hat's arm muscles were somewhat relaxed to wrench its head free and bite her captor viciously on the hand. She screamed shrilly with pain and anger.

"Damn the critter!" she cried, wrenching her hand loose and stuffing the offending head back under her arm. "Lord love you, Judy, you hain't got no idea haow hard a goose kin bite."

"I have, too," answered Judith. "I bin bit more'n once."

"I wisht Luke had," said Hat, glancing darkly in the direction of her husband, as she settled herself to the task of plucking. "Have you hearn the last news abaout Ziemer Whitmarsh, Judy, an' the way he's been a-carryin' on with Minnie Pooler?"

"I ain't hearn nothing lately nor been nowhere," answered Judith. "I been a-feelin' so bad I ain't cared to go nowhere nor do nothin'. I'd jes as leave be dead as feel the way I been a-feelin' lately."

"Why, what kin ail you, Judy? You've allus been so strong an' hearty."

Judith began to tell Hat about how she had been feeling for the past two weeks or so. As she went into the details of her symptoms, a look of interest, of satisfaction, and of amused patronage came into Hat's face and widened into a broad grin which seemed to Judith at first disagreeable and then revolting.

"Why, Judy Pippinger, d'you mean to tell me you don't know what ails you?"

"Haow should I know? I don't know nothing about diseases."

Hat broke into a coarse laugh.

"You hain't got no disease, Judy, no more'n this here goose has a disease. You got a young un in yer insides. That's what's wrong with ye. You was kinda lucky it didn't come sooner."

With the last remark, Hat shot a swift, sharp glance at her visitor.

Judith was so taken by surprise that she scarcely noticed the meaning glance. It took her a full half minute to absorb the new idea. It was a possibility that of late had not occurred to her, although the thought of it had caused her some needless worry earlier in her relations with Jerry. She felt humiliated at disclosing what Hat appeared to consider such crass ignorance and disgusted at an indefinable something in Hat's attitude.

"But Hat, a caow ain't sick when she's a-fixin' to have a calf," she said at last, looking straight at Hat with her clear, level, searching eyes.

"Wimmin has troubles caows don't never even dream on. You'll find that out afore you're married long," said Hat darkly. From this cryptic prophecy she launched into a description of the pregnant state and went into the subject in all its ramifications. She did not tell Judith how it came that she who had never had a child knew so many intimate details regarding the symptoms of pregnancy. That after all was her own affair.

Judith listened with a mixture of interest and disgust. She wished to know all that she could find out on this as on any other matter that concerned her life. But she was revolted by Hat's whispered undertone and her air of salacious secrecy. She was glad to cut her visit short on the plea that she had work to do at home. When she left, the two men were still standing in the same attitudes by the wagon shed.

As she walked homeward along the top of the ridge, she was glad to look out over the broad expanse of clean earth, to draw in deep breaths of pure, hilltop air and to shake from her the close and fœtid atmosphere of Hat's hollow.

CHAPTER XI

SHE felt less abjectly miserable after she had learned the cause of her distress of body. As time passed, her symptoms became gradually less violent, and at last disappeared altogether. The nausea passed away, and she was able to eat again and enjoy her food. The pictures on the wall took on their old, natural look; and she got out Lizzie May's present from under the sheets and pillow slips in the bureau drawer and found it once more a delight to her eyes.

It was good to feel like herself once more and to be able to get pleasure instead of loathing from the multitudinous small things that make up the major part of life. It was like waking up from some dismal nightmare and finding the earth still a good and pleasant place. The happiness of freedom regained more than equaled the irk of the old bondage. And as Judith stretched and laughed and enjoyed the rain and the sun and ate heartily and loved Jerry more than she had ever loved him before and felt herself overflowing with physical well-being and spiritual content, she knew the joy of reacting to perhaps the most powerful stimulant in life, the elixir of sharp contrast.

And now that she was well again there was plenty of work for her to do. The tobacco, which had survived the warm, damp seasons fatal to many a tobacco crop, must be stripped and stripped quickly, so that Jerry could haul it off to market before the price dropped. Jerry had bulked the tobacco early in November, and had been stripping for some time. But it was slow work for one pair of hands. Now that Judith was able to help him, things went faster.

They got up in the dark, chilly winter mornings long before it was day, ate breakfast and did the morning chores by lamplight, and were ready to go out into the slow, gray dawn while the sky was still only faintly alight and the familiar outlines of the barnyard only dimly visible. The last thing that they did before leaving was to scatter food for the hens, which had not yet come from the roosts. Then they climbed the hill to the ridge path that led to the big tobacco barn.

At the far end of the ridge, the tobacco barn lifted its weathered bulk into the sky. Built on the highest point of land, the wide sweep of lonely fields and pastures dropped away from it in every direction. Its roofs fell from the ridge-pole with the broad sweep of a buzzard's wing; and it seemed like some great bird brooding over the wide, solitary expanse, or like some gigantic, incense-breathing temple built by these poor shanty dwellers to their one god, the all-powerful god of toil. From its point of vantage it dominated the landscape, somber, strong, and implacable.

But to Jerry and Judith it was only a tobacco barn and they hurried to it as the factory hand goes to his daily dungeon.

By the time they reached the little stripping room that leaned wearily against the tobacco barn, it would be light enough to begin to strip. They shared this stripping room with Hat and Luke, the two couples working at opposite ends of the little oblong box. Sometimes Hat and Luke would be there already, and in that case the fire would be lighted. If they were the first to arrive, Jerry would quickly light the fire in the little rusty box stove and they would settle down to work.

All day long they would stand stripping the soft brown silk leaves from the thick, woody brown stalks, tying them in bunches and assorting them according to color and texture. The softest, silkiest, most pliable, and lightest colored leaves were the best in quality. Descending from this there were many grades ending in the scraggy, reddish top leaves, torn and discolored leaves and leaves that had been touched by frost.

At noon the two couples, still at opposite ends of the room, would eat the lunches that they had brought with them and immediately fall to work again, working steadily until the short winter day was over and the twilight blurred the shades of brown before their eyes.

It was strange and unnatural how little conversation went on among these four young people as they stood working together day after day. Judith would have liked to talk and often wondered why she and the others did not talk more. Sometimes she made a deliberate attempt to start conversation; but it always ended in nothing. There hung over them always a heavy air of self-consciousness and constraint that smothered all natural spontaneity. There were several private and personal reasons for this. Jerry continued to nurse the old grievance of the stolen tobacco plants, and added to it the suspicion that Luke was getting away with some of the cream of his crop. He could steal a good many bunches without the possibility of their being missed, and Jerry opined that he was just the man to do it.

The minds of Hat and Luke dwelt largely upon the subject of money. They had one all-consuming desire in common, which was to get their crop stripped and on the market before the price fell. In this at least they were at one; aside from it their thoughts and desires were their own. Hat meditated upon what she had been reading in her latest copy of the "Farm Wife's Friend," mused upon her wrongs and Luke's shortcomings, and toyed gingerly, yet deliciously with thoughts of intrigue. Sometimes she lifted her black eyes to Jerry and saw that he was strong, healthy and handsome, then forgot him the next moment in thoughts of some imaginary lover.

Luke, in the short intervals of thoughts of gain, thought about the fox that he had hunted the night before and the good swigs of whiskey that he had had at Bob Crupper's out of a gallon jug stopped with a corncob. And he remembered how good the whiskey had made him feel. Not infrequently his mind wandered from these thoughts to dally with meditations more vague but more attractive. Sometimes when Judith lifted her head she met his little blue eyes fixed upon her with a look, the meaning of which was unmistakable. Instantly he would withdraw his eyes and work furiously at his task.

Once Jerry surprised one of these looks. His face flushed a dark, angry red and his fist involuntarily doubled, the knuckles protruding formidably. He opened his mouth, then thought better of it and closed it again. Luke had not noticed that he had been observed; and Judith, absorbed in her work of sorting, had not seen either Luke or Jerry. The little pantomime had taken only a second to perform and was gone as though nothing had happened.

Once Hat surprised this look and shot a lightning glance from under her heavy black eyebrows to see if Judith was answering it. Reassured from this direction, she turned her bold eyes and cast a black look of uncontrollably furious jealousy at her husband who was now bending again over his tobacco.

So the little human comedy went on; and Judith, the only one who was not cherishing ulterior motives or covert suspicions, found her natural desire for companionship swamped in this heavy undertow of suspicion, greed, craftiness and lust. There is an idea existing in many minds that country folk are mostly simple, natural and spontaneous, living in the light of day and carrying their hearts on their sleeves. There is no more misleading fallacy. No decadent court riddled with lust of power, greed, vice, and intrigue, and falling to pieces of its own rottenness, ever moved under a thicker atmosphere than that which brooded over the little shanty where these four fresh-cheeked young country people stood stripping tobacco.

They sighed with relief when the long job was over and the tobacco was ready for market.

Tobacco was an unusually good crop that year and Jerry's half amounted to nearly two tons. In addition to his own tobacco, he was hauling a small crop for one of the neighbors, so his load was a heavy one. It was an exciting morning when the great, towering load stood outside the tobacco barn with four horses attached in the first gray glimmer of the dawn, and Jerry, perched on the high seat, cracked his whip over the four broad backs, and started out on the thirty mile trip to Lexington.

When he came home next day there was a check for three hundred and eighty-four dollars and seventy-six cents folded in the inside pocket of his coat. His tobacco had brought the high average of ten cents a pound. He had never been so proud and happy in his life as when he opened the check and spread it before Judith's delighted eyes. There was money to finish paying for the horses and money to put in the bank. His joy was marred only by the knowledge that Luke had averaged a cent a pound more for his crop, a knowledge which confirmed him in the suspicion that some of his finer grades had been stolen.

As Judith's waist measure increased, and it became apparent to everybody who saw her that she was with child, she became the recipient of the advice and confidence of all the women of the neighborhood. The confidences were many and varied; and the advice of one woman often flatly contradicted that of another. But they were all alike delivered with an air of conclusive authority. She found that when these women spoke to her about her pregnancy they adopted a manner almost identical with that which had revolted her in Hat: an air of great intimacy and secrecy, as though the subject was of such a private nature that it concerned only the talker and listener and brought the two together into a close and exclusive atmosphere. With this was combined a certain archness and playful levity which seemed to Judith the very soul of lewdness. Jerry's mother, Aunt Mary Blackford, a well meaning soul according to her lights, was one of the worst offenders; and she presumed upon her relationship, as relatives have a habit of doing. Judith grew to dread the approaches of these women as one loathes and dreads a pestilence. She resented their insinuating interference in a matter which she wished to concern only herself and Jerry; and the manner of their interfering seemed to her vile and disgusting.

After having endured several lengthy visits, she learned to

lock the door and hide in the bedroom when she saw a female figure approaching over the brow of the hill. The visitor would try the door, and finding it locked would knock loudly and imperatively, then wait a short time and knock again. Having satisfied herself that there was no one at home, she would scrutinize the dooryard more or less closely, according to the extent of her curiosity, and at last turn away and plod up the hill again. Not until she was quite out of sight would Judith dare to open the door.

Sometimes, however, she was not fortunate enough to see the visitor in time to feign absence from home. This was the case one afternoon when Aunt Maggie Slatten, the mother of Hat, and of many other children, bore down upon her.

They had not long since finished dinner. Jerry had just left the house to go back to his spring plowing, for it was February, and Judith was washing the dishes, when the door was unexpectedly opened and disclosed Aunt Maggie occupying the major part of the door space. She heaved in and sat down heavily in a chair, which creaked at the onset of her tremendous weight.

"Land alive, Judy, it's a hard climb over them hills," she gasped, laboriously taking off her mud-encrusted overshoes and setting them under the stove to dry. "An' the roads is that deep in mud, a body kin hardly pull their feet along. But I hearn haow you was in the family way. An' knowin' it was your first an' haow you didn't have no mammy, I felt I jes had to come daown an' set with you a while. Well, an' haow air you a-feeling', Judy?"

Judith sensed at once the familiar aura that had become her abhorrence. There was an air of condescension, too, as from one who confers a favor. She had never liked Aunt Maggie.

"I'm a-feelin' all right," she answered coldly, and went on washing the dishes.

"Well, that's good, Judy. It's a great blessin' to be well."

Having disposed of her overshoes, she laid aside her black sateen sunbonnet and started to divest herself of her outer garment. This task proved too much for her.

"I reckon you'll have to give me a little he'p here, Judy," she breathed, already winded by her efforts. Judith went over and helped her to peel the wrap from her fat arms and shoulders. It was an ancient garment called some decades earlier, when it had been new and fashionable, a dolman. It was of broadcloth, now faded into a greenish tinge, and it was trimmed with fringe, which was somewhat greener than the cloth. She laid the dolman over the back of a chair with the care and reverence due to best apparel and sat down again, smoothing her white apron over her lap.

Aunt Maggie was a woman of great girth. She had a large, flabby face of the color of cold boiled veal, so many large chins that they quite obscured what might have been her neck, a colorless, thin-lipped mouth and small, piercing, light gray eyes which gave Judith the uncomfortable feeling that they were bent upon prying into the innermost recesses of her private affairs. She had a way of asking a question in a sudden, direct and commanding way and accompanying it with a swift, searching look from her keen gray eyes, which seemed to say that she was entitled to the whole truth and she meant to have it.

Undaunted by Judith's assertion of present perfect health, an assertion which seemed to Aunt Maggie to be somehow rather indelicate, she proceeded, as one vested with authority, to inquire into the earlier history of Judith's pregnancy and to wrest from her admissions upon the basis of which she launched forth into the subject that she had come to discuss. She had a hoarse male voice and the air of one accustomed to dictate to others. Glancing about from time to time, as though constantly mindful of the fact that walls might have ears, she related to Judith all the details that she could remember—and her memory was excellent—concerning her own many pregnancies and the pregnancies of various of her neighbors and kinsfolk.

After a while Aunt Maggie's stream of talk began to flag. There was no stimulation to be gotten from Judith, who asked no questions and made few comments. And even a woman of fifty-three who cannot read or write, but has had seven children and three miscarriages, cannot talk forever on the pathology of pregnancy without at least some little assistance from her listener.

The talk began to be punctuated by heavy silences.

The whole afternoon was spent in this way, the silences growing longer and heavier as time dragged on. Still Aunt Maggie made no move to go.

"And where's the baby clothes, Judy?" she inquired. "Fetch 'em an' let me have a look at the dear little things."

"I hain't got any made yet, Aunt Maggie," answered Judith, putting a stick of wood into the fire.

"What, no baby clothes yet! Why, Judy Pippinger, hain't you 'shamed of yerse'f? Why, I'd a thought you'd 'a' bin sewin' fer the baby this four months back."

"How many months' sewin does it take to cover a little infant a foot long?" inquired Judith. "I 'lowed I could run 'em all up in a day on the old machine at dad's."

Aunt Maggie was aghast at this sacrilege.

"I never put in a stitch for one o' my babies that wa'n't done by hand," she proclaimed self-righteously.

Judith mentally reviewed the members of Aunt Maggie's family, a heavy, snub-nosed, dull-eyed swarm, and wondered in just what way they showed the benefits of hand-sewn baby clothes. But she said nothing. Aunt Maggie was too dominating and forceful a personality to have her prejudices challenged.

At last the February day began to gray to a close. The little window admitted less and less light; and Judith, hoping to hasten Aunt Maggie's departure, lighted the lamp.

"It's sinful to waste kerosene, Judy," commented her visitor. "You could 'a' gone a good half hour more 'ithout the light. 'Waste not, want not,' is a true sayin'. Well, I'll hev to be a-gittin' back home an' see to supper an' the milkin'. The young uns don't stir hand ner foot if I hain't there to tell 'em."

With alacrity Judith helped Aunt Maggie on with her dolman, and even knelt down on the floor and put on her overshoes. Seeing her at last really prepared to leave, she felt of a sudden quite kindly toward her visitor and suffered a twinge of shame at having treated her so coldly. She smiled in a cordial and friendly way as she ushered Aunt Maggie out of the house.

But when the door had closed behind her visitor the smile vanished and a look ᴧf empty weariness settled upon her face. It seemed as though Aunt Maggie still sat in the room and with her all the other stuffy old women of the neighborhood. Their prying eyes leered at her out of the gloomy corners. From their presence issued a stifling and oppressive aura.

When Jerry came in he found her sitting slackly in the old rocking chair, her long hands hanging limp like dead things.

CHAPTER XII

AFTER the baby's birth the routine of life in the little house in the hollow fell along quite different lines. Judith no longer went with Jerry to the field to hoe or top tobacco. The baby could not be left alone in the house. Judith sometimes wished to leave him for an hour or two so that she could give Jerry a little help when work was pressing. But he would not hear of it.

"S'pose he took a fit while you was gone, Judy. Or s'pose a rat should come."

"But he don't never have fits. An' we hain't got rats this summer. They're all over to Hat's place since that big yaller cat come here."

"But sumpin might happen to him, Judy. You can't never tell. I'll make shift to git along. If anything happened to him we wouldn't never be able to forgive ourselves. Besides you got plenty nuf to do, now you got him to take care on."

So Judith stayed at home and looked after the house and the chickens and the vegetable garden and tended the baby, while Jerry did the field work in the corn and tobacco. When there was a rush of work he hired Elmer or his own brother Andy.

The baby claimed most of Judith's attention. It was astonishing that so small a creature should make such heavy demands. Nursing him, bathing him, washing for him, rocking him when he cried, remaking his cradle, changing his diapers, taking him up and laying him down, washing for him again, changing his diapers again, rocking him again, nursing him again, putting him back in the cradle again occupied her days and part of her nights in a round of small activities which, after the novelty wore off, began to fret her like the tug of innumerable small restraining bands.

It was not that she took less interest in the baby. Instead he became each day more engrossing. In her scarcely outgrown childhood she had never cared much for playing with dolls; but this live doll that laughed and cried and gripped her fingers with its tiny hands and looked so ridiculously like Jerry was the most fascinating of playthings. The fascination, however, did not extend to his diapers, his clothes always accumulating in the washtub, his insistent demands night and day for her continual presence at his side and for all sorts of constantly recurring small attentions.

But dislike her bondage as she might, she was his slave. Miraculously this little newcomer who a few short weeks ago had been nothing to her but a burden of the flesh, now occupied with undisputed assurance the position of the most important thing in her life. Everything was for the baby. His health and comfort were the only things that really mattered. All the activities of her life centered about him. He was her first thought in the morning and her last care at night. When she came back into the house after working in the garden or feeding the hogs and chickens her first step was toward the cradle. He was always in her thoughts. She could not let her mind dwell upon the desolate vacancy that would be left if he should be snatched away from her. And yet she became daily more irritated and harassed by the constant small cares that his presence demanded of her.

Sometimes, to break the monotony and loneliness, she would take the baby on one arm and walk across fields by the short cut to Lizzie May's or down into the hollow to Hat's or up along the pike to her father's. There she would visit for a while, returning in time to do up the evening chores and get Jerry's supper. She often walked many miles in this way, carrying the baby on her hip.

On Sundays Jerry would hook up and all three of them would drive off to spend the day at her father's or at his father's or at the home of one or other of their many relatives. Judith looked forward to these Sundays. She who had always despised visiting was now glad to escape from the tedium and monotony of home into the comparatively refreshing atmosphere of other people's kitchens and dooryards. There she would sit and string beans or peel apples and talk with the women of the house about chickens and babies and the sicknesses and deaths and scandals of the neighborhood, clutching eagerly at these tattered scraps of other people's lives, as they fluttered past her in the idle and haphazard talk.

Soon, however, it was no longer possible to go visiting every Sunday. The summer passed; and the early fall, warm and calm and caressing, the full blown flower of the year, faded quickly into late fall with its cold, driving rain, keen winds, and sodden depths of mud. After Thanksgiving there were very few days when the weather was such that she could take the baby out.

So she stayed in the house with him long gray day after long gray day and plodded through the dismal daily round of dish-washing, clothes-washing, cooking, sweeping, nursing, and diaper changing. Each day was exactly like the one before it. Each day the demands of the baby and the rest of the household were precisely the same. Even the cooking allowed of no variation; for now that winter was come, there were just four things in the pantry: coffee, corn meal, dried beans, and hog meat, with perhaps an occasional cabbage or squash that by some miracle had escaped the frost. From as far back as she could remember she had been accustomed to this winter scarcity and had never minded it much before. Now she found herself continually longing for something new, something different to eat, not so much from starvation of body as of spirit.

Through the winter months the sun rarely shone and for days together the rain dripped dismally down the window panes and filled the dreary little house with its monotonous murmur. From the window she could see nothing but twinkling tawny puddles, slick, tawny mud, the outbuildings gaunt and black in the rain and above and beyond them the unchanging lines of the hills.

She borrowed Hat's books and her copies of the "Farm

Wife's Friend" and read them through. But she could not get from them the mental stimulation that they had afforded to Hat. Instead of opening to her the door of romance, they seemed only flat, silly, and unreal. She was sure that no such people had ever existed. She had never cared much for reading any of the books that had fallen in her way. She got more satisfying entertainment from drawing pictures of the dog, the cat, and the chickens in the dooryard. She tried again and again to draw the baby, but could not make the picture look like him. She drew the view from the little kitchen window as it appeared from every position in the room. With each step that she took the view was a different one. But all the pictures had one thing in common: the sweep of hilltop lining itself against the sky. She amused herself by piecing these pictures together and making the whole line of hills that bordered the hollow on the window side.

She was glad when Jerry came home at night, and ran to meet him, listening eagerly to his talk of what had happened in the field or the stripping room. She devoured greedily his tale of how Luke and Hat had got into a quarrel about which of them was to light the fire in the stripping room; and how he, coming in in the midst of the quarrel, had settled it by lighting the fire himself. But Hat and Luke had not seemed to consider it settled, for they had not spoken to each other all day long.

When Jerry came home from his trips to town to buy sugar and coffee and get the corn ground at mill, she listened with the most lively interest to his rendering of the news gathered at Peter Akers' store. Young Jim Patton's wife had left him for the fourth time after a quarrel in which it was said that he had tried to use the hay fork and she the butcher knife. Ziemer Whitmarsh, driving home from a drinking bout over near Dry Ridge, had been arrested on the triple charge of abusing his horse, using profane and obscene language, and disturbing the peace. There had been a shooting affair over at Sadieville. A nigger had been killed and two white men wounded. Nobody seemed to know just how the trouble had started.

Black Joe, a half witted nigger of the neighborhood, had been caught stealing Uncle Sam Whitmarsh's chickens. And Uncle Sam, with a buggy robe clutched over the shirt and drawers in which he had nabbed the thief, had appeared at Constable Seth Boone's door at one o'clock in the morning, covering the frightened nigger with his gun.

Sometimes Luella came to spend the day with her and dandled the baby and helped Judith with the housework or with some piece of sewing. Luella was only twenty-two; but already she was taking on many of the looks and ways of an old maid. Lizzie May never came; she was entirely taken up with her own family concerns. Sometimes Hat dropped in, bringing the latest copy of the "Farm Wife's Friend" and her most recent tale of wrongs at Luke's hands, or old Aunt Selina Cobb slipped in and sat for the afternoon, patching an already much patched shirt for Uncle Jonah. Aunt Sally Whitmarsh, who lived in the nearest house on the pike, wended her way across the fields once in a while and brought up to date the news and rumors of the neighborhood from far and near; for Aunt Sally was a great hand to collect gossip.

Sometimes Judith felt a bit creepy as she looked at Aunt Sally. Could it be that this calm featured, self-contained woman who sat placidly mending drawers for Uncle Sam and telling the news as dispassionately as if she were the personal column of a country weekly, had sown the seed of insanity in more than one of her children? Judith thought of Bessie Maud over in Black Creek Hollow and wondered if it could really have come through Aunt Sally.

Once young Bob Crupper drew rein in the dooryard; and instead of hallooing from the horse's back, flung himself from the saddle, tied the horse to a fence post and came striding toward the house. He was a tall, strongly built young fellow, handsome like his father and with his father's fearless and dreamy eyes.

"Is Jerry hereabout?" he asked, standing holding the knob of the open door in his hand.

"No, he's strippin'," answered Judith, looking up from her sewing. "You'll find him in the strippin' room."

"I wanta see him 'bout buyin' that little crop I raised on Uncle Ezry's place," explained Bob. "I hain't hardly got enough to make it wuth my while to haul it, an' I'll let it go cheap. There hain't a lot of it, but what there is is durn fine terbaccer."

"Mebbe he might buy it," said Judith. "He hain't got a big crop this year. Anyway, you'll find him in the strippin' room."

Bob made no move to go immediately in search of Jerry. Instead he closed the door that he had been holding open and made a step into the room.

"Bin cold this last few days, hain't it," he said, scratching up under his cap. "But the wind don't git you daown here in the holler. It blows mean up our way."

Something made Judith glance up swiftly from her sewing; and she caught Bob's eyes, which had been gazing at her neck and the curve of her right shoulder. When she raised her eyes he turned his away and fixed them on the woodbox.

"I see Jerry leaves you plenty wood to keep warm with," he said, with a short, embarrassed laugh.

"Yes, it's more'n some men does. Hat Wolf's allus a-kickin' 'cause Luke leaves her most o' the wood to chop."

"Well, the big heifer might as well be a-choppin' wood an' a-usin' up some o' that extry fat she's got. Naow a gal like you's too fine an' purty to chop wood."

She cast a swift glance at him.

"That's easy fer you to say, Bob Crupper, seein's you don't hev to chop my wood. If I was your wife or sister you'd think diff'rent, no matter if I was as good lookin' as the Queen o' Sheba."

"I dunno haow good lookin' the Queen o' Sheba was," answered Bob, emboldened by this rallying. "But I do know you're the best lookin' gal this side o' Georgetown."

He took a step nearer, and she could smell the whiskey on his breath, which she had not noticed before.

"I'd feel proud to chop wood fer you, Judy."

"Seein's you don't hev to," she flashed back. "I notice men is allus proud to do things fer wimmin if it's sumpin they don't hev to do. You'd better git along an' see to sellin' yer terbaccer crop."

Something brisk and decided in her manner made him take a step backward toward the door. But the whiskey gave him a little courage.

"I hain't a man that goes araound talkin' private to other men's wives," he began desperately, in a pompous, whiskey fuddled voice.

"You mean you air," countered Judith, getting up from her rocking chair. "You take yerse'f along about yer business, Bob Crupper."

The sharp and quite decided tone of her voice made him take another step backward and open the door. She gave him a push which sent him over the threshold and slammed the door in his face. Peering out of the little window, she saw him kick his horse in the ribs and gallop away. As she watched him out of sight she suddenly saw him standing by Wolf's wagon shed talking to Luke. He turned and looked at her, said something to Luke, and the two men laughed. She resented the look and the laugh and felt angry and insulted by his recent quite uninvited advances. Yet deeper seated and longer lasting than the anger and the feeling of insult, there was a sense of pleasurable excitement. Her neck and right shoulder were still warmly conscious of the bold gaze of his eyes. She looked at herself in the glass and saw that her cheeks were glowing—not entirely with anger. It was a long time before her neck and shoulder could forget how they had been looked at; and she was not sure that she wished to have them forget.

"Did Bob Crupper come to the strippin' room to see about your buyin' his terbaccer crop?" she asked, when she and Jerry were at supper that night.

"No. Was he here?"

"Yes. He come by on that big roan mare o 'hisn. I told him he'd find you in the strippin' room."

"I wouldn't mind takin' a risk on a small crop if I cud git it reasonable," mused Jerry.

Sometimes old Jonah Cobb, bent almost double, would walk silently into the house and sit for hours. Just why he came Judith did not know, for he hardly ever opened his mouth. He had been a tenant farmer ever since any one could remember. Now in his old age he still made every year a weak attempt to raise a little tobacco. Each spring he would prepare a bed; and when the setting season came he and Aunt Selina might be seen in the first gray of the dawn trudging out to set their plants. The dusk of the long spring day would be closing in before they struggled homeward again, he plodding a few steps behind. The result of their labors never amounted to more than a mere handful of tobacco. They occupied a one-room tenant house which Hiram Stone had long allowed them to consider their own. Here they kept some chickens, half a dozen rabbits, and a few hives of bees. Of late years Uncle Jonah had devoted a good deal of his attention to the bees and had come to consider himself quite a bee man. Almost every time that he opened his mouth it was to speak of bees. He would sit in Judith's kitchen for half an hour or more without opening his lips except to spit into the woodbox, and at the end of his period of silence would say abruptly:

"Bees needs salt same's sheep or cattle. A man otter salt his bees every so often."

After another twenty minutes he would break the silence by saying:

"Sorghum makes good feed for bees in winter."

Sometimes old Amos Crupper, the father of Bob, came in after supper and spent the evening sitting by the stove talking of wars and rumors of wars. The old man was tall, large and broad-shouldered, full of health and vitality. He had a massive leonine head, covered with a shock of thick gray hair, which he held erect in soldierly fashion. His eyes were fearless and dreamy, like those of his son Bob. He always looked clean and wholesome and was circumspect about his tobacco spitting.

He was a veteran of the Civil War and loved to talk of those far off days when as a youth of twenty he had toted a musket in defiance of what was for him the right. In a deep bass voice vibrant with chest resonance he would tell again and again in the same words stories of the events of the war that had made the deepest appeal to the simple nobility of his nature: stories of romance of devotion and of heroism.

When he was not talking about the war he talked about the virtues of his dead wife. Late in life he had made a second marriage with a sister of Uncle Sam Whitmarsh, Aunt Amanda Baxter, herself a widow of long standing. He remained, however, an unwilling victim. In the neighbors' houses he talked continually about the beauty and sweetness of his first wife, alluding to her always as "My wife." He never spoke disparagingly of Aunt Amanda, but when he had occasion to mention her it was always as "That woman I'm a-livin' with naow."

Uncle Amos was fond of Jerry and Judith and spent many hours of undisturbed quiet sitting by their stove talking of the old war and of the wife of his youth.

Once in a while Joe Barnaby came over to get away from the thick atmosphere of home. Joe was a son-in-law of Uncle Sam, having married one of the latter's nine children, Bessie Maud by name. Bessie Maud had not spoken to her mother and father since the occasion of a quarrel which had occurred shortly after her marriage. That was eight years ago. She had also quarreled with several of her brothers and sisters and stopped speaking to them. Such long sustained family feuds were common enough in Scott County where slight grievances dwelt upon in solitude grew like a rolling snowball. But of late years Bessie Maud's temper had become so uncertain and her habit of mind so strongly anti-social that few even of the near neighbors ever went near her house. It was whispered that she had always been a little off. It was in the family, the neighbors said, and it was on Aunt Sally's side. Aunt Sally's father, old Abe Beasley, had been "queer," and so had several of her other relatives on the father's side. And of Aunt Sally's children there were others besides Bessie Maud who showed traces of the taint.

Although Joe was but little over thirty, his hair was streaked with gray, his chest sunken, his features drawn and pinched, his face clouded with a dull misery. How much of this was due to his having to provide for so many babies, to his affliction of chronic rheumatism, and to his domestic troubles nobody could say. The neighbors all felt sorry for him, but nobody was heard to waste any pity on Bessie Maud.

The visitor that Judith liked best to see push open the door was Uncle Jabez Moorhouse. Often the others wearied or annoyed her if they stayed too long. She always knew what they were going to say; and the men nursing the stove got in the way of her cooking. Uncle Jabez was the only one of them all who might say or do the unexpected. When he came in at the door, something of the outside came in with him; and as he stood spreading out his great hands over the top of the stove or sat and smoked meditatively by the oven door, it seemed to her as though a warmth and radiance reached out to her from his great, ungainly body. He was often silent, sometimes weary and cynical, rarely merry through these dismal winter months. Yet whatever his mood, she felt the same emanation from his presence: a heartened feeling, as if the pulse of life had grown stimulatingly strong and full.

Once when they were alone and he had been sitting silently by the stove for a long time, he said, re-crossing his legs:

"You know why I like to come an' set here, Judy? It's 'cause it's as good to me as a half pint o' whiskey in my belly."

The winter dragged slowly to a close, and on its heels came an early spring to hearten the mud-bound tenant farmers. The March winds and warm April sunshine dried up the mud and the shanties were no longer prisons.

"I've a mind to go to Georgetown nex' Court Day," said Jerry one April morning at breakfast. "I'd kinda like to see haow hosses is a-sellin' this spring."

"Let's both go," chimed in Judith eagerly. "I'd love to go. I hain't bin no place all winter; an' I hain't bin to Georgetown but onct in my life."

"But haow about the baby?"

"Luelly'll take care of him. Or we kin take him over to your mammy."

"I was countin' on ridin' over with Joe Barnaby. If you go we'll have to drive the cart an' let Joe ride by hisse'f. Why do you want to go, Judy?"

"For the same reason you wanta go," she flashed angrily. "Because I'm sick o' doin' allus the same thing every day."

Jerry tried to assume an expression of male dignity and importance.

"I'm goin' fer to see haow hosses is a-sellin'," he said.

"As if you need to go fer that! You know well nuf you kin ast anybody that's bin there. An' anyway you don't need to know; you hain't a-buyin' no hosses. Why don't you tell the truth? You wanta go fer a holiday; an' I wanta go fer a holiday. So we'll both go."

"All right. Have it yer own way," said Jerry. He had the air of making a concession, and he looked disturbed and annoyed.

CHAPTER XIII

On the evening of the great day, Jerry and Judith took the baby and his bottles over to Aunt Mary Blackford, who was only too glad to have charge of the little darling. Judith felt as happy and excited as though to-morrow was to be her wedding day. She was unrestrainedly voluble even to Aunt Mary. When she and Jerry got home, they scrubbed themselves in the washtub, laid out their clean clothes, and went to bed, setting the alarm for two o'clock.

When they heard the alarm clock's noisy ting-a-ling, they jumped out of bed as eagerly as two children on Christmas morning. It was one thing to get up early to set tobacco and a much easier thing to get up early to make a trip to Georgetown. They had breakfast and did up the morning chores by lamp and lantern light; and it was still night, with no light but that of the stars when Jerry tied the lantern underneath the cart and they clambered in and started Nip up the steep path that led to the ridge road.

The path was full of the smell of damp earth and growing grass, mingled from time to time with the heavy scent of flowering locust trees. As they swung out onto the smooth pike, the first rays of the sun came slanting across the fields, casting long morning shadows. To Judith there was something vastly exhilarating about this driving out of the night, out of the creeping gray, out of the dimly growing twilight into the full blue and gold glory of the morning. She had a sense of infinite freedom and gaiety, as though the whole world had become a holiday place. It was the first time that she had been away from the baby since he was born eleven months before. Out of pure exuberance she began to sing:

Oh, the bumblebee is a busy bird,
He bumbles all araoun',

169

He sucks the honey off'n the flower
An' puts it in the graoun'.

Jerry too whistled with joy of the spring morning. But it did not mean to him what it did to Judith. His nature did not respond to the stimulation of natural things; and he had not been shut up in the little house in the hollow all winter. To him the drive was only a little more enjoyable than many other recent drives; and the sway of the cart, the rattle of the wheels and the rhythmic pounding of Nip's hoofs did not mean to him, as to Judith, a triumphal progress.

She was wearing a new dress of white with tiny red dots, and a sunbonnet that she had cunningly contrived out of a big red bandana handkerchief. Under the red sunbonnet her dark yet delicate beauty glowed like the silken flame of a poppy.

Standing back behind its two gloomy hemlock trees, the little shanty in which Jabez Moorhouse lived was brightened into silver gray by the morning sunshine and smoke was pouring from the chimney. A few hens scratched about the door, and a white-breasted collie sunned himself on the step and looked intelligently about. Jabez was in the yard chopping wood to feed his morning fire. Half of his shirt tail hung out of his overalls, as it nearly always did, and his head and hairy chest were bare. He paused in his chopping as the cart came rattling gaily along the road and waved his hand to the young couple, who waved back to him. After they had passed he stood watching the retreating cart till it disappeared around a bend in the road.

A strange thought suddenly took possession of Judith. She found herself wishing that it was Uncle Jabez who was sitting beside her instead of Jerry. Together she and Uncle Jabez would notice all sorts of things; and they would point them out to each other and laugh and wonder and enjoy the beauty and strangeness of the world. Jerry was different. For a moment she felt cold and dreary.

As they trotted past Uncle Ezra's long white mansion, they glimpsed Cissy's face pressed close to the little kitchen window.

Jogging along toward Clayton, they saw the smoke of breakfast fires curling up in white columns and vanishing into the blue. About the houses that they passed dogs were barking, roosters crowing, and hens cackling. Men were leading horses to water, women milking, and children picking up chips around the chopping block.

"I'll bet Joe's most there by this time," said Jerry, as they swung out of Clayton. "He said he was a-goin' to leave at midnight so's to be there fer the fust tradin'. Funny the way he does. He hain't never got the money to buy nuthin, an' he hain't got much to trade with neither. An' yet he don't hardly miss a Court Day in a year; an' he's baound to be there fer the fust dog shootin'. An' Gawd, haow he does drink! He says it helps him to fergit his troubles."

"It looks like Bessie Maud don't git much chanct to fergit *her* troubles."

"Well, she makes 'em fer herse'f."

It was about nine o'clock when they pulled up in the main street of Georgetown and gave Nip a drink from the fountain. They had traveled a little over twenty miles.

"We'll tie up in there," said Jerry, nodding sidewise in the direction of a grassy back street. "It's a nice, quiet place to eat our lunch, an' there's grass fer Nip."

Judith sprang out of the cart and together they started out to see the town.

Trading was already in full swing. The main street was lined on both sides by buggies and spring wagons, with here and there an automobile. The side streets, too, were quickly filling up, as farmers' rigs of various kinds came rattling into town looking for a place to tie up. Riders galloped along the street, sometimes leading one or more horses behind them. And in a vacant lot that flanked one of the hotels a human ring had formed itself around a group of restive mountain cattle in the midst of which a sun-browned young fellow was gesticulating and talking loudly. From this ring one could see the back quarters of the hotel piled with heaps of boxes, crates, old lumber, and refuse swarmed over by flies. From the in-

evitable large pile of scrap iron and tin cans, a few as yet un-
rusted surfaces reflected the sun's rays like mirrors.

The street in front of the hotel was thronged with a crowd
of men wearing, not the clothes they put on for funerals, but
something a little better than the clay-caked overalls of daily
wear. The swinging doors of the bar were already active on
their limber hinges, and a smell of beer oozed out into the
street, carrying a suggestion of kegs and coolness.

As they passed these swinging doors, Joe Barnaby came out,
wiping his mouth on the back of his hand.

"Howdy, there, yo'all. You jes come?"

"Jes tied up," said Jerry.

"Me I bin here this two hours past. There's bin some mighty
smart tradin' a-goin' on. Two bunches o' maounting cattle
sold dirt cheap. If I had a place o' my own I'd like to git me
a few head o' them maounting cattle an' slick 'em up with good
feed an' mate 'em to a short horned bull. They'd sell good
when they come fresh, an' there'd be money in it. But anybody can't do nuthin 'ithout capital. The young uns eats up
everything I kin make fast's I make it. So there you are.
'Ithout land or capital a feller goes raound year after year the
same old turns, like a squirrel in a cage, an' comes back at the
end right where he started from."

It was not at all like Joe to make so long a speech; and both
of his listeners looked at him a little surprised. The smell of
mingled beer and whiskey on his breath gave the explanation.

Georgetown could boast of a population of only a scant five
thousand. But with the crowded streets and the bustle and
activity of Court Day, it was a metropolis to these dwellers
in lonely hollows. The three strolled along, looking curiously
at the people they met and being looked at by them in turn.
It was an excitement to see so many of their kind at once.
Most of these people wore in their eyes and about their mouths
that look of vague, mild blankness characteristic of country
people in Kentucky. The attention of every one was divided
between the crowds and the shop windows, in which the Georgetown tradesmen had cunningly placed on view such articles

as they considered would most appeal to the Court Day crowds. The hardware merchants had taken their lawn mowers, carpet sweepers, and phonographs to the back of the store, and displayed instead rows of cheap, tin-plated wash-boilers, gray enameled sauce pans, sheep shears, tobacco knives, hoes, rakes, shovels, and cheap butcher knives. The windows of the dry-goods stores were full of overalls, corduroy trousers, work shirts, apron ginghams, and sleazy but bright colored calicoes. The two druggists had withdrawn their tooth brushes, toilet soaps, and cosmetics, and vied with each other in a tempting array of patent medicines, nursing bottles, sheep dips, and veterinary remedies.

The Town Hall, where the Court sat, showed unusual signs of activity. Boys swarmed over the stone steps; and one of the two policemen of the town walked up and down the side-walk in front of the entrance. From time to time some one would hurry up or down the steps. More likely than not such person was baldish, parchment skinned, dressed in a rusty black suit, and carrying a leather satchel.

On every side there was uproar. Horses whinneyed and neighed, wheels rattled, small boys yodeled for joy of the crowds and excitement. From every direction came the sound of men's voices proclaiming loudly in the familiar phrases of the horse trader the virtues of the animals that they had to sell or trade.

Listening to the peans of the traders, one would be led to believe that all the horses for sale or trade were splendid animals, young, healthy, vigorous, and docile. A glance around, however, belied this impression. Very few conformed in any way with the descriptions of their enthusiastic would-be vendors. There were old horses with hanging heads and sagging haunches, bowed like an old man at the knees and shoulders. There were vicious horses, with evil, suspicious eyes and ears that they laid back ominously. There were weak, spindly horses, with no breadth to their backs and haunches that sloped away into nothing, like the shoulder of a ringleted mid-Victorian female. There were old race horses, once good for the track, now good for nothing whatever. There were horses with clumsy, ill-shaped legs and awkward feet, that could hardly raise one hoof without setting it down on another. There were horses, naturally of good disposition, which had been made irritable and vicious by bad training. There were horses with all sorts of bad habits. There were horses with the heaves, horses with ringbone, spavin, stringhalt, and a dozen other equine diseases and defects.

The really good horses were very few in number; because a good horse can readily be sold near home and for a good price. The farmer used Court Day as an occasion for trying to get rid of the maimed, the halt, the blind, and the aged.

Everybody knew this; and yet everybody who had a little money in his pocket and many who had none at all, bought and traded horses on Court Day. It had become a passion which swayed in spite of reason, like the lure of the lottery or the seduction of the gaming table. Horse trading, with the drinking which accompanied it, was to these lonely tobacco growers their one joyful extravagance. It was their dissipation, their romance, their single oblation to the god of life and joy.

Around the corner of a side street, the Blackford party glimpsed Uncle Sam Whitmarsh in conversation with a lithe young man wearing a broad felt hat over a face that betokened life in the open air. Each man was holding the bridle of a horse. Coming up to see what it was all about, they found that a trade was in progress.

Uncle Sam was never so taken up with a trade that he had no time for his friends. He beamed a welcome on his good neighbors and his son-in-law.

"Howdy, Jerry. Howdy, Joe. Waal, Judy, you're a-lookin' like a rose in May. You don't mind a old man like me tellin' yer wife she's handsome, do you, Jerry? . . . No, stranger, the mare's too light. I hain't got no youst for her no more'n a hen has for teeth."

The horse that Uncle Sam held by the bridle was a heavily built iron gray work horse apparently about twelve years old.

He was a bit clumsy looking, but on the whole sound and healthy in appearance.

The stranger's horse was a beautiful cream colored mare with large, intelligent eyes, small ears, a gracefully arched neck and slim yet strong looking legs, the very perfection indeed of shape and proportion. Not even a track horse could be daintier in appearance. Uncle Sam tried to look at the animal with disdainful indifference; but for all his experience in the art of dissimulation, he could not keep out of his eyes a covert gleam that glinted of admiration and coveteousness.

"I'd suttenly never dream o' lettin' her go under a hundred," the young trader was saying. "But I jes can't take her a step fu'ther 'ithout shoes, an' I hain't got the money to git her shoes. I've had hard luck lately, stranger. Gawd, what hard luck I've had! Many a time this past month my three babies hain't had all they cud eat; an' me an' my wife has gone hungry fer days together. The two linin's o' my pocket has got to know each other good these past weeks. Lookit the shoes I got on, willyuh? I can't git shoes fer myse'f, let alone fer the mare."

Uncle Sam looked down at the shoes and saw that they were badly scuffed and that the young man's foot was bulging from a slit in the leather on the side of one of them. A good deal of the stitching on the other one had come loose; and it was laced with a shaggy scrap of binder twine. Whether the soles were through or not Uncle Sam could not see.

"An' lookit my shirt. It's the on'y shirt I got, I swear it is; an' it hain't a-goin' to cover my nakedness much longer."

He turned around with a broad grin and showed a long slit over the shoulder blade, through which his healthy, sun-browned skin shone with a satiny sheen.

"Naw, even if she didn't have nothin' the matter with her feet, the mare's too light. I hain't got no youst fer her."

Uncle Sam took a sidewise step, spat over the edge of the curb, and made as if to jump into the saddle.

"I tell yuh, an' I'd swear it on the Holy Book, there hain't a thing the matter with them there front feet. The poor beast's footsore, that's all's wrong with her. If you'd come from Williamstown this mornin' 'ithout shoes, wouldn't you be dead on yer feet? Gawd, them rough, stony roads is hard on a good shod hoss, let alone one that hain't got no shoes at all. I wouldn't think o' tradin' fer that awkward lout o' yourn, not fer a minit if it wa'n't he's new shod. I gotta be on the road tonight agin, an' I gotta have a hoss that kin travel along."

"Naw, she hain't nuthin to me. She's too light."

"But look what a beauty she is! Wouldn't you be praoud to drive a hoss like that? Wouldn't yer wife be praoud to drive her? Lookit the color of her. Look haow she holds her head. Lookit them round haunches. Lookit them slim, dainty legs. If she hain't sound an' perfect in wind an' limb you kin take this las' shirt off'n my back."

"Naw, I can't use her."

Uncle Sam made another move toward the saddle.

"I'll let you have her for twenty-five dollars boot. Bejasus, that's givin' her away. But what kin a man do when his pocket's flat? A baby kin have the best of him."

For about the twentieth time Uncle Sam looked into the horse's mouth and assured himself again that she was in very truth only five years old. Then he carefully ran his practised hand down each of her legs, feeling for bumps and finding none. Then he meditatively scratched his head.

"Waal, I tell yuh, stranger," he said, after a long period of deliberation. "I hain't got a passell of use fer the mare; but I'll give yuh five dollars boot. That's the best I kin do."

After a great deal of further parley, they compromised on ten dollars boot. Uncle Sam took two five dollar bills out of his well worn billfold and handed them to the trader, put his own saddle and bridle on the cream colored mare, wished the young man the best of luck, and the trade was made.

By this time it was getting on toward noon, and they went to the place where they had left the horse and cart to eat their lunch. Joe and Uncle Sam accompanied them, unfolding the lunches that they had brought in their coat pockets; and the four made a festive picnic meal together, supplementing what they had brought from home with peppermint drops and ginger snaps contributed by Uncle Sam, who was always a free spender on holiday occasions.

As they were eating, Uncle Sam entertained the little company with the tale of how he had that morning started out from home with a pocket knife and by a series of successful trades ended by possessing a fine new Colt automatic. He drew the revolver out of his pocket and caressed its smooth surfaces with his finger tips, a satisfied smile spreading over his foxy, fun-loving, and kindly face.

"The knife wa'n't a heap o' good," he said in his deliberate drawl. "So I up an' swapped it fer a dawg. I knowed I'd sholy have trouble gittin' the dawg back home, me bein' on hossback; so I traded him fer a watch. I had a purty good notion the watch wa'n't no timekeeper; so I traded it to Tom Pooler fer hisn that I knowed was a good un. Then I traded the watch fer a shot gun. It was a good shot gun; but I got two shot guns home; so I looked raound till I faound this here trade. She's a beauty an' she's jes the same as new."

He fondled the blue metal of the little death dealer with loving fingers.

"An' that's a rare beauty of a little animal I got yonder," he went on, nodding sidewise toward the cream colored mare. "When she gits shoes on her feet, she'll be fine as a fiddle. All in all, I'm praoud of to-day's tradin'. Some folks, 'specially wimmin, thinks a trader lives a idle life. But I tell yuh, tradin' hain't sech child's play. It takes hard work an' stickin' at it—an' it takes injinooity."

Uncle Sam's eyes turned meditatively inward and reposed upon himself, apparently not ill pleased with what they saw there.

"An' that there young feller thinks he's got a work hoss off'n me," he went on, musingly rubbing his lean chin with his lean hand. "Howsomever, 'twa'n't me that clipped the harness marks onto him. It was Edd Patton done it after he faound the hoss wouldn't work nohaow. All I done was jes to keep 'em trimmed a little."

After the meal was over, the three men sauntered away on manly pursuits, their steps leading them in the direction of the swinging bar door; and Judith was left to gather up the remains of the meal. As she was doing this, she saw the young man who had just traded with Uncle Sam come up and join the party belonging to a covered wagon which had tied up a few yards away. They were evidently his wife and three children; and the five ate dinner together, boiling coffee and frying bacon and eggs over a little gipsy fire of twigs and chips built between two large stones. The young trader seemed to be in high spirits and laughed and played light heartedly with the children. He recognized Judith as the young woman who he had seen standing by while he was trading; and frankly admiring her youthful good looks, he cast several bold glances in her direction, which his wife tactfully pretended not to notice.

After the meal was over, he went away again. Judith, giving herself up to an after dinner feeling of pleasant languor, sat on the grass under the big beech tree and watched the three little girls as they played house with a piece of board for a table and a handful of flat pebbles for dishes. Their mother, a faded, harassed looking woman, who was probably in the late twenties, although she looked much older, gathered up the broken egg shells and threw them on the fire, washed the gray enameled mugs and plates and put them away in the covered wagon. The three little girls were named Curlena, Sabrina, and Aldina. The faded mother, when she had occasion to speak to the children, called them by these names in a way which suggested that she derived pleasure from the sound of the long, euphonious, and unusual appellations.

After dinner lethargy does not last long in the young; and Judith soon grew tired of sitting idly under the tree. She got up, shook out her skirts, felt to make sure that she still had her little purse in her pocket, and started toward the town.

As she passed the covered wagon she paused; for country people do not go by each other without a word of greeting.

"Howdy, ma'am. You come from far?"

"From Williamstown this mornin', ma'am. My husband's a hoss trader an' he follers the court days. We're most allus on the road."

"You like the road?"

"No, ma'am. My husband likes it well enough; but I hain't never cared fer the road. It's a hard life—'specially with three young uns; an' you can't have things much better'n what the gipsies do. 'Tain't so bad purty weather like this; but then comes rains an' we have to take to somebody's barn, an' sometimes stuck there fer four or five days hand runnin'. It's hard then to dry the young uns' clothes an' to git any kind o' warm cooked food fer 'em. An' if they was to fall sick, I dunno what I would do. I'm allus glad when winter comes an' we have to go into lodgings somewhere. But 'tain't like havin' your own home."

"Would you rather your husband was a farmer?"

" 'Deed I would, ma'am," answered the woman eagerly. She seemed to be glad to have some one of her own sex to talk to. "There hain't nothin' I'd like better'n to have a little home o' my own an' never have to move out'n it. I'd have flowers in the yard an' lace curtains on the front winders; an' I'd keep my three little gals dressed nice an' have a white cloth on the table. But seems like folks hain't in this world to git what they want, 'specially wimmin. Well, it's the men that has to earn the livin', an' I s'pose they gotta do it the way seems best to 'em."

She sighed resignedly.

Judith felt sorry for the woman. To some extent she could understand her point of view. It was as if sister Lizzie May, with all her finnicky little housewifely instincts, had fallen to be the wife of a wandering horse trader. She herself thought the life would be a jolly one, if one had no babies.

She turned away with a word of good-by and went on into Main Street, where she made delightful explorations in the dry-goods stores. Here in the dim coolness that smelt alluringly of new cotton goods, she wandered around with other back country women, fingering this and admiring that and looking lingeringly at the things that she was not able to buy.

Most of these women were stolid-faced, ungainly, flat-footed creatures, even the young ones wearing a heavy, settled expression, as though they realized in a dim way that life held nothing further in store for them. Some carried babies on their hips or had older children peeping shyly from behind their skirts, overawed by the strange surroundings. They looked at and fingered the pretty voiles, ginghams, and summer silks, then bought unbleached muslin, dress lengths of calico and spools of white cotton thread.

Judith bought some bright calico for dresses for the baby, and a piece of embroidered white muslin to make him a bonnet and a Sunday dress. Then, not being able to resist a certain pretty flowered muslin gay with pink rosebuds, she bought enough of it to make a dress for herself.

As she was loitering along Main Street looking into the shop windows, Bob Crupper came up from behind and looked at her admiringly with his boyish eyes.

"Hey, Judy, what you a-doin' here in the big taown?"

"Same thing you're a-doin', I reckon: a-loafin' an' a-idlin' an' a-spendin' what little money I got."

"Yaas, I expect that's about what we're all a-doin','" said Bob, and walked along beside her.

Now and then they saw in the crowd the familiar face of some one from their neighborhood; and Judith was conscious each time of a certain constraint in the look and greeting of these people, which would not have been there if she had been alone. Since her marriage she had begun to learn that a married woman cannot appear in the company of any man other than her husband without "making talk." She looked at the people she knew, from under her heavy eyebrows, with a challenging boldness that was half amusement, half irritation.

In front of the Town Hall they met Jerry, who turned and joined them. She caught the same expression on Jerry's face. This look which had caused her only a vague annoyance when seen on the faces of the neighbors, brought a surge of quick anger, when she saw it sneaking out of Jerry's eyes; and she began to joke and banter with Bob in a hectic way quite unbecoming to a married woman of the tobacco country. Her gaiety sent Jerry into a fit of the sulks; and he walked along beside them silent and glowering. The more he sulked and glowered, the more feverishly Judith laughed and joked. The smell of whiskey, that powerful stimulant of the male propensities, was strong on the breath of both the young men, and was in a great measure responsible for Bob's animation and Jerry's sullenness. Judith, however, was not intoxicated, and did not know enough about the effect of alcohol to make it an excuse for her husband's behavior. Under her levity there lurked a growing spirit of quite sober and very cold appraisal.

When they reached the place where Nip and the cart were waiting, the young horse trader had come back and was busy greasing his wagon and making other preparations for pulling out. He looked at Judith again but not quite so boldly, out of respect for her husband's presence.

Obeying that magnetism which draws people of the same sex together, the three men gathered in a little knot beside the trader's wagon and began to talk about horses, saddles, and guns. Judith went over to the woman, who had spread a gunny sack on the grass and was sitting on it mending one of her little girl's dresses, and they began to talk of babies, of cooking, and patterns for pieced bedquilts.

As the woman prattled scarcely heeded at her side, Judith felt stirring strongly within her a deep exaltation. The break in the deadening monotony of her days had affected her like a strong stimulant and she was keenly alive to things, tasting deliciously the full savor of life. She had forgotten her irritation at Jerry. All her perceptions seemed strangely sharpened. Her eyes took delight in noting niceties of tone and line and color, things for which she had no words but which were becoming with each year of mental growth more pregnant with suggestion.

She was so taken up with the delight of gazing about that she hardly noticed that Joe Barnaby had passed by and beckoned Jerry away, probably for the purpose of some further communion of spirits over the bar. Still less did she observe that after Jerry's departure the two men beside the covered wagon looked several times in her direction and dropped their voices to a very low tone. The trader's wife prattled on.

Suddenly and quite without warning, the whole scene went black before her. Against this blackness certain words stood out bright red. Her ear had caught only these few words; but they made the meaning of the whole sentence just spoken by Bob Crupper quite unmistakable.

When the black melted and she could see again, she felt herself tingling all over as if pricked by a million needles. She looked sidewise at the trader's wife to see if she had heard. The woman was running on about how hard it was to keep children in garters, too busy with her own chatter to notice anything said by anybody else. Judith knew that she was spared this much at least. She got up, made a stammered excuse about something that she had forgotten to buy, and almost ran from the hateful place.

She did not go toward the town, but in the direction of the deserted back streets. Among these she walked, at first with feverish haste, stumbling over clods and stones; then more slowly, as her rage and burning sense of insult subsided into dejection and misery. As she walked, she went over certain things in her mind. She saw Bob Crupper and Luke Wolf standing in easy attitudes by the spring wagon down in Hat's hollow. Bob said something to Luke, who turned and looked at her, and the two men fell to laughing together. She remembered certain looks from Luke that she had accidentally caught while they were stripping tobacco. She could see his little pig eyes squinting at her above his fat red cheeks. She called to mind all the details of Bob's visit to the house in the hollow. She remembered other things: whispers, looks, dark sayings that she had thought nothing of at the time; but that now flashed out of the past with vivid and sinister significance. She saw again the looks of the people that she had met on the street that afternoon while walking beside Bob. They were all too clearly explained by these few words that her ear had inadvertently caught and that now seemed to be burnt into her brain. It was the talk of the neighborhood, then; and there was only one person who could have betrayed the secret. It was desperately hard for her to force herself to this conclusion; but she made herself admit that it was the only one possible. That spirit in her which gave her eyes their level, searching look, which made her see through the flimsy shams and hypocrisies and self-deceptions of the people about her, forced her to look at her own situation with the same undeviating gaze.

She wandered about through sleepy, grass-grown back streets and lanes drowsing in the hot afternoon sunshine and deserted as a graveyard. She met nobody but an old man hobbling with the aid of two crutches. She had a feeling that the old man looked at her as if he knew and blushed furiously when she accidentally met his eye.

She took no note of the passing of time, and did not see that the shadows had begun to grow long, when she heard Jerry's voice anxiously calling her name and immediately after saw him appear around the corner of a fence.

"Hey, Judy! What the devil?" In his tone was the irritation which follows upon relieved anxiety. "Where you bin a-hidin' to? I bin a-lookin' all over taown fer you. I was beginnin' to think sumpin'd happened you."

Without waiting an instant, she turned upon him and accused him of what he had done. Even while she accused him, she felt herself buoyed up by a quite unreasonable hope that he would be able to deny her charge. The sight of him had for the moment restored her confidence in him. The moment, however, was a short one. Instantly she saw by his face that it was true, unbelievably but inexorably true. He stood before her sheepish, contrite and ashamed.

"Why did you do it?"

She flashed the words at him as if each one was a sword.

"Judy, I was drunk. It happened a long time ago, afore we was married; an' it was about the one time in my life I bin drunk enough not to keep my tongue in my head. Even so I could a bit it off soon's I'd said it."

She turned without a word and started to walk back toward the town. Disgust, like an avalanche of dirty dish water, put out the clear flame of her anger. The one thought left in her mind was that she was going back only because she had to go where the baby was. Jerry came up beside her and tried to take her hand; but she snatched it away and put it behind her back.

"Judy, it ain't sech a *dreadful* thing," he pleaded. "Course I hadn't otta done it, an' I wouldn't if I hadn't been drunk. But if you knowed haow most men is, an' haow they brag about everything like that, an' oftentimes when there hain't a bit o' truth in it, you wouldn't think so hard of me for one little slip."

He went on in this way, stumblingly trying to convince her that he was not a monster. But his pleadings fell on deaf ears, hard, young, intolerant ears that had learned from life no principles of judgment, yet were all too eager to judge. It was impossible for Jerry, out of his small experience of life and with the few words at his command, to tell her how deeply rooted in the young male is the urge to publish abroad his sexual achievements. She felt only that he was low, vile, and contemptible, no better than his cronies, the drunken young loafers whom he had, with such an unspeakable lack of delicacy, taken into his confidence, and who had been busy ever since rolling her secret on their dirty tongues. She loathed the whole odious pack of them, Jerry more than the rest. She walked on beside him silent and cold, without answering a word. Being able to make no impression on her with his pleading, Jerry too fell into sullen silence, musing on how hard she was. He felt chilled by a feeling that she was far away, that she did not belong to him, that she never had and never would belong to him as he did to her. A bitter feeling of estrangement and mutual distrust grew out of the silence like a dividing wall.

Turning the corner, they came upon Uncle Sam talking to

Joe Barnaby and holding the bridle of a stolid, heavily built plow horse, not over young, but healthy and tough looking and apparently good for many more years of useful labor.

"What's went with the purty mare?" asked Jerry, trying with poor success to make his voice sound natural.

"She's changed hands, bless her shapely carcass," laughed Uncle Sam. "This here is one time when the old man was trimmed good, Jerry. After I left here, I took her over to John Hornby, the blacksmith, to git her shod, an' he ses to me:

" 'Sam,' ses he, 'you're jes about the eleventh sucker that's brought me that there mare to hev her shod through this past winter an' spring. I'd jes as leave steal stovewood out'n a widder's back yard, Sam, as charge yuh money to put shoes on the feet o' that there animal.'

" 'What's wrong with her?' I asks, anxious like.

" 'What's wrong with her is she hain't no good fer nothin' whatever. She's track horse stock, but I wouldn't back her agin a mud turtle. She's part paralyzed in them there front legs. Everybody buys her thinks she's footsore; but after they've kep her a spell they find she's got a footsoreness that don't wear off. She's a purty animal an' it's a pity she's that way. But that's the way she is.'

" 'Thanks, John,' I ses. 'I allus knowed you wuz a friend o' mine.' An' I leads the mare away.

"Twa'n't twenty minutes after I'd left the blacksmith's shop afore I had her traded fer this feller. He hain't no beauty, an' he hain't no fancy saddle hoss; but he's a hoss I kin use on my place. An' when I hain't got use fer him, I kin allus trade him easy. He's a good, solid, dependable beast, hain't you, Dobbin?"

He patted the horse's gray neck affectionately.

The sun was beginning to slant low in the sky, and a cool late afternoon breeze had sprung up. Carts and buggies and spring wagons rattled through the streets on their way toward the open country; and horsemen cantered past them, going in the same direction. Uncle Sam mounted his plow horse and with a farewell wave of the hand trotted ponderously away with the rest of the procession.

Jerry and Judith followed in the cart. As they passed through Main Street they were greeted by pervasive scents of stale beer and whiskey. The ground was littered with lunch wrappings, egg and peanut shells, and banana skins. The crowd had thinned out. Most of the family parties had already started for home; and of the unattached males who remained some were reeling and lurching about the sidewalk noisy with drunken laughter and ribaldry, others stood propped up against a hydrant or a telegraph pole, portentously solemn and self-important, arguing in declamatory fashion with companions as ridiculously drunk as themselves. Here and there a little knot had formed about men who were quarreling over some fancied grievance, their angry voices rising harsh and ominous as the whiskey seethed in their fuddled brains and they strode threateningly nearer each other and gripped the handles of the revolvers in their pockets.

Through the hubbub of this sordid bacchanalia the young couple drove in cold and sullen aloofness and passed out into the heavy silence of the country.

CHAPTER XIV

JERRY had a fine bed of tobacco plants that year and together he and Judith set out four acres. Now that the baby was weaned, Judith could leave him with Luella or Aunt Mary while she worked in the field. Her help was badly needed this year, for Jerry had no money left to pay a hired hand. She was glad to do this, for even setting tobacco was a change from the dreary sameness of the household. At a cost of oozing rivers of sweat, of untellable weariness, stiffness, lame backs, and aching necks and hands worn almost to bleeding, the four acres were set at last and they sighed with relief.

"Naow if there on'y comes a good rain," said Jerry, "they'll git a start."

But the good rain did not come. Day after day the sky was cloudless, the flame of the sun clear and hot. Day after day the hard clay hillsides baked harder and the tobacco plants shrank into themselves, turned from green to gray, from gray to brown, shriveled and dried up and blew away in dust.

"Gawd, hain't it discouragin'!" Jerry would say, looking darkly at the clear, blue expanse of sky.

At last it rained. It rained all day and all night; and the next day the "season" was on.

With the infinite patience of those who have to humor the caprices of nature in order to wrest a living from the earth, they went over the whole four acres once more. Jerry had kept his tobacco bed well watered and there were plenty of plants.

"Bejasus, if Luke had stole 'em this time," he said to Judith, "I'd a gone daown there an' bust his jaw fer him. On'y reason he didn't steal 'em, he made his bed clost by a spring this year an' he's got lots of his own."

More than two thirds of the plants were dead and had to be replaced.

"They're a bit late," commented Jerry, "but if the season's
187

any good, they'll grow into good terbaccer yet. It don't take terbaccer long to make itsse'f."

It rained several times through June and the plants began to spread out green and lusty. Then with July the weather turned dry again and intensely hot. The clay hillsides baked harder than ever, so hard that the clods were more like stones than lumps of dried earth. Jerry, in an attempt to save his crop by making cultivation take the place of rain, went through his corn and tobacco again and again with the cultivator, then followed the rows of tobacco with his great sharp hoe, loosening up the ground around each plant. Judith tried to help him at this task but had to give it up. The ground was too flinty, the hoe too heavy; and the sickness of pregnancy which was coming upon her for the second time made her arms weak and nerveless.

No rain fell during July; and in blinding light and blazing heat August set in. It seemed to Jerry, who anxiously watched the sky, as though nature, not content with defrauding him out of the fruit of his labors, was amusing herself by making a fool of him and playing with him as a cat plays with a mouse. Sometimes the sky would grow overcast and all the signs of approaching rain appear, only to be swept away with the next wind. Occasionally even a light shower would fall, enough to partly lay the dust and irritate the anxious tobacco growers. Then the sky would clear again. Often they would see it raining on the horizon, over near Cynthiana or Georgetown or up toward Cincinnati. But no rain fell to refresh their own thirsty fields. Sometimes on hot afternoons great black storm clouds gathered in the west and rolled up into the sky, then passed away obliquely and disappeared toward the south. Through the heavy, sultry night, when it was hard to get to sleep, heat lightning played incessantly around the horizon. This long continued strain of watching for rain and seeing it approach only to go away again began to wear on the nerves of both Jerry and Judith. They became touchy and irritable and snapped at each other over trifling matters.

Judith tried to keep her garden alive by frequent hoeings.

But with the increasing heat and drought it wilted and withered up till there was nothing left but a few dried stalks. They had the milk from their cow, some salt meat left over from the winter before and some dried beans. These with corn meal cakes and coffee made up their daily fare.

By the middle of August wells and cisterns were getting low. and springs and streams were drying up. Some of these latter were already bone dry, with the hoofprints of the cattle that used to drink in them baked hard into the flinty clay. Water for stock was growing scarce. The Blackfords' well was dropping lower every day, and Jerry, afraid that it might go dry altogether, would not let Judith use any of the precious water for washing clothes. When wash day came, he would hook up Nip or Tuck to the cart and drive her and the baby and the tubs and the bundle of clothes to a spring further down the hollow where water was still to be had. The spring was low and the scant water fouled by the feet of cattle; but it had to serve. Here he had put up a rude bench on which to set the tubs, and here, as there was now nothing for him to do in the field, he would help Judith to rub and rinse the clothes through the muddy water and spread them on the grass to dry, while the baby crawled about through the wild weed jungle and grasped with his helpless, chubby hands at butterflies and flecks of sunlight.

These little excursions were not picnics, as they might have been under more favorable conditions. The failure of their crops had cast a gloom upon the young couple which was deepened by the change that had come over Judith. The debilitating effect of the long continued heat added to the nausea and nervous irritability of an unwelcome pregnancy had induced in her a state of body and mind in which, in order to endure life at all, she instinctively closed herself up from it as much as she could. With something of the feeling of a creature of the woods, she sought to shut herself up with her weakness and misery. She plodded through the round of her daily tasks like an automaton. Even to the lifting of an eyelid, she made no motion that was not necessary. Her feet dragged, her eyes seemed as if covered by a film and her face wore a heavy, sullen expression. She avoided meeting people, answered them in monosyllables when they spoke to her, and took no interest whatever in the doings of the neighborhood. When Jerry tried to talk to her, she scarcely looked at him or answered him, until, chilled by her lack of response, he too would fall into gloomy silence. Sometimes when Jerry, in his inexperience with the washing of clothes, did something particularly clumsy and awkward, she would scold him sharply then relapse into her habitual impassivity. When the clothes were dried and gathered up, they rode home in silence, Jerry driving, Judith holding the baby on her lap.

Beat upon by the fierce heat and the hard, white light, the face of the country took on every day more of the appearance of drought. Each day vegetation shrank and the exposed surface of bare, caked earth increased. Corn dwindled and yellowed and bluegrass turned dry and brown. The alfalfa stretched its deep roots far down into the soil and managed to keep its rich dark green color, but grew never an inch. The roads lay under a thick coating of this fine powdery dust, soft as velvet to bare feet. When a wagon or buggy passed along it traveled hidden from sight by its own dust and left a diminishing trail behind like a comet. Hens held their wings out from their bodies and panted in the deepest shade of the barnyard. In the pastures cattle and sheep stood all day under trees; and even horses rarely ventured forth into the full glare of the sun. In the evening when the sun slanted low and a grateful coolness stole across the fields, all these creatures, like their human brothers, shook off the torpor of the heat and began to feel more like themselves. The hens scratched for a living among the chaff and dung. The sheep and cattle, banded together after their kind and with their heads all turned in one direction, cropped the scant bluegrass. The horses, aristocrats of the pasture, went apart by themselves, scorning the company of these humbler creatures.

The tobacco plants, owing to their sturdy weed nature, lived through the heat and drought; but they might as well have died, for their leaves were as thin as paper. By the middle of August the tobacco growers, including even Jerry, had given up all hope of getting a crop that year.

With the failure of their crops, every day became Sunday for the men; and they began to visit in each other's barnyards. Different degrees of success, with the inevitable accompaniment of work, self-seeking, greed, jealousy, and disappointment, would have divided them. But the universal bad luck brought them into community of spirit and ushered in an era of neighborliness and good feeling. Lounging on the shady side of each other's barns, whittling aimlessly at bits of stick, chewing straws and tobacco, the men talked about the springs that had gone dry and those that were going dry, inquired about the state of each other's wells and cisterns, and complained about how far they had to drive their cattle to water. They compared notes on the subject of prickly heat and other skin rashes, and talked of the hotness of beds at night. Uncle Jabez Moorhouse quoted copiously from his one book on the subject of drought, a favorite topic with the prophets, and all the old men called to mind former dry years, citing chapter and verse as to the exact date of the arid year, the time the drought began and the number of weeks it had lasted. The calendar for the past fifty years was thoroughly gone over from this point of view and each dry year carefully compared in all respects with the current one. There was matter here for much discussion and argument among the older men, their memories often telling stories that were widely at variance with each other.

The first days of August brought news that sent a buzz of excitement through the groups of barnyard loungers. Although there was no newspaper to carry it, this news flashed rapidly into even the innermost recesses of Scott County. The most unschooled tobacco grower living in the loneliest hollow did not have to wait long for its arrival. The more advanced and intellectual, who subscribed to a religious or agricultural monthly, got the tidings long before the next issue of their magazine was dropped in the rural mail box. The magic word *war* is powerfully and swiftly winged and scorns modern methods of broadcasting. Standing about the coldly monumental August stove, the loiterers in Peter Akers' store spat into last winter's sawdust and talked over the news that the Cincinnati-Lexington train had brought. Driving homeward in their several directions, they pulled up alongside of every passing wagon.

"Hey, d'yuh know there's a big war on?"

At home they told their wives, their neighbors, everybody who passed by the house.

Having done this, they had, however, told all they knew. The words Germans, French, Russians, floated about in the air, but to most of the tobacco growers meant nothing whatever except that the war was a long way off. There was, however, a general realization that it was a big one, that somewhere far away the world was in great turmoil and excitement. The outermost ripples of this excitement shivered through Scott County.

The women inquired anxiously as to the likelihood of their sons and husbands having to go to war. Their fears relieved on this vital point, they poohhooed the whole matter and went on about their housework, instantly transferring their attention to matters of real importance, such as the rendering out of hog fat and the patching of overalls.

"It's ridiclus," said Aunt Abigail, on one of her visits to Judith, "the idee o' them folks a-goin' to fightin' each other. It's a shame an' a disgrace an' it'd otta be put a stop to. Even if they air on'y ignernt furrin folks, they'd otta know better."

To the men it was meat and drink. When they gathered in each other's barnyards, the talk was all of war. To sit in the peaceful warmth of a summer afternoon, placidly chewing the mild Burley of their own fields and express their views about the fighting of the foreigners was a rare treat, combining luxuriously the thrills and excitements of war with the comfort and security of peace. They had virtually no basis upon which to form opinions; but opinions they had, none the less. They were as excitable, argumentative, and dogmatic as any group of men in any other walk of life. Each man held his own convictions in as high esteem and those of his neighbor in as thorough despisal as if he were a successful manufacturer of toothpaste or a United States senator. The discussions on the war were as animated, as heated, as intelligent, and as generally representative of the different types of male humanity as if they had occurred in a metropolitan club. The fact that on the shady side of Jerry Blackford's cowshed the basis of fact was somewhat more vague and flimsy than that in a Union League clubroom made no essential difference. Each man aired his own ideas as loudly and impressively as he could, and paid no attention whatever to those of any of the others; and there was much honest joy and satisfaction.

"They'd otta have us fellers go on over there an' beat 'em all up. We cud do it easy," opined Ziemer Whitmarsh, who had a prominent chin and the long arms and heavy shoulders of a prize fighter. " 'Twouldn't be no chore fer us, would it, Bob?"

"No, siree," chimed in young Bob Crupper. "They'd otta let us at 'em." Bob's chin did not protrude unduly; but he had eyes fearless and dreamy, like those of his father. He was ripe for adventure of any kind: war, women, anything. His eyes wistfully sought the horizon.

"I wish 'twa'n't so durn fur away," he fretted.

Bob's father, old Amos, who was a veteran of the Civil War, had subscribed to a Georgetown paper, and was thus placed in a position of authority as regards facts. But it was the romantic and chivalrous aspects of the war that most appealed to the old soldier, as in the days of his youth; and out of his rich nature he was quick to set up heroes to worship and weave a mythical fabric of glory and chivalry.

"Some o' them generals must be powerful men," he would thunder out in a deep rumble of bass ecstasy. "This here von Kluck, he must be a mighty powerful man. An' the Roosians is a fine people, a strong, powerful people. Them Roosians hain't afraid to die fer their country."

"It'll fetch up the price of tebaccer," mused Uncle Sam Whitmarsh, sagely stroking his lean jaw, "—an' hosses. Terbaccer and hosses is things they used up fast in war. An' terbaccer an' hosses is what we got here in Kentucky. An' everything else'll go up too: hog meat and butter and eggs."

"Yaas, an' flour an' sorghum an' coffee alongside of 'em," grunted old Jonah Cobb pessimistically. "I mind me in Civil War times— "

"Aw, don't croak, Jonah. War times is good times fer the farmer. If we kin git a good price for our terbaccer, we hain't a-goin' to kick about payin' a little extry fer a sack o' biscuit flour."

"A sound of battle is in the land and of great destruction," quoted Uncle Jabez Moorhouse. "Woe onto them, for their time is come, the time of their visitation. The earth shall be utterly emptied and utterly laid waste. Behold, Jehovah maketh the earth empty and maketh it waste and turneth it upside down and scattereth abroad the inhabitants thereof. The earth shall stagger like a drunken man."

He loved the sound of the sonorous rhythms and rolled them on his tongue ecstatically.

"I done heard it was a-coming' this way," hazarded Gus Dibble timorously. "Did any o' you folks hear it was a-comin' this way? If it comes this way, they say we'll all hev to go into it."

Gus Dibble was a skinny, pallid fellow with very bad teeth. He had a wife and two small children and tried to raise tobacco to support them. He also had consumption, asthma, and a hernia.

"Aw, what kind of a notion hev you got, Gus?" scoffed Bob Crupper, who from association with his father had become enlightened. "Don't you know you gotta go acrost the ocean to git to where they're a-fightin'?"

"I dunno," answered Gus, humbly and vaguely. "All I know is they said it was a-comin' this way."

For Judith Blackford and the rest of the women in the solitude of their isolated shanties life moved on as stagnantly as usual, except that the heat and the scarcity of water made it somewhat more disagreeable and difficult. For them there was no such thing as change nor anything even vaguely resembling a holiday season. Families must be fed after some fashion or other and dishes washed three times a day, three hundred and sixty-five days in the year. Babies must be fed and washed and dressed and "changed" and rocked when they cried and watched and kept out of mischief and danger. The endless wrangles among older children must be arbitrated in some way or other, if only by cuffing the ears of both contestants; and the equally endless complaints stilled by threats, promises, whatever lies a harassed mother could invent to quiet the fretful clamor of discontented childhood. Fires must be lighted and kept going as long as needed for cooking, no matter how great the heat. Cows must be milked and cream skimmed and butter churned. Hens must be fed and eggs gathered and the filth shoveled out of henhouses. Diapers must be washed, and grimy little drawers and rompers and stiff overalls and sweaty work shirts and grease-bespattered dresses and kitchen aprons and filthy, sour-smelling towels and socks stinking with the putridity of unwashed feet and all the other articles that go to make up a farm woman's family wash. Floors must be swept and scrubbed and stoves cleaned and a never ending war waged against the constant encroaches of dust, grease, stable manure, flies, spiders, rats, mice, ants, and all the other breeders of filth that are continually at work in country households. These activities, with the occasional variation of Sunday visiting, made up the life of the women, a life that was virtually the same every day of the year, except when their help was needed in the field to set tobacco or shuck corn, or when fruit canning, hog killing, or house cleaning crowded the routine.

Late in August, when the tobacco and corn were past saving, the rains came in floods and filled up the wells and cisterns, set the creeks to running again, washed great gullies in the plowed hillsides and refreshed the thirsty pastures.

There followed a lean fall and winter. There was no corn to fatten hogs; so the tenant farmers had to get rid of what hogs they had. The hogs, being lean and forced upon the market, brought only a poor price. The stunted, half filled out nubbins that the corn fields had produced that year were all carefully saved to make into meal for household use. The hens, too, had to go; for hens are too greedy-natured to keep through a time of scarcity. Jerry bundled them into a coop and took them to Clayton and sold them for thirty-five cents apiece, all but a dozen or so which Judith insisted upon keeping "for company," as she expressed it. These scratched and ranged for a living, and kept alive, though they laid never an egg.

Jerry dug his potatoes, most of them not much bigger than marbles, a slow and disheartening task; and Judith cooked them, while they lasted, with the skins on, so that no part of them might be wasted. They were greenish and bitter; but when they were all gone they were sorely missed. The few dried beans and peas that had managed to come to fruit before the dry spell caught them were carefully pulled and shelled and stored away. Hickory nuts and black walnuts were gathered and spread out on the floor of the loft to dry. There were no blackberries that year and only a few stunted apples. Jerry searched through the woods looking for stray apple trees that had sprung up from seed, and brought home an occasional bushel or so of wormy runts. These Judith made up into apple butter which she stored away in crocks and jars.

By January all these things were gone and there was nothing left but some corn.

Work by the day was hard to get; for there were many more men than jobs, and would continue so until the spring rush came on. Jerry fretted at his forced idleness and was always on the watch for a chance to earn a day's wages. When he managed to pick up an occasional job, he bought flour for biscuits, canned salmon or a piece of bacon. Then there was a feast royal. These feasts, however, were widely scattered oases on a great desert of corn meal. This had to be eaten without milk; for there was not much food for the cow, and the small amount of milk she gave was all taken by the baby.

Judith was big with her second child. She had recovered from the sickness of early pregnancy and regained some of her old health and spirits. Grown accustomed perforce to the life made necessary by the baby, she chafed less at the monotony and restrictions of the household. But she was no longer the Judith that Jerry had married. The year and a half since the birth of the baby, which had made no noticeable change in Jerry, had left their print upon her. The youthful curves of her face and body were still there; the youthful color was in her cheeks in spite of the spare diet. But her body had lost its elasticity, her eyes their light and sparkle. The buoyancy and effervescence of youth were gone. It was as if the life spirit in the still young body had grown tired. She rarely sang any more, and was not often heard to laugh. Sometimes, in a feverish burst of gaiety, she would romp uproariously with the baby and seem for a little while like a child again. Then all at once she would let her arms fall at her sides as though suddenly tired and go about her work a little more soberly than before. Sometimes she would sit for a long time abstractedly looking out of the window at the sweep of hillside lined against the sky and take no notice that the baby was crying or tugging at her dress with his strong little fists or eating out of the dog's plate on the floor. Then she would rouse herself with a start, as though shaking something from her, and go on about her sweeping or washing or whatever she had to do.

One Saturday night in late February, the Blackford's door was flung open and Jabez Moorhouse stalked across the floor and stood warming himself by the stove. Snow was falling outside and his cloth cap and broad, stooping shoulders were powdered with white. He loosened the ragged gray woolen muffler that was knotted about his neck and beat the snow from his mittens on the side of the woodbox.

"The wind's sholy keen to-night," he said, spreading out his big hands over the grateful warmth of the stove. "It goes through clothes that hain't none too new like that much tissue paper. 'Tain't no night to be a-travelin' the roads. But I come on a special errand. I want you two and the young un to come over to my place to-morrer long about 'leven o'clock.

There's a-goin' to be a s'prise party. Now I gotta be a-gittin' on, 'cause there's others I wanta bid. To-morrer 'bout 'leven, or any time in the forenoon fer that matter. The earlier the welcomer. Don't say nothin' to nobody."

He was gone, with a significant parting smile and wink; and Jerry and Judith looked at each other in astonishment. Behind him he had left an air of mystery, of wonder, and surmise.

"A s'prise party," mused Jerry. "What the devil has Uncle Jabez got to make a s'prise party with? He hain't had no work this winter."

"We'll go an' see anyway," said Judith, a glow in her cheeks. Breaking thus unexpectedly into the dull monotony of their lives, the suddenness and mystery of the invitation thrilled her with excitement.

Next morning, when they arrived at the little shanty behind the big hemlock trees, Judith was surprised to find her father and Uncle Sam Whitmarsh standing talking together just outside the kitchen door where two walls meeting at right angles formed a sheltered nook, pleasantly warmed by the midday winter sun.

"What *you* a-doin' here, Dad?"

"I dunno yet, Judy," answered Bill. "I seem to be a-waitin."

Judith pushed open the door and stepped inside, the baby on her arm. She was greeted by a smell, an all-pervading, ineffable, intoxicating smell, the most delicious aroma that ever set a hungry mouth to watering. As she eagerly sniffed the savory odor, she felt a soft, pleasurable, almost erotic sensation tingle through her body, and her lips curved into a smile, such a smile as might have answered a lover's kiss.

"Looky here, Judy, my gal."

Jabez opened the oven door, which had lost its handle and had to be operated by means of a pair of pliers, and drew toward the front of the oven two large sizzling pans, one on the oven floor, the other above it on the grating. As she looked at these pans and sniffed the appetizing smell that steamed up from them, Judith felt once more creeping over her body he same soft, pleasurable, almost erotic sensation and her lips fell again into that smile which might have answered a lover's kiss. In each pan was a large, upcurving mass, delicately brown, casting up a savory steam and oozing succulent juices into the rich, bubbling gravy beneath. With a big tin spoon Jabez lifted this steaming essence from the bottom of the pan and poured it over the big brown mounds. Some of it penetrated into the meat; some trickled appetizingly down the sides and back into the gravy pool.

"Is it near done, Uncle Jabez?"

There was a strained tenseness in the question.

"You damn betcha. We'll be a-lightin' into it afore ten minutes is past. The Bible says the full belly loathes the honeycomb; but to the hungry every bitter thing is sweet. So I reckon them two hind quarters'll slide daown kinder easy."

Uncle Jonah Cobb, who had been pacing up and down the floor, stopped at the arresting word *honey* and looked disappointed when nothing further was said about it.

"They don't do good 'ithout salt," he mumbled to himself, continuing his walk.

Corn cakes were frying on the top of the stove. The big table, roughly made of unplaned pine boards, was drawn into the middle of the room; and Jabez had unearthed from somewhere a tablecloth that had once been white. It was yellowed from long lying away and much creased and crumpled. But it was a tablecloth, and as such suggestive of feasts and holidays. With a strange assortment of broken handled knives and forks and cracked and crazed plates, the table was set for eight.

The overpowering aroma, acting upon the intensity of her craving appetite, affected Judith like a drug which makes the near and real seem vague and far away. She had afterwards a dim recollection of people moving restlessly about, striding up and down the floor and asking if it was time to sit down. But she hardly realized what was going on about her until she found herself seated at the table. Silently as if they had sprung out of the earth, Uncle Jonah and Aunt Selina were found sitting

opposite her. Uncle Sam Whitmarsh was at her right hand and
Jerry at her left. Her father and Uncle Amos Crupper were
at the other end of the table.

Jabez brought one of the big roasting pans and setting it
down at his end of the table on top of a piece of pine board
began to carve. It must have been that all the others seated
there felt like herself; for they seemed rapt and taken out of
themselves as though they were religious devotees assisting
at some sacred rite. There was a tense look in every face and
every eye gleamed and glittered. Judith thought she had
never seen such a light in any eyes before. She had seen the
light of love, of anger, of jealousy shining from people's eyes.
But such expressions were weak and volatile compared with
this. It was a look that expressed something more basic than
anger, more enduring than love, more all-compelling than
jealousy. The eyes were all fixed steadily upon one object, the
roasting pan at Jabez' end of the table. The silence was tense
with ravenous expectancy.

As each guest was served, he fell to eating, without waiting
for the others. Those who were still waiting began to shift
uneasily in their chairs, while their eyes ranged restlessly from
the diminished hind quarter to the plates of their more fortunate neighbors.

At last everybody was eating and Jabez filled his own plate
and fell upon the contents. A silence followed, broken only
by the crackle of the fire and the click of the knives and forks.
In a patch of sunlight on the floor the baby sat and played
with a skunk skin that Jabez was saving to make into a cap.
"Ki-ki, ki-ki, nice ki-ki," he kept saying, as he stroked the
soft fur. When a large cat walked out from behind the stove,
purring and arching her back, he forsook the skin for the
living animal.

A heaping plate of corn cakes was set at each end of the
table, from which the guests helped themselves at their will.
These, with the meat, formed the whole meal.

For a long time no voice spoke, no eye was lifted. There
was nothing but the play of knives and forks, the sound of

munching, and the constant reaching out of hands toward the corn cakes.

It was only when the second hind quarter had been carved, served, and partly eaten that the diners began to lift their eyes from their plates, lean back in their chairs, and exchange occasional remarks.

Coffee, which had been boiling on the stove in a big granite stewpan, was now served by Jabez in whatever utensils he could find. Judith got hers in a jelly glass. Aunt Selina had a granite mug, Jerry a tin cup. Uncle Jonah was honored with a large, imposing, and very substantial mustache cup ornamented with pink roses tastefully combined with pale blue true lovers' knots and bearing the legend "Father" in large gilt letters.

Down at the far end of the table, Judith glimpsed her father's familiar habit of turning a spoon over in his mouth. He liked to soak his corn cakes in coffee and eat them with a teaspoon. He put the spoon in his mouth in the usual way and invariably brought it out bottom side up.

When Jabez had served everybody else, he used the dipper to hold his own portion of coffee; and holding it aloft by the long handle, he stood up at the end of the table and rapped for attention.

"Neighbors," he began, "I wish I might give youall sumpin' better'n coffee to drink a toast in. But this here's a dry year. I never reckoned the winter'd come that I'd spend 'ithout a drop o' whiskey on the shelf. But this is that winter. The Bible says that he that tilleth the soil shall have plenty o' bread; an' anybody'd think he'd otta. But you an' me knows, none better, that he don't allus have plenty o' bread, an' still less o' meat. Another thing the Bible says is that the poor man is hated even of his own neighbor; an' I reckon there's heap more truth in that sayin' than in the other one. The earth's a mean an' stingy stepmother, an' she makes the most of her stepchillun pretty mean an' stingy too. A hard life makes 'em hard an' close an' suspicious of each other. They cheat an' they git cheated, an' oftener'n not they hate their neighbors. But if a hard life breeds hates, it breeds likin's too; an' it's because youall is folks that I'm praoud to call my friends, that I ast you to come here to-day. Friends, let's drink a toast to the health of our landlord an' neighbor, Uncle Ezry Pettit. This here is his treat."

A perceptible tremor went around the table. Everybody started slightly and looked half apprehensively at everybody else to see how they took it; then at the door as if Uncle Ezra might be expected to appear there at any moment and claim his property. Uncle Sam Whitmarsh chuckled into his tin mug. Uncle Amos Crupper held his cup poised half way between the table and his lips, deliberate, thoughtful, turning it over in his mind. Judith, glancing sidewise at Jerry, saw a look of shock pass across his face and felt a disturbing aura of disapproval suddenly surround him. But he went on eating.

"Haow did yuh come to git away with her, Jabez?"

It was her father asking the question. He tried to make his voice sound off-handed, but it had a strained, unnatural sound.

"Waal, Bill, it was this way. Friday evenin' on towards night I was a-comin' home raound by the back of Uncle Ezry's old terbaccer barn; an' there she stud caught in the wire fence. I was jes' fixin' to pull her aout, when it come over me all of a sudden haow good she'd eat. After that idear'd took a holt of me, I jes' didn't hev the heart to turn her loose. I tuk a good look all raound, an' there wa'n't a soul to be seen on hill ner holler. It come into my mind haow Abraham when he wanted sumpin to offer up to the Lord fer a burnt offerin', faound a ram caught in the thicket. An' I ses to myse'f a wire fence was jes as good as a thicket any day fer ketchin' sech critters, an' mos' likely I needed the ewe more'n Abraham did the ram. So I jes hit her a whack atween the eyes with the hammer I was a-carryin'. She dropped like a sack o' meal, an' I drug her into the brush. Come dark night I went an' fetched her; an' here she is. She was a fat ewe."

"She was that," assented Uncle Sam Whitmarsh, wiping the grease from his mouth with his pocket handkerchief.

"Waal, I reckon Uncle Ezry won't die in the county house

fer lack of her," opined Bill in the tone of one who has justi-
fied himself to his conscience. "Gawd, there hain't nothin'
like a good meal o' meat to make a feller feel like a man agin.
I didn't have no idear I was that meat hungry till I smelt her
a-roastin'. Then wild hosses wouldn't 'a' helt me back. It
sholy feels good to have yer belly well lined."

Bill sighed, stretched out his long legs luxuriously, and
reached into his pocket for a chew of tobacco. The other men
pushed back their chairs and also sought their pockets. Aunt
Selina brought out her corn cob pipe from the pocket of her
patched skirt and filled it with swift, practised movements of
her small fingers. Having done so she approached Judith and
sitting down beside her plied her with questions about herself
and the baby.

All the time the old woman's bright, youthful brown eyes
sought Judith's face, as though trying to bridge the gulf of
years.

From a child, Judith had been fond of Aunt Selina. There
was something about her alert, birdlike, patched little person,
so frail and skinny, yet so full of a certain humming, quick
pulsating life that drew all children to her, as like is drawn
to like. For Aunt Selina, in spite of her years, her corn cob
pipe and her ability to spit like a man, was still more than half
a child. Judith's early liking for her had persisted through
the years; but to-day the old woman seemed a more than
usually attractive person. Judith answered all her questions
with great animation. She told all about the trouble the baby
had had cutting his teeth. She was enthusiastic over plans for
raising a big flock of chickens in the spring; and she discussed
exhaustively the relative merits of stripes, checks, sprays, spots,
and all over patterns in dress goods.

She scarcely knew what she was saying and could remember
almost nothing of it afterward. She only knew that she felt
warm, strong, happy, full of life and vigor, alive with interest
in everything. She seemed to be surrounded by a rosy mist
through which things appeared vague and somewhat removed
but replete with infinite possibilities for joy and achievement.

A small amount of alcohol would have had a similar effect. She was meat drunk. It was the second time in her life that she had tasted mutton.

The others seemed to be affected in much the same way. From about the stove where the men had collected came the sound of animated talk and of bold, assured, unrestrained laughter, such talk and laughter as were rarely heard in a tenant farmer's house except when whiskey was one of the guests. The language, however, out of deference to the two women present, was somewhat restrained and guarded.

"Mebbe you'll call to mind, Amos," Uncle Sam Whitmarsh was saying, "the day we helped tote Uncle Ezry's bar'l o' whiskey daown into his cellar. I reckon it's a good thirty-five year past; but it seems on'y like yestiddy to me. My haow time goes. There was you an' me, an' there was Ned Tyler that left here an' went over into Indianny an' there was Abner Sykes that's dead an' buried this thirty year. You mind that day, Amos?"

"Yaas, I mind that day, Sam; an' I mind well the heft o' that bar'l o' whiskey." Uncle Amos smiled reminiscently. "We was young men them days, Sam."

"Yaas, we was young, an' Ezry was young, an' he drunk a heap o' whiskey in them days afore he got so old he couldn't hold it no more. It was terbaccer harvest an' we was all there a-helpin' to cut. The bar'l come that mornin'. After dinner Ezry ses: 'Boys,' ses he, 'I wish you'd gimme a hand with this here bar'l afore you go back to field.'

"There stud the bar'l as big as a maounting; an' there stud the cellar steps, steep an' narrer. Ezry never so much as laid hand to it; he jes stud there an' told us what he wanted did. Waal, we four took a holt o' that there bar'l an' we tugged an' pulled an' wrestled an' strained an' sweat till we got her daown them steep narrer stairs. Then Ezry wa'n't satisfied with that; but he had to hev it put way back into the fur corner where it was dark an' cool. After we'd got her there an' blocks set under her to hold her level an' everything all shipshape, Ezry ses: 'Thanks, boys, you kin go naow.' An' we all troops back up the cellar stairs as dry as we come. I kin see the look on Abner Sykes' face to this day. He's dead an' gone, but that look is a-livin' yet. Yaas, he's got a close fist, has Ezry."

Judith, who had heard this story more than once before, felt herself dropping to sleep again and again. She would catch herself napping, straighten up with a sudden start and open her eyes very wide, only to fall into another doze. The sound of a snore roused her from one of these naps, and looking in the direction from which it had come, she saw that Uncle Jonah, sunk into the depths of an old rocking chair, had fallen fast asleep with his chin resting on his breast. The air in the room was close and heavy with Sunday afternoon dullness. Her eyelids kept falling over her eyes of their own weight. She longed with an intense physical craving to throw herself down somewhere—anywhere—and sleep, sleep, sleep.

Gradually the men stopped talking and lost interest in what their companions were saying. More and more they sagged in their chairs, their legs stretched out lazily toward the stove. Chins dropped, and the sound of muffled, fragmentary voices grew faint and far away. At length even these ceased, and only an occasional faint snore stirred the silence.

Judith was aroused by Jerry gently shaking her shoulder.

"Judy, Judy, it's near night an' time we was home. The baby's awake an' cryin'."

She roused herself with an effort and fetched the baby from the inner room where she had laid him on Jabez's bed. The others were all preparing to go, except Uncle Jonah and Aunt Selina, who still slept on peacefully.

"Leave 'em take their rest," said Jabez. "They hain't got nothin' to go home for."

As they were driving home, Jerry suddenly broke the silence.

"Uncle Jabez hadn't oughter of stole that ewe. I'm sorry I et any."

"But you kep' on a-eatin' after you knowed she was stole."

"Well, God damn it all, Judy, I was hungry."

"So was we all. So was Jabez when he knocked her in the head."

Her voice had a dry and final sound.

Jerry could find no words with which to express the complexity of his feelings. So he kept silence. From time to time he glanced sidewise at his wife with a look of uneasiness and mistrust. She gave him never a look, but sat staring straight in front of her over the baby's head. His mind stirred uneasily with a baffled, futile feeling, very disquieting to his male vanity, that she did not think it worth her while to discuss the matter with him. An intangible film which, ever since the Georgetown Court Day had been spreading itself between them, seemed to grow momently denser and more permanent in quality.

CHAPTER XV

I⊤ seemed that winter as if the spring would never come, as if there would never be an end to the arid routine of corn meal mush and coffee for breakfast, corn meal cakes and coffee for dinner, and coffee and corn meal cakes for supper. March dragged its weary length into what seemed more like a year than a month. February had been full of mild, springlike days, days of strengthening sun and greening grass that had cheered the hungry tenant farmers into hopes of an early spring. But March closed down grim and inexorable. Bitter winds blew all day under a cold, gray sky, a dead, frozen sky, all one blank, even tone of pale gray, dreary and disheartening. They dried up the tender grass that had been springing in sheltered places. They whirled the fine dust of dried clay about the barns and houses. They pierced like knife blades through worn-out underwear and sleazy cotton dresses and threadbare jackets and made the doing of barnyard chores a shrinking misery.

There were not many chores. Judith had only her cow to milk and care for and her hens to feed. Often, however, she had wood to chop; for Jerry was busy now with the spring plowing and was not so attentive to the woodpile as he had been during their first year together. When she had finished these chores, she fled back into the house as a woodchuck scuttled to the protection of his hole. The bitter, dust-laden wind seemed to suck the moisture from her skin and from her very bones. She felt as bleak, dry, desolate, and soulless as the landscape. Looking out of the little window at the bare garden patch where she had planted a few onion sets and some seed of lettuce and radishes, and which as yet showed no hint of green, she felt dismal, hungry, and hopeless.

During these last weeks of the winter, she grew daily paler and more listless. It was time for the baby to be born, and she was heavy with a great lethargy, as if the life within her, in its determination to persist, were slowly and steadily draining her, leaving her body nothing but a shell, a limp, nerveless, irritable, collapsing shell.

She understood now why snakes and woodchucks crawled into their holes in winter. She wished she had a hole to crawl into, a hole where there were no meals to cook, no fire to keep going, no fretful child to pacify—a nice, dark, quiet hole where nobody ever came and where she could curl up and be at peace.

Little Billy was a strong, stirring, loud-voiced, and self-willed child. Often when his clamorous demands became too much for her nerves, she would slap him savagely and force him to blubber into silence, gasping and choking and catching spasmodically at the heaving surges of breath that rose in him like tidal waves. He learned to be afraid of her in these moods and would sidle away and hide under the bed or behind the stove till the storm had passed, peering out at her with scared, watchful eyes, as a puppy watches the foot that has just kicked him. In such moments she hated them both, the born and the unborn, two little greedy vampires working on her incessantly, the one from without, the other from within, never giving her a moment's peace, bent upon drinking her last drop of blood, tearing out her last shrieking nerve.

Sometimes she would give way to one of these fits of irritation when Jerry was in the house; and he would rush to intervene and save the child.

"Why do you act so mean to the young un, Judy?" he would demand, his voice harsh with anger.

"Mebbe you'd act mean too if you was shet up with him all day long, like you was in a jail."

Her mouth set into hard lines, and her level brows contracted darkly.

When she said such things he always looked at her in a puzzled, hurt, and somewhat impatient way.

She no longer looked forward to Jerry's homecoming at night. When he came in from the day's plowing, tired but still ruddy and vigorous in spite of his diet of corn meal, she felt more dragged out and irritable than ever. Out of her own weakness and nervelessness she grew to hate his ability to relax, his aura of excess vitality, that strong, male vitality of which she was becoming the victim. After a day at the plow he could still whistle and sing, fling the baby to the ceiling or ride him on his back about the kitchen. His thoughtless, boyish good humor made her feel hard, bitter, and morose.

While he took his ease in the evenings, she went about the kitchen silently, fried the corn cakes, and made the coffee, washed the grime from the baby's hands and face, and fed his milk and corn cake. After they had eaten, she would wash the dishes and undress the baby and put him to bed. Then she would come back and sit by the little lamp darning socks or mending rompers or putting great, coarse patches on the knees of overalls.

Sometimes Jerry, looking at her under the light of the lamp and noting the tense, drawn look on her pale features, would fume within himself with impotent rage. He blamed it all on the lack of proper food. Things were in a hell of a mess, he told himself, when a man could work from sun-up to sundown and not be able to give his wife even the food she needed. He felt himself burning with a fierce anger against the order of things which prevented him from giving her anything she could ask for. He wanted to be the source of all good things for her and for her children; and here he was scarcely able to keep the breath in her body. It never for a moment occurred to him that she could ever want anything which he could not supply if he were only given a decent chance. Yes, he was placed in a nice hell of a hole, he told himself. But of course this was one year in a hundred. His corklike optimism reasserted itself. Everything would be all right as soon as the new crop came on.

In bed he would put his arm over her protectingly.

"Things'll be a heap better, Judy, soon's garden truck begins to grow."

And she would sigh lightly, glad of the comfort of the bed

and his warm, muscular arm, and fall into a deep, exhausted sleep.

It was on one of these bleak, windswept March days that the second baby was born, a surprisingly fat and healthy little boy, whom they named Andrew after Jerry's father. His health and vigor, however, had been obtained at the expense of his mother. For days after his birth she lay half unconscious, scarcely moving a finger, hardly lifting an eyelash.

"The girl must have nourishment," said Dr. MacTaggert. "Milk."

So Jerry scurried around and found where he could get a half gallon of milk a day without immediate payment; and at once she began to revive. He slaughtered one of the precious hens; Luella, who had come to take charge, made chicken broth which Judith sipped while the rest of the family gorged ravenously on the meat. The neighbors came bringing out of their great scarcity little delicacies for which in many cases their own mouths were watering: a pot of peach jam or a little jar of apple butter or a few new laid eggs. Aunt Selina brought a block of honey in the comb; and Jabez came carrying the first young onions and the first tender leaves of lettuce which he had grown under a window sash in a sheltered spot against his kitchen wall. To Judith, now rapidly growing stronger, these bits of green tasted better than anything else. Such succulence and flavor in the young onions! She had known every spring what it was to be hungry for green things; but young onions had never tasted so delicious before.

After the first half conscious days of exhaustion, she began to enjoy her convalescence. The strained tension of the long winter months was gone and already almost forgotten, and it was good to stretch luxuriously in bed and give way to the weakness which ignores all cares and responsibilities. Aunt Mary had taken little Billy over to stay with her. Luella was full of quiet competence. The new baby slept most of the time, and the house was still and orderly. Sunk in the utter relaxation that follows upon childbirth, she felt at first that there could be nothing more delicious than to lie motionless on her back and look lazily through the window at the slope of hillside, listen to the song of the returning birds, the cheerful cackle of the hens, the barking of the dog, and the subdued sounds made by Luella as she moved about quietly and adequately in the kitchen.

Soon, however, she grew restless with returning vitality and was glad to sit propped up with pillows and mend little Billy's clothes or sew on a dress for the new baby.

Sometimes she would ask Luella to bring her a pencil and a piece of paper; and using a pine shingle for a drawing board, she would amuse herself by sketching faces, some human, some animal, some half and half, as she had used to do when she was a little girl at school. Luella, looking over her shoulder, was scandalized.

"*Why* do you draw sech ugly things, Judy? It's a shame, when you kin draw so good, you don't draw sumpin purty an' nice. I wisht you'd draw me a nice pitcher in colors fer to hang on my wall."

"All right. There's some in the cupboard drawer, that Jerry bought for Billy to mark with."

Luella brought more paper and a handful of colored crayons; and Judith, not much interested, but rather curious to see how it would turn out, drew a picture in colors: A little house, a bit of rail fence, an apple tree in blossom, a hill rising steeply behind. Then she took another sheet and drew a large bunch of pink roses. Luella was delighted with the pictures, especially the roses.

"My, haow kin you draw 'em so good, Judy! Naow that's what I call nice work. I'm a-goin' to put frames on 'em an' hang 'em in my room."

Luella carried away the pictures in triumph, and Judith went on drawing her heads.

In a few weeks there was an abundance of garden "sass." The season was as bountiful as the year before it had been stingy. It rained and the sun shone hotly and the seeds in Scott County's fertile clay soil stirred, reached up their heads

to their God, like millions of little sunworshipers and covered
the earth with green.

Weeds grew too, tender and succulent from abundant moisture and rapid growth. They were easy to get rid of if they
were attacked in time. One stroke of the hoe killed hundreds
of them. Lying on the moist, steaming earth in the fierce heat
of the sun, they shriveled and dried up in a few hours. But
if they were allowed to live, they grew with incredible rapidity
into great, tough giants and overtopped the vegetables in no
time.

Judith spent all the time that she could spare from the babies
and the house working in her garden, chopping out the weeds
while they were still young and tender, hilling up the potatoes,
hoeing the rows of lusty beets and beans and turnips, training
the pole beans to climb on their poles and tying up the tomato
vines to stakes. She liked this work. She liked the feel of
the hot sun on her back and shoulders, the smell of the damp,
warm earth. Some magic healing qualities in sun and earth
seemed to give her back health, vigor, and poise. When she
had hoed in the garden for an hour or two, she felt tired from
her exertions, for her strength had only partly returned after
the birth of the baby. Yet, in spite of the ache in her muscles,
she was refreshed and in a way invigorated, more able to cope
with the washtub and the churn, with the baby when he cried
and refused to be pacified and with little Billy when he danced
up and down and choked and grew purple in the face with rage.

It was a hard spring and summer for Jerry. He had put in
five acres of tobacco; and this year there was no help to be
had from Judith. Even if she could have left the children, she
was much too weak for field work. So Jerry had to tackle it
alone. Five acres of tobacco and ten acres of corn—a good
full summer's work for three men, four if they worked union
hours. But Jerry did not work union hours. He was determined that this year he was going to provide for his wife and
family. The alarm clock was set every morning except Sunday for half past three. By half past four, he and the horses
were jingling out of the barnyard. At eleven he came home

for dinner; and noon saw him starting away again. That was the hardest wrench of all, to get up after eating and drag his swollen feet and aching muscles out into the hot noonday sun, before him the long broiling afternoon of endless plodding after the plow. It was not so bad after he had been working for an hour or so; he got his second wind and went along tolerably enough. Five o'clock came—quitting time for those who work for others; but it was only a little past the middle of Jerry's afternoon. Six o'clock, and the sun was still quite high in the sky. It was only when the sun dropped below the horizon that he clicked cheerfully to the horses and turned their heads toward home.

It was hard, too, on the horses. They grew gaunt and stringy-necked, their coats bleached by the sun into a dead, lusterless drab. Better, however, that they were thin; for then there was small danger of their dropping dead of the heat, as a fat horse might do. Jerry was a little sorry that he had not bought mules. They stood the strain of heat and hard work better than horses.

In the evening, after he had eaten supper, he rolled into bed in the same shirt that he had worn all day, or if it was very hot in no shirt at all. He was dirty, sweaty, unshaven. Tired in every muscle he fell asleep instantly. Judith had nothing to fear from his excess vitality. She, too, slept the sleep of exhaustion.

The weeds grew with such lustiness and vigor that Jerry had to cultivate his corn and tobacco again and again to keep the plants from being smothered. As soon as one generation was laid low another came to take its place. The earth teemed with the seed of this useless but vigorous and persistent life. By early July, however, Jerry saw the reward of his toil. By then the tobacco had spread its broad leaves and shaded the ground, and the corn had shot up thick and tall and dark green. When it had reached this stage, his crop needed no more cultivation. The weeds might continue to germinate all they liked; they could not grow if they did not see the sun. He took an occasional day off now and an extra hour or so at noon to loaf and play with Billy. If a neighbor happened by, he was willing to stop and chat with him. His vigor and good spirits began to return.

"Bejasus, I've got a good crop this year, Judy," he said, his face beaming with honest, simple satisfaction. "The corn's made. Nothin' can't hurt it. It's same as if it was in the crib. Of course a dozen things cud happen to that there terbaccer yet; but not likely. Everybody says terbaccer's a-goin' high this year. If I kin steer her safe to market, she'll bring us a neat little penny."

On Sundays they usually hooked up and went visiting. Often they went to Lizzie May's for the sake of Billy, who liked to have other children to play with. Jerry and Dan, too, were good friends and enjoyed an all day chat. Lizzie May had two children now: Granville, a year or so older than Billy, a stodgy, round-faced chunk of a child, and Viola, a little girl with yellow curls, her mother in miniature. Motherhood had improved Lizzie May. She had taken on flesh and seemed to have discovered some source of strength and vitality inaccessible to Judith. She beamed with maternal pride and satisfaction on her children. She kept their clothes and her own dresses and aprons washed and starched and fastidiously ironed; and she was always busy scrubbing, dusting, polishing, never tiring apparently of the endless cleaning of things just to have them get dirty again, a species of well doing of which Judith constantly experienced weariness. Her stove was always polished, her kettle shining, her floor scrubbed, her children clean and decent and neatly patched.

In addition to all this, Lizzie May had a "front room," an apartment rarely found in the houses of tenant farmers. It had a bright rag carpet on the floor made of rags all sewn by Lizzie May's own hands. Braided rag rugs were laid over the carpet in places where the wear might come if the room were ever used. There were lace curtains at the window, a bed with a white spread and pillow shams embroidered in red, a little what-not in a corner loaded with knick-knacks, two crayon enlargements on the wall, and a framed motto over the door. In this room the blinds were always drawn and sunlight entered only through chinks. It smelled of new rag carpet and freshly starched pillow shams and a slight mustiness, sweetish, and not altogether unpleasant. It had an air of cool, clean, quiet sanctity. After the children it was Lizzie May's greatest pride.

Judith often wondered why it was that Lizzie May got on so much better than herself. It was not hard to see why she was a better housekeeper. She had always liked housework and taken an interest in it. Besides, she did nothing else, never even venturing as far as the barnyard. Dan did all the outside chores and when he needed help in the field he called on one of his younger brothers.

But she was a better wife, too, for just what reason Judith did not know, though she was beginning to have vague thoughts on the subject. There appeared to be between her and Dan a settled, comfortable intimacy based on as perfect an understanding as can exist between a man and a woman. She bullied and nagged him a good deal about various things: his habits of drinking and fox hunting, his muddy shoes, his carelessness of her company table cloth. But she did not mean a great deal by the scoldings and he took them complacently. He on his side, though decidedly selfish in personal matters like most husbands, adored his family and considered his wife the sum of all perfections. Judith was quite sure that Jerry no longer regarded herself as perfect. What was worse, she felt her feelings gradually numbing into a growing indifference toward him. She saw quite clearly that Lizzie May and Dan got on much better than she and Jerry.

As a mother, too, Lizzie May was better than she. She hardly ever slapped her children or fell into a rage with them. They did not seem to annoy her. Why was this, Judith asked herself uneasily. She thought she loved her children quite as much as Lizzie May loved hers. Perhaps she did; but then quite possibly she did not. What was the matter with herself that she should be a failure? She began to brood and look into herself.

There was not the least doubt that she was a failure. It did not need comparison with Lizzie May to convince her of this. When she thought about it, as she did increasingly long and often, she faced the fact quite calmly and almost coldly, as she was in the habit of facing facts. She had always disliked housework. Now she loathed it as the galley slave loathes the oar. She let things slide as much as she could. The floor remained unscrubbed and the stove unpolished. Fluff collected in feathery rolls under the beds, and layer after layer of greasy smut formed on the outsides of the pots and pans. In the dark corners of the cupboard mice made nests of torn up bits of paper and rag and left little mounds of corn hulls and little black oblongs to show where they had feasted. When she opened the cupboard door, a stale and pungent smell testified to their presence. Dust collected on the shelves, cobwebs in the corners, and bedbugs in the beds.

Once in a while when the house got too distressingly dirty, she would have a grand clean up. She would spend two or three febrile days going into everything, cleaning the cupboards, sweeping down the walls, taking the beds apart, and soaking them with kerosene, washing the windows, polishing the stove. At such times her eyes sparkled and her cheeks glowed with excitement. When it was all done she would sink back, tired but happy, and register a determination to keep things looked after in future so that such a thorough going over would never again be necessary.

It seemed to her that she was an even greater failure with the children. She cared more for them than for anything else in her life, she felt quite sure of that. She was consumed with anxiety lest they should fall sick. In summer she cooled and strained the milk with the greatest care, fearful of dysentery; and in winter she was anxiously mindful of draughts and chills, worried as to whether the babies were warmly enough dressed and constantly on the watch for the first signs of the much dreaded colds so common in all the leaky, draughty shanties during the winter season.

Nevertheless, in spite of her anxiety about the health and

comfort of the children, she felt more and more that she begrudged them something. She did not serve them wholeheartedly, devotedly, joyfully, like Lizzie May. She wearied of the constant putting on and pulling off of little garments. More and more she chafed against the never relaxing strain of being always in bondage to them, always a victim of their infantile caprices, always at their beck and call seven days a week through weeks that were always the same.

They were so imperious, so rigorously demanding in the supreme confidence of their complete power over her. They were so clinchingly sure of their ascendancy. They gripped her with hooks stronger than the finest steel. If only she could have been a willing victim, like Lizzie May. But she could not. She strained away, and the hooks bit into her shuddering flesh, unalterably firm, enduring, and invincible. She knew that they would never let her go.

She found herself longing ardently for a single day, even a single hour when she could be by herself, quite alone and free to do as she chose.

At first when this wish formed itself in her mind the nostalgia of the fields and roads took possession of her. She imagined herself taking a long, carefree ride on horseback or following a turkey hen over the hills and hollows; and having found the hidden nest, coming back leisurely, aimlessly, enjoying the warmth of the sunshine and the touch of the wind on her face, feeling herself, as she had used to do, a part of the out of doors, untroubled by thoughts and happy that she was alive. Later on, in the winter, when the strain of her captivity dragged more and more wearyingly on exhausted nerves, she forgot the old nostalgia, forgot even to look out of the window, and longed for only one thing: quiet and peace—peace and deep, long sleep.

CHAPTER XVI

SUMMER months go quickly by. The summer and early fall were soon gone, and the long season of cold and rain set in. The tobacco was a heavy crop. It had been cut and hung in the barn, had survived the moist, warm spells that so often cause tobacco to heat and spoil, and was ready to be bulked. For this it was necessary to wait for right weather conditions. Jerry was impatient and every morning and evening he scanned the sky anxiously.

One morning in early November when he went out to draw a bucket of water, a soft, mild wind was blowing from the south under heavy clouds. It was not raining, but the air was full of moisture. He sniffed critically.

When he got back into the house, he set the bucket down with a hasty thump that splashed some of the water out onto the floor.

"I'll be off, Judy, as quick as I git sumpin to eat. It's fine bulkin' weather. I think the terbaccer'll be nice an' soft. An' you'd best put me up a lunch so's I won't hev to quit work long at noon."

For several days, whenever the weather conditions were right, Jerry worked at bulking the tobacco. At last it was done and the long job of stripping began.

Judith had to help with the stripping, or it would never be finished in time to get the tobacco to market while the price held. The price had a disconcerting way of dropping when the great bulk of tobacco began to come on the market.

Through the short gray days of late November and December the alarm clock was set for four. Bed was never so seductively delicious as during the few moments after its impertinent ting-a-ling had startled them awake. They curled together luxuriously in the warmth and softness. It was Jerry who had the strength of mind first to throw off the covers and bound out into the icy blackness. As he hurriedly poked kindlings into the cold stove, he cheered himself by singing, to the accompaniment of chattering teeth, a little song that he had heard somewhere and into which he had fitted his own name:

> Jerry git up in the mornin',
> Go out an' feed the foal.
> Jerry git up in the mornin',
> Bejasus hain't it cold!

"Naow, Judy," he would exhort her when the fire was going strong, "it's nice an' warm an' no chore at all to git up." And he would throw a coat on the floor by the stove, so that she could stand on it to dress.

When they arrived at the stripping room Jerry lighted a fire, while Judith arranged a bed of coats for the baby. When the heat of the box stove began to make the room heavy, Billy too would begin to nod and Judith would lay him beside the baby to finish his sleep. Then the long day began.

Hat and Luke shared the stripping room with them. Things were easier for Hat because she had no children to bother with. Judith half envied her. Compared with her she felt in a manner degraded and in bondage.

In the stripping room there was even less conversation than there had been two years before. For now even Judith felt no desire to talk. Instead she was the most preoccupied and indifferent of them all. When she met Luke's little pig eyes fastened upon her she felt no stir of excitement of any kind, neither interest, nor aversion, not even disgust. Always tired and always sleepy, her body and mind alike numbed into a dull torpor, she saw nothing and thought of nothing but the browns and reds and yellows of the silken tobacco leaves. On account of her unusual sense of color and texture she had become the best tobacco stripper of them all. She could make seven grades where Luke and Jerry could make only three and four. Hat, who up to now had considered herself the queen of tobacco strippers, could make five. They stood upon gunny sacks or bits of board to keep their feet from the damp

ground. Endlessly and in a heavy, sodden silence they all
stripped and stripped and stripped.

Every three hours or so, when the baby cried, she stopped
to nurse him. She was glad of this chance to sit down, for her
feet and ankles ached from the strain of long standing. Sometimes when she sat beside the stove nursing the baby she dozed
and dreamed, wakened with a start, dozed, and dreamed again.

If the weather was not too bad Billy was wrapped up and
put outside to play. But he did not stay there long; he soon
came back hungry for company. Inside he got into people's
way and was often fretful and badgering. Sometimes he annoyed Luke and Hat, and they were not slow to show it. As a
general thing they treated him kindly enough, rallied and
teased him, and asked him if he didn't want to come and live
with them. Sometimes Hat even brought him a little paper
of sugared popcorn or a top or marble that she had found lying
about. Luke made him a trumpet out of a goat's horn and
painstakingly taught him how to blow it. It gave out a musical,
melancholy sound far reaching and resonant.

They both liked the child well enough and were inclined to
spoil him with petting and teasing when he was good. But
when he was bad they guarded jealously their sacred right as
a childless couple to peace and freedom from disturbance. Hat
was sometimes heard to mutter something under her breath
about "Other folks' snotty-nosed brats," and Luke looked at
the child with little cold eyes full of dislike and annoyance.

Mercifully the days were short. By half past four it was
too dark to see to grade and they bundled up the babies and
went home.

But Judith's day was not yet over, nor was Jerry's. While
he milked and fed the horses and did up the other outside
chores, she washed the breakfast dishes, swept and straightened
the kitchen, washed out the diapers, washed and fed the children, and got the supper ready. After they had eaten supper
she put the children to bed and washed the dishes and strained
and put away the milk and set the table for breakfast and
fried corn cakes to take with them for lunch the next day;

and at last she was through, at least until the nursing baby waked and cried in the night.

The next morning at four o'clock the same thing began all over again.

As they neared the end of the long job, a febrile uneasiness stirred the dull atmosphere of the stripping room. It was the anxiety about the market, the eagerness to get done, and catch the opening price. It was whispered that on account of the war in Europe tobacco was going to bring the biggest price in years. Hat and Luke came early and stayed late. Their fingers flew. They were far ahead of Jerry and Judith, because Judith had to stay home at least one day a week to wash for the children. Jerry fretted at the slowness with which the work went on. Daily the tension of his anxiety grew more strained.

Not only in the stripping rooms, but all over the face of Scott County excitement grew and spread as the time of the opening of the market drew near. The price of tobacco was such an unstable thing that it was always a matter for conjecture. It was not a thing that varied within limits and according to known conditions, like the price of hogs and corn. In its variations the price of Kentucky Burley scorned limits; and the circumstances that controlled it were to the tobacco growers a shrouded mystery. Wherever men met together, there was only one thing talked about: the price that tobacco was going to bring. Each man shook his head sagely and hinted darkly that he had inside information on the subject. In reality they were as babes unborn. Speculators great and small hung about stripping rooms, appraising the tobacco. The growers themselves began to dicker about buying each other's crops. Every man who had a drop of sporting blood in his veins was itching to buy, sell, to take some sort of a chance. Their wives coldly counseled them to sit tight and tend to their own business, which advice made them surreptitiously determined to stake something on the turn of Fortune's wheel.

Before they had finished stripping, Jerry caught a cold which developed into a sort of influenza. He kept on working, miserable with a swollen throat and aching head. Then one morning he was hot with fever and had to stay in bed. He was away from the stripping room for four days.

The day that he went back to work, Judith felt her own throat growing sore. The next day she, too, had to stay in bed. For three days she was unable to get up, and Jerry, who had to stay home and take care of the children, floundered about the kitchen with the clumsiness and helplessness possible only in a man who has been brought up by a devoted mother in complete ignorance of every domestic detail.

When on the fourth morning, weak and shaky in the knees, she got up and went out to the kitchen, she found everything in a dreadful mess. The floor showed no appearance of having been swept since she went to bed. The stove was covered with ashes, grease, and the charred remains of something that had boiled over. Dirty dishes and dishes with little dabs of this and that in them were to be found in the most unexpected places. The children's clothes were unspeakably dirty; and the few things that Jerry had tried to wash were of a pale drab color. The slop bucket was a thing of horror. Everything she touched felt sticky, greasy, or slimy. The room smelt of burnt grease, sour milk, and unwashed diapers. Disgust and anger rose in her.

"Seems like you might 'a' tried to keep the place a little better'n a hogpen while I was in bed," she snapped, wiping the top of the stove vigorously with a rag. "Anybody'd think you'd tried to see how much dirt you could *make*, let alone clean anything."

"Well, I don't lay claim to be no expert pot wrastler ner wet nurse neither," returned Jerry, shrugging his shoulders. His three days of forced kitchen service had not improved his temper. His mind was on his tobacco and he felt irritable with anxiety. He wanted to get back to his stripping.

As she went about trying to get the breakfast, she felt faint and ready to drop with weakness. The dirt and confusion staggered and bewildered her. From the bedroom Billy began to shout for her to come and dress him, and wakened the baby, who set up a shrill cry. A shudder of revulsion went over her. In that moment she did not know which she hated most, him or his clamoring young ones.

"Good Gawd, man," she exclaimed in exasperation, "air you so good fer nuthin' you couldn't even wash a cup clean?"

"Aw, shet up. You're too damn fussy," he growled, and flung out of the room with the milk bucket.

She glared after him, her black brows drawn together with concentrated fury. She was holding in her hand a little bowl. It had been rinsed through cold dish water and her fingers felt the inside smeared with grease. She gave a sharp exclamation of disgust and with a sudden movement threw the bowl against the stove where it crashed into a dozen pieces. For a moment she stood looking at the pieces of the broken bowl, and her lips curled into an upward twist of sardonic satisfaction. The lip was lifted from the teeth as a dog's lip is lifted in a snarl. Then a heavy dismalness settled down upon her. She swept up the pieces and went on drearily about her work.

The tobacco market opened with fine prices, some of the growers who had especially good crops getting as high as thirteen or fourteen cents a pound. Hat and Luke were excited beyond words. However, on the day that Luke hauled his crop to Lexington, the market had fallen off somewhat and he averaged only nine cents a pound. He and Hat would have been amply satisfied with this if some of the neighbors' crops had not brought higher prices. They were tormented by the thought that if they had been a few days earlier, or perhaps a few days later they might have got a cent a pound more. They calculated again and again how much this would amount to. Even half a cent a pound would have made a very considerable difference. Hat thought about all the things that she might have done with this difference. Luke, who was not so unlearned in figures as in letters, meditated on the change it would have made in his bank book. Being childless and stingy, he had become the owner of a small but steadily growing bank account. The minds of both burned and seethed with these restless promptings of avarice.

Hat permitted herself only one extravagance. She "sent

off" to Sears Roebuck for the reddest sateen petticoat in the whole catalog. She had long coveted this petticoat, devouring the colored picture of the flaming garment with greedy eyes. When it arrived, after examining it in the most minute detail, she laid it reverently in the bureau drawer; and for the first few days opened the drawer at least a half dozen times a day to make sure that it was still there. When she went visiting on Sundays she wore it.

Cheerfulness, like a gleam of winter sunshine, brightened the Blackford household after the last tobacco stalk had been stripped and thrown on the trash pile. There was a feeling of some heavy incubus thrown off and a resulting sense of freedom and relaxation. A morning or two of lying in bed until seven instead of turning out at four had an enlivening effect on their spirits. Jerry whistled and sang again as he went about loading his wagon for the trip. It was February; but the good prices were still holding. Judith gave the house a vigorous cleaning, washed and mended for the children, and enjoyed a feeling of satisfaction, as she always did when she had made a fresh start. To both of them it was an immense relief to be out of the stripping room.

Jerry borrowed his father's horses to help haul the tobacco to Lexington; and on the third morning after they had finished stripping he was ready to start.

They got up at half past three. It was bitterly cold that morning. Judith turned over the contents of the bureau drawers and found three pairs of socks, two undershirts and two pairs of drawers, all of which Jerry put on.

"They've all got holes," he explained, "but the holes don't come in the same places. So I reckon my hide'll be covered."

He was in festive spirits. As he went about getting ready for the trip, he hummed a little song of the tobacco region.

When we sell the 'baccy an' the corn crop too
  Susy Jane'll ride to church in a gaown an' ribbon new,
Slippers neat upon her feet. There won't be none like Sue
  When we sell the 'baccy an' the corn crop too.

"What do you want me to bring you from taown, Judy?" he asked in a pause of shaving. "I want to fetch you sumpin nice that you bin a-wantin', sumpin that's a real treat. Shall it be a new dress or what?"

A year or so ago the mention of a new dress would have filled her with delighted enthusiasm. Now she only smiled a little wearily. She felt years older than he.

"I don't go nowheres to need good clothes," she said. "Bring stuff to make Billy a warm coat. An' you'd otta git yerse'f one o' them corduroy coats with sheepskin inside an' wear it on the trip home. Your clothes hain't near warm enough fer sech a long trip. I'm afraid you'll be awful cold afore you git there."

She scurried about looking for wristlets, mufflers for him to put on.

"Aw, I hain't a-goin' to be cold," he reassured her. "If my feet gits cold I'll jump off an' walk a spell. I'll like enough walk up all the hills anyway."

She gave him a hot breakfast and put up a big lunch for him to take along. At last he was ready with his cap pulled down over his ears, his neck wrapped in mufflers, two pairs of gloves on his hands. He took her in his arms and kissed her warmly.

"Good-by, Judy, dear. When I come back I'll be wearin' di'monds."

The door clattered to behind him and he was gone. In the melting darkness outside things were just becoming visible and the hills lifted black shoulders against a paling eastern sky. She watched him through the window as he led the four horses out of the barnyard.

Outside the tobacco barn, the more than two ton load towered high above the hay frame. Jerry fastened the traces of the four horses, climbed to the high seat and gathered the lines in his hands. Under the overhanging mountain of tobacco he looked small and perilously poised. He spoke to the horses; they strained; the wagon gave a lurch forward and slipped back again. Three times they tried to start the load and each time it fell back into the ruts made by its own weight. The fourth time they pulled it out. Slowly, steadily, and with a certain majesty the great brown mountain behind the two span of horses passed along the top of the ridge. The small speck that controlled it whistled cheerfully into the frosty morning air. When she saw the wagon pass, Judith waved a dishtowel from the doorway and heard his answering shout.

It was almost midnight of the following day when he returned. She was waiting up for him with a hot fire burning and the kettle boiling ready for coffee. It was still bitterly cold. The window panes were white with frost and the biting cold crept in around the sashes. She had rolled up an old mat and laid it before the door to keep out the draught. When she moved about at the end of the kitchen farthest from the stove, her breath was seen in a white steam.

"My, how cold he must be on the road," she thought and shivered.

At last she heard far off the rumble of the wagon on the top of the ridge, then the creaking sound of the dangerous descent down the steep hill track over the bare, frozen ground. Peering out into the darkness, she could see the gleam of his moving lantern. She set a lamp in the window, made coffee and put on cakes to fry. As she laid the table and turned the frying cakes, she could hear him unharnessing the horses and putting them up. She was in a flutter of excitement. Tobacco is not sold every day.

At last she heard his step approaching and rushed to open the door.

"My, but you must be near froze, Jerry—Jerry, what's the matter?"

He did not kiss her nor speak a word, but walked heavily to the stove and stood warming his hands. She looked anxiously at his face and saw that it was set and heavy. The eyes had a glassy, inward stare.

"Jerry, what's wrong? Haow much did you git a paound?"

"Four cents."

"Four cents!" It was all she could say. She was speechless with astonishment and dismay.

"She dropped yestiddy. There wa'n't hardly no buyers there. The bottom fell out clean. If I'd a been one day earlier I'd a got nine or ten." His voice was dead and husky.

"Oh, Jerry, hain't it a shame! After all haow hard you worked an' slaved over that crop!"

"After all haow hard we both worked an' slaved," he corrected her harshly.

Suddenly he dropped to the floor beside her, and with his arms across her knees and his face laid upon his arms, broke into dry, convulsive sobs, harrowing to hear.

For a long time he shuddered and sobbed, giving way at last with a certain relief to the disappointment that had been eating his heart out through the thirty mile drive home. She stroked his hair and his cheeks, murmuring over him words of consolation.

"Never mind, Jerry, dear. Lots worse things might of happened. We kin manage along all right; an' mebbe nex' year we'll be lucky."

After the first shock, she did not feel any great bitterness of disappointment. She had never been able to take money losses very seriously. In spite of the daily object lesson offered her, she failed somehow to realize their significance.

"Oh, Judy," he quavered, when at last his storm of sobbing had spent itself. "I wanted you to have money so's you could buy things you wanted, an' the young uns could have plenty warm clothes an' new shoes. An' I hoped I'd be able to put some in the bank this year toward buyin' us a place. Naow we'll jes have to skimp along same's las' year."

He buried his face in her lap and burst into another storm of weeping.

She soothed him and at last he was quiet.

"Anyway, things can't be so terrible bad so long as we have each other, can they, Judy?" he said, slipping his arm around her waist and looking up at her with doglike eyes, pleading and questioning.

She met his look and tried not to flinch.

"No, things'll come out all right, so long as we have each other."

As she said it and gently stroked his hair, a dreary sense of aloofness came over her and she knew that she was lying.

"Come, Jerry, some hot coffee'll do you good," she rallied, lifting his head from her lap. "An' this pan o' cakes is burnt clean to a crisp. I'll have to fry another batch."

While she fried the cakes, he hunched over the stove, and shiver after shiver turned his cheeks pale.

"Seems like I can't git warm," he said, his teeth chattering. "The cold's gone clean into my insides an' don't wanta come out. Gawd, it was cold on the way home. I thought the road'd never come to a end. I walked most of the way; but even so my feet was like ice. An' when I come to unbuckle the harness I couldn't hardly make my fingers work."

He shivered again.

She dragged the table over to the stove, poured him out coffee and set fried bacon and hot cakes before him. He ate and felt better; but still the shivers kept going over him.

"Dan went to-day," he said, setting down his cup after a long draught of coffee. "I met him jes afore I come to George- town. I didn't have the heart to tell him the market'd caved in; so I jes waved my arm to him an' kep' on a-goin'. Poor Dan! It'll come hard on him, too. He was a-buildin' great hopes on this crop—same as me."

He fell silent, musing with his chin on his hand and for- got to eat. When he roused himself he poked more wood into the stove and put his feet in the oven.

"Gawd, I feel like I could bake forever."

The cold spell held on. It was unusual for such extreme weather to last so long. The next day was bitter. That night when they went to bed they piled on old coats over the quilts for extra warmth and put hot flatirons in the bed.

"My, but it'll be a cold trip for Dan comin' home," said Judith, as she snuggled down under the covers. "He'll be on the road now, poor feller."

"Yes, it'll come close to zero. An' the wind makes it that much worse."

In the middle of the night Judith stirred uneasily, then sat up in bed listening.

"Jerry," she cried, shaking him by the shoulder. "Somebody's a-hammerin' at the door."

He started up out of a sound sleep and sat for a moment dazed. The knocking began again.

He jumped out of bed, pulled on his overalls, and opened the kitchen door.

"It's Judy's sister, Lizzie May," Judith could hear in the bedroom. "She's takin' on awful. The horses an' empty wagon has come home, an' Dan hain't with 'em. She wants you to come on over."

She recognized the voice of Ziemer Havicus, a half-grown boy who lived with his parents, nearest neighbor to Lizzie May. As soon as he had delivered his shivering message the cold and dark swallowed him up again.

Judith sprang out of bed and began to dress feverishly. In the gripping cold her numb, bewildered fingers could hardly fasten her clothes; but it was terror more than cold that made her teeth chatter.

Jerry hurried out with the lantern and hooked up Nip to the cart. They wrapped the babies in blankets and plunged out silently into the bitter night.

From Lizzie May's kitchen window a light was streaming. Two or three lanterns moved about in the barnyard and dark figures and shadows moved with them. There were sounds of horses being put to.

When they opened the kitchen door, she rushed to Judith and fell shuddering into her arms.

"Oh, Judy," she cried, clutching her sister hysterically. "What do you s'pose has happened to him? Judy, don't tell me he's been hurt. Don't say he's got hurt, Judy."

Jerry went out with the lantern. A little later he came in again and nodded silently to Judith in sign that he was leaving. His face was set and serious. He was going with the searching party to look for Dan. A few moments later the two women heard the wagon creak past and rumble away into the distance.

The terrible minutes of suspense dragged by like hours. Outside the night was cold, black, and silent, inscrutably hiding its secret. Inside, Judith, having put her children to bed, kept the fire burning and tried to deaden for Lizzie May the torture of waiting.

It was heartrending to be with her, to try to calm her with false hopes and lying assurances. Judith under the strain began to catch the infection of hysteria. She found herself trembling all over and could hardly keep back her tears. She could hardly believe that only twenty-four hours before she and Jerry had themselves felt calamity stricken. In the face of this, their misfortune seemed less than nothing.

The minutes dragged by. Outside the night remained cold, black and silent, inscrutably hiding its secret.

It was growing daylight when at last they heard the creak of wheels. For hours they had been listening for this sound with mingled dread and eagerness. Now it came all unexpectedly like a sudden blow, like a stab. Lizzie May heard it first and rushed to the door. Judith followed her.

The wagon was coming at a rapid trot. It creaked loudly in the intense cold. Jerry was driving. Judith knew him at once by his red muffler. And there were men sitting on the sides of the wagon box. On the seat beside Jerry was a figure that Judith did not at once recognize. For one foolishly glad moment she thought it was Dan. She looked again and saw that it was Jake Tobey, the coroner. Her heart contracted with a sharp pain and involuntarily her eyes moved to the wagon box. In the middle of the wagon box was a long, motionless object covered by a horse blanket.

Lizzie May had seen and understood it all much more quickly than Judith. With a terrible scream she rushed out to the wagon.

They brought him in and laid him on the bed in the best

room, composing his frozen limbs as best they could. He was frozen solid. On one side of his head was a deep gash where he had hit against something hard and sharp when he had fallen from the wagon. In the inside pocket of his coat they found a check for a hundred and seventy-three dollars and eighty-six cents, the payment for his year's work.

The coroner, a little parchment-skinned man, found that he had come to his death by freezing.

"Like enough he started to freeze an' lost his senses an' fell off the wagon," he said to the men assembled in the barnyard. "An' he would of come to when he fell if the blow on his head hadn't 'a' stunned him. Well, it's a dirty shame. He's gone, poor lad, an' one o' the best fellers I ever knowed."

"He wouldn't of started to freeze if he hadn't a been drinkin'," put in Bob Crupper, who had himself just got back from Lexington. "He was a-drinkin' heavy in taown yestiddy. He tuk it hard—the drop in the market—an' he drunk a good many drinks to try an' cheer hisse'f up. Then on the way home the numbness set in on him. If I'd ever had a notion what was a-goin' to happen to him I'd a kep' alongside of him on the way back. But anybody can't know these things till it's too late."

"That's what comes o' bein' a drinkin' man," said Uncle Joe Patton, who was one of the few total abstainers of the neighborhood.

"Waal, he's saved hisse'f a lot o' disappointments," opined Jabez Moorhouse. The old sayin' is the good dies young. But if I was havin' it my way I'd say the lucky dies young. They don't live long enough to find out haow little there is to make life wuth livin'."

"I dunno about that," drawled Uncle Sam Whitmarsh in his deliberate way. "I'm a-goin' to be seventy-one, come the twenty-eighth o' nex' month. An' I can't say I call to mind any time I've wished the pigs'ud et me when I was little. Dan wanted to live, an' he had a right to live, poor feller, an' it's all the fault o' the God damned terbaccer company that won't give us close markets fer our crops. The idee of havin' to pack yer terbaccer thirty miles in the dead o' winter to git to a market! Nobody but us growers'd stand fer sech a thing a minit. An' if yuh send it on the cars, the freight charges is so high yuh might jes as well give it away. The railroad an' them lousy buyers has got us by the throat."

"You damn betcha," growled Bob Crupper. "An' the dirty haounds pays us jes what they've a mind to. They let on they're biddin' agin each other; an' the hull lot of 'em is all in together buyin' fer the American Terbaccer Company. Any o' them furrin buyers comes in an' offers to give a little more, they freeze 'em out. The hull pack of 'em hid out yestiddy tryin' to let on the market was glutted. Any dirty dodge to git out o' payin' us a decent price. An' Gawd, when a man goes to buy terbaccer he pays more for one o' them little bags or tins holdin' three-four ounces than they give us for that many paounds. Then come spring, jes afore the market closes, the price'll go away up agin, so's us poor fools'll sweat over raisin' terbaccer agin' nex' year. You damn betcha they got us by the throat."

He paced up and down the barnyard moodily, thinking about the three and a half cents a pound that he had got for his crop the day before.

As the morning grew and the news traveled on the swift pinions with which bad news is winged, the neighbors and relatives came driving into the barnyard. As if in mockery, the cold had abated. The wind had gone down and the winter sunshine began to melt the scant covering of snow that had fallen the day before. The men stood about in the barnyard talking over the accident and the drop in the tobacco market. The women hurried into the house and tried to comfort Lizzie May.

She was wild and hysterical in her grief. Her face swollen and distorted with weeping, she flung herself upon one or another of her sisters, aunts, and cousins, sobbing out to them again and again her anguish and desolation.

"Oh, Judy, Judy, what's a-goin' to become o' these poor little young uns 'ithout no daddy? He was allus that sorry fer little orphans. He never thought how soon his own'd be orphans. Oh, oh, oh!"

"He was too good," she kept saying in her calmer moments. "That's why he was taken away. He was too good."

She had never entertained nor voiced such a sentiment during his life. But now she said it and believed it too.

In a far corner of the kitchen Aunt Nannie Pooler sat and mourned softly for her dead boy.

"He was too good," sobbed Lizzie May, burying her face on Aunt Selina's bosom. "Oh, Aunt Selina, he was too good."

Tears streamed down the old woman's leathery cheeks. She had seen many die, but yet death was not an old story. She could still weep as in the days of her youth.

With each new arrival who came to offer her tribute of sympathy to the widowed girl, she went over it all again with convulsive sobs and fresh bursts of weeping.

"It's better she talks," whispered Aunt Mary Blackford to her neighbor. "Some jes sits an' thinks. An' them's the ones that feels it most."

Some of the women busied themselves doing Lizzie May's work for her. They sent one of the men to milk the cow; and when the milk was brought in strained it and put it away. They washed and dressed and fed the children, wiped the stove clean and swept the floor. They made coffee and offered a cupful to Lizzie May, telling her that it would do her good. She tried to drink it, but her throat refused to swallow.

She could not keep still a moment. When she was not pouring out her grief to some newcomer she wandered restlessly here and there about the kitchen. Everything she saw reminded her of Dan and brought forth new bursts of anguish.

"There's his work cap. Oh, Luelly, he hung it on that nail. An' naow he won't never take it off agin."

"Oh, Aunt Abigail, it was Dan put up them shelves. He made that there little table. He used to whistle so happy when he was a-fixin' things araound the house. Oh, I can't think he won't never whistle agin."

Having done up all the chores, the women stood and sat

around in little groups, talking together in hushed tones. They slipped in to look at Dan lying so cold and motionless on the white bed; and after shaking their heads over him, turned to eye with scarcely less reverence and more lively interest the bright new rag carpet, the lace curtains, the shiny what-not with its load of gimcracks and the cane-seated chairs.

"Poor Lizzie May, my heart jes bleeds for her," said Hat Wolf. In truth her large, bold eyes were softened by tears. She wiped away two that had started to run down her cheeks. "I wish Dan hadn't never planted that cedar tree by the house. Luke told him while he was a-plantin' it that come time it growed large enough to shadder a grave there'd be a death in the fam'ly. But he on'y laughed an' said Lizzie May wanted a tree an' went on a-diggin' the hole."

"Yes, I've allus heard cedar trees is unlucky," sighed Aunt Sally Whitmarsh.

"I wonder what she'll do now Dan's gone," continued Hat. "If she goes back to live with her dad she'll like enough have a auction sale. If she has a sale I'd like to bid on the carpet an' curtains. They're both jes the same as new."

"I dunno what she'll do," returned Aunt Sally, who was also taking a curious survey of the things in the room. "She takes on terrible, poor thing. But of course she'll git over it. She'll likely go back to her dad fer a spell. But I don't hardly think she'll stay a widder long. People that has nice things had best hang onto 'em. If I was her I'd lay the things by so I'd have 'em." Aunt Sally slid back quietly into the kitchen.

Hat hesitated a moment before following her. On the little what-not amid the collection of shells and pincushions her sharp, inquisitive eyes had spied a little square looking-glass in a gilded frame in which were set bits of colored glass imitating jewels. There were many other knick-knacks, but none that seemed to Hat so desirable as this one. The trinket fascinated and held her eye. She glanced furtively about the room. The door into the kitchen was closed, and there was no one else in the room but the dead man. With a swift, snake-like movement, she darted out her hand toward the looking-glass and slipped it into her pocket, then went back rather hurriedly into the kitchen.

The undertaker came bringing a coffin and they laid Dan out in the middle of the best room. When she saw him stretched out straight in the long, shiny coffin, Lizzie May realized to the full the hard inexorableness of death. It came to her as though she had not know it before, that Dan was really dead, that her life with him was over, that her children were without a father. Beside the hard, cold coffin she burst into new paroxysms of grief.

When they were all gone back into the kitchen, Aunt Nannie came and hung dumbly over the body of her boy.

The neighbors and relatives began to go home, slipping away unobtrusively. They had their own affairs to attend to. There remained at last only Dan's family and Lizzie May's father, her sisters, and brothers. They decided among themselves that Dan's mother, Lizzie May's father, and Luella should stay with her over night. Toward the close of the afternoon the others went home to look after the horses, the cows and chickens.

As Jerry and Judith were driving home, she roused herself from the daze into which Dan's death had cast her to ask herself if she would have felt as desolate as Lizzie May if it had been Jerry who was brought home dead. Often of late she had wondered if she loved Jerry as Lizzie May loved Dan. For a moment she imagined him lying cold and stiff, a great gash on the side of his head, never to speak to her again nor whistle nor laugh nor throw the children to the ceiling. The thought was unbearable. For reassurance she looked sidewise at his healthy weathered cheek and snuggled close against the warmth of his body.

In the evening, after the children were in bed, she came to him where he sat by the stove thinking of Dan, slipped her arms about his neck, and kissed him again and again with mingled tenderness and passion. Instantly he forgot Dan. He was happy, and eager with warm and joyful response. It was a long time since she had given him such kisses.

CHAPTER XVII

Two days later, when they got home from Dan's funeral, she thought on going into the kitchen that it smelled stale. Jerry was outside putting up the horses. She set the baby in the rocking chair and started to make a fire. A puff of acrid wood smoke blowing into her nose seemed all at once to have an intensely disgusting smell. She gripped the corner of the table to steady herself and her features contracted into an expression of mingled rage and horror. She knew that she was with child again.

Wednesday of the following week was hog-killing day for Jerry. Joe Barnaby came over to help him butcher. From the kitchen window Judith could see the men going about getting things in readiness, putting up three sets of crossed poles from which to hang the carcasses, arranging a scraping table, setting up the scalding barrel at a convenient angle and building a fire under a large, flaring iron kettle. It was a gray, frosty morning and they had their caps pulled down over their ears. Their breath came in white puffs.

Inside she had a roaring fire and the wash boiler on the stove to make more scalding water; for the hog-killing kettle that they had borrowed was not a very large one.

"There hain't no day I like better'n hog-killin' day," said Joe, warming his hands over the fire while they waited for the water to heat. "Some folks hates to see butcherin' day come. But I say to dress a hawg clean an' neat is as nice a job as there is a-goin'; an' it's a job a man kin put some heart into, 'cause he knows he hain't throwin' his work away. More'n that, he's got company by his side, an' that means a hull lot."

Joe's long, melancholy face showed its nearest approach to satisfaction, as he went out with Jerry, who had the sharpened butcher knife in his hand.

Judith stood over the wash tub rubbing out children's

clothes. The baby crawled about on an old quilt spread on the floor. Billy, as was his three-year-old habit, had been spending his time getting from one mess of mischief into another. His latest adventure had been to fall backward into the slop bucket, from which he emerged with deafening screams. She had had to take off all his clothes from the shirt out and put on clean ones. The dirty clothes had gone to join the others in the tub. The heat and stale smells of the kitchen made her feel faint and sick. Her head swam dizzily. She wished she could go into the bedroom and lie down.

She heard the shrill squealing of the pig as its throat was cut, and a little later saw Joe and Jerry carrying it to the scalding barrel. Billy in his red cap bobbed excitedly behind. Snap and Joe Barnaby's dog careened alongside, Snap with loud barks of joyous excitement, the strange dog silent and respectful as befitted a dog not on his own ground. Then men came hurrying in for the boiler of hot water.

"Fill her up agin, Judy—not full, jes half," Jerry called back, as he hurried away after bringing back the empty wash boiler.

She threw an old jacket over her shoulders and went out to the well for water. Coming back into the stuffy heat of the kitchen from the fresh, frosty air, the place seemed more foul and stinking than ever. Her stomach heaved tumultuously. Her knees trembled and she sank for a few moments into the old rocking chair.

Through the window she could see the men sousing the hog up and down in the scalding barrel, pulling him half way out, turning him a little and plunging him back again. The steam from the hot water rose up into the frosty air like a cloud of white smoke.

The baby began to cry and she got up wearily and warmed some milk for him, then crumbled a corn cake into it and fed it to him from a spoon. Having put him into dry diapers, she set him back on the quilt and went again to her washing.

The second hog and the third were soon killed, scraped, hung up, and disemboweled. Joe was a hog butcher of much experience and prided himself upon the quickness and neatness with which he could do the work. The three carcasses hung with stiffly spraddled hind legs from the three gibbets, trim, bright, and spotlessly clean against the dun-colored frowsiness of the yard. Snap, puffed up with the pride and arrogance of butchering day, stalked about the carcasses and would not let even a hen approach the enticing little pools of blood that dripped from their noses. When the cat attempted to sniff delicately at one of them, he ran her off onto the nearest fence; and when Joe Barnaby's dog tried to sidle up unobtrusively, he flew at him with bristling hair. Ominous growls alternated with sharp, excited barks.

Suddenly the kitchen door was flung open letting in a cold draught of fresh air, and Joe and Jerry, their coats and overalls streaked with blood, appeared bearing between them a galvanized iron tub full of steaming pig guts. They set the tub down in the middle of the floor with a heavy thump and made for the door.

"You'd better run 'em through quick, Judy, afore they git cold. An' I think there's one that's cut into. Watch out fer it," Jerry called back. He was already outside.

She scowled darkly at the tub, her black brows drawing together. The bluish viscera, bubbling up in innumerable little rounded blobs, filled it almost to overflowing. Bloody fragments emerged along with the masses of intestines. The outside of the tub was daubed and streaked with blood. An unspeakable stench rose from it, mingled with the stale heat of the kitchen and grew every moment denser, more nauseating, more unbearable. She gagged and reeled. Then, with a quick movement of sudden determination, she threw on an old coat of Jerry's that hung beside the door and a faded cap that she wore when she milked or chored about the yard, and went out, slamming the door sharply behind her.

Going swiftly through the yard, looking neither to right nor to left, she passed the two men.

"Where you a-goin', Judy?" Jerry called after her in surprise.

"I'm a-goin' to git away from that tub o' stinkin' pig guts you set in the kitchen. It kin stay there till it rots afore I'll tech hand to it."

Each word she uttered was hard and sharp, like the point of a nail. She paused not a second in her rapid walk and in a moment was gone from sight around the corner of the shed.

Jerry stood looking at the place where she had disappeared with an expression of dazed bewilderment, changing to annoyance and embarrassment. His pride suffered humiliation at this open affront from his wife before another man.

Joe came magnanimously to the rescue.

"That's jes the kind o' tantrums my woman goes into, on'y worse," he said. "An' she's allus a heap flightier when she's in the fam'ly way. But I never knowed Judy was given to them fits."

"She hain't," Jerry hastened to assure him. "I never knowed her to take on in sech a way afore. She's run guts many a time, like all the wimmin, an' never made no fuss."

"It grows on 'em," said Joe, ominously.

"Well, I s'pose we better pack it out," said Jerry, turning toward the house. "I hain't a-goin 'to bother with the guts. There hain't but three four paound o' lard there at best. The pigs was too young to have much fat on their guts. We'll jes take an' heave it out back o' the shed where the hens kin peck it over."

The last sound Judith heard from the yard as she walked away was Snap fighting viciously with Joe Barnaby's dog, who had dared to approach too near to one of the blood pools.

She climbed the hill to the ridge road and walked and walked and walked. She no longer felt at all tired or sick at her stomach. A sense of burning indignation gave her power and energy. She wanted to keep on walking forever and put a longer and longer distance between herself and all that she had left behind: the hot, foul smelling kitchen with its odious tub of guts in the middle, the tub of filthy clothes, the steaming wash boiler, the screaming, insistent children, the men going smugly about with cheeks reddened by the frosty air, and trying to foist upon her the only part of the job that was tedious and hateful. The more she thought about it, the more redly her own cheeks burned with hot anger. She felt as if she could walk to the end of the world.

Her eyes, instinctively reaching out for freedom, sought the long view that sweeps from the top of the ridge to the horizon. It lay bleak and bare under a gray winter sky. Its bareness and monotony of tone made it more far-reaching than in summer. It seemed endless, as she imagined the ocean might be. Out of its calm and magnitude a sense of peace welled up and gradually enfolded her. Her step slackened into a measured, meditative pace. She half forgot the things that she had fled from and in a little while felt almost happy with the happiness that comes of peace and solitude and wide spaces. It was more than three years since she had been by herself in the open country. It was like meeting with an old lover who has not lost his power to charm. The cold air smelled good in her nostrils. She breathed deep and rested her eyes with a sense of quietness and calm on the long, dun stretches of winter fields.

Then it came upon her again quite suddenly. She felt that she had neither the courage nor the strength to go through with it all again, and so soon after the last time. Her flesh cringed at the thought and her spirit faltered. And when the child was born it was only the beginning. She loathed the thought of having to bring up another baby. The women who liked caring for babies could call her unnatural if they liked. She wanted to be unnatural. She was glad she was unnatural. Their nature was not her nature and she was glad of it.

She felt suddenly tired and sat down on a stone under a maple tree, her elbows propped upon her knees and her chin in her hands. A heavy cloak of misery hung about her its cold and clammy folds. The thought of her own utter helplessness against her fate settled upon her like the weight of something dead. For a long time she sat looking out over the winter landscape and seeing nothing. Her gaze was turned inward upon her own horror and despair.

After a while she began to cry, not passionately, but in a slow, cold, bitter way, as though even the relief of tears were denied her.

In the midst of her misery, thoughts of anxiety began to obtrude themselves. Suppose Jerry had let the fire go out. If he had, the baby would surely take his death of cold. Or he might have fallen head first into the slop bucket. Suppose Jerry had left Billy alone in the kitchen and he got to playing with matches or to poking bits of stick into the fire to set the ends burning. He could easily set fire to the house. And if anything happened to them it would be all her doing, because she had gone away and left them.

She began to shiver and became aware that her feet were like lumps of ice. She got up and turned hastily toward home. Looking about she was astonished to find how far she had come. As she hurried homeward her anxiety increased. Her heart began to beat fast and she stumbled over clods and bits of underbrush. The afternoon was fast drawing in to night.

When at last she reached the house and opened the kitchen door, the room was almost in darkness. Jerry was sitting by the table with the baby on his lap feeding him warm milk and corn cake. Billy was sitting on the floor eating some of the same mixture from a bowl. The room was frowsy and unswept. The washing was just as she had left it.

She had come back half prepared to be friendly with Jerry. But the look of aggrieved and self-righteous accusation that he cast at her as she opened the door was quite enough to kill feelings that at best were only struggling for existence. Her anger rose again as if it had never died. She returned his glance with a long, hard, black, piercing look and went to light the lamp. His sense of injury was changed into uneasiness and a vague anxiety. He would not admit it to himself; but he was afraid of her.

Silently she fried the corn cakes and some liver from the hogs that had been killed that day. When they had eaten and she was clearing the table, Jerry spoke.

"Lizzie May was here," he said, clearing his throat. "I had

to tell her you'd stepped over to see Hat Wolf. She don't seem to know what to do with herse'f, poor gal. She feels dreadful about Dan."

"The more fool she. She dunno when she's well off," she answered brutally in a harsh, grating voice, and went on clearing the table, slapping the plates together viciously. Her own words shocked her; then she felt defiantly glad that she had said them.

He started, where he sat by the stove, and looked at her in astonishment. As she went on silently about her work, he kept glancing at her askance, questioningly, and with a vague uneasiness.

That spring they moved to another house close to several acres of fresh tobacco ground. Tobacco exhausts the soil in about three years and has to go through a renovating period. An old couple who aimed to raise only a patch of corn and perhaps an acre of tobacco moved into the house that they had left.

Lizzie May had taken her children and gone back to live with her father; and Jerry had thought of taking Dan's old house. But Judith did not feel that she could go to live in the house to which Dan had been brought home dead.

The house to which they moved was less than a mile from the one they left. It was built of pine boards roughly nailed together and neither sealed nor plastered. It had three bare, box-like rooms and a rickety back porch floored with boards many of which had rotted away from the nails that once held them. When you stepped on one end of these boards, the other end flew up into the air. The house stood on the top of a rather high ridge and commanded a broad view. Near it there was neither tree nor shrub; but there was a little clump of locust trees by the horsepond. Like Dan's old house it was bare, stark, and open to the sky.

A large and very dirty family of Pattons had lived there the year before. They were probably distantly akin to Uncle Joe Patton, although both families disclaimed all relationship.

Judith spent days cleaning up the house and yard. The walls and ceiling of the kitchen were dark with soot and pendulous with dust webs. The floor was sticky with a long accumulation of grease and grime. Frying pan spatterings and the splashings from dish pan and wash basin showed just where the furniture of the Patton family had stood.

The yard was littered with rags, broken boards and old iron; and scraps of baling wire tripped the unwary foot.

She threw the old iron and baling wire into a pile behind the backhouse, and raked up the rest of the rubbish into several heaps of which she made bonfires to the delight and excitement of Billy, who hovered perilously near to the licking flames.

When it was all done there were still left many traces of the former occupants. In the packed dirt of the yard, old floor rags that had been trodden into the ground were continually coming to light. When she took hold of them to pull them out a rotted fragment came away in her hand and the rest clung obstinately to the dirt in which it was embedded. Billy, too, was continually crawling under the house and triumphantly dragging out filthy scraps of overalls, old shoes, stiff, and moldy, frayed fragments of straw hats, ghastly skeletons of corsets, eaten with mildew and rust, but preserving faithfully the shape of the female form that they had once embraced, old, rust-eaten shovels, broken rat traps, and the frowsy stubbs of ancient brooms.

These things she poked into the stove when Billy was not looking or relegated to the old iron scrap pile behind the backhouse. But the child was always bringing out more. It was an enticing mine of treasures.

As in almost all the other tenant houses, the windows were few and small, set high in the wall and placed without the slightest regard for comfort, convenience or symmetry. From the outside the house looked like a weathered packing case into which some one had sawed at random two or three small holes.

In spite of the dark rooms and the bare surroundings, Judith liked it better than the little house in the hollow. It was open to the wind and sky. From the tiny windows she could see far off. In the morning the first ray of sunlight brightened the top of the ridge; and at the end of day the sunset filled the house like a presence.

CHAPTER XVIII

ALL that summer, with the unwelcome baby growing in her body, she was tart and irascible and closed herself up morosely from Jerry and his affairs. She showed no interest in his work in the field. She never asked him about his corn and tobacco or made any offer to help him. When he came in with a story of a broken plowshare, strayed cattle that had got into his corn, fences that the sheep had broken down, she showed no interest nor sympathy. In the chill of her indifference he too grew sullen and irritable.

"Seems like you might take a little interest in a man's troubles, Judy," he said sulkily. "Mammy allus did."

The mention of his mother did not tend to increase her good humor.

"I hain't yer durn mammy," she answered tartly. "An' mebbe you think I hain't got my own troubles to tend to."

She had never felt much sympathy for him in his ambition to save money and buy a home of their own. The thought of such a home had never made any very strong appeal to her. When Jerry had talked about his place, as he often did, she had tried to look interested. But oftener than not she caught herself thinking about something else. Jerry sensed with vague irritation the chill of her lack of sympathy.

Gradually her feeble interest had diminished like a thin cloud on a hot summer day. She no longer made any pretense of caring about the prospective home.

"You know durn well you'll never save enough money to buy a piece o' land," she said to him brutally. "Tenants never does. If you ever git a chanct to own a place it'll be when yer dad dies. That's the on'y way."

Her voice sounded bitingly hard, cold, and bitter. He looked at her reproachfully, like a dog that has been kicked.

245

"What ever's got into you, Judy, to talk so hateful?"

She shrugged her shoulders and went on frying the inevitable corn cakes.

She grew more and more shiftless and slatternly about the house. More and more mechanically she dragged through the days. As she hung over the washtub or plunged the dasher up and down in the ancient oaken churn or stood by the stove frying three times a day the endlessly recurring corn cakes, her body moved with the dead automatic rhythm of old habit. Her face was habitually sullen and heavy, her eyes glazed and turned inward or looking out upon vacancy with an abstracted stare.

In October the baby was born.

It was a girl this time, a skinny little mite weighing not much more than five pounds. Judith had very little milk for it, and their one cow was nearly dry; so Jerry began to look around to see where he could get another cow cheap and on time.

One Sunday morning when they had overslept they were wakened by a light tap at the window and Uncle Sam Whitmarsh's genial voice penetrated their drowsiness.

"Waal, naow, if you two hadn't otter think shame to yerse'ves sluggin' abed with the sun a-shinin' an' the crows a-cawin' outside. Why, it's most seven o'clock, an' the whole countryside been up an' about this two hours. It's queer, too, what things'll happen to some while others sleeps." Uncle Sam's voice took on a serious if not tragic tone. "While you two was a-sleepin' here like babes, she's bin a-turnin' me out o' my home. Yaas, sir, already here afore breakfast she's up an' slammed the door in my face. Whatcha think o' sech carryin's on? Turnin' a old man past seventy, the father o' nine chillun, out o' the home that he's worked an' slaved to keep a-goin' this past thirty year an' more! I ast you, Jerry, if I hain't put more work onto that place'n what the place is woth a dozen times over? An' all 'cause she's got the deed to it in her name she shets the door in my face. I hain't a-goin' to stand fer sech goin's on no longer. I hain't no dirty dawg to be kicked outdoors when he gits underfoot an' whistled back when they want the caows brung home. Yaas, sir, Samuel Ziemer Whitmarsh is a old man; but he hain't a-needin' no repairs put on him yet; an' I reckon there hain't many young fellers kin learn him much about tradin' an' fetchin' in the money when it's needed. Nex' time she looks to me fer money, she's a-goin' to find it's buyin' some other woman a bonnet. An', speakin' o' tradin', Jerry, I hearn you was a-needin' a fresh caow fer Judy an' the baby, an' it jes comes lucky I kin lay my hands on the very caow to suit yuh. She's a nice black fam'ly caow, eight year old no more, a easy milker an' fills the bucket. She's got a purty red calf by her side, an' the calf goes along with her. She's yourn, calf an' all, fer sixty dollars. I don't ast fer no cash, jes a little note comin' due in three months' time an' you kin pay me when you sell yer terbaccer. Whatcha say?"

"I'll be over to have a look at her, Uncle Sam," said Jerry, stretching his arms above his head. "Got her at Uncle Amos's place?"

"Yaas, she'll be in Amos's barnyard. Come early afore somebody else grabs her up. Waal, I'll be steppin'."

"Is this the eighth time she's turned him out, or the ninth?" yawned Judith, as she slipped her petticoat over her head. "Funny haow he allus says exactly the same things. An' then when she's minded to take him back he goes back jes like a little lamb."

"I wonder what's wrong with the caow?" mused Jerry.

After breakfast he went over to see the cow and came back about noon leading her. She was a tall, slimly built cow with a long neck. The calf ran alongside.

"I think she's a purty good buy, Judy," he said, as they stood inspecting her. "'Course she hain't none too young; but she seems sound an' healthy an' she looks like a good milker. An' then most people that has caows to sell jes naow wants cash. It's sumpin to be able to git her on time. Uncle Sam hain't a stingy ole skinflint neither. He gimme this good rope an' halter. She seems cheap, calf an' all. Mebbe there's sumpin wrong with her. If there is I s'pose we'll find it out soon enough."

They found it out next day. In the morning when Judith went out to milk her, her teats were as flat and flabby as if the calf had just sucked her dry. The calf was tied in the shed and had not been with her. When Judith came back into the kitchen Jerry was dumbfounded at the sight of the empty bucket.

"Well, I'll be damned," he said, and stood scratching his head in perplexity. Then his face brightened with an idea. "I tell you, Judy, I'll bet she sucks herse'f. She's got the build of a caow that kin do it."

Through the day they watched her and found that it was even as Jerry had surmised. He threw on his cap and went over to Crupper's place where Uncle Sam, being the brother of Aunt Amanda Crupper, was staying.

"Say, looky here, Uncle Sam, whatcha mean by sellin' me a caow that sucks herse'f?"

Uncle Sam looked up from the piece of harness that he was mending for his brother-in-law and smiled a little quizzically.

"Waal, Jerry, somebody's gotta be the owner of a caow that sucks herse'f, hain't they?"

"Aw, come on naow, Sam, you know that's a dirty trick to play on a neighbor." Jerry kicked into the ground savagely. "Whatcha goin' to do about it?"

Uncle Sam looked a little hurt.

"Naow, Jerry, don't git mad. When I'm a-dealin' with a neighbor I like to tell him the truth, an' mos' allus I do tell him the truth. But there's times when it comes jes a little hard to tell him *all* the truth, an' this here is one o' them times. Naow, Jerry, a caow that sucks herse'f is jes as good as any other caow pervidin' you don't let her suck herse'f."

He went back into the stable and came out with a wire contraption dangling from his hand.

"You jes fasten this here little muzzle on her nose an' she won't suck herse'f no more. When she's a-grazin' it falls away off'n her nose and lets her eat, an' when she tries to suck herse'f it's there. You jes put that on her an' she won't give you no more trouble. I'll stand back o' what I said that she gives good milk an' lots of it. Judy an' the baby'll take on flesh fast when they git to drinkin' that good milk."

Warmed by the glow of Uncle Sam's genial personality, Jerry had to smile.

"Why didn't you gimme it yestiddy, along with the rope an' halter?"

They laughed together.

"Waal, Jerry, I won't say I didn't know you'd be back after it."

They named the little girl Annie.

The winter after she was born was a hard one with unusually frequent cold spells. In Scott County the weather is never very cold for long periods. Most of the time it is dull and cloudy, with dismal rains and deep, sticky mud underfoot. Sometimes, however, the wind sweeps icily from the north, freezes the mud, and sends the thermometer for a night or so down to zero.

In the house in the hollow the Blackfords had been protected from gales; but now they knew all the changes of the wind. Perched shakily on the top of the ridge, the flimsy little house rocked and strained before the raging northwesters and piercing northeasters. The loose-fitting window sashes rattled; the doors stirred uneasily. The bits of old rag carpet laid upon the floor rose in waves as the wind billowed under them. The unceiled house, no snugger than a wagon shed, let in wind and cold everywhere. The wind fluttered the towels over the wash bench and rattled the saucepans that hung on the wall beside the stove.

On cold, windy mornings, when Jerry got up to light the fire, the house was no warmer than the out of doors. The water bucket was frozen. The milk in the pans was crusted with ice. Cold boiled potatoes left over from the day before were frozen into rocks and eggs were cracked open. The slop bucket on the floor in the corner was frozen solid and the bucket sprung from the force of the expanding ice.

On such mornings it took a long time to get things thawed out so that they could have breakfast; and even the fire did not have much effect on the icy atmosphere. If the wind was from the west it created such a strong draught that it drew all the heat up the chimney. If it was from the east, the stove drew badly and belched forth intermittent clouds of smoke and spatterings of ashes. The fuel, too, was not of a sort that makes much heat. The tobacco growers take no thought for the morrow in the matter of wood. The wood is cut each day as it is needed, frequently by the women. It is usually green saplings or half rotted fence rails. These latter are often sodden from recent rains and have to be dried out in the oven to make them burn at all. When at last they do burn they give only a faint glow of heat.

Judith grew waspish when the fire would not burn. On Sundays, when Jerry was home from the stripping room, she raged at him for not providing better wood. He was churlish and disheartened because much of the tobacco that he was stripping had been bitten by frost. He snapped back at her and sulked and when she was not looking sneaked away to the kitchen of some neighbor who had a warmer house and a less irritable wife.

She was left alone in her prison with the chilly and restless children. On cold days she kept the two boys dressed in all their outdoor clothing, even to their mittens. When she took the little girl out of her cradle, she wrapped her in shawls and blankets.

Jerry had raised a patch of cane that year. He hauled up cane and stacked it all around the house to try to turn the wind. The cows, drawn by the smell of the cane, kept breaking through the rickety fence; and soon had it all eaten up. He stacked up more; but as fast as he stacked it, the cows broke in and ate it up. All around the house they left hoofprints and round, brown cakes of dung the size of a large dinner plate.

All day long for days together, as long as the cold spell lasted, the slop bucket stood frozen solid in the corner, anchored to the floor by a surrounding island of ice. When at last the thaw came and the ice melted, the leaky bucket, its bottom sprung outward, teetered unsteadily and slowly dribbled its dirty contents.

While the cold spell lasted Judith kept keyed up, energetic and irascible. With the thaw she relaxed into an exhausted torpor. As she wearily heaved out the contents of the greasy slop bucket and washed up the floor under it she sighed and her eyelids fell together asking for sleep.

There were war prices for tobacco that year. They ran as high as forty cents a pound. But the summer had been a dry one and the tobacco was light and of poor quality. Much of it, too, had been nipped by an early frost. Jerry thought himself lucky to get a check for two hundred and thirty-six dollars. Out of this he had to pay forty-seven dollars for hired help.

Guss Dibble, whose wife had a new baby, traded his crop for a cow, and considered that he was doing well.

The winter was a constantly recurring round of thaws and cold spells. It lasted far into March. It seemed as if it would never end. At last the change came all of a sudden and it was summer again.

CHAPTER XIX

COMING suavely and benignly after the cruel winter, the warmth fell like a softly enfolding presence. Spring is a gracious season in Kentucky, full of the smell of flowering locusts, of birdsong, and happy mornings. With sunlight falling through open doors and windows, the children playing outside and the baby asleep in her cradle, the house that all winter had been a cluttered, stinking prison became by contrast quiet, spacious, and restful.

Stimulated by the change, Judith cleaned house, raked up the yard, and burned the winter accumulation of rubbish, set out her garden and even planted some seed of sweet peas and nasturtiums about the house. The caressing spring days filled her with a sense of calmness and passive wellbeing.

She never sang or romped any more. She could not rejoice and be glad with these things of nature. But out of her calm torpor she looked at them as through a thin mist and they sank upon her spirit like healing on a wound. She grew very fond of sitting on the doorstep.

It was that spring that the United States began to make preparations to send young men to Europe to fight for democracy.

A black wave of fear darkened the sunshine of Scott County when it became known that the United States had entered the war. Gus Dibble's vague apprehensions that the trouble might come their way had incredibly been realized. Out of the mouth of a fool the truth had come, and the impossible had happened. The war had crossed the ocean and was among them and was going to take them away from their homes. A few restless and physically fit young blades like Ziemer Whitmarsh and Bob Crupper found in the news the glorious promise of adventure. A few hailed it as a hope of deliverance from irksome conditions of life. But to most of these simple youths who had never been more than twenty miles away from their own dooryards it brought terror, stark and appalling: terror of the unknown into which they would be dragged from the security of their home cabins and tobacco patches, terror of death and of the unknown after death. In the tired bodies and shrinking minds of these underfed young men there was little to foster a thirst for adventure, still less any feeling of adherence to such a middle class luxury as patriotism. No newspapers nor shouting demagogues came to them with the lies that create and feed an artificial frenzy. For them there were neither crowds nor music nor public acclaim: no showy paraphernalia to hide the stinking carcass of war; only the naked certainty, faced and pondered upon in solitude, that inevitably that dreaded and all-powerful machine known as the law would reach out for them, take them out of their homes, away from the comfort of familiar faces, and place them they knew not where. Knowing nothing of the law and its processes, they feared and respected it beyond all other things. To them it was a god much more real and powerful than the still less known God of the Bible.

It was the most timid among them who developed the boldness of desperation and dared to hide themselves from the recruiting officer. They dropped out of sight, fled away to the hill country. Often they were brought back ignominiously and given a year in jail. Sometimes they were never heard of again.

For the most part, the young men shambled mechanically about the barnyard and behind the plow, trying with indifferent success to cultivate stoicism, afraid of being thought cowards, waiting in cold terror until their time should come.

Fear and hate lay at the hearts of the mothers. And having fewer pretenses to keep up than their sons and less respect for vested authority, they gave free voice to their feelings. Mothers whose sons had been caught in the draft said hard and bitter things behind the backs of the more fortunate ones whose offspring had escaped. There was weeping into midnight pillows, there was terror and dismay, envy, and hard suspicion.

Elmer, the second oldest Gibbs boy, shot himself in the foot while he was out hunting. Nobody knew why or what he was hunting at that time of year. He was lamed for life, so Dr. MacTaggert said; but he didn't have to go.

Marsh, his elder brother, was all agog to get into the fray. He had been listening to the talk of Bob and Ziemer; and being something of a braggart like his father, he had begun to lust for military adventures.

One afternoon when he was plowing near by, he took refuge in the Blackford kitchen from a heavy thunderstorm. From time to time, as he sat close to the door, he cast a swift glance at Judith who stood by the table ironing a Sunday shirt for Jerry. When she went to the stove to change her iron, he followed her movements with eyes that peered furtively from under the brim of his frayed straw hat.

"Well, Marsh," she said, "I hear you're a-goin' into the war."

His face brightened.

"You betcha. Me an' Bob an' Ziemer is a-goin' to clean 'em up good."

"An' what you a-goin' to fight for, Marsh?"

"I dun—" He checked the word before it was out of his lips. "What we a-goin' to fight fer? Why, fer our rights, o' course. An' we're a-goin' to lick 'em, too, the hull lot of 'em."

"Haow do you mean, the hull lot of 'em? Who all air you a-goin' to lick?"

"Why, all them furriners o' course: the Germans an' the Turks an' the Eyetalians an' the French an' the whole lousy shootin' match."

Among the women a few bright particular spirits like Aunt Eppie, who had no sons of an age to come within the selective draft, burned with righteous zeal against the Hun. And as the tigress is more fierce and pitiless than her male companion, so the hatred in the hearts of these women burned with a more cruel, intense, and implacable fury than a man's heart is able to sustain. Aunt Eppie, who had gloried in her neutrality before the United States went into the war, considering the belligerents all equally despicable and trifling, now could not find enough words of praise for the Allies, nor heap sufficient ignominy on the Germans. When Aunt Eppie spoke of the unspeakable Hun and the idolatrous Turk, her cold gray eyes flashed with the steely gleam of a scimiter, her false teeth came together with a fierce click, like a rat trap closing down on an unfortunate lover of cheese, and her imperious, bony knuckles rapped the table with a sound as suggestive of finality as the driving of nails into a coffin.

Jerry's mother, Aunt Mary Blackford, was another who was consumed with the fires of hate. At any mention of the enemy Aunt Mary's personality changed from kittenish to tigerish. It was an uncanny thing to see this small, frail woman, so given over to the service of others, so devoted to her husband, her sons, and her grandchildren, so kind and friendly toward her neighbors, turn into a spiteful, vicious virago at the mere mention of people of whom she knew nothing whatever. As the cat's claws are sharp and pitiless, so something hard, cruel, and implacable stretched itself at this crisis out of Aunt Mary's velvet exterior. Her blue eyes, ordinarily mild and childlike, could flash with as cold a gleam as Aunt Eppie's gray ones. Her mouth could shut in lines as hard and pitiless. Her babylike hands, fluttering in excited anger, seemed to Judith even more savage claws than Aunt Eppie's imperiously tapping knuckles. The younger woman felt something akin to hate rise in her own breast as she turned coldly away from Aunt Mary's demonstrations of righteous indignation.

"I reckon," she said, looking with coolly level eyes at her mother-in-law, "if you'd been born a German you'd be the fust one to hate us Americans same's you're a-hatin' the Germans naow. An' either way there'd be about as much sense to it."

Aunt Mary bridled fiercely under Judith's cold gaze.

"Well, I'm thankful I hain't one o' them that's without no nat'ral human feelin's," she spat out, then was silent, unable to find words to express her irritation and chagrin. The atmosphere was dense with the intensity of the two women's dislike for each other.

"When times like these comes, they show up folks in their real nater," sniffed Aunt Mary, after an angry pause.

"Yes, they do," answered Judith, with cold incisiveness.

Jerry, the only true devotee of peace, was made miserable when his wife and his mother sparred about the war. He shifted uneasily and looked from one to the other with dumbly beseeching eyes, like those of a gentle dog.

One morning when she was churning on the porch, Bob Crupper sauntered around the corner of the house.

For some time he hung about, talking of this and that: last night's rain that would bring the tobacco beds along, the new flagpole that they had just set up in the school yard, the big price that the sheep men were going to get for their wool. As he talked, he sat on the edge of the porch and whittled aimlessly at a stick or trundled a toy wagon up and down the porch floor with his hand.

At last, after a silence broken only by the thump of the dasher in the churn, he roused himself and stood up.

"Well, I must be a-goin'. I'm off to-night for the trainin' camp. So I'll say good-by."

She released the dasher and gave him her hand. He took it in his which was large, firm, and warm. His face twitched with embarrassment.

Suddenly she felt his face close to hers and heard his voice in a quick, hoarse whisper.

"Judy, mebbe I won't never see you agin. I'm agoin' to hev one kiss anyway afore I go."

She felt herself melting into his arms as he kissed her on the mouth long and passionately. The next moment he was gone.

Her hands trembled as she took hold of the dasher again. Had she kissed him back or had she not kissed him back, she wondered. For a long time her lips burned from his kiss, as once before her neck and shoulder had burned from his look.

In June the neighborhood was thrown into a flutter of excitement by the coming of two evangelists. People said that they were from a little sect in the hill country. They stopped with Uncle Joe Patton, who was himself a religious man and a total abstainer, and they were to hold their meetings in Uncle Joe's house. All the neighbors were urged to attend the meetings.

Jerry was again working beyond his strength. He was determined to have a big tobacco crop this year. It was whispered that the price of tobacco would go sky high on account of America being in the war. He was becoming grouchy from the strain of overwork. Judith, with three babies to care for, could give no help.

"I hain't a-goin' to be drug to none o' their godforsaken meetin's," he said testily to Judith, when she mentioned the evangelists. "I'm too damn tired nights to do anything but turn in. But there hain't nothin' to keep you from goin' if you've a mind. I'll be here in the house with the young uns. All I ast is don't wake me up when you come home."

The thought of the evangelists piqued Judith's curiosity. Her life was easier now that summer had come; and her peaceful apathy was beginning to be stirred by slight tremors of returning interest in things. She had never listened to an evangelist since that half forgotten night when she was ten. She decided to go.

On the way she called for Hat. She knew that Hat would be going. As she expected Hat was preparing to start and had made elaborate toilet preparations. She had frizzed her hair so that it stood out violently on all sides, and she was wearing a stiffly starched pink calico dress. Under the dress Judith glimpsed the red petticoat.

Luke, in his sock feet, stretched luxuriously in an old rocker.

"I reckon you two is spilin' fer sumpin to do," he said, giving them a swift disdainful glance, as he spat into the woodbox. "An' if them lousy preachers'd foller the plow a spell or do a little wrastlin' on the end of a shovel through the day, they wouldn't be so spry about draggin' the wimmin out nights."

"Aw, shet up," returned Hat. "I guess seekin' the Lord nights is jes as good as huntin' foxes anyway. You don't need to hand out no lip."

They walked across fields to the Patton home, each carrying a lantern, for there was no moon. The night was warm and sweet with the smells of summer. Blackberry bushes reached sharp tentacles out of the dark and made Hat gather her precious dress more closely about her.

"I wisht the meetin's was held anywheres but at Patton's place," she fretted. "It's so durn hard to git to, an' when you git there it's so lonesome lookin' it seems like it's hanted. The old folks all says it's hanted. It gives me the chills."

They crossed one creek on a plank and another on a log. Hat's great bulk teetered uneasily on the log and she thought of her clean dress and white stockings.

"Durn hard place to git to," she muttered.

The light wind was balmy and full of woodsy fragrance. In one place a whiff from a flowering alfalfa field came to them on the warm air heavy and sweet.

In a corner of a pasture their footsteps startled some sheep invisible in the darkness. A shivery sound of the movement of many soft bodies and then the patter of innumerable small feet told them that the sheep had scampered away. A few who had become separated from the main flock bleated inquiringly. The others answered: "This way, sisters, this way."

Judith felt strangely stirred and elated. It was an adventure, this coming out into the warm, soft, fragrant night. She thrilled to hear the sheep pattering away into the darkness calling to each other.

A rough wagon track down the side of a steep hill covered with brush and stunted trees brought them to the clearing about the Patton house. It was a tall old house built of heavy logs that had once been whitewashed. It rose corpselike in the dim light of the stars. Small dark windows piercing the thickness of the logs looked out from the pallid walls like eyes.

The house was hemmed in on every side. On the north, from which they had approached it, the hill rose abruptly. East and west the woods crept almost to the doors. On the south was Stony Creek, a torrent in winter, a wide, half dried up river bed in summer. Wagons to get to the place must either come down the steep hill or ford the river. The house was shaded by aged gray willows. Of evenings it was swathed in vapors from the river bed.

There was a vague story whispered about the place: a story of one of those atrocious murders that occur from time to time in out-of-the-way places, where solitude and the emptiness of life teach the mind to brood. Such morbidly brooding minds sometimes flare out into sudden, grim passions, craving the sacrifice of blood.

Such a story was told about the Patton place. Perhaps it had a basis of fact. Perhaps it was only a myth grown out of the sinister appearance of the house and the dark-crannied minds of the tobacco growers. It was old and vague and told with many variations.

"Land alive, but it's a pesky, shivery place," complained Hat. "An' it's damp an' dirty, too. I despise sech a place. I wouldn't live here fer no money."

Light shone from one window of the Patton house, and several low-burning lanterns stood by the door. They added their own to the gleaming cluster and pushed open the door.

Uncle Joe Patton was praying. In the half light cast by a tall, thin glass lamp with a tiny wick, a dozen or so women and perhaps half a dozen men knelt upon the floor before planks laid from chair to chair. Two dogs sat at respectful attention and one was curled up under the table. A large black cat slept on the flattened patchwork cushion of the only rocking chair in the room. The heavy beams of the low ceiling, blackened with smoke and hung with cobwebs, seemed to absorb into their gloom the light of the small lamp.

Uncle Joe's prayer was long and meandering, like all his talk. He was a very old man, and like many other old men harped constantly upon a certain few things, saying them over and over again, each time as impressively as if they were quite new to the patient listener. He addressed the Lord in like manner. His voice rumbling along in the level monotone appropriate to prayer was as drowsy as the humming of bees over a clover field. Judith, who had been standing at the washtub most of the day, caught herself nodding into sleep as she knelt at the end of one of the planks.

She was roused from one of these dozes by Uncle Jabez's dog poking his moist nose into her face; and she began to peer about from under her sunbonnet in quest of the two strangers. She found them easily enough; but their heads were so devoutly bowed in prayer that there was nothing of them to be seen but backs and shoulders. She saw Hat's eyes traveling in the same direction as her own, and encountered the bored gaze of Uncle Jabez and the twinkling gray eyes of Uncle Sam Whitmarsh, who was taking a look around after having consulted his watch.

She dozed a little; and when she roused herself and fell to peeping again she caught an exchange of looks between Abbie Gibbs and Ziemer Whitmarsh.

Aunt Jenny Patton, who suddenly remembered that she had forgotten to put the yeast into the rising of bread, rose at this moment and slipped unobtrusively into the back kitchen. The cat in the rocking chair yawned and stretched, then curled again deliciously. Still Uncle Joe droned along. The kneelers stirred more and more uneasily trying to relieve their cramped legs and aching knees.

At last, when they had almost lost hope, Uncle Joe droned to an end; and they all stood up with sighs of relief and were led into a hymn. The two evangelists and Jabez Moorhouse were the only ones who really sang. The others made vague, inarticulate sounds, took breath gaspingly and quavered uneasily into silence. Uncle Joe, in an aged tremolo, tried hard to follow, but was like a dog that has lost the scent.

When the harvest is past and the summer is gone,
And summons and prayers shall be o'er;
When the harvest is past and the summer is gone,
And Jesus invites us no more.

The evangelists were both rather good singers, and Jabez had a sonorous bass. The tune went wailing to the smoky rafters, wistful and melancholy.

During the hymn Judith and everybody else gazed curiously at the evangelists.

They were farmer folk like herself she knew by the sure intuition with which people know their own kind. One was tall and flimsy of body, with a receding chin, bulging eyes light blue in color, prominent teeth and a large Adam's apple. She seemed to have seen him before or somebody like him. He made her think of a fish. He looked innocent, kindly, and stupid.

The other was shorter and more compactly built. There was nothing remarkable about his face or figure except that he had strange, arresting eyes that seemed to smolder with a dark, inward flame. The eyes fascinated her. Again and again she felt her own drawn toward them. Twice during the singing she met his gaze and turned away her own abashed and in confusion.

When the singing was over, the evangelist with the strange eyes began to preach a sermon, taking as his text the words, "Repent ye, for the Kingdom of Heaven is at hand." As soon as he began to speak, she knew that his voice matched his eyes. It was glowing, fiery, and under the fire rich with tenebrous depth. He talked about sin and the wrath to come, the raging fires of eternal damnation and the worm that never dieth. As he talked the smoldering glow of his strange eyes burst into flame. The familiar cant phrases of revivalist exhortation falling glibly from his tongue took strength and color from the fire of his dark fanaticism. In the dim light he seemed to grow larger. A potent magnetism issued from him and held the listeners spellbound.

At the end of his discourse he swept them into a hymn.

> Almost persuaded. Summer is past.
> Almost persuaded. Doom comes at last.
> Almost can not avail.
> Sad, sad the bitter wail.
> Almost is but to fail.
> Almost—but lost.

The music, lovingly hugging the words, combined with the rankling pain of remorse and the bitterness of despair the iron clang of inevitable doom. Of its kind the hymn was a masterpiece. During the singing the simple tobacco growers and their wives, not used to spiritual stimulation, looked vaguely troubled, flustered and ill at ease.

When the hymn was over and the preacher sat down the spell was broken. Virtue seemed to have gone out of him. With all his fervor he had uttered nothing but strings of stock phrases used by every ranter about hell fire. They had heard it all before. When the glow of his personality no longer enfolded them, his listeners were left empty-minded and their thoughts reverted instantly to their own affairs, to the kitchen, the barn, and the tobacco field.

Judith did not ponder upon what the preacher had said. For her hell fire had no terrors. Her spirit was of a pagan soundness that shed such tainted superstitions as a duck's down sheds water. But she could not forget the man's darkly glowing eyes and darkly vibrant voice. Through the thick gloom as she walked home she saw the eyes burning before her, heard the voice vibrating through the fragrance of the summer night.

"Ouch!" exclaimed Hat, "if I hain't done gone an' stuck my foot into a mud hole. An' me with white stockin's on, too. Drat the durn lantern, it don't give light enough fer a flea to go to bed by."

In the same spot where it had greeted them before came a whiff from a flowering alfalfa field, not clover nor heliotrope, but a mixture of the intensest sweetness of both, subtle, and disquieting.

"Say, Judy, don't you think the short feller was good lookin'? An' what was it about his eyes—an' his voice, too? I dunno— sumpin."

All the way home Hat talked about the preacher's good looks, about Luke's slovenliness, a new dress that she was making, and a sunbonnet pattern that she had made up herself out of her own head. Through her unheeded patter of talk Judith saw the strange eyes looking at her out of the darkness, heard the dark voice vibrating in the fragrance of the summer night.

On the way home Amos Crupper said to Sam Whitmarsh in his deep chest tones:

"Waal, that there was a fine sermon the young feller preached —a strong, powerful sermon. I like to listen to a good sermon an' read the news about the war. It makes a man feel like life hain't all but jes plantin' an' diggin' taters an' hoein' ter-baccer."

"Yaas," agreed Uncle Sam, "sech things livens a feller up a bit an' makes him realize this life hain't all. I hearn you was needin' a buggy hoss, Amos. I got the finest little mare— dark bay—awful purty color—six year old no more, an' I'd—"

"No, Sam, she hain't fer me," Uncle Amos interrupted him smiling genially. "I knowed that there little mare when Pete Akers had her, an' I know she's twelve if she's a day an' she's had the heaves since she was little more'n a colt. You fix her up with a little dose o' birdshot to cover up them heaves an' take her to Georgetown on Court Day. You'll be able to trade her good an' mebbe put a little piece o' money in yer pocket."

On the way home Jabez Moorhouse, walking somberly alone, thought how his life had been wasted.

"I cud a made a preacher," he said to himself, "or a con-gressman or a jedge or learnt to play the fiddle good if I'd on'y had a chanct. But all my life I hain't done nothin' but dig

in dirt. An' all the rest o' my life I'm a-goin' to keep right
on a-diggin' in dirt."

He spat tobacco juice into the grass and uttered his favorite
exclamation of disgust. It was a phrase of his own contriving,
a rich verbal arabesque of profanity and obscenity cunningly
inwrought.

Having thus partly relieved his feelings, he took a long pull
from a bottle that he always carried in his pocket.

After several long pulls he felt much better and sang into
the night a ballad with the oft-recurring refrain:

"You can't have my daughter without the gray mare."

On the way home Ziemer Whitmarsh overtook Abbie Gibbs,
who had purposely hung behind the other members of her
family, wound his arm about her slim, consumptive waist and
drew her aside from the path.

On the way home Joe Barnaby and young Marsh Gibbs hesitated where a road making gang who were widening the pike
to Georgetown had left their roller and other tools by the side
of the road.

"D'yuh know what I spied Gus Dibble a-doin' the other
day?" said Joe in a tone of infinite disgust. "I seen him
a-stealin' a log chain out o' these here fixin's. What d'yuh
think of a feller'd steal a log chain, hey?"

Joe himself had for many years eked out his small means by
doing jobs of lumber hauling and was hence amply provided
with log chains.

"I dunno," mused Marsh. "Mebbe he needed the log chain.
I know I need a new shovel awful bad, an' they've riz up awful
high in price since the war come on. That there long-handled
one over there is jes the kind I was a-wantin'."

He looked wistfully at the shovel.

"Oh, well, of course a shovel's diff'rent," Joe hastened to
assure him. "If I wanted the shovel I'd take it along 'f I'z you.
The dod gasted road comp'ny kin buy more. 'Tain't like takin'
anythin' off'n a neighbor."

"That's so," agreed Marsh, taking loving hold upon the
handle of the shovel.

"The young uns lost my last pair o' pliers yestiddy," confided Joe. "I made the little buggers look everywhere fer 'em, but o' course they didn't find 'em. Hardware's awful high these days. I never knowed hardware to be so high. I reckon I'll jes slip this pair into my pocket, an' nobody'll know where they went to 'cep you an' me, hey, Marsh?"

"Sure," agreed Marsh heartily, as he shouldered the shovel. "You might's well have 'em as any other night walker. Durn careless of 'em to leave these small things lyin' about anyway. Serve 'em right if they hain't here when they come back."

When Judith crept into bed beside Jerry and closed her eyes inviting sleep, she saw the burning eyes of the evangelist looking at her out of the darkness.

CHAPTER XX

A FEW weeks before the arrival of the Evangelists, Hat had sent away a dime and a two cent stamp to certain parties who had advertised in the "Farm Wife's Friend" that for that sum they would teach you how to develop your personal magnetism and to exert it in such a way that you could control the people with whom you came in contact and make them do whatever you willed that they should do. She received in answer a typewritten letter informing her that hers had been one of the very few letters received by them which indicated beyond a doubt that the writer was a person possessed of a tremendous amount of latent magnetism, a mighty force with untold possibilities of being turned to the owner's advantage. For ordinary people the fee for further instruction was ten dollars. But for her, with her intensely interesting personality and wonderful latent power, they would make the exceptionally low rate of three dollars. For this trifling sum her special case would be taken up and studied in the minutest detail by the greatest specialists of the world, all of them congregated for this important purpose in Toledo, Ohio.

The letter brought to Hat's bosom considerable conflict of impulses. She was flattered and thrilled to know that she was the possessor of an interesting personality full of great magnetic power. In a vague way she had always suspected something of the sort. Now of course she knew for sure. She pondered upon the advantages that the use of this magnetic influence would bring. Of course her first exercise of it would be upon Luke, to make him change his socks oftener, eat less disgustingly at the table, get up first and light the fire in the morning, and chop the stove wood instead of going off and leaving it for her to do. She would also influence him to be fairer in money matters and let her have her just share of what she earned and put it into a bank account in her own name. Since her marriage her disputes with Luke on the subject of the division of their money had been frequent and heated.

Having reformed Luke in this way, she was by no means sure that she would be entirely satisfied with him. She was ready to be convinced that there were nicer men in the world than Luke. Her thoughts rambled away into shadowy and devious paths, imagining lovers of many sorts. With this great power in her possession what avenue in life would be closed to her?

But three dollars! It was too much! How could she bear to take three whole dollar bills and put them into an envelope and send them away? With a two cent stamp or a dime or even both it was different. But three whole dollars! She thought of all the finery that three dollars would buy if she had a mind to spend the money on finery. She thought of all the eggs that she would have to take to Peter Akers' store to get three dollars. No, she just couldn't send away three dollars.

But the idea of having her personal magnetism developed was too fascinating a subject to be easily forgotten. She figured and pondered, almost sent the three dollars a dozen times, but could not bring herself to the final mailing of the letter.

On the day after the first revival meeting, Hat found in her mail box another letter from the cultivators of personal magnetism which fairly made her heart bleed. It began:

"Dear Harriet Wolf: If my own sister had failed to answer my letter, I could not have felt more disappointed than I was at not hearing from you. Many a night I have lain awake thinking of the tremendous power in your extremely interesting personality which is being wasted, thrown away, scattered to the idle winds."

It went on for two and a half typewritten pages in the most personal and poignant manner. Hat could hardly keep from shedding tears of mingled gratification and self-pity. She was a stranger to the devious ways of the advertising business; and the mimeographed form letter, with her own name so skilfully inserted that it took a trained eye to tell it from the rest of the type, was to her a personal missive from one overflowing heart to another. Besides, the price was reduced fifty cents. For two dollars and fifty cents, if she acted quickly, she could now have her personal magnetism developed.

As she walked home from the mail box through the sweet June weather she thought of the dark eyed evangelist and of her own great undeveloped possibilities. She was stirred by a feeling that life was on the point of opening out for her. She decided to send away the money.

At home she got out the two dollars and fifty cents from a secret place in which she kept such money as she could manage, by various roundabout methods, to get out of Luke's hands, and dropped it into a jar on the clock shelf ready to buy a money order when she met the rural mail carrier next day. But by the next day her ardor had cooled to such an extent that the money looked too good to part with. She put it carefully back into the secret place.

After the second revival meeting she arrived at the conclusion that it was her duty to give a party to make the strangers feel at home.

"It looks like it's up agin me," she said to Judith, with something of the air of a martyr, "seein' nobody else hain't come forrard. O' course the fixin' an' bakin'll come kinder heavy on me, bein' as haow it's terbaccer choppin' time. So I wouldn't mind a bit if you brung along a little cake or sumpin like that to he'p me aout."

She must have thrown out the same subtle suggestion to all the invited guests, for few of the women came without a package in their hands.

The party, as seemed fitting, opened with prayer and a hymn and partook throughout of the nature of a prayer meeting. Out of respect for the preachers there was no dancing, neither were there any boisterous kissing games. The men lounged in the kitchen handy to the stove and woodbox and talked about the war. The women sat about in little groups in Hat's best room and from time to time broke the heavy silence by isolated remarks about babies, sicknesses, and the best ways of rendering out hog fat. Even the men talked in subdued tones; and over everything there was a hushed atmosphere of restraint and respectful decorum. Nothing disturbed the decent calm but occasional giggles and titters from the young and unmarried who had a tendency to disappear in couples.

Hat, who entertained her guests with several songs, accompanying herself on the violin, avoided the more jaunty and jiglike airs of her repertoire and sang instead a doleful ballad of many stanzas, the gist of which is contained in the following two:

> Just one year ago to-night, love,
>   I became your happy bride,
> Changed a mansion for a cottage
>   To dwell by the waterside.
>
> And you told me I'd be happy,
>   But no happiness I see,
> For to-night I am a widow
>   In the cottage by the sea.

Though her voice was a bit strident and her fiddling rather noisy and vigorous for the conveying of these soft sentiments, the listeners, especially the women, seemed none the less deeply touched at the poor young woman's loss of both her man and her mansion.

As she sang she sought more than once with her bold, dark glances the magnetic eyes of the more attractive of the two preachers. Her chagrin was great and very poorly concealed when toward the close of the song about the unfortunate young lawbreaker, she saw the glance that she coveted traveling straight toward Judy Blackford who sat in a corner with her hands folded in her lap looking strangely demure and more than usually beautiful. The eye of jealousy is quicker than the eye of love to perceive beauty. Hat glared and in deep bitterness cursed the fate that had not given to herself outward charms in keeping with her qualities of soul. She wished that she had sent away the two dollars and a half.

Out of respect for the guests of honor, very little whiskey flowed at this party. The small amount of drinking that went on was done surreptitiously from pocket flasks in the dark of the outer night. The beverage served with the cake was water.

"It's pure," Hat boasted proudly, as she passed it about in tumblers, goblets, teacups, and jelly glasses. "We got the best well this side o' Sadieville."

When the guests had washed down their pieces of stack cake with this innocent and economical drink, they began to think about going home. As Judith was tying on her sunbonnet, she glimpsed under the bed where Hat had hastily shoved them, the corners of several cakes.

"Her an' Luke'll live on stale cake fer the nex' month," she whispered to Jerry.

The two young preachers stationed themselves at the door and shook hands with all the "friends" as they passed out. And though the handshakes were a bit solemn and prayermeetinglike, they were kindly meant. When it came Judith's turn to take the hand of the preacher with the strange eyes, she felt herself hesitating. Then, having given him her hand, she withdrew it hurriedly and passed out. She felt Hat's searching eyes fastened upon her. Her fingers tingled and her heart thumped as she climbed into the cart and sat down beside Jerry. She was glad of the darkness, for she knew that her cheeks were in a flame.

A compelling fascination lured her again and again to the revival meetings. There through the meaningless droning of the prayers, the wail of the hymns and the exhortations of the evangelists, she sat in a half hypnotized state conscious only of a pair of darkly burning eyes, a darkly vibrating voice. Not once but many times during the service her fascinated gaze met that of the preacher and swerved from it, confused and abashed. Once, by an effort of will, she met his look with her own dark, level gaze and did not turn her eyes aside. He started and turned abruptly away; and in the dim light she thought she saw a dark red flush pass across his face.

Having found that she had this power, she was constantly prodded by the urge to exercise it. She knew nothing about self-discipline. All her life she had known no guide but her impulses. Now as always she followed where they pointed. It was not mere coquetry, but an irresistible force stronger than herself that made her dart her level, penetrating glance like a keen sword into the dark turmoil of the evangelist's smoldering eyes. He winced as if the sword had pierced him. Through her temples the blood pounded tumultuously. She was seized with a delirious, half frenzied joy. She held her breath so that she would not scream. Out of the corner of her eye she watched Hat.

Once they sang an old fashioned hymn, now rarely heard in churches:

> Oh to be nothing, nothing,
>   Only to lie at his feet,
> A broken and empty vessel
>   That the Master's use may meet.
> Empty that he might fill me
>   As forth to His service I go,
> Broken and unencumbered
>   That His light through me may flow.

When the evangelist sang he gave his whole soul to the singing. His breast heaved with more than the expansion of his lungs. His strange eyes dilated and burned. An aura of ecstasy welled out from him. He was a man transfigured and beyond himself. The tune, unutterably wistful and rich with passionate longing, surged through the little room. With music, the only tongue that can voice passion, it spoke mightily to the two who had ears to hear. It throbbed in Judith's temples, in her heart, in all the arteries of her body. Irresistibly she sought the eyes of the evangelist. This time he did not turn away. A shaft of dark fire reached out to her from his transfigured face, bold, compelling, and masterful; and it was she who with a hot blush dropped her gaze to the floor. By a lucky chance Hat was not there that night.

In the darkness of the summer night he overtook her on the way home. All the way she had been listening for him. She knew that he would come. He came up with her where the alfalfa field spilled its subtle fragrance into the warm night air. His arms about her were strong and imperative. His hands were hot. His kissing mouth was insatiable. With an ecstasy transcending anything that she had ever felt in her life, she yielded herself to his passion.

She moved through the succeeding weeks in an unquiet trance, treading not upon hard earth, but upon some substance infinitely buoyant and elastic. She scarcely knew that she washed and milked and churned and worked over butter, that she cooked and swept and hoed in the garden and dressed and fed the children. She performed these tasks as one drives a horse through a pitch black night, leaving the lines slack and letting the animal feel his way. Her body, well broken to household routine, went forward by itself without guidance of the mind. From daylong labors done in this way she came forth strangely fresh and unwearied.

Always she was intensely conscious of her body, deliciously aware of the roundness of her arms, the softness and whiteness of her breasts, the slim grace of her ankles. Never before had she given such things more than a passing thought. In other times when she had thought about the appearance of her body it had been in relation to new dresses. Now the beauty of her body lived and moved with her continually, a part of her consciousness. She gazed long into the little looking glass at her cheeks, radiant with a warm flush, her eyes softly luminous. Something of the cool, level quality had gone out of the eyes leaving a deep radiance. Looking into the glass she laughed little soft, shivery laughs and felt the blood rise tingling into her cheeks.

Sitting on the doorstep to peel potatoes or shell peas, she

stretched her slim, brown, bare feet out into the sunshine and looked at them with eyes that saw their beauty. She twisted a strand of her lustrous black hair about her finger, made it into a glittering curl and dangled it in the sunlight with a foolish little laugh.

In the yard not far from the kitchen door stood a rose bush, a poor, battered, stunted thing, scratched and nipped by the hens and broken back again and again by straying hogs and calves. Nothing was left of it but a few spiny stalks almost denuded of leaves. On one of these stalks she had noticed a red bud swelling.

One morning when she came to the door she saw that the bud had blossomed into a rose, not a frail pink blossom, but a silken, scarlet thing with a great, gold heart, heavy with dew and fragrance. Gorgeously it flaunted on its distorted stem. Against the drabness of the dooryard, now bare with summer drought, it flamed rich and vivid. She knelt on the ground beside the rose and smelled of its perfume. Inhaling the fragrance and looking into the deep richness of the scarlet leaves, she felt carried beyond herself with a great uplifting of the heart. Tears from some strange, hidden source welled into her eyes.

After its one rose had shed its leaves, the little bush, discouraged by the drought and the continual pecking of the hens, dried up and leveled itself with the ground.

Fearful of shrewd looks and whispering tongues, she did not go often to the meetings. They had other places of rendezvous. One was a deep hollow pungent with the smell of mint, where the creek splashed over moss covered stones and a weeping willow trailed its gray leaves in the water. Here on the hottest July afternoon the overhanging boughs of many trees and saplings made a green coolness. The place seemed remote as a cave until one day Uncle Jonah Cobb came along the little cowpath that bordered the creek. They heard him pushing aside the branches that grew across the unfrequented path and had time to dive back into the underbrush. Half blind and more than half deaf, he took his slow way through their little bower and, like an old ox whose neck bends by second nature to the yoke, never once lifted his head.

"I wonder was Uncle Jonah ever young?" she whispered, when he was safely out of hearing.

After that she would never go there again. The place seemed as open as a public square, as bare to the world as a housetop. She could never think of it without seeing Uncle Jonah plodding through it, his eyes fixed on the ground, a long blue patch on the back of his gray shirt, his denim trousers, much too large for him, hitched half way up his back by his greasy galluses.

Hemmed in between two steep hills and smothered in brush that had grown up about it was the shell of an old shanty that had been forsaken of man as long as Judith could remember. Near it was neither wagon track nor cowpath. Nobody ever came that way. On the floor, streaked and stained by many rains, they made themselves a resting place of cedar boughs and last year's leaves.

Mocking birds had built that year in the locust trees by the horsepond. How many she did not know. Perhaps there was only a pair or two, but it sounded like a dozen. She could see their pert little gray and white bodies darting about in the branches. Sometimes one of them would perch on a fence rail or the rooftree of the smokehouse and flirt his long tail saucily as he preened his feathers. These little choir boys to Pan, in whose small bodies the spark of life burned with such an intense flame, who lived only to love and to sing, kept the air vibrant almost all day long with their insistent, soul disturbing melodies. For a few hours the noonday sun lulled them into luxurious rest and a deep quiet fell, treacherously haunted by erotic echoes. The meadow larks that sang over and over again at regular intervals their one slender ripple of song were with their few guileless notes like poor little parlor singers beside these great masters of bird opera. There was no sound in the language of birds that they could not make. They chirped, chirred, trilled, twittered, caroled, ran again and again through all the scales a bird's voice ever compassed. Just to show what they could do, they imitated with perfection of accuracy the song of the finch, the robin, the meadow lark. Then, soaring far beyond the compass of these humble singers, burst forth rapturously into such floods of melody that the sunlight seemed filled with a rain of bright jewels. With delirious abandon to love and joy, the music welled from their little throats, palpitatingly, delicate, piercingly sweet. The enraptured rush of it, the sudden turns of it, the mad surprises of it penetrated Judith's being and swayed her like the master passion of which they were the voice.

They did not often sing in the night. But once a wakeful wooer sat on the ridgepole of the smokehouse and poured into the white moonlight floods of wild melody. For a long time Judith stood at the window looking out at the dim sky with scarcely a star showing and the world lying blanched and black under the light of the full moon. The locust trees by the horsepond looked dark and mysterious. The shadow of the smokehouse gable lay sharp and black against the whiteness of the yard. On the ridgepole she could just distinguish the little dark speck whose music thrilled the night. She leaned her head on the window sill and felt herself melting, dissolving away into music and moonlight.

All at once the bird stopped singing and a silence fell like the hush before doom. She shivered in her thin nightgown and crept back into bed. Sobs were rising in her throat. She tried to stifle them in the pillow; but her whole body shook in the grip of the hysteria.

Jerry stirred uneasily in his heavy sleep of exhaustion.

"Don't cry, Judy," he murmured sleepily, winding his arm about her. "Things'll come out all right."

It was blackberry season and she had a good excuse for leaving the children with Aunt Selina. Aunt Selina was genuinely glad to have them. Like most other back country women she was ready with glib lies to suit any occasion. But Judith knew that she was not lying when she said: "Fetch 'em over soon agin, Judy, the little darlin's." The old woman dearly loved the company of children. She chirruped and twittered to the baby and prattled in an unending stream to the two boys as they followed her about while she fed the chickens and tended the rabbits and hoed the cabbages and the rows of beans. She loved to put cookies into their chubby little grimy hands and twists of sugared popcorn in the pockets of their overalls. She had a sweet tooth herself, so she nearly always had such things about the house. They were near of an age, all four, and happy together.

He would meet her on the edges of the pasture slopes where the blackberries grew and help her fill her tin bucket with the large, juicy berries. Here in the embrace of the sun the earth swooned with midsummer heat. Bees drowsed over the patches of steeplebush. Here and there tall stately stalks of ironweed lifted their great crowns of royal purple. The scent of flowering milkweed distilled out into the hot sunshine was heavy and sweet. Heavier and sweeter was the smell of purple alfalfa blossoms blown across the pasture in warm whiffs.

As they strayed about over the close cropped grass among the brambles and dock and patches of steeplebush, they spoke to each other scarcely at all. Only sometimes when he came beside her, he gripped her hand in his which was strong and dark. When the berry bucket was full he drew her unresistingly down between the steep hills to the old shanty.

Through these hot summer weeks she felt small need of sleep. When in the half light of the early morning she and Jerry took their milk buckets and went through the yard to the cowlot, she felt awake, alive, a creature of the morning. She thrilled to the feeling of newness, of life born again, that stirs through a summer dawn.

As the summer advanced, an uneasiness that was something other than erotic unrest began to assail her. She tried to dismiss it, to ignore its existence, to lose herself in the old preoccupations. Untiring as a weasel intent upon the blood of chickens, it kept coming back upon her with stealthy persistence. She knew that it was trying to awaken her from her dream. She did not want to be awakened; yet more and more surely she realized that the waking hour was at hand. When she looked into her mirror she met a cool, level gaze looking calmly out at her through radiance that was growing dim. The blood no longer rose warmly into her cheeks.

At first the dark-eyed stranger had power to charm away this disquieting intruder and bring the dream back. For this she sought him out at all times and places, unmindful of the tongue of slander, forgetting prudence, forgetting everything but the desire to be kept within her dream. He felt gratified at first, as a man is gratified by evidence of his power to attract. Then, fearing whither her recklessness might lead, tormented too by fears and dark conflicts that were an outgrowth of his nature, but had no part in hers, he tried to show her the folly of her lack of discretion. When he began to do this she was filled with bitter contempt for what she called his cowardice. She looked at him grimly, with a hard light in her eyes, and knew that she must surely awaken.

She began to go less often to look for berries; and the little shanty between the hills saw them more and more rarely. When they met in the pasture lands she was sullen and irritable. He too gloomed and grouched.

One day when she saw him coming toward her in the blackberry patch, her eyes instead of seeking his fell upon the lower part of his face. It was not a bad face as the faces of men go; but of a sudden it seemed to her revoltingly stupid, sullen, and almost bestial. She restrained a mad impulse to fling out her arm and slap it with the back of her hand.

The blackberry season was nearly over, and the berries were becoming few and scattered. They ranged far searching for the luscious fruit. She kept as far away from him as she could. Something about his presence seemed to make the air stuffy.

He picked into a little folding cup that he was in the habit of carrying in his pocket. When he brought the cup full of berries and emptied it into her bucket, she looked at him with cold, sardonic eyes.

When the bucket was half full she took it resolutely on her arm.

"You don't need fer to pick no more," she said coldly. "I'm a-goin' back home naow."

He looked at her at first beseechingly. Then a look of relief spread over his features.

"It's best so," he muttered huskily. But he turned and walked beside her.

"Fall'll soon be a-comin' on," she said. "See that there maple branch is red a'ready. That there one big branch allus turns red in August, long afore the others."

He quoted from one of his hymns:

> The harvest is past and the summer is gone,
> And Jesus invites us no more.

She was mastered by a cruel desire to make him suffer.

"I shouldn't reckon Jesus'd invite *you*," she scoffed, "after the way you bin a-actin'. Hain't you askairt you'll roast in hell fire forever for the way you bin a-doin'? An' you with the face to keep on standin' up an' preachin' diff'rent all the time!"

He started violently, as though she had thrust a knife into him where it could hurt the most. The struggling demons of lust and religious fanaticism that made for themselves a battle ground of his wretched body and spirit looked at her out of his darkly smoldering eyes. It was a look to call forth pity. But she was not in a mood to feel pity.

"God forgive me and save me from you," he groaned, covering his face with his hands, "you scarlet woman!"

She laughed derisively.

"Huh, I reckon I hain't no scarleter'n what you air. An' anyhaow I don't *feel* scarlet, an' you do. I don't do things I'm ashamed o' doin', an' I hain't a bit askairt o' hell fire neither."

He turned and fled away from this monstrous creature, this cold and sinful woman who knew neither fear nor shame.

She laughed a mocking laugh; then turned toward him suddenly, overpowered with deep disgust.

"I couldn't stummick to swaller the dirty berries you picked," she called out, and threw the berries after him, with the swift motion of a spiteful little quarreling schoolchild. Then she walked away and never once looked back.

For weeks she had been struggling against this unseen force that she knew was trying to awaken her from her dream. She had been edging away from the thought of waking, shivering with apprehension. Now that she knew herself broad awake, she felt of a sudden glad, bold, and strong. A sense of freedom, of relief from some clinging burden that had grown clogged and foul, passed through her like a strong wind that scatters cobwebs and made her breath deep and lift her head high in the sunlight. Swinging the empty bucket with happy abandon, as a child its dinner pail, she strode with long, free steps across the pasture and along the ridge road, delighting in the sun and the sweet air, feeling clean, sound, and whole, her mind untroubled by regrets, unsullied by the slightest tinge of self-abasement.

In Aunt Selina's clean-swept dooryard she called for the children and went on toward home walking like some primal savage woman with movements scarcely less strong and free for the weight of the baby on her arm. The boys, half carrying, half dragging the empty bucket, frolicked about her in circles.

At supper that night she looked about at her family as though she were seeing them for the first time after an absence. As is usual after absence, she liked them all better, felt more kindly disposed toward them and more solicitous for their welfare. Also she saw them more clearly as with the eyes of a stranger.

The boys, greedily devouring their milk and corn cakes and champing valiantly up and down ears of green corn that she had boiled for supper, were hale and ruddy little fellows. But on their baby faces she saw already appearing traces of a look that she had learned to dread, a look that stamps itself upon the faces of those who for generations have tilled the soil in solitude, a heavy, settled, unexpectant look. It seemed cruel that such a look should come upon the faces of little boys long even before their time for doing barn chores. Looking at them she was filled with a vague unhappiness.

When she turned from the boys to the little girl she felt a more poignant sting. Annie was the kind of little girl one sees often in country places and very rarely in towns. She had a puny, colorless, young-old face, drab hair thin and fine, that hung in little straight wisps about her cheeks, a mouth scarcely different in color from the rest of the face, and blank, slate-colored eyes. There was neither depth nor clearness in the little eyes, no play of light and shade, no sparkle of mirth or mischief, no flash of anger, nothing but a dead, even slate color. They were always the same. In their blank, impenetrable gaze they held the accumulated patience of centuries. Looking into these calm little eyes, Judith shrank and shuddered.

At the other end of the table Jerry sat and swilled down numberless cups of strong coffee. When she looked at him she was startled to see the creased hollows under his eyes and the heavy look of toilworn despondence that merged his features into a dull sameness. With a sharp stab of pain she realized that before her eyes he was turning from a boy into an old man. He ate and drank soddenly, bestially, without lifting his eyes, his head sunk between his shoulders. He was beginning to talk in grunts, like old Andy, his father. When after supper he walked across the floor to get a broom straw to pick his teeth, he lurched in his weariness like a drunken man. His legs were bent at the knees, his step in his great plowing boots heavy and dragging.

When she came beside him to put more fried meat on his plate, she let her hand rest upon his shoulder with a caressing touch. He looked up at her quickly, his features suddenly brightened by a smile of surprised pleasure at this unexpected token of her affection. Something about the smile smote her cruelly, something pitiful and heartrending. She felt that she could not bear it. She made haste to go to the smokehouse for another piece of meat; and there amid the hanging sides and shoulders she shuddered convulsively, clenched her hands, and bit into her under lip, struggling against tears.

In the night a strong wind sprang up and the sky grew overcast. In the blackness she lay awake feeling the house rock in the gusts, listening to the rattle of window sashes, the uneasy creaking of doors, the flapping of loose shingles on the roof. A broken molasses jug lying under the edge of the house, caught the wind in its funnel and whistled eerily. The shed door swung on its hinges and banged intermittently as the gusts of wind slammed it violently shut. From time to time a rat scampered the length of the loft over her head.

The baby in the cradle by the bedside, also lying awake, talked to herself, making soft, cooing little noises, delicate little purling sounds as sweet as flower petals. Jerry slept heavily.

Lying between her husband and child, she felt alone, cold and dismal, alone yet inextricably bound to them by something stronger than their bonds of common misery. Their future lives stretched before her dull, drab and dreary, and there was nothing at the end but the grave. She began to cry into the pillow, repressing her sobs so as not to wake Jerry. For a long time she cried in a stifled, bitter, despairing way. As she wept the baby's babblings ceased and she fell into the sleep that in puny children seems closely akin to death. Toward morning Judith, too, fell mercifully asleep, pale from tears and bitter thoughts; and when the ghostlike dawn peered into the little window it saw them all three lying stretched out stark and pallid like corpses.

CHAPTER XXI

In September the thing she had begun to dread happened. She found herself with child. To her bodily misery and disgust were added a misery and disgust more deeply seated, more hateful and appalling. How could she bear to bring this child into the world? How could she keep her mouth shut and allow Jerry to accept it as his? The whole thing was too horrible and monstrous to think about. And yet she must think about it. She must find some way to keep it from happening.

She was informed now about many things of which she had been ignorant when her first child was born. She had listened to the whispered confidences of other women and from their dark hints had learned that unwilling mothers had sometimes succeeded in doing what she now felt that she must do. Hitherto a powerful physical revulsion had prevented her from trying to interfere with nature in its course. Pain had always terrorized and maddened her; and from the idea of self-inflicted pain she shrank like a child. From the thought of such an instrument as a knitting needle her flesh writhed away as if the needle were heated white for torture.

Now, however, in the extremity of her need, she forced herself to think calmly of a knitting needle. She found one half buried in a crack of the cupboard drawer, hidden away under a frowsy accumulation of tangled scraps of twine, half empty spools, rusted fishhooks, odd washers, screws and nails, and crumpled grocery bills. Having pried it out with a hairpin, she laid it away in a safe place to be ready against the time when she could summon courage to try to use it.

There was another method, for her much less repugnant, which she decided to try first. She waited and watched for an opportunity.

One day Elmer, who had come over to give Jerry a hand with the tobacco cutting, left Pete, the chestnut mule, tied in

282

the shed. Pete was no mere plow mule. He had fire and spirit. The men had taken their lunches with them to the field and would not be back before night. After she had washed up the breakfast dishes and swept the kitchen, she put clean things on the children and took them over to Aunt Selina's.

"I gotta go to mill," she explained, "an' git a sack o' corn graound up. I didn't know we was so near out o' meal till I come to mix up the cakes this mornin'."

When she got home again she saddled and bridled Pete and, stepping with some diffidence into the saddle, turned the mule's head toward the road.

It was years since she had ridden horseback; and for the first few moments she felt awkward and perilously poised. Then the familiar undulation of the animal's flanks under her and the old feel of the lines in her hands restored her confidence; and all at once, as if a good fairy had breathed new life into her, she felt her spirits rise and began to realize the September morning, clear, blue, and sparkling, the caress of wind and sun, the exhilaration of change and motion.

Out on the pike she urged Pete into a gallop and passed Aunt Eppie's house riding like the Wild Huntsman, her old red cotton sweater flying out behind.

Cissy, hearing the beat of the mule's hoofs, ran excitedly to the kitchen window.

"Well, if there hain't Judy Pippinger a-gallopin' past like mad on her dad's mule, her hair a-blowin' out jes like she used to ride when she was a little gal. What's fetched her away from home, I wonder?"

All along the road she drew similar comments from the neighbors who were fortunate enough to live on the pike. The conclusion generally arrived at was that only urgent need of the doctor could satisfactorily explain her appearance. Otherwise it was an unheard of and hence unseemly thing for a married woman the mother of three children to be seen out alone on horseback and going at breakneck speed. But then, after all the things that had been whispered about her, anything might be expected of Judy Pippinger.

Unmindful of the prying looks cast after her from stuffy kitchens, Judith galloped on, feeling as light as a puff of thistle-down blown through the September morning.

When the first wild exhilaration of the ride had spent itself and she became aware that Pete was sweating and breathing hard, she pulled the mule down to an easy trot and turned him from the pike onto a grass grown wagon track that wound in and out at the foot of gently sloping hills.

It was such a peaceful, meandering, sleepy, sun-steeped wagon track that before she knew it she had let the lines drop along the mule's neck, and she and Pete were lazing along in the sunshine like two natural born loafers as though there never had been and never would be a furrow to plow or a floor to scrub. Since the day when she had fled from Jerry's tub of hog guts, she had never been away from the house in the morning. Yet now the hundreds of dreary mornings spent in the stuffy clutter of the kitchen fell away into unreality like a dream and she was a girl again, free to come and go as she liked, happy and careless.

The grass grown wagon track, bordered by golden rod and sprays of little purple asters, dozed so sweetly and calmly in the sun that it seemed removed by the width of the world from human filth and fret. Soon, however, it wound around a curve where there was a gap between the hills and she could look out over acres of alfalfa, fields of corn and tobacco and the shanties and pigsties of those who tilled them. In the middle distance she saw three men cutting tobacco, going along the rows with the precision of machines. How small they looked to her eyes.

In another field she saw men cutting corn and stacking it in shocks. In the spaces where they had cut the scattered pumpkins appeared bright and golden. The whole made a pretty picture to look at. But she knew that now in the noonday heat the men's arms and backs were aching and the sweat pouring from their faces as they worked.

Over a bluegrass pasture cattle and sheep browsed. They were at ease and at peace among themselves. Three young colts raced up and down in an alfalfa field, brimming with health and the joy of life.

In the dooryard of a shanty not far away a frowsy woman was chopping wood. In another dooryard another woman was frantically chasing a pig that had broken out of its pen. Her long slatternly skirt tried to trip her as she ran. She heard the wail of a baby and the harsh scream of an older child, followed by the still harsher-toned reprimand of the harassed mother. A skinny-armed girl, little more than a child, with a long flaxen pigtail down her back, was rubbing out clothes at a washtub by the door.

Seated easily on the mule's back and commanding with her eyes the wide stretch of country, she indulged for a moment in the dark fancy that she was God looking out upon these poor children that he had made in his own image and condemned to a life of toilsome grubbing in the dirt that ended only with the grave. Then a flood of the old nausea swept over her and with it a terror and she faced the abysmal truth that she was not God, but only one of these pitiful, groveling creatures, doomed to the same existence and the same end.

She turned the mule's head and rode toward home slowly and dejectedly. From time to time, mindful of the purpose for which she had come, she tried to urge him into a gallop, to make him take a fence or a ditch. But Pete was tired and his rider's hand had grown listless. She felt herself overcome by a great weariness of all things.

By the time she reached home in the late afternoon, the whole neighborhood knew that she had been out and just how long she had been out. And having satisfied themselves that there was no sickness in the family, the women drew their own conclusions.

When she had given up hope that the ride was going to have any effect, she forced herself to try to use the knitting needle. But she was shrinking and clumsy, and at the first stab of pain she flung the instrument violently to the other end of the room. Afterward she dropped it through a wide crack in the kitchen floor so that she would not be able to find it again.

She searched out pennyroyal and tansy and other noxious herbs in the places where she knew they grew, and took to brewing nasty smelling decoctions over the stove and sipping gingerly at the brackish liquor she poured off from them. But all that these evil brews did was to increase her sickness and lassitude. Drearily she shambled about the kitchen through the dragging days and felt too sick and weary for despair.

One night in late October she woke from her first sleep with a mind preternaturally wide awake. Free for the moment from the nausea and dragging weariness of the day, she was left bare to the attacks of the things that prey upon the mind. It was raining in a fine, slow, steady downpour, and she lay listening to the patter of the drops on the roof, looking blankly at the dimly outlined oblong that was the window. At such times the numberless trivialities that clutter the day are sunk into insignificance, leaving the path to the grave straight and plain.

What real difference did it make after all whether the baby was born and lived to be a hundred or died in the womb?

Nevertheless, the moment after she had asked herself this question, she got out of bed and moving cautiously so as not to waken Jerry gathered together her clothes in the darkness and slipped with them into the kitchen, closing the door behind her. She dressed hastily and without putting on shoes or stockings, jacket or sunbonnet, stepped out into the rainy night.

She shivered and hesitated as the first cold drops fell on her shoulders through her thin cotton dress. But the next moment she plunged out boldly straight across the swimming mud and filth of the cowlot. The moon, far in its third quarter, gave only a feeble glimmer of light from behind the clouds, but it was enough to guide her to the horsepond, which was deep and full from recent heavy rains. There was no slackening of her steps as she came near the tawny pool, but rather an increase of speed; and when she reached the edge she flung herself instantly into the water and disappeared as inconsequentially as if she had been a stone or a clod of dung.

She came up swimming. She had forgotten that she knew how to swim. She had not been in the water since she was twelve years old. Yet now she swam, vigorously and toward the bank. Even above humiliation and despair there rose in her a sense of power and triumph as she realized that she was master of the water.

Her long arms rising alternately above the muddy smoothness brought her in a few strokes close to the bank. When she was within a few feet of it she remembered suddenly that she had not come to the horsepond to take a swim. She relaxed her body and tried hard to sink. The next moment her feet touched the slimy ooze of the bottom and she saw that the water was not above her shoulders. Standing there breast high in the muddy water with the ooze welling up between her toes, she caught herself thinking that she was glad she had not put on her shoes, which were nearly new. Suddenly she began to laugh, wildly, hysterically into the rainy night.

As she waded to the bank, still laughing insanely, she cut her foot on some sharp object that lay at the bottom of the pond, a piece of old stovepipe perhaps or a broken bottle. She gave a sharp scream of pain, then laughed again.

But when she had climbed up the slippery incline of mud and crouched on the wet ground in the rain there was no hysteria left. Slow tears of misery and despair welled into her eyes.

She thought of trying once more. But what would be the use, she told herself dejectedly. She would only wade out again.

She began to shake with cold. Shiver after shiver passed through her and her teeth chattered. All at once she felt as if she had never been so cold in all her life. Still she crouched shuddering on the soggy ground and hugged herself in a vain attempt to get warm.

At last she got up and plodded slowly back to the house that she had thought never to see again. There she squeezed the water out of her hair and rubbed herself dry, piled her clothes in a dripping heap on the porch and turned the washtub over them and crept miserably into bed. Jerry stirred in his sleep, turned over and wound one arm around her, as his habit was. From the comfort of his warm body and circling arm peace came to her and she fell asleep.

The next morning the Slatten boys butchered a hog. Aunt Maggie Slatten, coming over in the late afternoon to borrow the Blackford sausage grinder, found Judith writhing and screaming on the bed. The two boys were standing solemnly by the bedside looking at their mother with scared eyes. The baby, not aware that anything was wrong, crept about the floor. She had been dabbling deliciously in the slop pail and her face and hands were smeared with its contents. The unwashed dinner dishes were still on the table, the floor was scattered with many things; and some washing that had been brought in from the line was piled in a heap in the rocking chair.

Aunt Maggie's experienced eye took in the situation at a glance. She sent Billy back to her place with the sausage grinder. Then she set about doing the things she knew to be necessary. She made up a fire and heated water. She put hot flatirons to Judith's feet and hot stovelids to her back. She rummaged around among the drawers and cupboards for sheets and old cloths, and did not neglect her opportunity to peer curiously and critically into all the household arrangements. When Jerry came home she sent him out to chop up more wood so that the fire could keep going all night. And when at last the struggle was over and Judith lay white and semi-conscious, she fixed her up as clean as she could, swept and straightened the house, plunged quantities of blood-soaked clothes into a tub of water on the porch and helped Jerry to get together something for them to eat. Jerry wanted to sit up; but she waved him aside, bent upon doing her whole duty. When the others were in bed she made herself comfortable in the old rocking chair and dozed till morning.

Not a word did she utter to the sick woman of inquiry or reproach. But the next day, talking privately with Aunt Sally Whitmarsh by the kitchen stove, with the door into the bedroom closed, her tongue was loosened and she billowed with self-righteousness and the joy of scandal.

"You'd never bring yerse'f to believe it, Sally, the state I found things in," she said in low but impressive tones. "O' course I fell right to an' done everything I could. Judy Pippinger hain't never acted none too neighborly to me; but jes the same I aim to do allus like I'd be done by, an' Jerry says he'll haul the boys' terbaccer fer what I done fer Judy. It pays to treat yer neighbor right, Sally.

"I sez to her, sez I, 'A sow when she's a-fixin' to farrow finds herse'f a bed. Anybody'd think you'd make out to be clean as a hawg, anyway.'

"She looks up at me with them big black eyes o' hern.

"'Haow did I know this was a-comin' on me?' she whines fretful like. 'It come on all of a suddent when I was a-fixin' to gether up the dishes.'

"'Mebbe it did,' I sez, 'an' mebbe it didn't. But I got a notion you bin kinder lookin' fer it right along.' An' I looks right at her, cool, an' meaningful. She never said a word to that, but turned her face araound to the wall."

"Well, Judy was allus a wild young un an' a wild gal," said Aunt Sally, glancing cautiously at the bedroom door, "but I didn't hardly think she'd ever come to sech a pass as this." Then, lowering her voice to a scandalized whisper: "The talk that went araound about her an' the preacher in the summer was a disgrace. He wa'n't helpin' her pick blackberries fer nothin'."

"Yaas, an' this here's what's come of it, if I hain't much mistaken," said Aunt Maggie, setting her thin lips together with grim satisfaction.

"An' 'tain't as if Judy'd ever had anything to complain about," continued Aunt Sally, smoothing the piece of patchwork over her knee. "She's got three nice chillun an' the best man that ever worked his hands to the bone fer a woman."

"You've spoke the truth there, Sally. There hain't a steadier man than Jerry Blackford this side o' Georgetown. He don't drink, he don't hunt an' he don't idle his time away.

He's done everything a man kin do fer that woman. An' that's the thanks he gits fer it. Trouble with Judy, she dunno what she does want."

"I reckon not. If she had to put up with the things some wimmin has, she might have sumpin to complain about."

"Yaas, if he spent every cent on whiskey an' come home drunk an' blacked her eyes, like Teenie Pooler's man."

"Or run after every petticoat he saw, like Lambert Patton."

"Or went flighty, like Melvin Brewer, so's you couldn't know what he might be a-goin' to do with the butcher knife."

Aunt Maggie could have bitten off her tongue before the last speech was out of her mouth. It slipped out before she remembered to whom she was talking. She had not meant to encroach upon the sanctity of her listener's family skeleton.

Aunt Sally Whitmarsh's placid features did not alter in the least. But Aunt Maggie knew by a subtle change of atmosphere that her breach of the rules of conversation had not slipped by unnoticed.

"It's purty weather naow; but it'll likely rain agin to-night," said Aunt Sally, looking out of the window.

Later in the afternoon, Jabez Moorhouse pushed open the kitchen door. Nobody was there but the baby taking a nap in her crib. After a moment the door into the bedroom opened and Aunt Sally stood holding the knob in her hand.

"Howdy, Aunt Sally. I bin over to Gibbses' place grindin' up some tools, an' they told me Judy was took sick. Could I step in an' see her a minute?"

Aunt Sally hesitated and looked at him coldly. It was not the custom in Scott County for men who were no relation to be admitted to the bedsides of sick women.

"He'd better be off about his work, the idle loafer," she said to herself. But aloud she said, "She's a-feelin' pretty poorly," and held the door gingerly open for him to pass through.

He had come into the house from the midst of a blue October afternoon, still, sweet, and sunny, and with just enough freshness of chill in the air to make one take deep breaths and step lightly along and whistle the end of a tune. He passed into a room where the air was chokingly hot and heavy with the smell of sickness and of many breaths. The one small window was tightly closed; and the green paper blind, full of white creases and pinholes, was drawn three quarters down.

Aunt Abigail sat knitting on one side of the bed. On the other side Aunt Maggie Slatten dozed ponderously in the rocking chair. She wakened as Jabez came into the room and sat bolt upright looking at him with eyes full of hostility.

Aunt Sally, after dropping some more pieces of wood into the little sheet iron stove, came and resumed her seat on Aunt Abigail's side of the bed. She was nearest to the window and she had in her lap a bit of patchwork that she was piecing together.

In the middle of the big bed, Judith's face was very white in its frame of black hair. Her thin body hardly raised the patchwork quilt. Heavy and somber the tall walnut headboard rose behind her. In her wasted youth she looked more ready for the grave than any of the old duennas about her. As Jabez looked he had a vision of her as he had seen her how few years before in the walnut bed, fresh, gay, and rosy after the birth of her first child.

She opened her eyes as he came toward her and greeted him with a shadow of the old flashing smile.

The three old women glanced at each other with meaningful looks. After all they had done for her, she had not smiled once for them.

"Waal, Judy," was all he could say, as he stood awkwardly by the bed, his cap in his hands. The darkness oppressed him, the stinking heat of the room made his eyeballs ache. He felt the three pairs of vixenish old eyes fastened upon him with dark suspicion and cold hostility.

"Waal, Judy, I hope you'll git well right quick," he said after an awkward pause and turned and went out of the house. As he passed over the ridge and down on the other side, he neither whistled nor sang, and the weight of his great shoulders seemed to be dragging them to the earth.

CHAPTER XXII

WHEN she was able to be up and around again, she began to be possessed by a great dread and loathing of the thought of the coming on of winter.

One late afternoon in early December, when the thick mud and heavy skies of winter had laid hold upon the country, Jerry came into the kitchen carrying a crooked nail covered with blood and rust.

"Looky here, Judy, what I took out'n the side o' Nip's leg. The damn fool hoss'd done gone an' laid hisse'f daown on it. It was in near up to the head. Where's the turpentine?"

"My, it's an ugly lookin' one. Jes thick with rust, hain't it?" she said, as she rummaged for the turpentine. "Some heats the nail red hot an' sticks it back into the hole."

"I know, but I kinder hate to do it. I'll soak it well with turpentine an' that'd otta fix it. I can't fer the life of me see haow so many old boards with nails stickin' up in 'em gits laid about in the barnyard. All the time I keep pickin' 'em up, more keeps a-comin'. It looks like they growed there. Is that the turpentine? Give it here. The quicker I git it in the better."

He went out, slamming the door violently in his haste.

The wound healed over and Jerry had almost forgotten to worry about it, when about ten days later he noticed that the horse was not acting just like himself. He was nervous and fidgety and there was a stiffness in the injured leg. Looking at the sore he saw that it had broken again and there was a thin trickle of ugly looking matter oozing from it.

The next morning when he went into the stable to feed the horses, Nip was frothing at the mouth. The stiffness had extended to all his four legs, and he held them extended as if to keep himself from falling. He looked at his master with wide, startled eyes that showed much of the whites and from time to time a shiver ran through his body.

Jerry saw himself faced with one of the most serious disasters that can befall a tenant farmer. Without going back to the house for his breakfast, he saddled Tuck and galloped away in search of Doc Beasley, the veterinary.

They came back a couple of hours later riding side by side. As soon as Jerry laid eyes upon the horse, he knew that he was much worse. The shivers had changed to convulsive shudders, and pain and terror looked out of the animal's dilated eyes.

The veterinary, a lean old grayhound with a face of tanned leather, shook his head.

"You'd best put a bullet into him, Jerry, an' have done with it. I cud cure him, but it'd cost yuh more'n what the hoss's woth. That damned antitoxin fer lockjaw's high's hell an' it takes so much fer a hoss 'tain't practical nohaow. If yuh wanta take a chanct on it's helpin' him, I kin give him a shot o' some other stuff that sometimes does the trick. It'll cost yuh five dollars, an' I hain't promisin' that it'll cure him. But onct in a while it does. Anyhaow whether yuh take it or whether yuh don't take it, I won't charge yuh nothin' fer comin' here, 'cause I'm on my way to Joe Patton's sick caow an' I know yuh hain't no millionaire."

"Let's try it, Jerry," implored Judith, who had come into the stable behind the men. "It seems a shame not to let him have one chanct."

"All right, Doc," agreed Jerry a bit huskily. "Go ahead an' try what you kin do. If I had the money I'd feel like tryin' the big cure. But I hain't got the money. So that settles it flat."

The horse doctor cleansed the wound, took a big syringe from his kit satchel, filled it with a yellowish fluid, and gave the horse an injection in the leg close to the wounded spot.

"There," he said as he replaced the syringe, "if he hain't a heap better agin to-morrer mornin' he hain't a-goin' to git no better. Anyhaow, you hain't got the hardest luck there is, Jerry, ole man. Two o' Jim Summerfield's hawgs has got the cholera, an' the whole thirty-odd'll be dead afore the week's gone. So you see you might a had it worst."

With this cold but well meant comfort he was gone.

The next morning when Jerry went into the stable, the horse was down, his jaws were locked and he was writhing in agony. Tuck, tied at a little distance, looked at him with mild, questioning eyes.

He went to the house for his revolver. Judith said nothing. When she saw him take the gun out of the dresser drawer she did not need to ask what it meant. A few moments later she heard a shot and knew that it was all over for Nip.

It was war time and horse hides were worth four dollars or more. So, although he loathed to do it, Jerry skinned the poor animal that for so many years had been his friend and the companion of his labors. When the carcass was skinned he tied a chain about the hind legs, attached the other end to Tuck's harness and, taking the lines in his hand, said, "Git up, Tuck."

Restless and unhappy from the odious smell of blood, the horse started uneasily, shied a little and looked around with dilated nostrils and eyes that showed the whites. Then, seeing his master, hearing his voice and feeling his familiar hand upon the lines, he went forward with his usual steady step, dragging his dead companion.

Judith, watching sadly from the porch, saw the little procession pass across the pasture. It had snowed during the night and the ground was still white. Against the whiteness the dark figures of the man and horse plodded with bowed heads. Behind them trailed a long thing of an evil scarlet color. The front legs stood up stiffly in the air. The inert head and neck, preternaturally long, trailed behind like a snake. Behind the dragging head a dark streak marked its path from the barn.

On the far side of the pasture lay a deep gully. Here Jerry halted Tuck and manœuvered him back and forth so as to get the dead animal as near to the brink as possible and in the position he wanted. Then he unloosed the chain from the hind

legs and, using a fence rail as a pry, worked with the carcass
until it went crashing over the brink. The noise startled Tuck,
who looked around uneasily.

Returned to the stable he sadly salted the hide, while Tuck,
surprised to find an empty stable, nickered and whinneyed
and waited impatiently for his friend.

The buzzards did the rest.

For days they hung in the air over the gully. From the
kitchen window Judith could see them moving on widespread
wings. They would circle a while in one spot, then fly off a
little distance and circle again, as though loath to give up their
habits of search. The motion of these silent creatures, slow and
steady, with no perceptible vibration of the sweeping, horizontal wings, was as beautiful as the flight of sea gulls. When
they tilted, the sunlight caught the under side of the black
wings and turned them gleaming silver. Watching the stately
grace, the balanced dignity of their movements as they circled
alone in the wide emptiness of the winter sky, Judith felt herself enfolded in a deep sense of calm, as though Nature had
laid upon her brow a firm, soothing hand and told her to be
at peace. The flight of the birds added beauty and dignity
to the thought of death; and for the first time in her life
it seemed a thing to be looked upon with calmness. She was
affected as she might have been by a Greek tragedy or by
Bach's coldly austere music. She felt no sense of shrinking,
but rather a solemn uplift of the heart in the thought that some
day she too would return to the ground; and that always,
when she was no longer there to see it, sunshine in winter
would be a lovely thing, and other buzzards, foul smelling birds
though they were, would soar and tilt with incomparable grace
and stateliness over other dead horses and dead dogs that like
her had had their day.

After the buzzards were gone, she was still followed by the
thought of death. But it was no longer a beautiful thought.
She shrank from it and tried to turn her thoughts to other
things.

The horse's death brought them many visits of condolence.

The men sat around the stove of an evening and told Jerry just what he ought to have done to save the horse and just what they themselves would have done if the horse had been theirs. Having exhausted this topic, they drifted to other things: the victories over the Germans, the high and ever climbing cost of flour, the scarcity of sugar, the unheard of prices that were being charged for overalls and shoes and stoves and hay forks and wire fencing.

"Waal, if we kin git forty cent a paound fer terbaccer this year, 'twon't pan out so bad," opined Uncle Sam Whitmarsh. "An' eggs an' butter is fetchin' a good price."

"You was allus a joker, Sam," said Columbia Gibbs, spitting into the woodbox. "You know dern well there hain't one of us in twenty'll git forty cent fer terbaccer. Mebbe a few lucky ones'll draw a big price; but the most of us'll be on'y too glad to drive back home with ten or twelve. An' if butter an' eggs is high, they hain't high compared with flour an' coffee. Afore the war I cud drive into taown with five, six dozen eggs an' the same number o' paounds o' butter, an' I cud git me a sack o' flour, a couple o' paounds o' sugar, a paound o' coffee an' a paper o' candy fer the young uns. Naow I take in that same lot o' butter an' eggs an' I can't hardly git me a sack o' dirty flour chuck full o' bran an' middlin's. I gotta go 'ithout the coffee an' sugar an' the young uns has gotta go 'ithout the candy."

He looked about the group clinchingly and made a feint of wiping away the streams of tobacco juice that had begun to dribble from the corners of his mouth.

"I wisht Roosevelt was back in agin," spoke up Gus Dibble. "When he was in the price o' mule colts was a heap better. One year I got fifty dollars fer a mule colt. An' las' year I didn't git but forty fer a better one out'n the same mare. I'd like to see Roosevelt back in."

Two weeks after Nip's death Uncle Amos Crupper received word that his son Bob had been killed, blown to pieces by an exploding shell.

The old man was broken by the news. Bob was his only

son, the son of the wife of his youth whose memory he had cherished for twenty years. He wandered about restlessly from neighbor to neighbor, seeking comfort and finding none. As he sat hunched over the Blackford stove, his usually erect shoulders bowed into a semi-circle, it seemed to Judith that winter had descended upon him over night, as snow falls on the hills.

She, too, as she went about her work, kept thinking of Bob —and of death.

The thought that he was dead would waylay her suddenly, startingly, and she would see him as she had known him in life, his lithe, muscular body, his boyish smile, his clear eyes, fearless and dreamy.

Once with a dustrag she slapped a fly on the wall. It fell mashed and mangled to the floor.

It came over her suddenly that he had died like that. With all his health, vigor, and charm, his power to make women love him, he had died like the fly. Some great, pitiless engine of war had mashed these things out of him and left only a few bits of stinking flesh.

"What are we all anyway but flies," she said to herself bitterly.

One morning when it was mild and the sun was shining she went out to clean the rain barrel that had grown slimy with a green scum. Bent over with her head and shoulders in the almost empty barrel, she scrubbed the sides vigorously with the scrubbing brush. When she had finished, her wrists felt weak and shaky. Taking hold of the top of the barrel with both hands she tried to tip it to drain away the dirty water and was suddenly aware that it was too heavy for her. She could not understand it. She had dumped the same barrel many times before with the greatest ease. She struggled with it and for the first time in her life felt herself overcome by a sense of physical powerlessness. Some virtue had gone out of her long, muscular arms trained from childhood to do heavy work. Her breath came in short, quick gasps and she felt her knees weaken and tremble in a way that she had never felt before.

When at last she succeeded in tipping the barrel and returning it to its place, she sank down on the ground gasping with
exhaustion, her knees weak like water beneath her.

After that whenever she drew a full bucket of water from
the well or carried slop to the hogs or stood too long over the
churn or the washtub, she felt creeping over her this strange,
tremulous sensation of extreme weakness. Countless times before she had known what it was to be tired. But this feeling
of sinking knees, of shivering powerlessness was something
new, something quite different from anything that she had
experienced before in her life.

With it came an increased impatience with the chatter and
wrangles of the children, a growing lack of interest in the affairs of the neighbors or even in those of her own household,
a desire to retire within herself, to be alone and apart.

Ill luck seemed to love their company that winter and, like
a hungry stray dog, would not leave their door. Luke Wolf
said it was all because Jerry had torn the shoes from Nip's dead
hoofs and later used them in shoeing Tuck.

"Nine times out o' ten," he said to Jerry impressively, "if
yuh shoe a hoss with shoes taken off'n a dead animal, he'll die
afore the year's out. An' if he don't die some other kind o'
bad luck'll foller yuh."

Tuck did not die; but, as Luke had prophesied, other bad
luck followed apace. When Jerry hauled the tobacco off to
market he was caught in a drenching rain, and hundreds of
pounds of what would otherwise have been a fine grade of tobacco were changed to the sort that brings a cent or two a
pound. The tobacco should have been covered to protect it
against such a contingency. But a tarpaulin is an expensive
luxury which few tenant farmers can afford to buy. Most of
them use their wives' rag carpets. But Judith had no rag
carpet.

When Jerry had paid off the help that he had hired during
the year and settled the store bill that had been accumulating
for many months and bought some tar paper to nail over the

north and east sides of the house, he had a hundred and eighteen dollars left, most of which would have to go to buy another horse. Fortunately the corn crop was a fairly good one that year.

It was a hard winter, a winter of pinching and skimping and doing without, doing without sugar, doing without coffee, doing without even the salt meat to which they were accustomed, for hogs were worth too much to be consumed at home. They had to be sold to meet the exorbitant cost of shoes and overalls and underwear to keep the children warm.

Since the beginning of the war these things had become of very inferior quality. It seemed as if Jerry was always cobbling the boys' shoes and Judith always putting patches on their overalls. And in an incredibly short time their feet were on the ground again and their knees out. Like all the rest of the women, Judith pinched and contrived, tried to make clothes for the children out of old garments that were fit only for the ragbag, made flour sacks into pillow slips and even into underwear and carefully saved the smaller pieces of everything for the bedquilts that were always wearing out and having to be replaced.

As she sat by the little glass lamp of an evening making over flour sacks or mending overalls, her face had not the dull, sullen look that Jerry remembered from other times, but rather a hard, grim, half defiant expression. Watching her covertly his own face took on an ugly look.

More and more, as the days went by, she was confirmed in the stand that she had taken after getting up from her last sickbed. She was through forever, she told herself, with having children and with running any risk of having children. She wanted no more children that she could not clothe, that she could hardly feed, that were a long torture to bear and a daily fret and anxiety after they were born. Her flesh recoiled and her spirit rose in fiery protest against any further degradation and suffering. Too long she had been led along blindly. Now her eyes were open and she would be a tool no more of man's lust and nature's cunning. She would see her path and choose it. She would be mistress of her own body. She would order her future life as seemed best to herself.

It was the imprint of these thoughts that Jerry saw on her face as she sat sewing under the lamp; and the covert looks that he cast at her were ugly and ill omened.

For her there was stimulation mental and physical in such thoughts, and she began to grow stronger. It was this determination stubbornly adhered to and constantly borne in mind that made her arms powerful to rub the coarse clothes up and down on the washboard, that set the dasher thudding against the bottom of the churn more noisily than need be and drew the broom with brisk, emphatic strokes across the floor. When she gathered up the dishes she slapped the plates together with the emphasis of one who is indifferent as to whether they crack or not, and when she cleaned house the dust and feathers flew mightily. At the woodpile she was merciless to the saplings and rotted fence rails that Jerry had dragged up.

Often at the end of a day of such emphatic housekeeping, the old insidious weakness would slip into her bones, her knees would tremble and sink and she would drop with sudden exhaustion into the old rocking chair.

As she lay with her head against the bit of patchwork that was tied to the back of the chair, her eyes, the only parts of her that were not tired, would wander restlessly about the walls and ceiling. The winter before, in a vain attempt to keep out the cold, she had bought for a quarter a bundle of old newspapers and pasted them over two walls and part of the ceiling. She had intended to buy another bundle and finish the job, but had never gone beyond the intention. The papers had pulled apart over the cracks between the boards, they were yellowed with smoke and blotched with rain; but they still displayed their wealth of pictures. There were pictures of society people grinning and squatting on the sand at Palm Beach, pictures of smug, well fed dignitaries of church and state, pictures of business magnates, still smugger, fatter, and more rigorously curried, pictures of kings and generals pompously pin-

ning medals to the coat lapels of heroes of war, well brushed
and subdued for the solemn occasion, pictures of dismal, stuffy
people who had been given new life by Tanlac or Lydia Pink-
ham's Vegetable Compound, pictures of actresses and movie
stars, some simpering and insipid, others with grace and charm
diffused over the pure lines of youth, pictures of people who
had been killed in automobile accidents, pictures of murderers
and the murdered.

Her interest was only mildly stirred by all these pictures of
strange people in strange walks of life that she would never
tread. They seemed, with but few exceptions, solemn and
sodden creatures in no way to be envied. From them her
eyes traveled with heightening interest to the streaky discolora-
tions that the rain beating through the walls had made on the
papers. There she never failed to find pictures that beguiled
the eye and inspired the imagination.

Often when the children were at play out of doors she sat
a long time looking at these weird freaks of water. At such
times her hectic energy and the determination that lay back of
it were gone, and with the graying twilight there came instead
dark thoughts of the emptiness and purposelessness of life,
of Bob who had died and of the death that lay in wait for her
and hers. When the corners grew shadowed and the rats began to peer out of their holes with bright, furtive eyes, she
would get up with a heavy sigh and begin to mix the batter
for corn cakes.

As the weeks went by her relations with Jerry grew daily
more strained. She rarely spoke to him except to call his attention to an empty woodbox or a broken door hinge or a loose
board in the floor or the fact that the boys' feet were on the
ground. Daily he grew more morose and evil tempered. A
brooding animosity looked out of his eyes as he furtively followed her movements about the house. At the least excuse
this smoldering fire broke out into the fierce flame of violent
and brutal quarreling. The quarrels usually ended by his taking his hat and slamming the door behind him as he went to
seek diversion in some neighbor's barnyard. For her there was

no diversion. When the quarrel was over neither of them could remember what had caused it.

Christmas brought a truce. By a tacit mutual understanding it was agreed between them that on this day, if only for the children's sake, there should be peace and some measure of goodwill.

The children were up with the dawn, uproariously and gloriously happy over the few ten cent gimcracks that Jerry had brought home the day before and that Judith had stuffed into their stockings. She caught the infection of their happiness, laughed with them over the antics of the Jack in the box and the monkey on a stick, and beguiled them with descriptions of Santa Claus and his swift reindeer, his home built of ice far up in the frozen north, his shop where he and his wife work all year to make playthings for good little boys and girls and his long, exciting gallops over the snow on Christmas Eve.

Having done up his morning chores, Jerry, feeling leisurely and luxurious in clean overalls, stretched himself in the rocking chair and listened contentedly to the prattle of the mother and children, showed the boys how to spin the tops and fell to carving them a whistle apiece to supplement the toys that Santa Claus had brought.

Annie was happy with a doll which she hugged maternally to her bosom, then absent-mindedly dragged about the floor by one leg.

Jerry had killed a hen the day before, and there was a gala dinner of stewed chicken, hominy, sweet potatoes, and a boiled pudding with sauce. They all gorged mightily.

After dinner Jerry took up his hat and strolled out through the barnyard. Judith was left alone with the children, now grown cross and fretful, the litter of broken toys and clutter of dirty dishes.

The dinner had been late, and it was after four o'clock and already growing twilight in the room before she had washed the last greasy pan. When she had finished everything and washed the table and hung up the dishrag, she pushed the frowsy strands of hair back from her face and sank into the rocking chair. Annie began to whimper and, putting her little hand over her stomach, said that she had a pain there. She gave the child a drink of water to help dissolve the colored candy she had eaten, then took her up and rocked her, crooning a song. The boys who had been wrangling all afternoon and constantly appealing to her to settle their differences, now fell to fighting, rolling over and over on the littered floor. She got up and slapped them both smartly.

"Naow, then," she said, administering a last cuff to Billy, "you'd otta think shame to yerse'ves, the way you been a-actin'. You jes set right to work the both of you an' pick up all them things an' put 'em in the box, an' don't let me hear nary word out'n you."

They subsided from loud wails to whimpers, then set to work sullenly picking up the toys and throwing them noisily at the wooden grocery box in which she had tried to train them to keep their things. When they thought their mother was not looking, they angrily nudged and pinched each other. Then, forgetting enmity, they began to make a glorious game of it and threw the playthings in all directions, trying to hit anything but the inside of the box. She tried to tell herself that they were only children having childish fun; but to her irritable nerves they seemed like little fiends. She felt a wild impulse to turn her back on everything, even the sick baby, and flee away along the roads, into the woods, anywhere where there was quiet and peace.

She put up with the turmoil for a while, sitting with closed eyes silently rocking the little girl. To the casual eye she looked passive and acquiescent enough; but her whole body and soul were one strung up tension of screaming protest. It was not until a tin railway car hit her on the side of the head that she got up and slapped both the boys again and reduced them once more to a sullen putting away of the toys.

Jerry lurched into the house, his hat over one eye, smelling of whiskey. He shambled into a seat by the stove, and she knew by the evil looks he cast at her that he was in an ugly drunk, a strange thing for him who was usually silly and good natured under the effects of alcohol. As she caught his glowering eye the smoldering sense of injury that she had been nursing all afternoon flared into hate and fury. If it came to a test of ugliness she could be more than his match, she told herself and her lips set together in grim lines.

Jerry saw the sinister setting of her mouth, and his own face darkened into a black scowl.

Annie had fallen asleep, and she slipped off the child's shoes and outer clothing and carried her into the other room. When she came back the kitchen was almost dark. Jerry still sat by the stove, his head sunk on his breast.

"Air you a-goin' to do the milkin' to-night?" she asked in a dry, dead voice.

"No, I hain't."

She threw on an old cap and jacket, took up the milk bucket with an emphatic rattle and bang and went out, slamming the door so that the house shook.

When she came in again the room was so dark that she could hardly see the outlines of things. The boys had dropped asleep on the old sofa behind the stove. The fire had gone low and the room was chilly. Jerry still sat by the stove, his head sunk lower on his breast.

She lit the lamp, strained the milk and mixed the corn cake batter, then came by the stove to make up the fire. He bulked obstinately between her and the woodbox. For a minute tense with their mutual aversion she stood waiting for him to move.

"Air you a-goin' to move or hain't you?" she asked at last in the same dry, dead voice.

He glanced up at her with a hateful leer, then dropped his head again to his breast.

"I hain't."

For another moment she stood eyeing him with a look of exasperation mingled with cold despisal. Then red fury burst in her and she grasped the handle of the stove lifter.

"You git out o' that chair, you damn filthy haound. Hain't it enough that I gotta spend the hull day scrapin' greasy burnt pans an' puttin' up with them pesterin' young uns, 'ithout havin' you lurchin' in here with a dirty drunk an' plantin' yer carcass right where I wanta git the supper? I hain't in no humor to put up with none o' yer drunken sulks. You git away from this yer stove an' do it mighty quick too."

He did not move nor even glance at her. He bulked big and sullen, a silent affront.

Trembling all over she uttered a scream of rage and swung the stove lifter in fury. It descended sharply on his skull.

With a thick curse he sprang up, wrenched the stove lifter from her hand and flung it to the other end of the room. It fell into a pan of milk and the milk splashed in every direction. Then, grasping her by the shoulders, he began to shake her. He shook her so violently that her teeth chattered and her furious screams of rage came in a shrill tremolo hideous to hear. Like a tigress she struggled in his grasp. If she had had a knife she would have plunged it into him.

Her frenzied struggles drew them close to the wall; and it was the sound of her head beating with a hollow noise against the boards that at last penetrated his drunken fury and brought him to his senses. With the movement of one who drops hot iron, he let fall his hands from her shoulders and fled out into the darkness, leaving the door swinging open behind him.

CHAPTER XXIII

THAT night she set up an old stretcher in the kitchen and made herself a bed out of buggy robes and ragged quilts that had been discarded and used as pads on the wagon seat. She used it the next night and the night after that. It was a chilly and uncomfortable bed and on cold nights she had to sleep in all her clothes; but week after week went by and she showed no signs of wishing to leave it. After a few contrite but clumsy attempts at reconciliation, Jerry, too, took the stretcher as a thing accepted and permanent.

A sort of cold respect for each other grew up between them after the quarrel on Christmas day. To both it had been a warning of the abyss toward which they were tending, and they strove to maintain the outer decencies of human intercourse. This was best done by avoiding each other, having little to say and tending strictly to their own affairs, interfering as little as possible with those of the other. After their long siege of violent quarreling and mutual recrimination, this silence that had settled down between them seemed almost like peace. But at meals, over the corn cakes and rank salt hogmeat, they looked at each other with hard, inimical eyes. When they spoke it was in tones flat and dry from which all life had gone. A dreary oppression, dull, heavy and deadening, weighed upon the breasts of both of them, went with Jerry to the field and stayed with Judith as she shambled about the kitchen. When he came in at night from the field she rarely spoke or looked at him. Silently she slapped the corn cakes and fried meat on his plate and they ate in a hostile silence which was not disguised by the prattle and clamor of the children.

The stimulation that had come to Judith out of her determination to have no more children died away as all stimulation must, leaving her listless and slack. Daily she grew more slovenly about her work. More and more her mind turned in upon itself, indifferent to her surroundings, thinking its own thoughts. Through the dismal, shut-in months of late winter and inclement spring she gradually drifted into that way of life, perhaps because it was the only way in which she could continue to endure the burden of existence.

When spring came at last in earnest and the mud dried up, Hat came quite often to visit her and talked glibly of Luke's injustices, of troubles with chickens and geese, of paper patterns and calicoes and the latest bulletins from the "Farm Wife's Friend," and of new songs that she had learned for the violin. She was rather glad of the break these visits made in her monotony and envied Hat her diversity of interests.

Once Hat came over with the triumphant news that she now had a bank account of her own. She had sold the bay mare which was, she declared, her rightful property; and before Luke could get hold of the money had taken it to Clayton and deposited it.

"An' naow," she concluded, "I'll hev sumpin' woth while to think about, seein' haow much I kin put to it."

Once she brushed a spider from her skirt.

"There, naow, Judy, that means a new dress. It's a sure sign. Jes fer that I'll drive into taown to-morrer when Luke's to work an' buy me the goods. Las' week I seen jes the piece I been a-wantin'."

And in truth Hat blossomed that spring in new dresses, frilled aprons and sunbonnets. Preoccupied though Judith was with her own misery, she could not help sensing a change in the bold, dark, childless woman. Her talk consisted mainly of complaints about one thing and another; and yet she gave Judith the feeling that she was especially well satisfied with life and with herself. She seemed more than usually self-assertive and blatant. She peered with more insistent curiosity into all the details of her neighbor's household. Shafts of excess vitality radiated from her and invaded irritatingly the younger woman's languor and listlessness. Often in her presence Judith was seized by a shrinking feeling as though she was a rabbit and a bird of prey was hovering above her.

Sometimes a strange look sprang out of Hat's eyes, a look at once questioning, cunning, mocking, and triumphant. It flashed only for the swiftest moment, then retired behind the mask of impassivity with which country people cover their faces.

It was in April that they took Joe Barnaby's wife, Bessie Maud, away to the insane asylum. For a long time she had been given to fits of destructiveness, when she would break dishes, smash window panes and try to tear up the furniture. These fits had of late been more frequent and violent. One day in April she was seized with this urge to destroy, and building a bonfire in the yard had thrown onto it chairs, bedding, and clothes. She had done such things before; but this time her mania had taken a worse turn. Joe, seeing the smoke from the fire and knowing only too well what it meant, had run up just in time to save the baby, which she was about to throw into the flames. That night they took her away to the asylum. It was too bad, the neighbors all told each other. But it wasn't as bad as it would have been a few years earlier when the children were all small. Now Ruby, the eldest girl, was eleven and big enough to cook the meals and take care of the baby; and at last Joe would know what it was to have peace in his house, and that was something.

One Saturday afternoon in May Jerry had gone to town for groceries and was late getting home. When Judith had given the children their supper and they had run away to play she sat on the doorstep to watch the sunset, leaving the flies to swarm over the unwashed dishes. It occurred to her that perhaps Bessie Maud had not been able to draw comfort out of the sunset and the late twitter of birds, and that was why life had gone so hard with her.

The sky was streaked with bands of light cirrus cloud, like sheep's wool washed and teased apart. White and fleecy and ranked in regular rows, they spread out over half the heavens like a great feather fan. Toward the earth they gradually thickened until they formed a solid bank. As the sun sank behind this bank, the light, fleecy clouds, which grew sparser, finer and whiter as they neared the zenith, took on a soft flush that turned the whole western sky into a harmony of faint rose and tender blue.

Jabez Moorhouse, passing with a hayfork over his shoulder, stopped for a few moments' chat; and they looked at the sky together, talking of crops and of rain.

As they looked the faint, frail pink gradually deepened into a richer rose, then glowed for a few passionate moments the color of intense flame. The little delicate shreds high up in the sky were each a slender whiff of spun gold, fine and pure. The under edges of the clouds burned with the amber and scarlet of flame against a background of shaded grays and purples. The grayish purple bank that lay along the horizon was slashed here and there by bright swords of fire. The burning clouds hung low, as if one might reach up and touch them. A rosy flush hung over everything.

It seemed as if no color could be warmer, deeper, richer. And yet incredibly as they gazed it grew before their eyes richer, warmer, deeper, more vivid and intense, more full of living fire, until Judith involuntarily held her breath in sympathy with nature in this her supreme moment.

Short-lived it was, like every other supreme moment. A second after it had reached the height of its intensity it began to fade and fall away into ashes. As if a cold breath had passed over them, the little tendrils of spun gold in the zenith turned almost instantly to gray. Lower down the deeper colors lost their glow more slowly, melting back into the surrounding purple. Soon there was left nothing but a somber interweaving of purple gray and dull magenta.

"It's a heap like a man's life, hain't it," said Jabez, spitting into the grass. "It begins happy an' simple, like them innocent pinks an' blues; then turns flame colored when he grows to be a man an' learns to know the love o' wimmin. But it don't stay that color long. Fust thing you know it's gray, like his hair, what he has left of it. Yaas, Judy, the young time's the on'y time. It's the same in dawgs an' mules, an' the breath they draw hain't no diff'rent from ourn."

Looking at his bowed knees and shoulders, his great seamed hands, his weatherbeaten face and the grizzled locks that curled behind his big ears and straggled over the brick-red creases of his neck, she thought how coarsened was every part of him except the fine, delicate lines about his mouth.

"Hain't life woth livin', Uncle Jabez?" she asked.

He laughed a short, harsh laugh and fell silent.

"Waal, I dunno, Judy," he said at last, meditatively shifting his quid of tobacco. "I reckon it makes a big diff'rence who you live it with an' a bigger diff'rence yet what work yuh lay yer hand to. Both o' them things, as I see it, is a matter of luck. An' if luck hain't with yuh—"

"Luck hain't been with you, Uncle Jabez?"

"Well, I reckon not. When I was a young feller I dearly loved to play on the fiddle. I thought about fiddlin' all day an' dreamed about it all night. But there wa'n't nobody to learn me haow to play, an' I didn't have much chanct to try to learn myse'f, 'cause as soon as I was big enough I had to make a hand in the field same's other boys. I was raised up in one o' the dark counties where they grow the dark terbaccer.

"When I was nineteen I married a purty, light-headed little gal, an' for a while I forgot all about the fiddle. I loved that woman, Judy. I poured out my heart like water for her. After a while I faound out she liked another feller better'n me, an' I told her she'd best go off with him. After she was gone I learned I'd been the laughin' stock o' the whole countryside fer months. I was the last to find out about the other feller. Sech things, you know, Judy, comes to every pair of ears but one."

He paused and looked meaningly at her. She avoided his looks, pulled a blade of ribbon grass and began splitting it between her long fingers.

"Well," he went on, "when I faound that out I took my clothes on the end of a stick an' come over here where nobody knowed me. Since then I've lived a spell with diff'rent wimmin' but I hain't never let none of 'em git a holt on the tender end o' my feelin's. They cud quit me termorrer or hev all the other men they liked fer all o' me. By sech way o' livin' a man gits peace, but not much besides. Wimmin won't stay long with a man that feels that way. Naow, I'm old an' eat my morsel alone, I feel more satisfied than when I had a woman in the house, I kin go an' come when I like, eat when I like, smoke an' drink all I like, set over the stove of evenin's as late as I like, work as little as I like. Sech life suits me purty good."

He paused and looked at her with a fine, sad smile of gentle irony. How delicate, how inexpressibly fine and delicate, she thought, were the lines about his mouth.

"Which would have meant more to you," she asked, "the fiddle or the woman?"

He came and sat down on the step beside her.

"I reckon the fiddle, Judy. The world's chuck full o' wimmin; but a man hain't got but one set o' gifts. If I could a learnt to play the fiddle good I'd like enough forgot her long ago an' loved some other woman. As it was, I couldn't take my mind away from thinkin' about her. An' the kinder hard part of it is, if I saw the woman again to-day she wouldn't mean no more to me than any other woman. On'y the feelin's I had for her then I hain't never been able to forget."

"An' air you glad you're alive right naow?"

"I can't say I hain't, Judy. I reckon livin's made up more out of a lot o' little things than any one big thing; an' there's a heap o' little things I git injoyment out'n. Mebbe there hain't nobody in Scott County likes a smoke an' a chew better'n what I do. Terbaccer an' a quiet back door yard—sun 'ithout no wind—an' my mornin' glories an' rose bushes to look at, them things gives peace and comfort, Judy. Naow, I hain't got no woman araound to sweep me off'n the stoop, I set there through a good many mornin's. I like my coffee an' corncake an' my bit o' fried hogmeat when I git up; an' after it I like my pipe with the blue an' gray streams o' smoke a-driftin' up into a sunbeam an' a-curlin' raound among the little specks o' dust. I like to hear hens sing an' cackle an' watch kittens play an' dawgs stretch theirse'ves in the warm sun an' growl in their sleep a-dreamin' they're nippin' the heels o' caows. I like the fust feel o' spring with frogs singin' in the holler, an' the fust nip o' frost in fall, the smell o' burnin' leaves an' cold, yaller sunsets. You stand a long time in the gray cold an' look at them; an' when you go in it's dark inside an' you make up a fire an' it feels good. I like to see the low sun shine along a field o' young corn in spring an' through a grapevine in September. I like the sound o' rain on the roof an' snow drivin' past the winder when the wind whistles in the chimley. An' when there hain't much outdoors but mud an' clouds I like fire. Fire's a rare fine thing, Judy. Naow I hain't got no woman araound I kin set over it all I like. Sometimes when I set late over the blaze my thoughts runs a bit gloomy; but that hain't the fault of the fire. I git to thinkin' about when I was young an' life was ahead o' me an' I'm like Jerusalem that remembers in the day of her affliction an' her miseries all her pleasant things that were from the days of old. When sech thoughts gits too bitter, there's sumpin that's more comfortin' yet than fire, an' that's whiskey, good strong corn whiskey."

"Why do you drink so much whiskey, Uncle Jabez?"

" 'Cause when I got whiskey warmin' my belly I feel like I was really the man I onct hoped I was goin' to be. Hain't that reason enough, Judy? I'm a old man now an' my spirit's broke, an' a broken spirit dries up the bones. I gotta hev a drink now an' then to limber me up. You know the Bible says: 'Give strong drink to him that is ready to perish an' wine onto the bitter in soul. Let him drink an' forget his poverty an' remember his misery no more.' "

The last words vibrated into the gathering night like a melancholy bell.

"Then you air bitter in soul, Uncle Jabez, spite of all the things you enjoy?"

"Yes, Judy, I can't say I hain't."

In the pause that followed he turned his head and looked at her keenly. She was sitting staring out toward the disappearing horizon, her shoulders sagging, her arms hanging limply at her sides. Lassitude physical and spiritual spoke in her blank face and slumping body.

"It makes me feel bad, Judy, to see you go like all the rest of us, you that growed up so strong an' handsome, so full o' life an' spirits. I've watched you sence you was a baby growin' like a pink rosebud, an' then blossomin', so beautiful to see. And now—"

Huskily his voice went silent. He made squares and triangles on the ground with his heel.

"Sometimes I've thought that mebbe if you an' me'd been of an age, an' not me near old enough to be your grandaddy, you an' me together, Judy, might a made sumpin out of our lives, anyway got in a little play along with the grind. Mebbe so, mebbe not. Whichever way it don't do no good to figger about it—ner no harm neither."

He smiled again his fine, dry smile.

After he was gone and she had watched his broad, bowed back disappear down the side of the ridge, she sat looking out across the wide expanse of country to the horizon. The glow of the sunset had faded and there was nothing left but a few broken horizontal bars of pale saffron, backed by gray and lavender. Between her eyes and the saffron bars the long stretch of hills and valleys was sinking swiftly into darkness. They looked at her palely across the gloom-filled distance with a sad, horizontal gaze, sad and level, like her own.

At last she got up abruptly from the doorstep and went into the house and to the bottom shelf in the cupboard where Jerry kept his rarely used demijohn of whiskey. She took out the corncob stopper, poured a few spoonfuls into a teacup and tasted it gingerly. It burned her lips and throat and some of it went down the wrong way. She made a wry face, coughed, gagged, rushed to the water bucket and drank a dipperful of water, then slackly set about gathering up the supper dishes.

She made no further attempt to find the cheer that lay in the demijohn; but as the weeks went by something of Jabez' poise and calm seemed to have settled on her spirit. Often, thinking of their talk and seeing in memory his fine, sad smile, the irritations of the household fell away from her and she seemed as if enfolded in a twilight peace. Having discovered its charm, she began to wear this memory as an amulet.

Through the spring and summer she spent much of her time in the garden and barnyard, leaving the house to clean itself. She raised chickens, geese, and turkeys and even bought a pair of rabbits from Aunt Selina and started a little rabbit colony in hutches built against the south side of the shed. Here the children were happy running about barefoot, digging in little gardens of their own, feeding the geese and chickens and poking carrots and clover into the rabbit hutches; and for the first time in their lives the mother and children moved together in harmony. When Jerry came home from the field and found them in the yard shutting up the broods of little chicks for the night and listened to their excited chatter and prattle, he passed on into the house feeling lonely and morose.

"I reckon I hain't much good here fer anything but to fetch in the money fer the shoes an' groceries," he said to himself, as he splashed the water over his face.

The young fellows were back from the war now—those who had not been killed. Ziemer Whitmarsh came home shell-shocked and good for nothing. He hung about the neighbors' barnyards drooling silly talk and remembering nothing. "What could you expect," everybody said, "when it was in the family anyway?"

"A sword is upon the boasters an' they shall become fools," Jabez Moorhouse was heard to mutter, as he looked after him with a shrug that was half pity, half contempt.

Marsh Gibbs bragged unceasingly about his exploits and his power to turn shot and shell and was listened to with respectful interest until it became known that he had got no further than Panama, where he had done nothing more exciting and dangerous than drive a mule team.

With the return of the men from the war an infectious restlessness and discontent pervaded the barnyards. The talk was all of hard times, of war prices that were not coming down and of the foolishness of bothering with tobacco. Some spoke of

moving over into Indiana, others of going to Cincinnati, though
few had the courage or money to go beyond talk. There was
much robbing of hen roosts and stables and a general and oft
expressed feeling among the old folks that things were going
from bad to worse.

With August the grasshoppers came in great numbers. Luke
Wolf said it was the hard times that brought them. Grasshoppers and hard times, he declared, were never far apart.
However they did little to make the times harder, as they could
do but small damage to the crops. Tobacco they would not
touch and corn was beyond their reach. They were a bit hard
on alfalfa and garden stuff, but they made up for it by fattening
the geese and turkeys.

It gave pleasure to Judith and delight to the children to
tend and watch the little chicks and geese and turkeys as they
grew into strong, stocky birds. And at sundown, when they
all came up to the roosts, the yard was as crowded and busy
as a town on fair day, noisy too with the crowing, quacking
and gobbling of the young males who grew daily in self-import-
ance. But as the fall came on and the young turkeys ranged
further afield and found abundance of food and grasshoppers,
they began to fail to come up for the evening scatter of corn,
a tree in the woods often seeming to them a pleasanter roosting
place than the barn roof. Judith did not like to have them
roosting away from home. She knew that if any of the neighbors happened upon them they would disappear one by one.

Once, when she had not seen them for several days, she left
the children with Aunt Selina in the late afternoon and started
out to look for them. Loitering through the late glow of the
September day she half forgot the turkeys in the pleasure that
came to her from asters and goldenrod, red maples, and yellow
beeches. Almost without thinking what she was doing she began to stray along the path that led in the direction of the old
shanty between the hills.

When she came within sight of the deserted house, the roof
of which was just visible above the rank growth surrounding
it, she stood for a moment looking across the last red shafts

of sunlight that fell toward it through the trees. A half smile of weary cynicism lifted her upper lip, and with a scarcely perceptible shrug she was about to turn away.

Suddenly she drew quickly back behind the trunk of a tree.

Peeping around the tree, like a child playing hide and seek, she saw Hat Wolf appear on the outer edge of the shrubbery that grew about the old house. As she came out, Hat craned her neck and peered cautiously on all sides, scanning carefully the length and breadth of the hollow and the hillsides beyond up to the rim of the sky line. At last, feeling satisfied that no one was looking, she bolted as fast as she could, and her great hips and broad back were soon lost from sight in the nearest thicket.

It was turkeys that usually took Hat away from home. Judith looked around for turkeys. There was not a turkey in sight, nor, strain her ears as she might, could she catch any sound suggestive of their near presence. Perhaps some other business than to see if turkeys were making it a resting place had brought Hat to the old house. Judith had begun to shrewdly suspect what the business might be when she was confirmed in her conjecture by seeing a man emerge from the thicket in the same place that Hat had appeared. He did not peer about as Hat had done but walked away slowly, his head sunk on his breast, his hands plunged deep in his pockets, careless whether he was seen or not. In the dim light she did not recognize him at the first glance. When she looked again she saw that it was Jerry.

A hot wave of anger surged through her, her fists clenched and for the moment her whole being was one great hatred of Hat. Then a dozen conflicting emotions seized upon her, seeking to claim her at the same time. She wanted to run after Hat and spit in her face and call her the names that rose unbidden to her tongue. At the same moment she wanted to run in the opposite direction after Jerry and say to him things that she knew could bring the twitch of agony to his features. This desire had hardly risen in her when it was merged into the impulse to throw her arms about his neck and weep away her storm of struggling passions on his breast. He alone she knew had power to comfort her. But could she go to him for comfort? No, nothing in the world should make her go to him. For a long time she was unable to gather herself together. Her whole being seemed some inert, passive instrument through which impulses, thoughts and feelings came and went of their own accord without any power of her will to control them. Thoughts of Hat made her clench her fists again and flare with lightning flashes of anger. Thoughts of Jerry brought mingled emotions that, whether she would or not, fought frantically within her. Helplessly she fluttered and struggled like an old rag blown this way and that in some bleak dooryard where the winds meet.

Gradually the struggle weakened, and the old cold oppression closed down upon her, stonier, more inexorable than before. She felt drearily lonely and aloof as on the day when she had run away from the stripping of hog guts. Only this time she did not cry. She seemed to have grown too old and hardened for tears.

As her emotions sank and her mind began to work, she told herself coldly how silly she was to care, how stupid to be surprised, how unreasonable to be angry, how senseless every way she looked at it.

Yet she had to keep on looking at it, turning it over and over in her mind, viewing it from this angle and that angle. If it had been almost any other woman it wouldn't have seemed so bad, she told herself. But Hat! How had he allowed himself to sink so low? She felt herself drenched in a bitter flood of contempt for him—and for herself.

The sun had gone down long ago and it was growing dark when she moved at last from the place where she had been standing. But instead of going toward home, she went on down the hill to the old house and peered in at the gaping black doorway. Yes, it was there, looking just the same, the bed of branches and dry leaves that she and the preacher had made. It was still warm, she had no doubt! And suddenly the walls of the old house rang with a hard, sardonic laugh. Whatever sordid tragedies they had witnessed, and doubtless they were many, the rain-streaked walls had never echoed to an unkinder sound. With a shrug she turned away.

Nevertheless, when she started to open up the stretcher that night to make her bed, she found herself hesitating; and there was a softened moment when she almost fled to Jerry. The impulse passed without her giving way to it, and she continued to unfold the ragged quilts.

CHAPTER XXIV

THE great after war pestilence called "flu" swept across Scott County that fall and winter, sparing neither the old men nor the young virgins. It knocked at many doors, and often where its knuckles had rapped the undertaker hung his bunch of crape. Sometimes the crape was a rusty black, often a rather soiled white. It took away Uncle Jonah Cobb and left Aunt Selina alone with the bees and rabbits. It took one of Joe Barnaby's children and Aunt Abigail's son, Noey, and Evalina, Aunt Maggie Slatten's second youngest girl. It took babies in arms and young men that the war had spared and women with child. It took Uncle Sam Whitmarsh away from his cheerful traffic in dogs and horses.

"It's allus this way," said Jabez Moorhouse. "War an' pestilence goes hand in hand. The bigger the war the bigger the pestilence. The Bible says them that's near at hand'll fall by the sword an' them that's afur off'll die o' the pestilence. We're a hell of a long ways off, but we're a-dyin' o' the pestilence jes the same."

He hunched his shoulders over the stove, feeling suddenly cold.

Once again winter settled down on the wind-shaken little house on the ridge. Judith, peering from the window at the mud and clouds of December, felt the old oppression sink upon her, heavier because so drearily familiar. How many years would it go on, she caught herself wondering.

It was nearly a year since the quarrel. Since then they had treated each other with the chilly politeness of strangers who do not much like each other's looks. In summer when life dragged less oppressively it was not so hard to bear. But now that winter was come her heart sank within her.

Christmas came and went and there was no change.

319

It was not until after Christmas that the flu came to them. Jerry had a light attack which kept him away from the stripping room for two weeks. Then when he was almost ready to return to work, Andy got it and was followed in a few days by Billy.

"If Annie gets it, it'll likely go hard with her," said Jerry, looking anxiously at the pale, self-contained little girl who was his favorite among the children. "We can't take her to mammy's 'cause dad's got it."

"An' I can't take her to my folks, 'cause Luelly's jes a-gittin' over it."

Judith did what she could to keep Annie away from her sick brothers. But one morning about a week after Billy had been taken sick, when she went to dress the little girl she saw that her cheeks were flushed with fever.

"I knowed there was no gittin away from it," she said grimly to Jerry, as she mixed a dose of castor oil with warm coffee.

On the third day Annie was so much worse that Jerry rode over to Clayton for Dr. MacTaggert.

It was late that night when the doctor's mud-spattered Ford came panting up the long hill and stopped before their door. The little man looked haggard and hollow-eyed·from his constant attendance at sickbeds and his long hours of bumping over rutted roads and up and down steep, perilous trails to the tobacco growers' lonely shanties.

"It's pneumonia," he said, as he straightened up from his examination of the child's chest.

The blood sank away from Jerry's face, leaving it a sickly gray color, and he grasped the bedpost to steady himself.

"Can't you see your shakin' the child's bed," said Judith crossly in a grating voice.

The doctor said that she would have to be watched and tended carefully both day and night. Jerry let the tobacco stripping go and stayed at home to help with the nursing. The boys were now well on the way to recovery and beginning to be fractious and noisy. The father and mother took turns at nursing the little girl and trying to keep the boys quiet; and through the night one watched while the other slept. As Judith sat by the bedside of the sick child that she had begrudged to life before it was born, her heart failed her at the thought that the little one might die. She felt that to see her die, to have her cold little dead body put into a narrow coffin and laid in the frozen ground would be more than she could bear. Her thoughts skirted these images and fled away aghast not daring to face them. Keenly she suffered with the sufferings of the child. When she anxiously watched her breathing hard she felt her own chest racked by tearing pains. She had to summon all the courage that remained to her to enable her to bear the sight and touch of the limp and wasted little body. Never had the child seemed more inextricably bone of her bone, flesh of her flesh. She felt herself eager to make any sacrifice if only it would bring the little one back to life and health.

And yet at the same moment that she yearned over the sick child, another set of thoughts, strange and sinister, came forward with startling boldness, thoughts that had come to her at other times and before which she had quailed, as, in the darkness of a wakeful night, one quails before thoughts of approaching death.

Of what use after all that this baby should live? She would live only to endure, to be patient, to work, to suffer; and at last, when she had gone through all these things, to die without ever having lived and without knowing that she had never lived. Judith had seen grow up in the families of the neighbors and among her own kin dozens of just such little girls as this one that had come out of her own body: skimpy little young-old girls, with blank eyes and expressionless faces, who grew into a prim, gawky, old-maidish girlhood and passed quickly from that into dull spinsterhood as Luella had done, or to the sordid burdens of too frequent maternity. Little Annie was just such a one. In every way she was a product of the life that had brought her into being, and that life would claim her to the end.

Why had she been given such a child? It seemed the cruelest irony of chance that had bound her by this strong added link to the sodden life of the soil.

Sitting by the sick child through the long vigils of the winter night, the mother dwelt upon these thoughts, facing them squarely. And following them out to the end they brought her relentlessly to the conclusion that it would be better that the child should die. But having come within sight of this conclusion, she turned with instinctive horror and fled away from it. No, she could not have her baby die. She must not die. And yet better children were dying on every side. Why not hers as well as another's? The mother shrank and quailed, feeling her burden greater than she could bear.

As she struggled with these bitter thoughts, the moon, which had passed the full, looked palely into the lamplit room through the tracery made by a dead grapevine against the uncurtained window and saw her sitting gaunt and hollow-eyed, her sharp elbows propped on her knees and her chin in her hands. Again she restlessly paced the floor or stood by the window looking out and taking no comfort from the dumb stretch of hills and valleys that lay dark and lonely under the waning moon.

When it came Jerry's turn to watch by the baby, he was troubled by no such conflict of feelings. His one thought was that the child must be saved. He loved her with all the tenderness that fathers of his nature give to an only daughter, and he saw in her no defect nor resemblance to any other child. She was his girl and she must not be allowed to die.

For nearly a week the child lay tossing and moaning, seeming to be kept alive more by the hectic flicker of fever than by any more stable vital throb. The mother and father alternated in watching over her, silently doing what they could. They grew pale and red-eyed from lack of sleep, frowsy and unkempt. Above the tense strain of the anxiety that held them in grip, the dark cloud of their estrangement hovered with cold oppression. They rarely spoke except when they had to. At meals they sat opposite each other in gloomy silence. When, as sometimes happened, their eyes accidentally met across the bed of the sick child, they turned hastily away with mutual aversion.

At last, after a long night of feverish tossing, there came a morning when the little one seemed somewhat better. She breathed easier and the fever had sunk away leaving her pale and weak but more like the child that her parents knew. Was this a change for the better? Or might it possibly be one for the worse?

About the middle of the morning Dr. MacTaggert came. As he made his examination of the child the parents stood behind him watching anxiously, but never once casting a glance at each other.

"Why, she's a heap better," he said at last, turning around to them. "There's not much of her, but she seems to know how to hang onto life better than some of the stouter ones. The worst seems to be over now, and I reckon you'll raise her yet if all goes well."

"Judy!" said Jerry, when the doctor had closed the door. The one word was full of many things, like a bubble drifting through sunlight.

She fled to him and fell sobbing into his arms.

CHAPTER XXV

WHEN little Annie had recovered and the danger of contagion was well over, Lizzie May came one Sunday to spend the day with her sister, bringing with her Granville and Viola in stiffly starched Sunday clothes and her new husband, Edd Havicus, who handled freight at the Clayton railway station. While Edd and Jerry and Columbia Gibbs and Joe Barnaby sat and whittled at sticks on the sunny side of the barn, the sisters visited together in the kitchen.

Lizzie May looked blooming and happy, and a layer of fat that was beginning to show just a trace of coarseness filled up the wrinkles that had lined her face after Dan's death.

She was continually rushing to the door to make sure that Granville and Viola were not playing in the mud, that they were not in the barn where they might go too near the horses nor anywhere in the vicinity of the horsepond. From the doorway she called out shrill admonitions and threats of future punishment. She found it hard to hide her pride in her own offspring and her disapproval of the dirty faces, muddy overalls and complete lack of manners of Judith's boys. The little girl was better, more clean, and quiet. But even she had not been taught to say "Thank yuh, ma'am," when you gave her a penny or a popcorn ball. If Lizzie May's children were ever negligent in this important matter she always admonished them reprovingly, "Well, naow, what d'yuh say?" and thus drew forth the belated avowal of gratitude. But Judith was shamelessly remiss in all such training. Lizzie May did not know whether it was from laziness or stupidity. She was grieved that a member of her own family should act so.

She was sadly shocked too when she looked about Judith's frowsy kitchen at the stove, innocent of blacking, the pots and pans crusted on the outside with a long accumulation of greasy soot, the floor that needed scrubbing, the smoked-up teakettle and the littered shelves.

"My," she thought with a shudder that almost turned into a shrug, "haow kin she keep a-goin' in sech filth?"

But she would not for the world have said anything; for the longer sisters live apart the more polite they become to each other. And because she wanted to guard against saying anything or looking anything, she chose the safer and much more absorbing topic of her own recently settled home in Clayton. She was voluble and expansive over the new oilcloth in the kitchen, the ingrain carpet in the best room and the set of pink-sprigged dishes that Edd's mother had given her for a wedding present.

"I'm sholy glad I kep' my things an' didn't give 'em away at a auction, Judy. Sech things goes fer nothing when you sell an' costs a heap when you buy. We'd a had lots more expense settin' up housekeepin' if we hadn't a had 'em. Course some of 'em is old fashioned an' not jes what you would choose if you was a-buyin'; but we can't afford yet to have everything to match an' all in golden oak, like young Mrs. Jim Akers. Her things is swell, Judy. Sometimes when I look at the old chair Dan used to set in nights when he come in from the field, I jes can't hardly keep from bustin' out cryin'. An' yet it seems as if things works raound fer the best. Edd's awful steady an' don't never hunt an' hardly never drink. An' it's a heap nicer livin' in Clayton, Judy. No caows to milk nor skimmin' nor churnin' nor botherin' with hawgs an' hens. Sidewalks right to your door so's you don't hev to slush through mud every time you set foot outside. So much easier to keep the kitchen clean, specially with the oilcloth on the floor an' the men not allus trackin' in. Nice neighbors to speak to over the fence or drop in on of an afternoon with yer sewin', an' the store handy to run to, an allus sumpin a-goin' on, an' yer husband drawin' his money regalar every Satiddy night. I dunno haow I ever could go back to livin'," she almost said, "like this," but caught herself in time and ended, "the way I used to."

Judith sat wondering why she could muster up so little interest and why she was not even offended by her sister's airs of superiority, as Lizzie May sang the praises of such urban elegancies as screen doors, garbage cans, and oil stoves.

"An' d'yuh know, Judy," she went on, "I hear there's talk of their startin' a picture show in Clayton. Wouldn't that be fine?"

"It wouldn't make no diff'rence to us," said Judith, smiling a little ruefully. "We're so fur off we'd never be able to git to it."

"Oh, but you must bring the young uns an' stop over night with me," said Lizzie May hospitably. "I got a grand new sanitary bed that his sister give us. All his folks seems to be well fixed. It's a pleasure, Judy, to be amongst people that's refined and has things nice."

Lizzie May seemed indeed to have assimilated the refinements of the town as the sponge sucks water. She was wearing high heeled pumps and nearsilk stockings, a skirt fashionably skimpy, a sweater of brilliant Kelly green and hair that had been put up over night in crimping pins. The mincing precision of her talk and ways had never been so apparent before, and she used the words "toilet" and "sanitary" with the connotations at once malodorous and antiseptic given to these once innocent words by urban Americans.

Judith felt a bit bewildered by all this newness: new clothes, new things, new words. "Toilet" and "sanitary," "swell" and "grand," were words that she had occasionally overheard in Clayton, but they fell strangely from Lizzie May's lips. She realized, with no particular feeling of regret, that the gulf between herself and her sister had widened.

She was glad when Lizzie May and her endlessly trained and endlessly guarded children were gone. Trying to pretend to be interested in her sister's chatter had made her feel tired and headachy and she lay back in the rocking chair and closed her eyes. What a long time it seemed since she and Lizzie May were children together in the little log house that still stood scarcely more than a mile from where she sat. How changed was everything, and yet how unchanged. The same houses and barns stood where she had always seen them, the same people, looking scarcely different, moved in and out. But everything was stark now, bald and bare that in her childhood had been softened by haze, mysterious and beautiful. Beautiful indeed and mysterious the world had seemed then. She called to memory many things out of her happy childhood, the scent of drying tobacco and autumn evenings when they legged it, all five of them, around the clothesline prop, sniffing the winy air like young hounds. There were delirious June mornings, too, when she scampered down the pasture to bring up the cows, and pure April twilights lilac-scented that quickened into being young tendrils of fancy as airy and opalescent as morning gossamer.

How glad and forward looking had been all that time, how forward looking all the thoughts and stirrings and bubblings of youth, always reaching out, reaching out—to what?

Snorting and neighing in the glorious make believe that they were a prancing team, the boys came around the corner of the house trundling a homemade wagon. Annie, driving the wagon, uttered shrill squeals and giggles of delight.

In the half gloom of the kitchen the mother smiled mournfully. It was their day now. But their day too would soon be over, and the question remained unanswered. To what?

She took up the milk bucket and went out to do up the evening chores. When she had fed the hogs and chickens and milked the cows and strained and put away the milk, she sliced some meat for supper and mixed the corncake batter, then sat down to mend a tear in one of Annie's dresses. As she sewed she lifted her eyes often to the window.

From the day that they had moved into the windy little house on the hill, the sunset had begun to reach out hands to her. She had grown into the habit of looking forward to the end of the day. Its approach meant that the waking hours of dismal tasks and constant frets and cares would soon be over, that the whines and wails and wrangles, the scraping of chairs, the tramping of muddy shoes, the whole meaningless turmoil would come to an end, and for a little while there would be peace. Sometimes, too, there was an hour of quiet for her when the work was done, the children out at play and Jerry not yet come in for his supper. From the westward looking window she could see miles of rolling country that stretched to the long sweep of the horizon. Through the day the prospect did not vary greatly and she had not much time to spend in looking at it. But at sundown the west drew her eyes like a magnet. There, with the passing of the slow months, she saw glow into being and fade away the placid gold and azure sunsets of early summer, the hot, smoldering saffrons of August, the clear wine colors of September and the cold grays and yellows of winter. There, after the rain had poured heavily all day long, she sometimes saw the thick, one-toned pall of the sky lift itself away from a narrow strip of intensely glowing horizon against which distant roofs and tree-tops made a black landscape fringe sharply silhouetted against the shining river of light. And after a day of squalls and driving clouds, massed storm clouds hung their dark, rainy fringes around lakes of amber and pure apple green.

The cloud pictures fascinated her even more than the water landscapes on the wall; for in them there was infinite variety and change. She saw stately, turreted castles built upon the tops of crags that rose perpendicularly from shining water; and on the other side of the water perhaps a grove of great trees with weirdly twisted limbs. And even while she looked the outlines of the trees changed, the castle dwindled or loomed larger and there was a new picture. When she looked again it was all gone and there was left a peaceful valley with a river winding through it, a little steep-roofed house on the river bank and a church spire in the distance.

Faces, too, came out of the clouds, faces that held her eyes more than the landscapes: droll, exaggerated faces such as she had tried to draw when she was a little girl at school, faces with bulbous noses and bulging foreheads, faces half animal, half human, crafty faces with little fox eyes, great flabby faces like Aunt Maggie Slatten's.

Sometimes too she saw grow out of the clouds great monumental heads, aquiline-nosed and lofty-browed, full of dignity and repose, as solid and eternal looking as though they were of carved rock instead of drifting cloud vapors.

With a pencil and a piece of wrapping paper, she sometimes tried to catch and hold the fleeting faces that most stirred her fancy. She had a little pile of such drawings laid away in the bottom drawer of the dresser.

It grew too dark to sew. She threw aside the half finished dress and stood looking out of the window seeking peace and a something more than peace which she had learned to draw to herself out of the sunset. It had been a soft, springlike day in March with a mackerel sky undecided between rain and shine. Now the western sky was dappled with a gray and silver sunset, like the spread-out wool of old, weather-beaten ewes backed by the shining fleece of lambs. She went out and stood on the rickety porch. The air was pungent with the smell of damp earth and springing grass. A silvery quiet, pensive but serene, spread from the sky through the soft air, and in the evening silence a returned robin twittered from the top of a tall hickory tree.

Far down the ridge Marsh Gibbs was bringing up Hiram Stone's sheep and lambs to house them in the tobacco barn for the night. The hundreds of woolly backs moving separately yet together made a soft, undulating carpet that grew grayer as the twilight shadows crept over it and at the edges merged imperceptibly with the earth. Mingled with the tremulous bleating of the sheep and the shriller ba-ha-ha of the lambs, the sheep bells tinkled faintly; and dominating all Marsh's long drawn "sheep-ee, sheep-ee," as he led the flock, was not a human-seeming sound, but weird and melancholy, like the cry of some creature born of the twilight. She could not see, but she knew, how trustingly the little lambs ran by their mothers. Soon they would all be at rest in the big barn, safe, warm, and quiet.

In the dooryard she saw the last chickens straggling up one by one, obeying the homing instinct that brought them always at night to the roost. Already the turkeys were perched in a row on the ridgepole of the shed, their big bodies outlined darkly against the sky. Now and then one of them would stretch out its long neck and look warily about to make sure that all was well. The last turkey flew up and joined the line, and with little chirrs of content they settled themselves to sleep. The dog in the corner of the porch sprawled luxuriously, and curled upon her friend's warm flank the cat slept. It was her favorite bed.

Standing wrapped in the growing twilight she felt herself like these humbler creatures an outgrowth of the soil, its life her life even as theirs. Quiet, peace and calm, these things belonged to them, a part of their heritage. These things in less measure her own life had to offer. These things at last she was ready to accept.

Since her reconciliation with Jerry in the joyful moment of their baby's triumph over death a new spirit had entered into her. Meltingly in that moment she had known by what strong ties she was bound to him. Convincingly she had realized the uselessness of struggle. Through the weeks that followed, long thoughts stayed with her as she went about doing her housework and she saw more and more clearly the path that the future laid out before her. Like a dog tied by a strong chain, what had she to gain by continually pulling at the leash? What hope was there in rebellion for her or hers? The boys would grow up to bury their youth in the tobacco field, as Jerry had done. Little Annie would be in years to come a prim and dull old maid like Luella or a harassed mother like herself. Which fate was worse, she asked herself, and did not dare to try to form an answer. She had grown timid about many things since the days of her forthright girlhood. Peace was better than struggle, peace and a decent acquiescence before the things which had to be. At the thought her sunken chest rose a little and the shoulders fell into less drooping lines; and there was a certain dignity in the movement with which she threw a long wrung sheet over her shoulder and stalking with it to the line spread it out to flap in the March winds.

Now, as she stood watching the pale sunset melt into darkness and listening to the distant bleating of the sheep, she told herself again that she was through with struggle and question, since for her nothing could ever come of them but discord. Henceforth she would accept what her life had to offer, carrying her burden with what patience and fortitude she could summon. She would go on for her allotted time bearing and nursing babies and rearing them as best she could. And when her time of child bearing was over she would go back to the field, like the other women, and set tobacco and worm and top tobacco, shuck corn and plant potatoes. Already people were beginning to call her "Aunt Judy." Some day she would be too old to work in the field and would sit all day in the kitchen in winter and on the porch in summer shelling beans or stripping corn from the cob. She would be "granmammy" then.

She felt that she would never again seek estrangement from Jerry. Divided, their life was meaningless, degrading and intolerably dismal. Together there would be if not happiness at least peace and a measure of mutual comfort and sustaining strength by virtue of which they might with some calm and self-respect support the joint burden of their lives. Peace in his house was a gift that she wished to offer him, not out of a sense of duty, but as a free and spontaneous return for his gentle goodness, his devotion to her and her children, his loving disregard of all her shortcomings as housekeeper, wife, and mother. Of this generous bounty she had received without stint, and she felt that at last it had brought forth response in her as grass springs up where warm rains have fallen.

She heard a step and turning her head saw her husband coming up the path. Even in the half darkness her eye, accustomed to all his moods, discerned in his hunched shoulders and heavy gait something more than the daily drag of the soil.

"I got bad news, Judy," he said, as he stepped shamblingly

onto the porch and stood beside her. "They found Uncle Jabez dead in his bed to-day—Aunt Selina found him."

"Uncle Jabez!" was all she could say; and a great void seemed to spread itself around her. Through the void she heard Jerry's voice coming as if from a long distance.

"Yes, it was the flu, I reckon. Nobody hadn't seen him for three four days. An', Judy, I won't never be able to forgive myse'f. Tuesday I was by his place an' he said he wa'n't feelin' a bit good an' strung me out some o' that Bible stuff o' hisn about how the Lord had made his flesh an' skin old an' broke his bones. He looked bad too. He said he reckoned it was the flu. Thursday I was past there agin a-chasin' the roan caow, an' I'd ought to a stopped in, an' I thought of it too. But the caow was a-gittin' fu'ther away every minute an' I kep' on a-goin' after her. An' if I'd on'y a stopped in he might a been saved, an' anyway he wouldn't a died there like a dawg with nobody near to turn a hand for him. It seems awful to think I never went in, don't it, Judy?"

She did not answer. In that moment the manner of his death and Jerry's negligence were nothing to her. All she could think of was that he was dead, that she would never again watch him warm his great hands over her stove, see the fine lines quiver about his mouth and hear the deep bass rumble of his voice, never again listen to his careless singing as he loitered boylike across fields, soaking in the sunshine, tasting the calm of the twilight, stalking giantlike through the light of the moon, and in the dark nights knowing the path with his feet as an old horse knows the road home. In that moment she realized that to know that he was dead was to fill her world with emptiness. What light and color had remained for her in life faded out before this grim fact into a vast, gray, spiritless expanse. Now for the first time she knew what his mere presence in her world had meant to her. The things that remained to her to raise her life above the daily treadmill were the things that she held in common with him: joy in the beauty of the world, laughter and contemplation. These things no one but he had ever shared with her. He had been the one real companion that she had ever known. Now he was gone and she was alone. A weight like a great, cold stone settled itself upon her vitals; and as she gazed out over the darkening country it seemed to stretch endlessly, endlessly, like her future life, through a sad, dead level of unrelieved monotony.

Jerry came and slipped his arm about her waist, as he used to do in the old days when he and she were lovers.

"It's sad, hain't it, Judy, so many folks we've allus been used to gone, an' all in one winter: Uncle Jonah an' Uncle Sam Whitmarsh—an' now Uncle Jabez." Then after a pause, "But you an' me's got each other yet, Judy."

His arm tightened about her and he bent down and kissed her on the lips.

"Yes," she answered a little huskily, "we've got each other."

In its mercy the darkness hid her face.

He went into the kitchen to wash up. She could hear him lighting the lamp, pouring water into the tin basin and splashing it over his face, while he cheerfully rallied the children who had followed him in from their play. The lighted lamp cast an oblique golden band across the porch. She moved a little to be out of the path of the light and remained standing in the darkness.

"Whatcha got for supper, Judy? I'm most powerful hungry, an' these here young uns is a-diggin' into the cold corncakes like so many wolf cubs."

It was the inevitable summons. In obedience to it she roused herself, as she had done so many times before, and went into the house.

THE END

THE UNPUBLISHED SCENE
Billy's Birth

An editor, probably Alfred Harcourt, excised these pages from the original edition of Weeds. *They would have followed Chapter XI. For a discussion of Edith Summers Kelley's reaction see Afterword, p. 361.*

JUDITH disliked, too, Aunt Mary's extreme femininity, her niceness and decency and care for the minutiae of the small properties of her little world. Her attention to detail in every tiny matter bored and wearied Judith and her fastidiousness annoyed her. She could not help thinking of Aunt Mary as a cat, a cleanly cat that attends to its toilet with great care and purrs by the domestic hearth and nurses its kittens tenderly and considers that the world revolves about itself and its offspring, and spits and scratches at anyone who approaches the kittens. She could not refrain from the pleasure of occasionally teasing the cat. She found that if she said anything disparaging about Jerry or any of his habits, the cat would bridle and raise its fur and stretch its sharp claws out of its soft, velvet paws. This amused Judith, and she often made such criticisms in order to get the inevitable reaction from her mother-in-law.

When Jerry returned with his mother, Judith had washed the dishes and put the house in order and made such preparations as she could for her confinement. Her pains were occurring only infrequently; and between the pains she felt no particular discomfort. But she was obsessed with a desire to be doing something, and kept finding more things to attend to so that she might not be left unoccupied. After the arrival of Jerry's mother she was all the more determined to keep busy; for she did not want to have to sit down and talk to Aunt Mary.

"Tain't a bit of use your goin' for the doctor now, Jerry," advised Aunt Mary, who was experienced in such situations. "This is Judy's first, an' it won't come in a hurry. Her pains ain't a-comin' near fast enough. The two of you had best go to bed an' try to git some sleep. You won't need the doctor afore mornin' anyway."

"But can't he give her sumpin to stop the pain?" inquired Jerry anxiously. A smile of amused condescension, in which Judith thought she detected a trace of malice, passed over Aunt Mary's face.

"I reckon she'll have to go through a deal more pain nor what she's doin' afore the baby's born. Fu'st babies don't come so easy. An' I kin tell you for sure the doctor won't be able to do a single thing for her. He'd jes' take a look at her an' go away agin."

Aunt Mary spoke with such conviction that the young couple were convinced. They went to bed in the kitchen, giving up their bedroom to their visitor. At first neither of them could sleep, Judith on account of the ever-recurring pains, which grew steadily worse, and Jerry because of his excitement and anxiety. At last, however, Jerry began to doze and soon fell from the doze into a deep, healthy sleep.

He was startled out of this sleep by Judith shaking him violently.

"Jerry, Jerry," she cried, "git up an' fetch the doctor quick. I've waited as long as I kin. I can't stand this no longer. It's a-comin'. I know it's a-comin'. An' there must be sumpin wrong. I'm jes' a-bein' tore up alive."

Her voice was vibrant with anguish and terror. It was different from any voice that Jerry had ever heard before in his life.

He leapt from the bed and struggled into his clothes, scarcely awake, yet keenly conscious of the one urgent thing that was required of him. They had left a lamp burning dimly in a far corner of the kitchen and it threw a faint light over the objects in the room. Judith was sitting on the foot of the bed clutching one of the posts, her hair hanging wildly about her face. He found the lantern and fumbled with the chimney, finding it in his excitement hard to open. At last he managed to open it and struck a match, which flared and went out. He cursed the match, struck another and at last had the lantern lighted and closed. Grabbing it by the handle he flung out of the door, and a few minutes later galloped past the house on Nip's back. There was no moon, but the sky was clear and the stars gave enough light for him to vaguely see the path. As he guided the horse up the steep hill that led to the ridge road, he heard, suddenly shattering the peace of the night, a terrible sound, a shriek of agony vibrating on two notes, shrill, piercing, utterly unearthly and seeming as though it would never stop. If it ever did stop, the end would surely be the silence of death. Nobody could scream like that who was not about to die. The prickly feeling of sudden sweat broke out all over Jerry, and he kicked the horse in the side to urge him on. The doctor! The doctor! He must fetch the doctor! He pounded along the top of the ridge with all the speed into which Nip could be urged. But he was sick with a dreadful certainty that however quickly he fetched the doctor, he would come too late.

In the meantime Aunt Mary had risen and lighted her lamp and came out into the kitchen with a shawl thrown over her nightgown. Judith was still clinging to the post at the foot of the bed, her cheeks flushed a bright scarlet. Drops of sweat stood out on her forehead and upper lip, and she constantly clenched and unclenched her hands. As Aunt Mary entered the kitchen, she was seized with the worst paroxysm of pain that she had yet had; and, gripping the bedpost, she uttered the scream that had struck terror into Jerry's heart as he was riding up the hill.

But the scream caused no such perturbation of spirit in Aunt Mary. She who went into spasms of anxious excitement over a mislaid male collar button, was here calm as the matron of a foundling asylum. She waited till the cry of agony and terror was over. Then she said,

"Try not to take on so, Judy. It on'y makes it seem worse when you screech."

Judith made no answer, but began to pace up and down the room, still clenching and unclenching her hands.

Aunt Mary went into the bedroom and put on her clothes. Then she came back and lighted the fire, filled the kettle and put it on, swept up the floor about the stove, and made everything neat in her fussy, meticulous way. Having done this, she went into the bedroom again and prepared the bed for Judith's confinement.

All the time Judith paced up and down the kitchen floor like a wild tigress newly caged. When the terrific spasm of pain would grind through her body, she would grasp the nearest object and utter, again and again, the strangely unhuman shriek, a savage, elemental, appalling sound that seemed as though it could have its origin nowhere upon the earth.

It did not, however, seem to greatly disturb the equanimity of Aunt Mary. She bustled about feeding the fire and putting on more water to heat and doing a hundred and one small things about the kitchen.

Having made every preparation that she could think of, she turned to Judith, speaking soothingly with an undertone of irritation, as one addresses a fretful child who has been causing annoyance.

"Naow then, Judy, you'd best come in the bedroom an' lay daown. I've fixed up the bed all nice, an' you'll be better off there. If you prance up an' down an' screech yer lungs out, you won't have no strength left when you'll be a-needin' it by an' by."

Judith only glared at her and made no answer. She continued to pace up and down.

The swift-coming summer dawn reached pale arms into the room, and with it came Jerry galloping back. He burst into the kitchen and could hardly believe his eyes to see Judith still alive and standing on her feet. With a great rush of joy and tenderness he took her in his arms and covered her face and neck with kisses.

"Judy, Judy, I was sure you was gone," he cried and broke into great, gulping sobs.

She gripped him by the shoulders and herself burst into hysterical weeping; then began to laugh foolishly. Jerry laughed too between his sobs; and they clung together, crying and laughing in one breath. Aunt Mary, forgotten and unnoticed, sat coldly by the stove.

All at once he felt her stiffening in his arms. As she stiffened, she trembled violently with terror of what was to befall her; and her hands clenched hard. He closed his arms about her as if he could ward off what was coming. But there was no saving her. In the iron grip of the demon, she grew first rigid as a statue, then bent, twisted, writhed in a hopeless, yet desperate, attempt to wrench herself away from his hold. Again and again came the dreadful shriek. When at last the fiend loosened his grip, she was left trembling, panting, breathless, and wet all over with the sweat of agony.

Jerry, almost as flushed and perspiring as she, stood aghast and speechless before this dreadful thing.

"My God, Judy, this is awful!" he managed to gasp out at last.

The spasm had left Judith exhausted. She sank back into a chair and her eyes closed for a moment. But it was only for a moment. She had gone past the stage when she was able to relax between the paroxysms. The fiend was now constantly at her side and would not leave her in peace a moment, but kept jabbing at her with sharp, vicious stabs which, although they were nothing like the great onslaught, kept her nerves taut and strained. At every moment she stirred uneasily, her knees trembled, and her hands alternately fluttered and clenched.

The doctor had not been at home when Jerry arrived at his house. He was away attending a critical pneumonia case, his wife said; but she would 'phone him to go directly from there to Jerry's. Jerry kept looking out of the window and imagining he heard the chugging of a car, although he felt sure the doctor would not arrive so soon.

In the meantime Aunt Mary had prepared breakfast and placed the steaming cakes and coffee on the table. Judith, between her spasms of pain, managed to drink a little coffee; and Jerry gulped down several cupfuls boiling hot, but could not swallow a mouthful of the cakes. Aunt Mary made her usual meal, eating as she always did in a dainty, pecking, birdlike manner. When crumbs fell on the table she brushed them away with her small, fidgety hands.

After breakfast Jerry went out to attend to the horses and feed the hogs and chickens. The barnyard seemed to him an unreal place and the farm animals mere painted creatures. He fed them mechanically, scarcely knowing what he was doing. Snap, the shepherd pup, now grown into a playful and intelligent young dog, barked joyfully at his heels, asking for attention.

"Down, Snap," he said absently, and kicked him gently aside. Even the dog seemed a phantom creature. The only real thing that penetrated to his senses was the shattering scream that came from the house. As he went about his chores, he found himself waiting for it, stiffening and gasping when he heard it, then waiting for it again.

When he went back into the house, he found that by some miracle the demon had left Judith's side for a few moments and she had fallen asleep of exhaustion. She lay back in the old rocking chair in which Uncle Nat Carberry had died, breathing heavily, her black hair dropping in a long, tousled wisp over the side of the chair, her features pale and drawn, her arms hanging limply, the long hands dangling from the ends like dead things. He moved about noiselessly so as not to disturb her.

"Ain't it dreadful that she has to suffer like this," he said more to himself than to his mother.

"It's God's will," answered Aunt Mary piously.

"Looks to me a damn sight more like the devil's will."

Judith was not allowed to rest for long. The first premonitory twinges of the great throe which was about to rack her roused her out of her sleep; and opening her eyes very wide she looked at Jerry with such horror and dismay, such abject fear, such beseeching, pitiful appeal that his knees went weak under him. She was asking him to help her, and he could give her no help. He held her and gritted his teeth till she had struggled once more with the demon and sank back limply in his arms.

About ten o'clock they heard the throb of an engine; and

rushing out of the door, Jerry saw Doctor McTaggert's battered Ford on the ridge above. The doctor got out and came down the hill on foot, carrying a small leather satchel. Jerry was so glad to see him that he ran to meet him as a dog runs to meet his master. Doctor McTaggert looked exactly as he had looked seven years before when he had attended Judith's mother in her last illness. He was still shabby, dust-colored, of unguessable age, and he still wore the same air of resignation to his lot. He was a very commonplace-looking little man; but the Angel Gabriel in all his heavenly finery could not have shone more gloriously in Jerry's eyes.

Eagerly ushered into the house by Jerry, he went up to Judith and held her hand with a firm, soothing pressure while he felt her pulse.

"You're getting along fine, Judy, my girl," he said, in the quiet, hopeful tone that experience had taught him to use toward expectant mothers. "You have a good, firm, steady pulse. Nothing wrong with *your* heart. Come now and lie down, and we'll see how far along you are."

In the bedroom the doctor made his examination.

"Haow is she?" demanded Jerry, anxiously drawing the doctor outside the kitchen door, when the examination was over.

"She's all right," answered the doctor in a low tone, "But it's a slow case. She's in absolutely no danger at present. Her symptoms are quite normal and natural so far. But the baby won't be born for a long time. Don't tell her that. She's always been a very active girl, and there's a good deal of muscular rigidity which must be overcome. We must leave nature to do it; and nature takes her own time. That's what makes the false pains so bad and makes them last so long."

"Good God, Doc, if these is *false* pains, what's the real ones like?" demanded Jerry.

The doctor smiled. "It's just a name that's been given them," he explained wearily. "I guess they're all real enough. Try to keep her courage up, and don't let her know how long it's going to last. I'm going home now to turn in. I had two hours' sleep last night and three the night before. I'll be here first thing tomorrow morning. If anything unusual happens, you can get me on the phone from Uncle Ezra's."

Tomorrow morning! Jerry was dumbfounded. Desperately he gripped the doctor by the front of his coat, as though to hold him against his will.

"But Doc, how's she a-goin' to *live* till tomorrow mornin' through such pain?"

The doctor smiled again. "She'll live all right," was all he said.

He was gone, and Jerry was left with his terrible task before him. Tomorrow morning seemed to stretch centuries away into the distant future. He gritted his teeth and went back into the chamber of torture where once more she was struggling desperately with the fiend.

"Where's the doctor? Why don't he come back?" she demanded eagerly, when the spasm was over.

"He's a-comin' back right soon, Judy."

All through the rest of the long day and all through the dreadful, crawling hours of the night, he was by her side. When the pains tore at her vitals and she shrieked and flung her arms wildly and aimlessly in the air protesting that she couldn't bear it, she couldn't bear it, she wanted to die and have it over with, he could do nothing but stand by the bedside feeling bitterly his own worthlessness. When she clung to him, as she sometimes did and dug her nails into his flesh, he supported her as best he could, glad to seem to be of some help to her, and waited, tense as she, through minutes that seemed like hours, till she fell back again into the pillows. During the short intervals when she was not suffering so keenly, he bathed her hot face, arranged her pillows, lied to her heroically, and tried to say a few soothing words of hope and comfort.

From time to time Aunt Mary offered to take his place, but Judith would have none of her. Her manner of offering suggested that she considered it a rather indecent thing for Jerry to be there at all. She had a way, which Judith hated, of suggesting things quite definitely without the use of words.

During the night it began to rain. The patter of the drops falling on the roof and beating against the window pane seemed to shut Jerry in with the tortured girl in a great loneliness, as though all the rest of the world had withdrawn itself far away and forgotten them.

As the night wore on and her exhaustion became greater, she slept in the intervals of the pains, short as these intervals had now become. The instant the demon relaxed his grip upon her, she would fall asleep, breathe heavily for a few seconds, then wake moaning with pain and terror of what was to come, as the inexorable iron grip tightened once more upon her. Outside the rain fell steadily and peacefully.

Toward morning she was granted a short respite. When Jerry saw that her body was no longer rent by pain, that she was not even moaning, and had actually fallen into a deep, quiet sleep, his nerves, strained tight for so many hours, all at once relaxed; and he dropped his head into the quilts at the foot of the bed and sobbed for a long time.

When he had emptied his reservoir of tears he felt much better and went out into the kitchen and awkwardly made himself a cup of coffee and devoured four large corn cakes that he found in the cupboard. Aunt Mary, who had lain down in her clothes and was sleeping fitfully, woke up as he was drinking the coffee and asked him why he had not called her to make it for him. When he went back into the bedroom Judith was still sleeping. He sat down in a low rocking chair and instantly fell asleep.

He awoke the moment that he heard her stirring and was on his feet and listening terrified to a sound that he had never heard before, a deep-toned, gutteral, growling sound that ended in a snarl. It was not like that of an ordinary dog; but more as Jerry imagined some wild, doglike creature, inhabitant of lonely waste country, might growl and snarl over its prey. Could it be Judith who was making this savage sound?

He was at the bedside looking at her. The veins in her forehead were purple and swollen. The muscles of her cheeks stood out tense and hard. Her eyes, wide open, stared at the ceiling with the look of eyes that see nothing; and her gums were fleshed in the snarl like the gums of an angry wolf. Her hands were clenched into iron balls, her whole body rigid and straining heavily downward. As she gave vent to this prolonged, wolfish noise, she held her breath. He watched in helpless, horrified suspense.

When at last the strange spasm passed, she took breath again with a gasp and looked up at Jerry as one who has returned from another world.

"That's better," said Aunt Mary, who had come into the room. "That means the baby'll be born afore long."

This news changed Jerry's terror into joy and helped to cheer him through the trials that were yet before him.

There were hours upon hours of this, dragging endlessly into eternity. Like the ever-recurring drive of some great piston which went on its way relentless and indomitable, the irresistible force drove through her quivering body, drew back and drove again. At first there was a moment or two of breathing space between the drives when she could look up at Jerry declaring that she could not bear it a moment longer, begging him frantically to save her, bring the doctor, do *something*. But as time passed the great drives became as regular and as incessant as clockwork, with no stop, no slightest pause, no abating of the terrific, invincible energy.

She no longer saw Jerry nor heard his voice nor cared anything about him. For her there was no longer any return from the ghastly No Man's Desert of pain into which she had been snatched by a strong, pitiless hand again and again for so many long hours. She was there now quite alone and cut off from all humankind. Out of it there led but one sinister canyon through which she must pass to come back to the world of men. All other ways were closed but this. Nature that from her childhood had led kindly and blandly through pleasant paths and had at last betrayed her, treacherously beguiling her into this desolate region, now sternly pointed her the one way out: the dread and cruel pass of herculean struggle through tortures unspeakable.

Through no volition of her own, but following only the grimly pointing finger, because follow she must, as a leaf is drawn upon a downward current, the girl entered between the towering entrance boulders of that silent canyon and passed far away from the life of the world. There was no time any more, nor space, nor measure of anything. It was her fate only to struggle on desperately, blindly, knowing only one thing: that each struggle meant the suffering of anguish that is unbearable and that yet must and will be borne; and to do this endlessly, endlessly, endlessly, without rest, without respite.

Her eyes were closed now, her face a dark purple with dreadfully swollen veins and salient muscles; her body driving, driving, driving, with the force and regularity of some great steel and iron monster. It seemed to Jerry impossible that a creature made of mere flesh and blood could struggle and suffer like this through so many hours and continue to hold the spark of life.

"If she'd been a caow, she'd a been dead long ago," he muttered; then started violently, shocked at his own comparison.

The rain stopped as the dawn began to grow in the room. With the approach of the sun, roosters crew and hens cackled in a chatty, gossiping way, as though nothing unusual were happening. Snap, the dog, full of morning vivacity, rushed among them and scattered them, barking joyously. They half ran half flew from his approach and cackled in loud tones, at first with fright, then with indignation, and went back to their scratching. Robins and orioles greeted the rain-washed morning with song; and a meadow lark, perched on a rail fence a few rods from the house, uttered at regular intervals its trill of melody. After the rain everything beamed, sparkled, and gave forth all it had of color and fragrance.

These things in which Judith was wont to take delight were all as nothing to her now. Stretched out on the bed as on some grisly rack of torture, she still gasped, strained, ground her teeth and uttered again and again the growl of struggle ending in the fierce snarl of agony. To Jerry's sleep-dulled mind she took on gigantic proportions. She was no longer Judith; she was something super-human, immense and overpowering.

The sun rose over the brow of the ridge and made the pattern of the half open window on the floor. Through the open door shaded by the grape vine came the pungent smell of flowering grapes exhaling their intense wet fragrance into the warm sunshine. Aunt Mary flitted about, doing such things as she deemed necessary; and Jerry, having done his morning chores, sat by the bed in a sort of dazed stupor. He was too tired now to care very much what happened.

The sun rose higher and higher, whitening with its glare the deep morning blue of the sky. And still the never-ending struggle went on, and still the doctor did not come. It was nearly eleven o'clock when at last Jerry heard, as if dimly through a dream, the chug of his engine. He came in and having felt her pulse nodded in a reassuring way.

"She's got a good strong heart all right," he said, as he washed his hands at the washstand. Having made his examination, he smiled with a sort of weary satisfaction to find that he would not have long to wait. He washed his hands again, and this time the water in the basin was red with blood.

"Is it all right?" asked Jerry anxiously.

"Perfectly all right. Everything normal. No complications."

"Now then, Judy," he said, bending over the struggling girl. "Try to bear down just as long and hard as you can each time, and you'll be out of pain before you know it."

He asked for a handkerchief; and having taken a little bottle of chloroform from his bag, poured a few drops on the handkerchief and handed it to Jerry.

"Hold that over her nose," he said.

She breathed deep of the sweet, suffocating, merciful fumes; and as she drew them into her lungs the intense, tearing agony changed to a strong but dull straining pressure, as though she were still being pulled apart but had lost most of the power of sensation. She still felt the great drives going through her, she still strained with all the power of her muscles, and she still felt pain, but in a dull-edged, far off way. Her mind, released from the present, wandered aimlessly into the past, picking up a shred here and a scrap there.

"Ain't he a handsome mule, Elmer? An' don't he smile for all the world like Uncle Sam Whitmarsh?"

"I'm a-goin' to have a pink dress an' a pink sunbonnet, like Hat's, on'y nicer made, an' slippers with two straps an' white stockings."

"Oh land, I wisht she'd go. I hate all these old wimmin. She smells bad too."

"You gotta let me have all them terbaccer sticks, Jerry, 'cause I wanta build a cage with 'em to break up my settin' hens. No, them old rotten pickets won't do. I want the terbaccer sticks, an' I'm a-goin' to have 'em. Hiram Stone's a rich man; he won't miss a few terbaccer sticks."

"All right, dad. I'm a-comin'. I'm a-fetchin' 'em. Git along, Blackie. He there, Spot. Land, ain't a caow a o'nery beast!"

The doctor stood over her with patient watchfulness, encouraging, exhorting. (Aunt Mary flitted about in the background.)

"Hold fast, Judy. A little longer. A little longer. It'll soon be all over. There. Once more. Just once more."

She heard him and instinctively responded with her body, although his voice seemed to be far, far away, and his words of but vague import.

There came at last one great drive that did not recoil upon her as the others had done from the impact against something hard, solid, and immovable. This time something gave way. Encouraged by the far away voice of the doctor and the more clearly heard accents of nature, she kept on straining, straining, straining, as though she would never stop. She vaguely sensed the doctor working rapidly above her, tense, sweating, straining with all his might even as she was straining. And miraculously something started to come and kept on coming, coming, coming, as though it would never have an end.

But there was an end at last; and with a great sigh she fell back into the bosom of an immense peace.

It was over, and the doctor triumphantly held up nature's reward for all the anguish: a little, bloody, groping, monkey-like object, that moved its arms and legs with a spasmodic, froglike motion and uttered a sound that was not a cry nor a groan nor a grunt nor anything of the human or even the animal world, but more like a harsh grating of metal upon metal. It was a reward about the worthwhileness of which not a few women have had serious doubts, especially when first confronted with what seems to the inexperienced eye a deformed abortion. Judith was too far sunk into semi-unconsciousness to care anything about it one way or the other.

Aunt Mary, however, entertained no doubts. It was her first grandchild.

"Ah, but ain't he the fine boy!" she cried, taking the creature from the hands of the doctor and wrapping it carefully in a woolen shawl, "Der naow, he was des the best boy his granny every had, yes he was."

She approached her face to that of the weird mannikin, waggling it up and down, and actually began to chirp and twitter ecstatically to the bloody little squirming object. The sight gave Jerry a shiver of revulsion. It did not occur to him that he himself had once looked just like this; and if it had his feelings would probably not have been different.

"Ain't he a splendid boy, Jerry?" she cried, carrying him over toward her son.

"Aw, take the durn thing away," growled Jerry impatiently, and bent over his wife.

It was astonishing how quickly the color came back into Judith's cheeks, and how soon her muscles, strained and aching from the two days of incessant struggle, became relaxed and rested. The baby, too, was greatly improved in appearance by being washed and dressed. Judith's first impulse was to dislike the child because, before she even saw it, she heard its grandmother in the other room making such a silly fuss over it. But when the little stranger, who seemed to have miraculously appeared from nowhere, was brought to her dressed in white muslin garments, she was completely captivated by the appeal of the soft, yet strong, little body, the perfect hands and feet, the eyes, bright yet vague, like those of a young kitten, and the foolish, groping little mouth. His finger nails, exquisitely pure and clean, were pink like the inside of a sea shell, and they had already grown too long. So she must have Jerry get the scissors and cut them at once, although Aunt Mary said that to cut his nails before he was a month old would surely bring bad luck to the baby. Jerry, too, who had been assured by Doctor McTaggert that the baby would "come out all right," began to take an interest in the child and to watch him curiously as he unfolded day by day into more human likeness.

"You know, Judy, he turns a diff'rent color every day," he said to Judith, when the baby was about a week old. "The fu'st day he was purple, the next day red, the next day a kind of Chinaman yaller; an' naow he's a-gittin' to be jes' nice an' pink an' white like a kid otta be."

The little house was beset with visitors. Everybody in the neighborhood dropped in to see the new baby; and the relatives came from miles around. An air of festivity clung about the house and the visitors, as though even in Scott County it was a good thing to be born. Aunt Abigail, whose hard, shiny black hair still showed no streak of gray, presented Judith with a cream colored baby cape which her son Noey had worn when he was a baby. Luella brought two white muslin dresses elaborately tucked and trimmed with lace. Lizzie May came proudly carrying her own child, a round-eyed, puffy-cheeked, rather stodgy-looking boy, now several months old, to whom she had attached the name of Granville. Lizzie May looked better and younger than before the birth of the child, and seemed to take Dan's shortcomings less seriously. Hat came and old Aunt Selina Cobb and Aunt Sally Whitmarsh and Cissy and Aunt Eppie Pettit and a dozen others. Most of these women brought their men with them and left them in the kitchen to chew and spit and talk about the dry spell while they themselves went into the bedroom and admired the baby and asked Judith how she felt.

Of the men only her father and Jabez Moorhouse came in to see her. Bill looked his grandson over and decided that he would pass.

"Purty good size an' strong fer bein' on'y a heifer's calf, Judy," he said, showing the twinkle in his gray eyes.

Judith laughed gaily. She was glad her father was pleased with the baby. These few words of praise from him meant more to her than the cooings and gurglings of all the women. Between Bill and his youngest girl there had always been a strong bond of silent sympathy.

Jabez was the only one of the visitors who did not say something "nice." He had not had a drink that day, and was in one of his melancholy moods. He cast an unseeing glance of indifference at the baby and then looked at Judith with eyes at once vague and intense that seemed to look through and beyond her into some gloomy and unfathomable distance.

"I s'pose it's a fine brat," he drawled. "They all are when they fu'st git borned. But somehaow I don't like to see you a-gittin' yerse'f all cluttered up with babies, Judy. There's plenty enough wimmin likes to mess about over babies in the kitchen. You'd otta a left it to the like o' them. It hain't fit work for a gal like you. But that's haow young folks is. You can't tell 'em nothing for their good. You can't tell 'em nothing. They gotta find it out for their selves—when it's too late. Ah well, it's nater. It's nater, that must have her fun with all of us, like a cat that likes to have a nice long play with every mouse she ketches."

He sat with his chin propped on one great, heavy-veined hand and looked gloomily out of the little window. He had dropped in on his way from setting tobacco and his hands were caked with dried earth. The buttons were gone from his faded blue shirt, and the lean cords of his neck vibrated above his hairy chest.

"This here stuffy bedroom hain't no place for you to be this fine day, Judy," he went on, sniffing the air, which was faintly suggestive of wet diapers. "You'd otta be out over the hills a-stalkin' turkeys or a-fetchin' up the caows, or a-ridin' hoss back over the roads up hill an' down dale, or else jes' a-runnin' wild with the res' o' the wild things: grass an' wind an' rabbits an' ants an' brier roses an' woodchucks an' sech. That's where you'd otta be, Judy. But I expect you won't never git back there no more. Waal, I s'pose the world has gotta be kep' a-goin'."

AFTERWORD

by Charlotte Margolis Goodman

Edith Summers Kelly's *Weeds* was published originally by Harcourt, Brace in 1923. Despite favorable reviews, it sold poorly and soon went out of print. It remained yet another "lost" novel by a woman until Matthew J. Bruccoli, professor of English at the University of South Carolina, Columbia, discovered it in a used bookstore and persuaded Southern Illinois University Press to reissue it in 1972.[1] (The first Feminist Press edition followed in 1982.)

After coming across Alden Whitman's laudatory review in the *New York Times* in 1973, I purchased Kelley's novel about the bleak life of the wife of a Kentucky tobacco tenant farmer, thinking that it might be pertinent to an article I was writing about rural women in American fiction.[2] Subsequently, as long as *Weeds* remained in print, I taught it to class after class of college students, who were always as moved as I was by the plight of Kelley's trapped female protagonist, Judith Pippinger Blackford.[3] They were surprised to discover, in a novel written so many years ago, that Kelley was very much aware of the ways in which the lives of women may be circumscribed by material circumstances, biological imperatives, and patriarchal attitudes. From what we now know about Edith Summers Kelley's own life, we can understand how her feminist consciousness evolved and came to be expressed in *Weeds*, in a second novel, *The Devil's Hand*, which was published posthumously in 1974 by Southern Illinois University Press, and in her short stories, poems, and essays.

Family members and friends described Edith Summers Kelley as "a golden-haired and shrewdly observant young person whose gentle voice and unassuming ways gave us no idea of her talent";[4]

a "Cherub";[5] a woman who was "even-tempered, undemonstra-
tive, unsociable, and usually expressionless, except when laughing";[6] a nature lover who "never put a flower in a pot or had a
caged bird";[7] an admirer of the poetry of Thomas Hood, Algernon
Charles Swinburne, and Heinrich Heine;[8] a skeptic who nevertheless could "quote the Bible by the yard."[9] The youngest child of
Scottish immigrants, she was born in Toronto, Canada, on April
28, 1884. She showed early promise as a writer, for she sold a
Christmas story to a Toronto newspaper at the age of thirteen.
The recipient of a scholarship to the University of Toronto, she
graduated in 1903 with honors in modern languages. Like the
protagonist of one of her unpublished stories, "Heart of April,"[10]
Edith Summers Kelley then settled in New York City with hopes
of pursuing a career as a writer. To support herself, she worked on
Funk and Wagnall's *Standard Dictionary*, incurring the eyestrain
that would continue to plague her for the remainder of her life.

A newspaper advertisement led to Kelley's next job, as secretary
to novelist Upton Sinclair. She worked for Sinclair from 1905 to
1906 at his farm in Princeton, New Jersey, and then at Helicon
Hall, an experimental cooperative community founded by Sinclair that was located in the elegant buildings of a defunct boys'
school on the outskirts of Englewood, New Jersey. Its members
included forty intellectuals, among them Sinclair's wife Meta, a
writer; writers Alice McGowan and Grace McGowan Cooke; edu-
cator Anna Noyes; suffragist Frances Maule; a medical student
named Helen Montague; and Stella Cominsky, Emma Goldman's
niece. American philosophers John Dewey and William James, as
well as Charlotte Perkins Gilman, author of "The Yellow Wallpa-
per" and *Women and Economics*, were among the colony's distinguished visitors.

The communal kitchens and centralized nurseries that Gilman
advocated in *Women and Economics* were two of Helicon Hall's
most notable features. In a recent, posthumously published mem-
oir of Helicon Hall, Kelley celebrated the fact that, because of
these kitchens and nurseries, mothers at Helicon Hall were able to

eat their meals in peace and converse freely with other adults, while their children enjoyed "a wonderful time and very desirable training."[11] A reader of *Weeds* cannot help but speculate how different life would have been for Kelley's protagonist, Judith Pippinger Blackford, had she been a member of such a community.

Several members of the Helicon Hall community were important figures in Kelley's personal life. These included its founder Upton Sinclair, whose naturalistic novel *The Jungle*, which he had just completed when Kelley began to work for him, appears to have influenced her own writing; Sinclair Lewis, to whom she was engaged for a brief time, and who helped her to get *Weeds* published;[12] and Lewis's friend Allan Updegraff, who soon became Kelley's husband and the father of her first two children.

Kelly later recalled, "To me, and I think probably to most of the others who shared that experience, Helicon Hall is one of the beauty spots of the past."[13] Unfortunately, this experiment in communal living ended abruptly on March 14, 1907. Awakened by noise in the corridor at 4:00 A.M., Kelley opened the door to her room to discover that the opposite end of Helicon Hall was in flames. "In less than an hour," she mourned, "our beautiful home with its billiard room, its pipe organ, its great fireplaces and tropical patio, was nothing but a heap of smoldering ashes."[14] After the fire she returned to Greenwich Village, where she began to earn her living by writing what she later described as "frothy and inconsequential" stories for magazines.[15] Four of her poems also were published in 1907.[16]

During the seven years Kelley lived in Greenwich Village, many Villagers were promoting both socialism and feminism. Village champions of women's rights included such political activists as Henrietta Rodman, Crystal Eastman, Ida Rauh, and Margaret Sanger, leader of the movement for birth control, as well as the writers Neith Boyce, Mary Heaton Vorse, Susan Glaspell, and Floyd Dell.[17] Although there is no evidence that Kelley knew all these Village radicals personally, during her association with Helicon Hall she had met many writers, artists, anarchists, and socialists. One of the Village writers who did become a friend was Susan Glaspell, a founder of the Provincetown Players whose play *Trifles* illuminates—as does *Weeds*—the harsh realities of life as experienced by the wife of a poor farmer. Floyd Dell, an editor of the periodical *The Masses*, also contributed to Kelley's evolution as a writer.[18] In 1912 *The Masses* serialized Emil Zola's *Germinal*, a powerful naturalistic novel that may have had an influence on Kelley's descriptions of the lives of tenant farmers in *Weeds*. *The Masses* also regularly published articles of interest to feminists, including editorials defending Margaret Sanger's crusade to distribute birth control information to the poor. Dell himself argued that feminism not only would improve the situation of women but would "make it possible for the first time for men to be free."[19] In the political atmosphere of Greenwich Village, Kelley's interest in the struggles of the poor and in feminism coalesced.

Little is known about Edith Summers Kelley's brief life with Allan Updegraff, whom she married in 1908 and divorced three years later. Their daughter Barbara was born in 1911; their son Ivor in 1913. During this period Kelley taught French and German at a night school in the Hell's Kitchen district in Manhattan. She and her husband spent their summers in the Berkshires, where they often visited with friends from their Helicon Hall days, including suffragist Frances Maule and her husband Edwin Bjorkman, who translated Strindberg's naturalistic plays into English, and writer Freeman Tilden. In 1913 Kelley and Updegraff published an English translation of Italian playwright Giuseppe Giacosa's plays *The Stronger, Like Falling Leaves,* and *Sacred Ground,* with an introduction they wrote together.

In Greenwich Village Edith also met C. Fred Kelley, a sculptor who had spent his youth on a prosperous wheat ranch in Oklahoma. After she divorced Updegraff she lived with Kelley, and in 1914 they decided to try their hand at raising crops, and moved to a tobacco farm in Kentucky. In "We Went Back to the Land," an essay chronicling the Kelleys' unsuccessful efforts to earn their living from the soil, she described the move to Kentucky:

A day and a half after leaving our comfortable New York apartment, we found ourselves in an unpainted, three-room tenant shack, a mere shell of four flimsy walls and a leaky roof, no sink, no closets, no cupboards, no shelves even, just four stark walls and a tiny, cobwebbed window high up in the wall of each room. I shall never forget the feeling of dismay with which I stood in the midst of this with the baby in my arms and my little girl clinging to my skirt.[20]

Edith Summers Kelley and her husband became the managers of a seven-hundred-acre tobacco farm they had rented in Scott County, Kentucky. Like the tenant farmers in *Weeds*, they experienced anxiety and dread whenever drought or weeds threatened their crops. "The weeds grew so fast that it was almost impossible to keep them from smothering the young corn and tobacco," she said of her own second summer on the farm.

Failing to make a profit on their investment in Kentucky, the Kelleys then purchased a farm in Newton, New Jersey. Edith Summers Kelley wryly observed that its "quaint looking old farmhouse—somewhat fallen into decay,"—looked like a "palace" compared to their former cramped quarters. However, it did not take them long to discover that they could not earn their living from the beautiful but infertile 140 acres of stony soil. Instead, they took in summer boarders, young men and women workers from the city who were drawn to the farm by the smell of hay, the fishing available nearby, the fresh farm food, and the home-baked bread that the Kelleys provided for a modest fee. Here Edith Summers Kelley's third child, Patrick, was born in 1917.

With three young children to care for and the boarders to attend to, the overworked Edith Summers Kelley found the summers stressful, while the winters in rural New Jersey were "tedious, dull, and cold." A posthumously published short story, "The Old House," which Kelley wrote during this period, may well have reflected her own state of mind. Its female protagonist, a portrait painter, is exiled to a house in the Berkshires when she marries a writer. She insists on drawing up a prenuptial marriage contract before she marries, stipulating that she will always be allowed to earn her own living, that she will have a separate bedroom and also a workroom, that she will be free to come and go as she pleases, and that she will not be expected to darn socks or sew on buttons or in any way minister to her husband's material needs;[21] however, she quickly discovers that the housework becomes *her* work, and she begins to wonder when she had "evolved from a happy, careless, life-loving Pagan into a sad, weary, discouraged female drudge."[22] In a passage reminiscent of the description in *Weeds* of the never-ending chores of a farm housewife,[23] Kelley's depressed protagonist thinks of what the coming of winter will mean:

> the ever-lasting building and keeping up of the fires, the clearing of paths, the emptying of ashes; the monotonous dazzling white without even a fence visible. It meant the snow drifting through the cracks and melting into pools onto the window-sills and about the kitchen door. It meant the sickening, ever-present odor of the greasy fried food which they had to eat to keep themselves braced against the weather. It meant going about the draughty old kitchen with her body weighed down with tons of clothes and yet with her feet in a chronic state of chilled numbness. It meant the primitive, never-ending fight against the cold—the fight that took up every ounce of her energy—for the sake of an empty existence that seemed far from worth the price paid for it.[24]

Her husband insists on remaining in the country for another year while he finishes the book he is writing, ignoring her protestations that she herself is unable to do any portrait painting in these surroundings. At the story's conclusion Kelley's despondent female protagonist sets fire to the house, though she does rescue her husband's typewriter and manuscript from the flames.

After living in New Jersey for five years, the Kelleys in 1920 were once again on the move, lured to the sunny Imperial Valley of California by a folder that extolled its beauties and the opportunities it offered to make money quickly by farming. "But alas," Edith Summers Kelley subsequently lamented, "how different it all was from what we had expected! The folder had said nothing about dust, dismal monotony of landscape, more dust, miserable shacks standing starkly on patches of bare, treeless, beaten ground, more dust, waste paper, tin cans, carcasses of dead cars, abandoned tracts going back to desert, more monotony and more dust."[25] Farming, too, was difficult. "As soon as the conditions of the ground would permit," Kelley explained, "my husband plowed the corn; and I tagged behind and pulled aside the masses of up-rooted weeds from the young plants." The "weeds" took root in her psyche, becoming a dominant motif in her first novel, which she began to work on here. In a letter she wrote to Sinclair Lewis during this period, she declared her intention of writing about the poverty-stricken Bluegrass region of Kentucky where she and her husband had lived earlier. Thanking Lewis for sending her a copy of his newly published *Main Street*, to whose trapped protagonist Kelley's Judith might be compared, she went on to say that her own novel would describe the tragic fate of a woman born into a "worn-out, in-bred, toil-sodden race" who "realized the hideous-ness, and at last the hopelessness of her trap."[26] The inspiration for Kelley's second novel, *The Devil's Hand*, can also be traced to this year, for she acknowledged that the two young women who farmed the land adjoining the Kelleys' property were her proto-types for the fictional Rhoda Malone and Kate Baxter.

The Kelleys' farm in the Imperial Valley was a financial failure, just as their other ventures in farming had been, and the next year found them trying to raise chickens on the outskirts of San Diego, an enterprise that ended disastrously when the chickens became ill and had to be sold to a butcher. To support his family, Fred Kelley then took a job in a slaughterhouse, where his task was the dis-tasteful one of pulling the wool from the decaying hides of sheep. Meanwhile, Edith tended to the house and the three children, sewed the family's clothing, milked the cow, raised and canned vegetables, cooked, and during the hours when the children were in school, completed the manuscript of *Weeds*, typing its pages on an ancient and massive office typewriter.[27]

In a letter she sent to Alfred Harcourt at Harcourt, Brace on February 26, 1923, she suggested to what extent she had identified with the struggles of her overworked protagonist, Judith Pippinger Blackford, a wife and mother who shows some artistic promise but whose circumstances do not permit her artistic talents to flourish.[28] "It has been a terrible task to write the book underneath the same roof with three irrepressible children who had nobody to care for them but me," Kelley wrote.[29] In a subsequent letter to Harcourt dated April 12, 1923, she requested a five-hundred-dollar advance so that her husband could quit his job at the slaughterhouse and raise chickens once again on their farm. As she hastened to explain:

> By making this change in our way of living, I could get at the work of revising the book promptly, could get it done earlier and make a better job of it, because my husband would be near at hand to keep the children out of the way while I worked. Indeed I hardly see how I can revise the book unless he is at home, for the writing of the book under the circumstances in which we live was a supreme effort which I now feel incapable of repeating.[30]

Three of Edith Summers Kelley's friends from the East—Upton Sinclair, Floyd Dell, and above all Sinclair Lewis—helped to promote the novel. It was Lewis, in fact, who originally contacted Alfred Harcourt and Donald Brace, the publishers of his own novels, and encouraged them to read the manuscript of *Weeds*. "It sounds to me as tho she had a novel here, as tho she had grown from the poetic yearnings she had fifteen years ago when I knew her best to real stuff for a good American novel," Lewis wrote them after receiving a letter from her in which she spoke about her plans for her novel.[31] Later, when Lewis had read *Weeds*, he wrote to them again, saying, "I think you have something big in her and in this book." Realizing her financial difficulties, he also urged them, "Don't let her fail for lack of encouragement—particularly in the hard dollars which will make it possible for her to work."[32] It is probable that Lewis also helped to persuade Jonathan Cape to publish a British version of *Weeds* in 1924.[33] He even offered to make the cuts to the manuscript recommended strongly by Harcourt and Brace; but he entreated the editors at Cape not to cut too much, reminding them that his own novel, *Main Street*, which the British house had recently published, had sold very well, despite the fact that it too had needed to be pruned.[34]

The issue of making cuts in the novel distressed Kelley, who insisted that eliminating sixty thousand words (about two hundred pages), as her publishers had requested, would remove material necessary to understand the Blackfords' life fully. "My idea in writing the book," she argued, "was to portray a narrow and intense private life against the background of a community which was of course more diversified."[35] She was particularly irate at her publishers' insistence that she delete the "poor little handful of 'bad words'" she had included deliberately to render a truer picture of the tobacco growers' language, as well as a scene describing the birth of Judith's first child. About the birth scene she wrote:

> I had never read in the works of a woman novelist—obviously a woman is the only one who could do it justice—an adequate description of childbirth, so I concluded that the job was waiting to be done by me.

Then, in a more conciliatory tone, she added, "Though it is in no way exaggerated, it reads a bit that way, and some people would be inclined to deduce from it that the whole book is hysterical."[36] She may well have been irked by the thought that twenty years earlier her friend Upton Sinclair had been permitted by *his* publishers to describe just such a scene in *The Jungle*. (This exised birth scene appears in the Feminist Press edition, immediately following the text.)

The publication of *Weeds* in 1923 was a source of both pleasure and disappointment for Edith Summers Kelley. Most disappointing was the fact that the book was not a financial success, despite favorable reviews by such luminaries as Joseph Wood Krutch and

Stuart P. Sherman, as well as by her friends Upton Sinclair and Sinclair Lewis. As she lamented to Upton Sinclair in 1926, she still owed her publishers 130 dollars of the 500 they had advanced her.[37] Her son Patrick recently remarked that his mother always believed the novel did not sell in part because of the publisher's failure to promote the book sufficiently,[38] and her son Ivor Updegraff remembers her remarking bitterly that the American public wanted romantic novels about women who got jobs in offices and married the boss, rather than realistic novels like *Weeds.*[39]

Discouraged by the reception of her novel but still determined to succeed as a writer, Edith Summers Kelley began to work on a second novel, *The Devil's Hand.* As a result of Upton Sinclair's efforts on her behalf she obtained a grant, without which, as she wrote to him, she could not have had "the heart to tackle another book."[40] However, her writing was interrupted when she and her family moved once again; while her husband was building a house for them in Ocean Beach, California, the Kelleys lived in a shed and she wrote in a small tent.[41] Describing the disheartening experience of two young women from the East who purchase a farm in the Imperial Valley of California, *The Devil's Hand* draws on her own experience in this locale as well as on the chicken farm. When the novel was later rejected by Harcourt, Brace, she admitted in a letter to Upton Sinclair that she was dissatisfied with the book herself but planned to revise it, explaining, "One trouble was that I tried to work on it when conditions were so unfavorable that I simply couldn't give it my best efforts or even my second best."[42] Several years later she was still working on the novel sporadically, although she indicated in a letter that her efforts had been interrupted once more, this time by "acute eye trouble."[43] It was not until 1974, eighteen years after her death, that this second novel was published after her son Patrick gave the manuscript to Matthew Bruccoli, who served as editor for the Southern Illinois University Press publication of the novel. Although reviewers pronounced it to be less accomplished than *Weeds,* they found it to be of considerable interest nevertheless.

Describing in *Silences* the circumstances that may dampen the spirits and restrict the literary output of writers, Tillie Olsen mentions financial pressures, domestic responsibilities, and the lack of a sympathetic audience.[44] All of these circumstances constrained Edith Summers Kelley. They perhaps help to account for the fact that, after the appearance of *Weeds*, she published nothing during the remaining thirty-three years of her life, although she did continue to write short stories and poetry. Her creative energies were further depleted by three more moves within California: in 1928 to Point Loma, in 1945 to Pacific Grove, and in 1946 to Los Gatos. Moreover, during the years of the Depression she worked briefly as a domestic in order to supplement the family's meager income. Fortunately, real estate investments that her husband Fred had made earlier, in part with profits earned from operating a still during Prohibition, finally brought the Kelleys economic security. During the last decade of her life, however, Edith Summers Kelley was not able to commit her energies fully to her writing.

In a poem called "Roses and Peonies," which might well have served as her epitaph, Edith Summers Kelley wrote of a worn-out "empty shell of a woman":

> She died among the roses and the palms
> But always to her secret heart there clung
> In shifting visions of its storms and calms
> The winter world she knew when she was young.[45]

Finding in California no community of artists and intellectuals like the one she had been a part of in her youth, she became more and more reclusive. Edith Summers Kelley once had confided to Sinclair Lewis that she would feel like a "jail bird" if she thought she would have to remain in California for the rest of her life.[46] Nevertheless, she continued to live there until she died of renal failure in her seventy-second year, on June 9, 1956.

In his afterword to the Southern Illinois University edition of *Weeds* that was published in 1972, Matthew Bruccoli pronounced it "a superb forgotten novel," describing it as "a quiet masterpiece" about farm life that belongs to the "realistic/naturalistic" literary tradition.[47] Indeed, Kelley's novel does have affinities with both American realism and naturalism, but the American writers within those traditions whose works are usually cited, particularly by male critics, are male. A case in point is Donald Pizer's 1982 study, *Twentieth Century American Literary Naturalism: An Interpretation*, which begins with a brief discussion of early naturalists Stephen Crane, Theodore Dreiser, and Frank Norris, and then focuses on works by later generations of male naturalists, including James T. Farrell, John Dos Passos, John Steinbeck, Norman Mailer, William Styron, and Saul Bellow. Ironic indeed is Pizer's failure to mention Edith Summers Kelley's *Weeds* even in passing, since both the 1972 edition of *Weeds* and Pizer's 1982 study were published by Southern Illinois University Press. Moreover, Matthew Bruccoli, the discoverer of Kelley's "quiet masterpiece," serves also as coeditor for the Crosscurrents/Modern Critiques/ New Series in which Pizer's study appears. Though Kelley's protagonist Judith Pippinger Blackford, an intelligent, once-vibrant, trapped wife of a poor Kentucky tobacco tenant farmer, would definitely fit Pizer's own definition of the "naturalistic tragic figure whose potential for growth is evident but who fails to develop because of the circumstances of . . . life,"[48] Pizer and the great majority of other male critics who have written about literary naturalism—or about the literature of the twenties or about working-class literature—do not mention the novel that Bruccoli himself describes as "first-rate: perfectly controlled, accurately observed, and carefully written."[49]

As Pizer's failure to include Kelley in his study of naturalism suggests, merely reissuing a "lost" first-rate novel does not necessarily guarantee its incorporation into the literary canon. What is necessary to secure a permanent place for a novel like *Weeds* is that it be discussed over time by critics who focus on its literary merits and also link it to other works with which it may be compared. As I shall suggest, Kelley's novel is, in fact, connected both in terms of genre and theme to other distinguished fictional works by women that are beginning to help define a number of women's literary traditions. Those traditions pertinent to a consideration of *Weeds* include female literary naturalism, which emphasizes the social and biological constraints of women; literary feminism; the female *Bildungsroman;* the female *Künstlerroman;* American women's regionalism; and women's working-class literature.

In his study of American literary naturalism, Pizer argues that during the twenties and beyond, modernism did not supplant naturalism but coexisted alongside it, as is demonstrated by the works of a number of first-rate male writers. Had Pizer also looked at *Weeds* and other naturalistic novels by women, he might have discovered additional first-rate examples of literary naturalism.[50] With its focus on the entrapment of a sensitive female protagonist whose spirit ultimately is defeated by the material circumstances, social constraints, and biological imperatives of her life, *Weeds* is a quintessential example of female literary naturalism. Judith Pippinger much prefers the outdoors to her confining tenant's shack and imagines herself "taking a long, carefree ride on horseback or following a turkey hen over the hills and hollows" (217). Once Judith marries and becomes a mother, she is forced instead to stay indoors most of the time. Never free of the burdens of housework, she also is tethered to her children, "always at their beck and call seven days a week through weeks that were always the same" (217). Abounding in images of nature that articulate a Darwinian "survival of the fittest" perspective, Kelley's bleak, deterministic novel concludes with the formerly rebellious Judith sadly resigned to her fate. "What are we all anyway but flies," Judith bitterly remarks when she learns that a former suitor, Bob Crupper, has been killed in World War I (297). Having become "timid about many things since the days of her forthright girlhood," (330) at the novel's end Judith sees herself as "a dog tied by a strong chain" who finds it useless continually to "pull at the leash" (330).

Another literary tradition to which *Weeds* belongs is the feminist tradition that is limned by Elizabeth Ammons in her study

Conflicting Stories: American Women Writers at the Turn into the Twentieth Century (1991). Ammons argues persuasively that instead of considering women who were writing during this period individually or ignoring them entirely, we should see them as constituting a group influenced by the women's suffrage movement to produce a body of literature that boldly addresses feminist issues.[51] In her tenth chapter, "Slow Starvation: Hunger and Hatred in Anzia Yezierska, Ellen Glasgow, and Edith Summers Kelley," Ammons discusses the difficulties all three women writers experienced as they struggled to bring their work to fruition, as well as the ways in which each writer transmuted her own difficult personal circumstances in her fiction. Whether we are looking at Sara Smolinsky, the feisty Jewish immigrant protagonist of Yezierska's *Bread Givers* (1925), who rebels against the patriarchal pronouncements of her Orthodox father, or Dorinda Oakley, the protagonist of Glasgow's *Barren Ground,* whom Ammons describes as growing "from a vulnerable adolescent into a tough, independent woman,"[52] or Kelley's Judith Pippinger Blackford, who continually chafes at the inexorable demands of housekeeping and motherhood, we can see the ways that a feminist consciousness about such issues as women's roles and the economic disadvantages of women are reflected in these novels.

Two other important literary traditions relevant to a consideration of *Weeds* are those of the female *Bildungsroman* and the female *Künstlerroman.*[53] Judith Pippinger, who resembles many of the assertive, frequently angry protagonists found in other female *Bildungsromane,*[54] caustically observes that because he is a male her brother is excused from tedious domestic chores. After she marries Jerry Blackford, Judith is furious when he, too, refuses to perform any of the household chores, even though she helps him with the work of the farm. Judith, who much prefers farm work to housework, disapproves of her more domestic sister, another character type that appears frequently in the female *Bildungsroman.* Focusing on the struggles of an assertive female protagonist to achieve autonomy in a patriarchal society, *Weeds* bears comparison with other, currently better known female *Bildungsromane*, such as Charlotte Bronte's *Jane Eyre* and George Eliot's *The Mill on the Floss.*

Related but not identical to the tradition of the female *Bildungsroman* is that of the female *Künstlerroman,* a novel that traces the growth and development of a would-be female artist. Distressed when she cannot reconcile the traditional roles she is expected to fulfill as a woman and her aspirations to be an artist, such a protagonist frequently is compared to a more conventional female character, who serves as her foil.[55] Like a number of other protagonists in the female *Künstlerroman,* Kelley's Judith Pippinger more accurately should be described as an "artiste manqué" rather than an artist, for though she eagerly draws figures on scrap paper of people and animals—pictures that Kelley describes as showing "great vigor and clarity of vision" (25)—Judith has neither the necessary funds nor the leisure to perfect her craft.[56]

Yet another genre of women's writing with which *Weeds* has affinities is American women's regionalism. American women regionalists from the nineteenth century to the present have portrayed sympathetically the language and customs of a particular region, often focusing in their fiction on the experience and culture of women.[57] Though Kelley, who was born in Toronto, resided in rural Kentucky only briefly, she renders in dialect the courting, funerals, dances, revival meetings, tobacco harvests, and hog butchering of rural Kentuckians.[58] Kelley also describes in graphic detail the culture of rural women during the first decades of this century, including several methods employed to abort a fetus. After Judith conceives as a result of a brief affair with an itinerant preacher, she gallops wildly on horseback, hoping her ride will precipitate an abortion. When her horseback riding fails to produce the desired results, she forces herself to use a knitting needle to abort the fetus, but "shrinking and clumsy," she flings the instrument away at "the first stab of pain" (285); finally, after the consumption of "nasty smelling decoctions" brewed from noxious herbs such as tansy and pennyroyal also fails (286), she wades into the icy waters of a nearby pond.

The inclusion of a selection from Kelley's work in *Calling Home: Working-Class Women's Writing*, edited by Janet Zandy (1990), also places *Weeds* within the tradition of working-class women's writing.[59] Such works make visible the underpaid and undervalued work of women in offices and cotton fields and mills and households. As Paula Rabinowitz has pointed out, descriptions of women's work often cover a terrain "marked by childwork, domestic work, and unorganized labor."[60] That *Weeds* is part of this tradition of women's working-class writing is evident to any reader of Kelley's novel, for as Fran Zaniello has observed, "It has some of the fullest descriptions anywhere in literature of the monotonous, back-breaking work of poor rural women."[61] The passage Zaniello cites is the one in which Kelley enumerates the never-ending chores of the typical poor rural farm woman of Scott County, Kentucky, during the era of World War I:

> Families must be fed after some fashion or other and dishes washed three times a day, three hundred and sixty-five days in the year. Babies must be fed and washed and dressed and "changed" and rocked when they cried and watched and kept out of mischief and danger. The endless wrangles among older children must be arbitrated in some way or other, if only by cuffing the ears of both contestants; and the equally endless complaints stilled by threats, promises, whatever lies a harassed mother could invent to quiet the fretting clamor of discontented childhood. Fires must be lighted and kept going as long as needed for cooking, no matter how great the heat. Cows must be milked and cream skimmed and butter churned. Hens must be fed and eggs gathered and the filth shoveled out of henhouses. Diapers must be washed, and grimy little drawers and rompers and stiff overalls and sweaty work shirts and grease-bespattered dresses and kitchen aprons and filthy, sour-smelling towels and socks stinking with the putridity of unwashed feet and all the other articles that go to make up a farm family's wash. Floors must be swept and scrubbed and stoves cleaned and a never ending war waged against the constant encroaches of dust, grease, stable manure, flies, spiders, rats, mice, ants, and all the other breeders of filth that are continually at work in

country households. These activities made up the life of the women, a life that was virtually the same every day of the year, except when their help was needed in the field to set tobacco or shuck corn, or when fruit canning, hog killing, or house cleaning crowded the routine (195).

Describing as well the hard work that Jerry Blackford does on the farm, Kelley does not suggest that the life of the poor tenant farmers of Scott County, Kentucky, is difficult only for women; however, she does devote more space in her novel to depicting women's work than men's. For her anthology Janet Zandy has chosen the passage now appearing as an appendix to the Feminist Press edition of *Weeds*—the formerly excised passage describing the birth of Judith's son Billy. This selection reminds us that bearing children and tending to them afterward has been a major focus of women's work.

Locating *Weeds* within a number of women's literary traditions may prove to be of value for readers of the novel; however, whether or not this novel will survive over time ultimately will also depend on its literary merits. I agree emphatically with Matthew Bruccoli's pronouncement that *Weeds* is a "superb" novel. In it we encounter not only Kelley's memorable female protagonist, Judith Pippinger, whom she describes as "a poppy among weeds" (88), but sympathetically drawn male figures such as Judith's husband Jerry and the elderly, embittered fiddler Jabez Moorhouse. Painstakingly rendering in simple yet eloquent prose the often monotonous everyday life of working-class rural Kentuckians during the first two decades of the twentieth century, Kelley poignantly describes the fleeting moments of pleasure that provide relief from the tedium of their daily toil, as well as the economic hardships and the personal tragedies that threaten to engulf them. Although *Weeds* is primarily Judith's story, one that empathically traces the downward trajectory of her life— from exuberant tomboy to worn-out, depressed wife and mother, Judith's tragic life is echoed in the diminished lives of others in her community. Vivid images of the daily lives of Kelley's characters remain in the mind long after one has finished reading her novel.

In 1987 Tillie Olsen, who has written about the tragic "silencing" of authors like Kelley, sent me a note of thanks for my afterword to the first Feminist Press edition of *Weeds*. Identifying with the struggles of Kelley and her working-class protagonists, Olsen said, "I keep up over my work table E. S. K.'s old face—from the jacket of the 1st hard cover *Devil's Hand*." Kelley's work has been celebrated not only by well-known feminist scholars like Olsen, but also by a whole generation of readers to whom *Weeds* became available once again in 1982, when The Feminist Press decided to reissue it. Writing about *Weeds* in 1986, Barbara Lootens described its importance: "The first step in the destruction of the myth of the artistic irrelevance of an ordinary woman's life, acceptance of *Weeds* is acceptance of the right of women to establish new literary traditions evolving from essential female experience."[62] Lootens speculated nevertheless about the ultimate fate of *Weeds*, wondering whether The Feminist Press's reissuing of the novel would "have the power to break Edith Summers Kelley's tragic silence."[63] Out of print again after the 1982 Feminist Press edition of *Weeds*, too, became unavailable, this work once more was in danger of being forgotten despite the fact that a handful of critics continued to celebrate Kelley's achievement. It is my hope that this new printing, along with the growing body of critical material about Kelley's moving, beautifully crafted novel, will both secure an enduring place in literary history for *Weeds* and guarantee that it reaches a wider audience.

NOTES

1. For an account of the rediscovery of *Weeds,* see Matthew Bruc-coli, afterword to *Weeds,* by Edith Summers Kelley (Carbondale: Southern Illinois University Press, 1972), 345–46.

2. Charlotte Goodman, "Images of American Rural Women in the Novel," *Michigan Papers in Women's Studies* I (June 1975): 57–70.

3. For a discussion of the theme of entrapment in Edith Summers Kelley's work, see John Earl Bassett, "Edith Summers Kelley: The Trapped Women of her Novels," *Ball State University Forum* 23 (Winter 1982): 2–11 and Charlotte Goodman, "Widening Perspectives, Narrowing Possibilities: The Trapped Woman in Edith Summers Kelley's *Weeds,*" in *Regionalism and the Female Imagination: A Collection of Essays,* ed. Emily Toth (New York: Human Sciences Press, Inc., 1985), 93–96.

4. Upton Sinclair, *The Autobiography of Upton Sinclair* (New York: Harcourt, Brace and World, Inc., 1962), 132.

5. Sinclair Lewis, quoted in Edith Summers Kelley, "Helicon Hall: An Experiment in Living" (manuscript posthumously edited by Mary Byrd David), *The Kentucky Review* 1 (Spring 1980): 85.

6. Patrick Kelley, "Edith Summers Kelley: A Postscript," in Edith Summers Kelley, *The Devil's Hand* (Carbondale: Southern Illinois University Press, 1974), 299.

7. Barbara Updegraff, "Edith Summers Kelley," Edith Summers Kelley Papers, Special Collections, Morris Library, Carbondale, Illinois (hereafter cited as Kelley Papers).

8. Patrick Kelley to Charlotte Goodman, Castro Valley, California, 26 June 1981.

9. Patrick Kelley, "Edith Summers Kelley: A Postscript," 300.

10. Edith Summers Kelley, "Heart of April," Kelley Papers.

11. Edith Summers Kelley, "Helicon Hall," 29–51.

12. Bruccoli, afterword to *Weeds,* 341.

13. Edith Summers Kelley, "Helicon Hall," 32.

14. Edith Summers Kelley, "Helicon Hall," 44.

15. "Author Has Unusual History: Friend of Famous People; Wife of Farmer-Sculptor," *San Diego Union* (November 4, 1923), quoted in Bruccoli, afterword to *Weeds,* 338.

16. Edith Summers Kelley, "The Sleeping Beauty," *New England Magazine* (January 1907); "Morning-Glories," *New England Magazine* (July 1907); "Magic Door," *Lippincott's Monthly Magazine* (November 1907).

17. For a discussion of the Greenwich Village feminists, see June Sochen, *The New Woman* (New York: Quadrangle Books, 1972).

18. Bruccoli, afterword to *Weeds,* 338.

19. Floyd Dell, "Feminism for Men," *Looking at Life* (New York: Knopf, 1924), 14.

20. Edith Summers Kelley, "We Went Back to the Land," Kelley Papers. This is also the source for the description of the Kelleys' farming experiences that follows.

21. Edith Summers Kelley, "The Old House," *Women's Studies* 10 (1983): 66.

22. Edith Summers Kelley, "The Old House," 71.

23. See Edith Summers Kelley, *Weeds* (New York: The Feminist Press, 1982; 1990), 195.

24. Edith Summers Kelley, "The Old House," 77.

25. Edith Summers Kelley, "We Went Back to the Land," 77.

26. Edith Summers Kelly to Sinclair Lewis, Herber, California, 29 May 1922, courtesy of Patrick Kelly.

27. Barbara Updegraff, "Edith Summers Kelly."

28. For a discussion of Judith Pippinger Blackford as an *artiste manqué,* see Charlotte Goodman, "Portraits of the *Artiste Manqué* by Three Women Novelists," *Frontiers: A Journal in Women's Studies* 5, no. 3 (Fall 1980): 57–59 and Elizabeth Ammons, *Conflicting Stories: American Women Writers at the Turn into the Twentieth Century* (New York: Oxford University Press, 1991), 177–180.

29. Edith Summers Kelley to Harcourt, North San Diego P.O., 26 February 1923, courtesy of Patrick Kelley.

30. Edith Summers Kelley to Harcourt, North San Diego P.O., 12 April 1923, courtesy of Patrick Kelley.

31. Lewis to Harcourt and Brace, 2 June 1921, *From Main Street to Stockholm: Letters of Sinclair Lewis 1919–1930,* ed. Harrison Smith (New York: Harcourt, Brace, 1952), 75.

32. Lewis to Harcourt and Brace, 28 September 1923, *From Main Street to Stockholm,* 140.

33. Bruccoli, afterword to *Weeds,* 341.

34. Lewis to Harcourt and Brace, 28 September 1923.

35. Edith Summers Kelley to Harcourt, North San Diego P.O., 29 March 1923, courtesy of Patrick Kelley.

36. Edith Summers Kelley to Harcourt, North San Diego P.O., 12 April 1923.

37. Bruccoli, afterword to *The Devil's Hand,* 292.

38. Telephone conversation with Charlotte Goodman, 3 August 1981.

39. Ivor Updegraff to Charlotte Goodman, Stamford, Connecticut, 22 July 1981.

40. Edith Summers Kelley to Upton Sinclair, 3 May 1925, quoted in Bruccoli, afterword to *The Devil's Hand,* 293.

41. Edith Summers Kelley to Sinclair, 7 May 1926, quoted in Bruccoli, afterword to *The Devil's Hand,* 294.

42. Edith Summers Kelley to Sinclair, 19 October 1926, quoted in Bruccoli, afterword to *The Devil's Hand,* 294.

43. Edith Summers Kelley to Cary McWilliams, 19 April 1929, quoted in Bruccoli, afterword to *The Devil's Hand,* 295.

44. See Tillie Olsen, *Silences* (New York: Delacorte Press, 1978).

45. Edith Summers Kelley, "Roses and Peonies," Kelley Papers.

46. Edith Summers Kelley to Lewis, North San Diego P.O., 9 October 1922, courtesy of Patrick Kelley.

47. Bruccoli, afterword to *Weeds,* 335.

48. Donald Pizer, *Twentieth Century American Literary Naturalism: An Interpretation* (Carbondale: Southern Illinois University

Press, 1982), 335.

49. Bruccoli, afterword to *Weeds,* 335.

50. See, for example, Josephine W. Johnson's *Now in November,* Fielding Burke's *Call Home the Heart,* Tillie Olsen's *Yonnandio,* and Louise Meriwether's *Daddy Was a Number Runner.*

51. Ammons, 3–19.

52. Ammons, 172.

53. For essays on the female *Bildungsroman,* see *The Voyage In: Fictions of Female Development,* ed. Elizabeth Abel, Marianne Hirsch, and Elizabeth Langland (Hanover: University Press of New England, 1983). Two critical works on the female *Künstlerroman* are Linda Huff, *A Portrait of the Artist as a Young Woman: The Writer as Heroine in American Literature* (New York: Frederick Ungar, 1983), and Grace Stewart, *A New Mythos: The Novel of the Artist as Heroine 1877–1977* (Montreal: Eden Press, 1981).

54. Other angry, assertive female protagonists in the female *Bildungsroman* with whom Judith might be compared are Jo March in Louisa May Alcott's *Little Women* and Molly Fawcett in Jean Stafford's *The Mountain Lion.*

55. See Huff, 4–11. In *Weeds,* Judith's sister, Lizzie Mae, serves as her foil.

56. Other female characters whose circumstances do not permit their artistic talents to flourish are Edna Pontellier in Kate Chopin's *The Awakening* and Gertie Nevels in Harriette Arnow's *The Dollmaker.*

57. For essays on female regionalists see *Regionalism and the Female Imagination,* ed. Emily Toth (New York: Human Sciences Press, 1982) and *American Women Regionalists: 1850–1910,* ed. Judith Fetterley and Marjorie Pryse (New York: W. W. Norton & Co., Inc., 1992).

58. Other Kentucky-born women regional novelists include Elizabeth Maddox Roberts and Harriette Arnow.

59. *Calling Home: Working-Class Women's Writing,* ed. Janet Zandy (New Brunswick: Rutgers University Press, 1990).

60. *Writing Red: An Anthology of American Women Writers,*

1930–1940, ed. Charlotte Nekola and Paula Rabinowitz (New York: The Feminist Press, 1987), 3. Another working-class novel with which *Weeds* might be compared is Agnes Smedley's *Daughter of Earth.*

61. Fran Zaniello, "Witnessing the Buried Life in Rural Kentucky: Edith Summers Kelley and *Weeds,*" *The Kentucky Review* 8 (Autumn 1988): 65.

62. Barbara Lootens, "A Struggle for Survival: Edith Summers Kelley's *Weeds,*" *Women's Studies* 13 (1986): 113.

63. Lootens, 105.

ABOUT THE AUTHOR

Born in Canada in 1884, Edith Summers Kelley graduated from the University of Toronto in 1903 and moved to New York's Greenwich Village. She worked as a secretary to Upton Sinclair, lived in an experimental community he founded in New Jersey, and participated in the rich social and intellectual life of the Village in the years before World War I. After a brief engagement to Sinclair Lewis, she eventually married his roommate, with whom she had two children. After that marriage ended, she lived for fifty years with C. Fred Kelley, a sculptor and the father of her son Patrick. Together the Kelleys tried growing tobacco in Kentucky, operating a boarding house in New Jersey, and raising chickens in California. There she wrote *Weeds,* first published in 1923, and a second novel, *The Devil's Hand,* which was published posthumously. She died in 1956.